JAZZ
JAZZ
JAZZ

JAZZ
JAZZ
JAZZ

A NOVEL BY
Patrick
Skene
Catling

Blond & Briggs

First published 1980 by Blond & Briggs Ltd.,
44/45 Museum Street, London WC1

Printed in Great Britain by The Anchor Press Ltd
and bound by Wm Brendon & Son Ltd
both of Tiptree, Essex

© copyright 1980 Patrick Skene Catling

SBN 85634 065 0

for

IRIS DIANA

PRELUDE

Jazz began with rape. Jazz was created by abduction, exile, enslavement, misery and desire. Jazz was an active verb. Later, when the word got around, it became a noun and an adjective and something like a philosophy. Jazz was a passionate idea of survival and freedom, an idea that attained a certain careless popular acceptance and at last an almost universal understanding.

Africans sold Africans to white slave-traders. They made the West African coast hideous with whiplashes and the cries and groans of captives. Sailors chained the slaves supine in congested rows in the dark holds of sailing ships to cross the Atlantic from Africa to the West Indies and America. The crossing of the Middle Passage was the cruellest voyage in the history of racial migration. These blacks from Africa were sick and melancholy and full of hate. But the survivors were strong, with a powerful urge to enjoy life.

Aboard one of the slave ships in the summer of 1826, in accordance with a custom of the time and the privileged opportunities of his rank, the master jazzed a young black girl. When he eventually delivered the cargo to New Orleans for auction and she was sold to a Louisiana cotton farmer, she learned she was pregnant. In the plantation slave quarters, in due course, she gave birth to a brown boy. His great-grandson turned out to be a pale-brown Creole by the name of Moses Decatur. An illegitimate child, he was cared for by Sarah Jackson, a black cook who worked for A. Chesley Poindexter III, the wealthy, aristocratic cotton broker. This was in New Orleans in 1913, long after Emancipation, of course, though not everybody had got the message. By then, to some people, jazz already meant a kind of music.

ONE

New Orleans, 1913

A fter a warm thunderstorm, the old French Quarter was steaming like a Cajun bayou. The setting sun was a pale-yellow blob in dull white cloud. The sky was low and heavy with the menace of more thunder to come. One would not have been surprised by a sudden pestilential downpour of the wet, lumpy toads that smell of drains and are used in the concoction of evil voodoo potions. In short, it was an ordinary September evening in New Orleans. As usual when he dined at home, A. Chesley Poindexter III was not in a good mood.

The Poindexter town house was one of the noteworthy architectural ornaments of Beauregard Street, behind St. Louis Cathedral. Visitors to the city were guided to admire the mansion's wrought-iron Spanish balconies, the eighteenth-century Colonial red-brick façade, the Classical white columns of the portico. The interior was equally dignified, equally opulent, and, to the owner, equally boring.

Chesley, as close friends and his wife were permitted to call him, sat at the head of a long mahogany table in the dining room. It was a large, formal room, with dull ochre tapestry-covered walls, a Venetian crystal chandelier and a black onyx fireplace, which contained an elaborate arrangement of dead flowers. On the high ceiling two wooden propellers slowly revolved, stirring the stale, humid air. At one end of the room tall windows overlooked the street; at the other end french windows gave onto a square patio. In the center of the patio water splashed in a circular white-marble fountain, and, in the center of that, a small plump white-marble naked boy balanced on one foot with upraised hands and outspread wings, looking like Cupid unblindfolded and disarmed – a godling without illusions and without power. The power of the house, if not the illusions, was Chesley's. But even power at that moment seemed to afford him little pleasure.

He was as handsome as it is possible for an ex-athlete to be by the time he has grown a second chin and a bulge at the back of his neck and his liver-function tests have begun consistently to indicate that he really should cut down on the bourbon. But his sandy-colored hair was boyishly short and his pale-blue eyes were fairly clear and his permanent golf-course sun-tan, accentuated by the white of his shirt and the blue and white stripes of his seersucker jacket, gave an impression of youthful vigor. The only really nasty feature of his appearance was his smile. In this respect, he differed markedly from the somber ancestral portraits on the walls beside him : his father and mother and their fathers and mothers all looked as gravely disapproving as Chesley's trustees.

"Is there any chance, do you think, that our son will honor us with his presence at the table this evening?" Chesley asked, smiling his usual acid smile.

His wife, Elizabeth, a faded red-head with a dull, pale complexion, furtively glanced at her gold wristwatch and made a feeble attempt to smile back. She was dressed in gray silk and pearls. She looked as insubstantial as ectoplasm.

"I'm sure he'll be right down," she said. "He's probably washing his hands."

"Washing his hands! Well! I wouldn't want to interfere with any new enterprise as noble as that. But perhaps you would ring the bell, my dear. Perhaps he has been detained by something less momentous."

Elizabeth picked up a small silver bell and delicately agitated it. Almost immediately a door opened and the black butler, in black tie and white jacket, silently entered the room with his eyebrows solicitously raised.

"Perhaps Benjamin will be able to help us to gather a quorum," Chesley said, as though he had not noticed the butler come in.

"Yes, sir, Mr. Poindexter?"

"Ah, Benjamin. There you are. We were wondering whether you could somehow manage to persuade Alan to join us for dinner."

"Yes, sir."

"Please try his room, Benjamin," Elizabeth said. "He's probably there." She gave the butler an encouraging, almost conspiratorial, nod. The butler sympathetically returned it.

"Is that where he is?" Chesley asked with a knowing grin.

"I'll go see right away, Mr. Poindexter," the butler said, backing and turning and leaving.

"Want to make a small bet?" Chesley asked his wife, as soon as they were alone.

8

"What do you mean, dear?"

"I mean I bet he isn't upstairs."

"I thought he was."

"I don't believe you," he said. "*Dear.*"

"He's only a minute or two late," she said.

"Why can't he be a minute or two early? Is that asking too much? As you know, it isn't often possible for me to get home for dinner, but when it is I make it on time. If I can be punctual so can he."

Chesley's sulky frown suggested that his family was callously indifferent to his efforts to achieve togetherness.

"No, dear," Elizabeth said.

"No?"

"I mean yes."

"Surely I have a right to expect rudimentary courtesy in my own home. Courtesy, at least."

"Yes, of course, **dear.**"

The door opened again, admitting a lanky thirteen-year-old boy in a light gray knickerbocker suit. Alan was tall for his age. His face was lean and pink and freckled and his inaccurately combed damp hair was bright auburn, almost orange, as his mother's had been before the years of marriage had subdued her. He nervously grinned, baring white teeth that looked a bit too big in his young jaw.

"Sorry, Mom," he said blithely.

"Excuse me, Mother and Father, for being late," Chesley corrected him. "Your necktie's crooked. Straighten it."

"Excuse-me-Mother-and-Father-for-being-late," Alan automatically repeated, tugging at the loose knot of his tie.

His mother laughed at the result.

"Come here, darling," she said. "Let me fix it."

Chesley rolled his eyes upward.

"Isn't the boy old enough to dress himself?" he asked the ceiling.

Elizabeth deftly arranged the navy-blue silk tie and patted the knot approvingly and quickly kissed Alan's cheek. Alan took his place, midway between his widely separated parents. Chesley threateningly smiled at him.

"By the way," Chesley said, with sinisterly exaggerated pleasantness. "Where were you just now?"

Alan swallowed without having anything to swallow.

"Daddy wondered why you didn't hear the dinner bell," Elizabeth lightly explained. "I said you must be washing your hands." She turned towards her husband. "With the water running – "

"There's no need for an interpreter. Alan's perfectly capable of speaking for himself. Aren't you, Alan?"

"Yes, sir."

Chesley suddenly leaned forward, in the manner of a tough prosecuting attorney. There was no smile now.

"Well, then. Where were you?"

The defendant made no attempt to cover up.

"In the kitchen, Father," he said.

Chesley sat back and beamed at his wife.

"Ah!" he exclaimed. "In the kitchen! Not upstairs at all. And what, may I ask, were you doing in the kitchen?"

"I wasn't there long," Alan said. "I was just lending Moses a book."

"You were *just lending Moses a book*, were you?" Chesley said, ponderously feigning incredulity. "But Alan! – correct me if I'm wrong – I thought I had made it quite clear that you are not allowed to consort with colored folk. Any colored folk, at any time, under this roof or anywhere else. Didn't I make that quite clear? Dear me. Benjamin and Sarah are good niggers. If they weren't they wouldn't live on my place. Moses, no doubt, is a well behaved child, in his way. That is not the point. You are a Poindexter. One day you will inherit the presidency of our brokerage company. There's a lot of loose, slovenly mixing in New Orleans these days, but you will have no part of it. White is white and black is black. You have your place and they have theirs. You have reached the age at which you and Moses cannot possibly play together. You are no longer infants. You have reached the age of reason and discretion. It is unfair of you to intrude into his world. He cannot enter yours. That is a rule of our society. I thought I pointed that out to you the last time we talked."

"We weren't *playing*, Father," Alan said earnestly. "I only visited the kitchen for a minute. I said hello to Sarah and lent Moses a book. That's all."

"Sarah took care of Alan when he was a baby in his cradle," Elizabeth said, more spiritedly than usual.

"So she did," Chesley agreed. "She was very useful. She still is. She is a conscientious servant. But I hope you didn't delegate too many of your responsibilities. And anyway: Alan is not a baby now, I trust."

"I only lent Moses a book," Alan muttered insistently. "Moses has lots of white friends."

"That's a *non sequitur*," Chesley said. "I cannot be held accountable for the eccentric ways of some of our neighbors. But, by God, we Poindexters have always maintained our standards, and, as long as I have my say, we always will. Enough. Let us have our dinner. Elizabeth, kindly ring the bell."

However, Chesley could not leave his son alone. After Benjamin served the chilled cucumber soup, Chesley said:

"Doesn't Moses still attend school? Doesn't his school supply him with books? What's this book that you felt compelled to lend him?"

"He wanted to borrow my Goodspeed and Manchester."

"A hymn book? Well, well," Chesley said, smiling. "Have you set yourself up as some sort of missionary?"

"He wanted the music of 'What A Friend We Have In Jesus.' There's going to be a spasm band – a bunch of the kids – at the Ethiopian Temple picnic. Moses has a new banjo. It's a real one."

Chesley gave his wife a significantly severe look.

"You see," he said. "A so-called 'minute' with Moses and our son is talking gibberish."

"Moses loves music!" Alan protested.

"Banjos do not make music," Chesley ruled. "That's a lot of darky foolishness. You're supposed to know better."

As if on cue, a street parade started suddenly at the end of what Chesley regarded as his block. The Poindexters heard a whirring roll on a snare drum, the thud of a bass drum, the whumping grunts of two tubas like swamp monsters in heat, the urgent bugle calls of two cornets in almost harmonious mutual incitement, the slow upward drone of a trombone, like a primitive flying machine laboriously taking off. At a medium pace, the small, ardent musical rabble, armed with battered percussion and brass instruments, approached like the vanguard of a revolution.

To Chesley, the increasing cacophony seemed like insolence directed toward him personally and a threat to social decorum and order. To Alan, the music was a beautiful promise. He failed to hide his pleasure.

"Listen, Mom!" he cried out. "That's them now! The Ethiopian Temple Band! I'm sure it is!"

"Those are they, I suppose you mean," Chesley said, as he got up and walked over to the windows, as the parade came into view.

A tall, thin, black man in a black top hat and a black tail coat, striped trousers and gray spats twirled a many-colored parasol at a crazy angle above his head, leading half a dozen black musicians in black-peaked white caps, maroon uniform jackets with brass buttons and unmatching civilian trousers. The marchers' steps had a strangely unmilitary little hesitant bounce to them, in time with the strong beat of the music but a fraction of a second ahead of it. The march was a jazz march for the happy part of a funeral, the survivors' return from the cemetery.

As the parade was passing by the windows, Chesley slammed them down, one by one. In the dining room, when he sat down again at the head of the table, the sound of the music was subdued.

"That's jazz," Alan said with proprietary pride.

"Hush now, Alan!" Elizabeth protested, with a nervous glance at her husband.

"Where did you pick up that disgusting word?" Chesley demanded. His tan reddened.

"It only means the new music," Alan explained.

"I thought we retained Dr. Frischauer to teach you the classics," Chesley said.

"Alan plays beautifully," Elizabeth said.

"Moses says – "

"I don't care what Moses says," Chesley said. "I won't have that nigger language used in this house. Not in this part of the house. Certainly not in front of me and your mother. Moses doesn't know any better."

"It's not a nice word," Elizabeth gently pointed out. "Nice people don't use it."

"Gutter talk!" Chesley exclaimed.

"But – "

"You'll understand when you're a bit more grown up," she said. "Now, please let's not discuss it any further."

"Moses – "

"That will be *all*," Chesley snapped.

But, of course, it wasn't all.

The music was diminishing further, as the parade moved on down along the street, but nothing could have kept the sound out absolutely, the insistent joy of it. Alan could still feel its pulse quickening his heart.

Soon the marchers were out of earshot, but they left behind a family irreversibly changed.

TWO

A lan told himself that he really loved his father. How could Alan hate him? Your father was always your father. But Alan subconsciously recognized that his parents – even his mother – and he now lived in two separate worlds. They and he were still visible to each other; they could touch each other but there was no more feeling; they could hear each other but without sympathetic understanding. The recognition of a shared identity, the awareness of the sameness of their blood, had gone.

Chesley Poindexter was clever enough to know that he did not know Alan and treated him with chilly circumspection. The man suspected the boy of disloyalty, even subversion. Alan realized intuitively that there was no trust, and he, too, became cautious.

In the early years of his childhood he had always told the truth, blurting it out with natural candor. Now there was a slight lag between the thought and the spoken word: he considered what he would say and its possible dangerous implications and repercussions before he said it. There were approved family topics and attitudes to them, and there were taboos. There were subjects in which he could not openly express interest with impunity. They happened to be the subjects that interested and excited him the most.

One of them was the warm, intimate world of the kitchen, in the basement beneath the dining room. The kitchen seemed to be the center of his life. The family he knew best, the butler, the cook and their foster son, slept in the servants' quarters, in a two-storey brick building across the patio behind the mansion. But during the day, from shortly after dawn until quite late in the evening, their home was the kitchen; the kitchen was a private black enclave in white territory. A basement kitchen in an old Colonial mansion was an apt metaphor for Negro status in New Orleans in the early years of the present century. Blacks lived in a social underground. The workers in the basement did all the drudgery that supported the tranquil order, comfort and elegance of the life above. Yet Alan envied them. On his furtive, illicit visits to the kitchen he felt that he was being allowed to enter a sanctuary of secret emotional privilege. Moses was his best friend.

He, too, was thirteen years of age, but he was three or four inches taller than Alan, and he had long bony hands and big feet, which suggested that in a few years he would be very tall indeed. Moses had a narrow face, with slightly protuberant brown eyes, an aquiline nose and poutingly curved, full lips. His short, curly hair was dark brown, almost black, with auburn glints in it. His complexion was a smooth, creamy beige, like *café au lait*. Girls called him "cute"; in fact, he was already almost handsome. He was a lazy, disorganized, quick-witted, popular student who got by with a C-minus average because the teachers liked him. Even they sometimes could not help laughing at his clowning in class. He was a natural, well-coordinated, relaxed athlete, excelling at the hundred-yard dash, the two-twenty low hurdles and the broad jump. Long distances bored him. He could throw a baseball so hard that it stung through a first baseman's mitt. When batting, he rarely struck out; he was usually caught, deep in center field : that was his style. If his teammates suggested that he should try to change it he good-humoredly chuckled. The only thing he really deeply cared about, in addition to his family, was music. He was devoted to it. But he managed to make even music seem unserious. He was never solemn about anything that made him happy. Alan admired Moses so much that he made Alan feel inferior. He hoped that Moses would not notice this inferiority and find it irksome. Alan was afraid that Moses was so quick and sharp and was developing so fast that Alan would be left behind, stranded, alone. If he had ever told Moses about this fear he would not have understood it. He lived insouciantly in the everlasting present.

As soon as Alan got home from school in the afternoon, he ostentatiously carried his satchel up to his room, as if to do his homework. He went up loudly, loudly closed his door, and a few minutes later quickly tip-toed down the back stairs to the basement. His mother, for the sake of peace and quiet and because she sympathized with him, pretended not to notice. In the absence of A. Chesley Poindexter III the whole household spontaneously organized in tacit connivance against his harsh rules.

This afternoon, late in September, when Alan reached the kitchen he found that Moses, as usual, had made it back home before him. There had never been any stated challenge but they both understood that there was a daily race. Their schools closed simultaneously. Alan's was seven blocks closer but he was handicapped by the slow detour through the front door and up and down stairs. Moses sat back in a corner chair. His hands were clasped behind his head and his legs were crossed in a posture exaggeratedly miming ease. He was trying not to breathe hard. He smiled.

"Hey, there, slowpoke!" he said. "What kept you?"

Alan attempted to compose his face into an expression of dignified indifference.

"Hello, Sarah," he said, looking over the cook's plump shoulder to try to see what she was busily slicing on the counter. "Hot, isn't it?"

"Yes, it is, Mister Alan. I noticed." She turned her head and smiled. Her black face was shiny with sweat. "You know where the lemonade is at."

"Yes. Inside Moses, most of it, I bet."

Moses raised a tall glass and tauntingly licked his lips. Though he was sitting behind her, Sarah was always aware of every move, every gesture, and even, apparently, every nuance of thought in her kitchen.

"There's enough for the both of you," she assured Alan. "There's plenty more water in the faucet."

He took a glass from the cupboard above the stone sink and filled it with homemade lemonade from a cold stoneware jug that he had found in its proper place on a plain wooden table as massive as a butcher's chopping block. Pieces of ice chimed as they tumbled into his glass. He drank the whole glassful without a pause and refilled the glass before he sat down near Moses.

"How was the game?" Alan asked.

"All right," Moses said.

"What was the score?"

"Three-one."

"Who won?"

Moses opened his eyes wide.

"Who *won*? What kind of question is that?"

"Gee, Moses. That's swell!"

Moses grinned. He could never keep a straight face for long.

"Now ask him about his arithmetic," Sarah suggested.

"Aw, Mom," Moses protested with a scowl. "Don't be like that. I told you they're going to let me take the exam over again."

16

"You ought to be studying up on it right now," Sarah said. "And what about *your* homework, Mister Alan? I swear, you two are too much, setting around gossiping and giggling like a couple of old grandmas that's gone soft in the head."

"I only just got here," Alan righteously pointed out.

"Yeah, sure. But that's what you're *going* to do, set around, gossiping and giggling and getting in my way." She shook her head and heaved a theatrical sigh. "I don't know what's going to happen to you boys. I really don't."

Moses placed his thumbs against his temples and wiggled his fingers and crossed his eyes and stuck out the tip of his tongue, and Alan, trying not to laugh out loud, did the nose trick, snorting out lemonade, coughing and spluttering.

"O.K., kids, O.K.," Sarah said calmly, because she wasn't actually in the least anxious about Moses' academic career – in fact, she didn't much care what he did in school as long as he didn't get into trouble. "Make fun of me, if you like. But you'll be sorry later if you don't heed me now."

An opening door saved them all from further discussion of scholarly opportunities neglected. Benjamin came in with a tray of coffee things.

"Oh, my Lord!" he said. "Are my eyes deceiving me, Mister Alan? That ain't you, is it? It couldn't be. Your father was real mad with me last night. He said the kitchen's strictly *off limits* and he said I was responsible to always take care to keep it that way. What are you trying to do, Mister Alan? Get me fired?"

"I just came down for a glass of lemonade," Alan said, holding up the glass as evidence.

"He ain't doing no harm," Sarah said firmly. "He'll be going up to do his studying in a minute. Won't you, Mister Alan?"

"Yes, Sarah."

"Well, as far as I'm concerned," Benjamin said, "you ain't even here. But you better not stay long. Still, if you are here you may as well have a slice of pie. Sarah?"

"I'm cutting it," she said. It was lime chiffon pie, one of her best, with buttery brown pastry that crumbled in the mouth. They all ate some, and then there wasn't any more.

"That's it, folks," she said, smiling proudly. "Now, Mister Alan, you just scat now, hear?"

Alan glanced at Moses. Moses, poker-faced, almost imperceptibly winked. Alan thanked Sarah and left the kitchen. Ten minutes later he and Moses met in the alley behind the carriage house, which was used these days as a garage for the Poindexter cabriolet automobile.

"Our families are getting tougher all the time," Alan said, as they cut across Jackson Square and headed for the river.

"You mean your family is," Moses said.

"Yes," Alan admitted. "I suppose you're right."

"It ain't your fault. You can't help being your daddy's son."

Alan flinched. He stopped, holding Moses' arm, and Moses stopped too. Alan knew he was no longer a match for Moses in a fight but had to pretend that he was game. Fighting with Moses used to be fun when they were the same size and there was nothing important to fight about. Alan intuitively realized that if they ever fought again the fight would be no fun at all, and it would probably be final.

"What's wrong with being my daddy's son?" Alan asked.

Moses soothingly patted Alan's shoulder.

"Nothing, Alan," he said.

They walked on, close together, side by side, without speaking.

They crossed the railroad tracks and climbed stone steps to the levee overlooking the Mississippi. Alongside the quay, a riverboat's stern wheel churned the brown water into pale froth. A whistle beside one of the tall black funnels, as narrow as stove-pipes, steamily hooted three times.

Moses and Alan sat on the granite parapet and watched the boat slowly pull out. This was where they often came to contemplate the future. The river joined New Orleans to the rest of the world.

"Do you wish you were going?" Moses asked. It was a question they often asked each other.

"Do you?" Alan asked.

"In a way," Moses said, sounding more cautious than most days.

"So do I," Alan agreed loyally, wondering why Moses seemed noncommittal.

"But not till after the picnic. And the day after that it's Mom's birthday. I'll have to be here for that."

Of course, the picnic.

"If only I could come," Alan said.

"Well, why don't you? Afraid of your daddy?"

"Don't be dumb. Do you think it'd be O.K. if I did come? Wouldn't your people mind?"

"Why should they mind? There'll be hundreds of others. Thousands, I expect. If you can get the ticket money, who's to stop you? You could go on your own and we'd meet. There'll be lots of music. The Ethiopians. The Holy Glory Jass Band. And maybe The Good Timers. There'll be all kinds of stuff to eat. And the fireworks when it gets dark. You'd kick yourself if you missed it. But don't come if you're afraid. I'll tell you all about it on Monday."

Alan irritably squirmed.

"I'll be there," he said. "My daddy'll never know. I could be over with a school friend. Anyway, he's out most weekends, at the club."

"Come on then," Moses said. "It's going to be the best picnic ever."

THREE

The picnic took place in a dusty, faded, sere public park on the south shore of Lake Pontchartrain on a brilliant Sunday near the end of September. The crowd was a spicy cultural gumbo. The people were black, brown and beige. They embodied a rich confusion of exotic bloodstreams – African predominantly, diluted by complicated mixtures of French, Spanish, English, German, Italian and those of all the other varieties of human jetsam that the seas had cast ashore in the Crescent City. The genes in the blood carried folk memories of ju-ju drums, operatic orchestras, string quartets, choirs and military bands. In the picnickers' heads were echoes of waltzes, schottisches, polkas and rags; marches, hymns, work chants and street hollers. Never before, nowhere else, had so many different kinds of music been so happily jumbled together.

Ancestrally from all Africa and all Europe and the Caribbean, the picnickers today had convened from all over town, some of them from the distant parishes south of the river. The population of New Orleans then was over two hundred thousand, and a large number of them had responded to the call to meet for something special. They had taken several hours to assemble, and now they looked as though they were settling down for a long stay. This gathering was an encampment, revivalist convention, a gluttons' saturnalia, a musical jamboree. The music was all the colors of the rainbow and beyond color, soaring in a radiant arc of light high above the earth.

Some of the musicians had arrived on horse-drawn bandwagons of the kind that advertisers used in the city streets. There were several bandwagons, decorated with red, white and blue bunting and painted banners that proclaimed the names of the bands and their sponsors. The bands were scattered about the park, each with its own audience of uncertain loyalty. Anybody who thought he heard what might be a better sound elsewhere unhesitantly headed for it. The bands were as far apart as possible but not so far apart that they could keep their music entirely separated from one another. The music peripherally overlapped in terrible discords. The louder the bands played, in their efforts to out-play their competitors, the less separate the music became. This was an all-day, all-night cutting contest, with no quarter expected or given.

The Ethiopian Temple had the biggest marquee (red and white stripes), near the edge of the lake. The temple band was making a joyous gospel uproar on a wagon between the tent and the long pine trestle tables where the food and drink were spread out. The ladies of the congregation had whomped up a mighty feast – great cauldrons of jambalaya, mountains of red beans and rice, crawfish, shrimps, frogs' legs, crabs, catfish, pigs' feet, hot dogs, chicken, ham, potato salad, cole slaw, beaten biscuits, cakes, buns, cookies, fruit salad and water melons. There were iceboxes containing tubs of ice-cream. There were glass coolers full of iced tea, lemonade, root beer and sarsaparilla. There were wooden barrels of beer, a stout regiment of them, and a truck laden with a lot more in reserve. There had been no shilly-shallying or fooling around. This was an all-out, honest-to-God *picnic*.

Family parties of three generations were seated on canvas chairs, cushions and blankets they had brought with them. White-haired grandparents dandled babies. Most of the adults and many of the children were dressed in their Sunday best. There were some fancy flowery hats and bright hair-ribbons and stiffly lacquered curls. Men in Panamas and skimmers grandly gestured with cheroots. Young couples strolled hand in hand, waiting for the night. Gangs of independent teenagers ran zigzag.

Alan found Moses where he had said he would be, close to the Ethiopians' bandwagon. The music and singing were so loud when they met that they could not talk. They simply beamed, congratulating each other in this way for being alive and in that place on that occasion. When the music paused, Alan cheered and clapped so hard that he hurt his hands. His demonstration of enthusiasm was so outstanding that one of the cornet players smiled and waved his dripping cornet at him, and Alan felt as if he had been awarded a medal.

After a while, Moses led Alan to the feast. They loaded cardboard plates with plenty of everything. When their stomachs began to feel uncomfortably full, they threw their plates into one of the bins and refilled their paper cups with root beer and set off to explore the rest of the picnic grounds.

"You were right," Alan said. "This is the best picnic of all time."

"Have you ever been to one before?" Moses asked.

"Not like this."

"This is my first."

"Mine too."

"Hah! Well, it *isn't* my first. I was just finding you out."

Alan felt stupid for a moment, but he didn't care. He was enjoying himself too much. He gave Moses a friendly knuckle punch in the biceps and they both laughed.

"O.K.," Alan said. "But it sure isn't going to be my last."

They listened to some of the other bands. They were good, but Alan and Moses agreed that the Ethiopians were better.

They raced around the softball diamond and to the shore road and back. Moses gave Alan a head start and still beat him both times. Alan did not enjoy the races.

"When are you going to play your banjo?" he asked.

"Soon. When the band takes its lunch break."

"I wish I had a banjo. Is it very difficult?"

"It isn't all that *easy*. Well, maybe it's kind of easy to start, keeping the beat with the bass and drums. But it sure ain't easy to play it real pretty."

"You're lucky, Mo."

"I'm lucky? Listen to him! You kidding? Piano's a whole lot better any day. You got control. I mean, when you want a note, you hit that note, and that's *it*. If you don't treat strings just exactly right they can go sour on you. And piano's got a bigger, prettier ring to it. That piano *sound*. You know?"

"But you can't carry a piano around with you wherever you go," Alan said. "Specially a lousy old grand piano. You can take a banjo and when you meet someone and you-all feel like playing you can play."

"There are pianos all over," Moses pointed out. "And everyone respects a piano player."

Moses envied Alan his music teacher, the music room, the formal lessons, the printed sheet music, the approved official hours of practice. Alan envied Moses his musical freedom and his easy access to the popular new living music of the streets.

Alan hated his teacher, who had long wispy gray hair around a shiny bald pate and wore silver-rimmed pinch-nose glasses and loose-fitting false teeth that smelled like a dentist's surgery. Dr.

Frischauer made music seem like a solemn task, an onerous duty, almost a punishment. When Alan made a mistake the old man wagged his finger like a metronome and crossly rebuked him.

"No, no, no, no, no!" he would say in his thick Viennese accent. He gurgled as if his mouth had been half full of whipped cream. "Not like that. Again! From the top, again. Accuracy, Alan – always accuracy! Music is like mathematics – exactly. You cannot cheat or pretend. If you do – phooey! – the sums come out wrong. Bach had excellent reasons for writing those notes, and no other notes. He was a genius. Those are the correct notes. He doesn't need changes by you, Alan, thank you very much. Now: *concentrate.*" He said it annoyingly, "*gon-zen-drate.*"

Alan and Moses came to a bandwagon on which the musicians were presenting themselves as grotesque comedians, wearing battered pink derbies, horseblanket-plaid jackets, vaudevillian baggy pants and black-face greasepaint with big white lips. There were a rinky-tink thrumming of banjos and a thumping and crashing of tambourines. The wind instruments sounded like mayhem in a farmyard – a growling wah-wah cornet, a screaming clarinet and a slide-trombone that hee-hawed and whinnied like a demented donkey.

"Minstrels?" Alan said, surprised and rather embarrassed. Minstrels made what his father contemptuously called "darky music".

"Colored minstrels," Moses said, "made up to look like white minstrels made up to look colored."

"I don't think that's very good jazz," Alan said cautiously. "Do you like it?"

"That ain't jazz," Moses said disgustedly. "That's darky music."

As they turned away, Alan tried to reconcile his father's and Moses' irreconcilably opposed though apparently identical hostile judgments. He decided that it would have to be enough to conclude that that kind of music was no damn good, no good for anyone whatsoever. Even without any sociological guidance, his own two ears could have reached that conclusion.

They walked back toward the Ethiopian Temple camp. For a short time neither of them spoke. Alan saw that Moses was frowning.

"They weren't any good on those banjos, were they?" Alan

said. "I bet you're a lot better than them. I bet you can get a lot more of a tune out of your banjo than that."

Moses did not reply.

"I didn't say anything wrong, did I?" Alan asked anxiously. "Did I say something wrong?"

Moses smiled and patted his friend on the shoulder.

"No, you didn't say anything wrong. Sorry, Alan. I was thinking about Mom's birthday. I still don't have a present for her. I just *got* to get her something nice. That's all I was thinking."

"Gee, Moses. That's a problem, all right. How much have you got to spend?"

"Nothing. I'm like to breaking my ass earning the payments on the banjo."

"Gee, that's rough."

"You don't happen to have a few dollars stashed away, do you, Alan? I could pay you back a little every week."

"You know I haven't. Daddy gives me the smallest allowance in the whole of New Orleans. It's good for my character."

"I thought I'd just ask."

"You'd be welcome to it if I had it. You know that."

"Sure. Thanks. Don't worry about it. I'll think of something."

"You know what? We have all kinds of silver stuff. I could easily let you have something. You could pawn it. Then when you saved up you could get it back. How about that?"

Moses stopped and seized Alan's shirt near the collar with two hands and angrily shook him and leaned close, face to face.

"Don't you *never* think of doing nothing like that, Alan!" he said. He released him. Alan staggered back a step, smoothing his shirt. His eyes glittered with tears.

"I was only trying to help," he said.

"Not like that," Moses said, his voice back to normal. "Thanks anyway, but think what'd happen. Sure as hell your mommy would notice a piece of silver missing. She'd tell your daddy and right away he'd blame my daddy and that would be the end of his job."

"I didn't think of that."

"If you were me you'd always think of things like that. When blame's being passed along it always finishes up at the end of the line. That's us. Even if you confessed, it would turn out to be my fault."

"I'm very sorry," Alan said meekly. He felt as though a gray cloud had obliterated the sun. But the feeling did not last long.

"It's all right," Moses said. "You couldn't know what it's like. Hey, listen! The Good Timers are playing 'Congo Square Stomp.' Ain't that something?"

Nobody could feel gloomy when The Good Timers were giving their all.

"That's Tony Rochambeau!" Moses said, when an enormously fat man in a white tuxedo got to his feet to play a cornet solo. He frowned and closed his eyes and his cheeks blew up like brown balloons as he leaned back and pointed his silver horn at the blue sky and screamed impossibly high notes and then higher still.

"They say he's the best since Buddy Bolden!" Moses shouted into Alan's ear. The solo progressed marvellously from jovial hysteria to apoplectic ecstasy. The final ensemble chorus, a headlong stampede over a cliff, was a relief. Tony Rochambeau slumped back on his chair and triumphantly brandished his cornet aloft, like a champion who had fought the music and won.

Moses and Alan walked on.

"He played with Buddy Bolden."

"I wish I could have seen him. I was too young."

"They say Buddy Bolden was the one who just about *invented* jazz. Those blue notes. They say when Buddy Bolden played here in the park on a summer evening and blew those big high C's you could hear him all over town. People would listen and say, 'That's Buddy Bolden, calling his children home!' "

"He must have been great."

"Buddy Bolden never had no music lessons. He taught himself and everybody else tried to follow him. He made a whole new kind of music all on his own."

"I can't help it if I have lessons."

"Buddy Bolden started off as just an ordinary poor working nigger," Moses said, easily slipping into the familiar story of the mythical jazz hero. "He worked in a barber shop. He bought a beat-up old accordion in a junk shop. He couldn't afford no fancy piano. He taught himself to play the accordion. He had a perfect ear for music and a perfect memory. If he heard a piece of music – any kind of music – just one time, after that it was his. He could play it right back, every note, and then he'd make it better, adding a few new tricks of his own; he'd make it better than anything the composer could have *dreamed* of."

"And then he found the cornet," Alan put in impatiently.

"Who's telling this?" Moses asked. "I'm coming to that. Then one day he was walking along the sidewalk, and what did he see there, laying in the gutter?"

"This is the part I like."

"He was just walking along, and the clouds opened a little, and the sun shined through, like a spotlight pointing down, and it sparkled like diamonds on that old cornet laying there in the gutter. That's how Buddy Bolden started to play cornet. It was like God just specially gave it to him and told him to blow. They say Buddy Bolden could blow louder than Gabriel. Tony Rochambeau is good and loud but they say he's only an imitation."

"I wish I could have heard him," Alan said.

"I heard him," Moses said proudly. "Buddy Bolden was my uncle."

"Was he *really*?"

"How many times do I have to tell you?"

"I believe you, Mo. But you're so lucky. I can't imagine what it would be like, having Buddy Bolden for an uncle."

When they got back to the Ethiopians' bandwagon, Moses' friends were already in their places, getting ready to play while the band were having lunch. The boys had a strange assortment of instruments – a kazoo made of an S-bend lead pipe from a derelict kitchen sink, a double-bass made of vegetable crates, a battery of timpani noisemakers that included a washboard, several tin pans of various sizes and a collection of wooden gourds, rattles and bells.

"You better hurry on up there," Sarah said with a broad smile, handing Moses his bright new banjo. "Everybody's waiting."

Moses scrambled up over the tailgate to be welcomed on board the wagon with some urgent muttering from his nervous fellow musicians. But Moses seemed quite confident. He liked being there, with an audience around him. He was the leader of the group, because he was a natural leader, and because his banjo was real. He stood in front of the others.

"Hello there, folks," he said. "First going to play our new song for you, a little number called, 'Lake Pontchartrain Blues.' "

Moses did the singing. The crowd's laughter was entirely sympathetic. At the end there was prolonged applause. Moses bowed in a professional manner and turned and pointed to the rest of the group and they stood up and bowed and visibly relaxed. They went on to play a medley of their lively, idiosyncratic versions of some traditional hymns and popular songs of the day. They turned Scott Joplin rags into something else, breaking down all the mechanical piano-roll regularity. After about fifteen minutes of strenuous exertion they took a couple of minutes out to discuss what they should try next. Alan took the opportunity to speak to Sarah.

"*Was* Buddy Bolden Moses' uncle?"

"Is that what Mo told you?"

"Some uncle!" snorted Benjamin, who had been getting fairly seriously into his own private supply of gin since their arrival at the park. Sarah gave him a brief discouraging look.

"Yes, Alan. You could say he was a sort of uncle. Buddy Bolden used to come and spend some time with us around the time Mo was born. That was before I came to work in your daddy's house." She gestured toward Benjamin. "Before I knew *him*."

"What was Buddy Bolden like?" Alan asked, willing to skip the intricacies of genealogy and domiciles. Buddy Bolden had been part of their lives; that was what counted. Sarah glanced warily at Benjamin, who was drinking out of a flat green pint bottle.

"He was a fine looking man when he was young," she said.

Benjamin wiped his mouth with the back of his hand, capped the bottle and stowed it away inside his jacket.

"Was he old when he died?" Alan asked.

"Buddy Bolden ain't dead. He went away."

"Sarah's boy friend suddenly had to get out of town."

"Please, Ben."

"That's right though, Alan. If you a jazzman you better watch out. That's what I tell Mo. If you a jazzman you better be ready to travel."

"Ben's only joking."

"Ladies and gentlemen!" Moses announced, trying to make his adolescent voice sound hoarse like Tony Rochambeau's. "Here's our latest – 'The Banjo Blues.' It's for Buddy Bolden."

"Sure," Benjamin said, as the kazoo elaborately introduced Moses' tribute to his absent hero ."I'm only joking. Buddy Bolden was only joking. Everything's all just a big joke."

27

FOUR

The next day after school, instead of racing Alan home, Moses walked over to Canal Street. This was the wide shopping street that divided uptown New Orleans from the French Quarter. The afternoon was hot and humid and Moses had a dull ache in his stomach. It was empty. He had eaten a peanut butter and jelly sandwich for lunch at school, and afterwards he had had to hurry to the toilet to throw up. As he walked slowly past the windows of the big stores, he felt sweaty and sick.

He stopped at the entrance of a department store. He was not sure that this would be the best place, but he would try. He still had not quite made up his mind about his mother's birthday present. She always said she didn't care about presents, but he knew that really she did care. Everybody cared about presents. He wished he were a famous bandleader, wearing a cream fedora and a cream sharkskin suit and two-tone shoes, brown and white, and riding in a shiny black automobile longer than the Poindexters'. He would have told the chauffeur to come into the store with him, to carry all the parcels. A white chauffeur in uniform. Moses wished he could buy all kinds of expensive luxuries – a diamond necklace, an alligator-skin handbag, a huge box of chocolates with soft centers, all different, an enormous bottle of imported French perfume, a gigantic bunch of red roses – and a new hat, with big feathers. Sarah said she was ashamed to be seen in her old hat. When he grew up and became a famous bandleader she could have a new hat every day if she liked. After she had worn a hat once she could throw it in the garbage.

The store was crowded with black shoppers, mostly women, hurrying in all directions, pushing past each other as if they were in search of the last bargains to be had before the end of the world.

Moses, bewildered, moved hesitantly from department to department, wondering what he could possibly get that Sarah would like. He wanted to get her something that was not at all useful and that she could not share with anyone else. She spent almost all her time cooking and cleaning and sewing for other people. He must find something she would never consider buying for herself, something that existed only for the sake of giving pleasure.

In one large hall, where they sold ladies' dresses, a tall, gray-haired man dressed as smartly as an undertaker confronted Moses. The man was black but he spoke with the authority of a white boss.

"Yes, boy?" he said. "May I help you?" The offer sounded like a threat.

"No, sir."

"Are you here on an errand?"

"Yes, sir. Through there." Moses pointed the way he was already heading.

"Get on with it then. Next time I look that way I don't want to see you hanging around."

"Yes, sir."

Moses did not loiter. He hurried through the archway to the next department. At the first glance, he knew that this was the one he was looking for. This was where they displayed the costume jewelry. Some people called it junk jewelry, but Moses had not heard the derisive term. There were long counters of open trays of brilliant baubles. He stared open-mouthed at the scintillating array of highly polished base metals and colored glass with the amazement and avarice of a magpie in Aladdin's Cave. The spectacle instantaneously dissipated all his doubts and fears.

He found the perfect present on the first tray of the nearest counter – a butterfly brooch, which was life-size and, he thought, lovelier than any butterfly that had ever lived. The brooch was outlined in delicately ornate golden filigree, and the colors of the wings, peacock green and peacock blue, were filled in with richly gleaming enamel. He knew that Sarah would love it.

Moses leaned close to the counter. He stretched his left arm forward to its full extent and picked up a pair of golden earrings and moved his head as far forward as possible, as though examining them with great interest.

At the same time, his right hand moved like a small furtive animal, crawling over the edge of the counter, over the edge of the tray, over the brooch.

Moses paused and looked up at the saleswoman in charge of that section of the counter. She was busy showing a customer how to fasten the clasp of a necklace.

The fingers of his right hand closed around the brooch and quickly withdrew it. He slipped it into the right pocket of his shabby brown trousers, while ostentatiously dropping the earrings onto the tray and shaking his head as though having decided against buying them.

He slowly turned from the counter and slowly walked toward the doors to the street. His innards seemed to be tied in tight knots and he could feel his heart-beats pounding in his head. He wanted to run but he was careful to maintain the same easy pace, casually looking from counter to counter on the way out, as if still considering the possibility of making a purchase.

He pushed his way around the revolving doors and emerged into the hot white dazzle of Canal Street. He heaved a deep sigh. And then he felt the heavy hand on his left shoulder.

FIVE

The magistrate of the Juvenile Court was in a benevolent mood. He had lunched well. There was not much on the docket. Flanked by the flags of the United States and the State of Louisiana and the city of New Orleans, he gazed over the gold rims of his spectacles with solemn attentiveness, his chin resting on his clasped hands, his elbows resting on the judicial bench, and allowed the social worker to recite her report. At last, after clearing his throat and neatly depositing the proceeds into his handkerchief, he delivered himself of his legal opinion, illuminated with a few homiletic personal comments. He handed down the court's verdict and pronounced sentence. The mill of justice ground exceeding small.

"Because the self-appointed guardian of this unfortunate illegitimate child, far from offering him the moral guidance needed in his formative years, evidently incited him to commit petty larceny for her benefit, and because nobody has been able to offer the court any documentary proof that she is cohabiting with her consort in a state of holy matrimony, my duty in the disposition of this case is quite clear.

"It is ironic, is it not, that this irresponsible couple and this child were privileged to live in the home of one of the most substantial citizens of our community? What ingratitude! But it is not for me to advise Mr. Poindexter as to what he should do about these cynical parasites who have abused his hospitality. No doubt he will know what to do.

"In the meantime, there is a child to be saved from further corruption and exploitation. Moses: stand up."

Moses stood up.

"Moses, in this court we are concerned not merely with punishment for wrong-doings, though, as you should now be aware, you have done wrong, and, in accordance with the law of the land, you must be punished. There is no getting around that. But, more important, in my view, we are concerned also with correction and redemption. You are still young, Moses, and your case is not hopeless, if you are prepared to make the most of the new life that lies before you. This court directs that you shall be given over to the care of the Colored Waifs' Home, for an indefinite term."

The magistrate smiled kindly and rapped with his gavel, which made a sound as conclusive as that made by an auctioneer at the end of a sale. While Moses was led away, a newspaper court reporter went to the bench to clarify a few colorful minor details that would help fill space on a slow August day, and the magistrate was most cooperative.

In the bar of his club before dinner that evening, Chesley laughed with more heartiness than he felt when a fellow member, an alert scrutineer of the evening paper, joshed him about the criminal activities that had been going on below stairs in the Poindexter home.

"Maybe you didn't contribute enough to party funds," the joker suggested, passing the paper around. "We Democrats don't usually have to take that kind of sass from our appointees." Chesley joined in the general merriment and ordered a round of drinks.

He dismissed Benjamin and Sarah the next morning.

Alan was grimly silent when he returned from school. He went up to bed early, without having to be told. A little later, his mother entered his room.

"Are you awake, Alan?"

"Yes."

"Do you feel unwell?"

"No."

"Don't you think it was rather impolite, going upstairs without a word?"

"Why did you let them take Moses away?"

"It had nothing to do with me, Alan. I didn't let them. Moses tried to steal from a store and the police arrested him. I hope he never tried to persuade you to do anything as wicked and foolish as that."

"It was only a little old brooch. It was for Sarah's birthday."

"Stealing is stealing. It wasn't the value of the thing that mattered."

"They didn't have to send him away to *prison*."

"Don't be silly now, Alan. The Colored Waifs' Home is exactly what its name says : it's a home for colored children who have no families to look after them. It's a school where he can live with other children of his own kind."

"You knew Benjamin and Sarah were the same as his father and mother. Would you send me away like that?"

"Really, Alan. Be reasonable. There's no comparison between our situation and theirs."

"Benjamin and Sarah loved Mo, and he loved them. You know that's true. Why did you let the police do that? I didn't even go down to the kitchen this afternoon. I couldn't have looked Sarah in the eye."

Elizabeth Poindexter was somewhat embarrassed. In a low voice, she informed Alan that Benjamin and Sarah had left the house. Alan was silent. Elizabeth could hear the tick of the bedroom clock.

"It's the best thing for everyone," she said. "We all felt terrible about Moses. They'll get over this episode much better in a completely new environment. I gave Sarah a nice present."

"What, a butterfly brooch?"

All his friends at school seemed to know all about it. Elizabeth patiently ignored the childish jibe.

"I gave her a check. For quite a useful amount, I can tell you. That's between you and me. Please don't mention it to anyone. Anyway, we've always treated Benjamin and Sarah most generously. We'll get a new butler and cook, a more mature couple, I trust. We've had enough melodrama in this house during the past few hours to last me a lifetime."

"Why didn't Daddy fix the police?"

"What *do* you mean, Alan?"

"He fixed them when he had his accident with the Pierce Arrow, didn't he?"

"I don't know what you're talking about. I won't have you talk about your father that way. Who ever suggested such a thing? Did Benjamin? The idea!"

"Daddy and you were talking about it. I couldn't help hearing. Daddy was shouting. I may be only thirteen, Mom, but I'm not deaf. And I'm not simple-minded."

"There's no need to be impudent. I know you're upset, but I think I'll leave you to sleep. I'm sure you'll feel much calmer in the morning. Goodnight, Alan."

Alan was silent. After a moment's uncertain hesitation, his mother left the room and shut the door.

SIX

Alan's parents did not pamper him. His father treated him with severe austerity, which was lightened at the best of times by nothing warmer than sarcastic banter and teasing. His mother would have dearly loved to lavish upon him all the privileges and indulgences within her ample means, but she did not dare to break the family rules. Alan always felt less free and less well off than any other children he knew. However, he *was* the only child of wealthy parents, his mother's only son. He was the possessor of a certain considerable potential power.

For the first couple of weeks after the departure of Moses, Alan was polite, quiet and sullen. When the new black couple made friendly overtures to him, he did not respond. They quickly gave him up as a rich white brat.

"What's the matter?" his mother asked.

"Nothing," he said.

His homework was beyond reproach and he played the piano in the prescribed manner for the ordained time. Although his technique was now excellent for one so young and he followed the music with precision, Dr. Frischauer of course realized that something was wrong. Alan's dispirited musical performances were like his behavior in general : his conformity was so coldly correct that he seemed to provoke and defy adult criticism.

During the lifeless rendition of a Mozart sonata, the music teacher threw up his hands in exasperation.

"No, no, no!" he protested.

Alan stopped playing and calmly awaited Dr. Frischauer's comments.

"This is the music of *love*, Alan. You must think of the blue sky, the spring flowers, the birds singing, a pretty girl. It's happy music! Please, Alan. Relax. Only melt a little. Play with feeling."

Alan grimly compressed his lips. What could a fat old gray-haired man like Dr. Frischauer know about pretty girls? Alan started playing again, as properly and as meaninglessly as before. Dr. Frischauer stared sadly out at the ragged dull green frond of a banana tree in the patio. Alan reached the end of the sonata and stopped.

"All right," the old man said. "Enough. Perhaps next time you'll feel better."

After the lesson, Dr. Frischauer asked Mrs. Poindexter whether he might have a few words with her alone.

"Alan's musical progress is disappointing," he mildly informed her.

She looked alarmed and guilty.

"He practises every day. He never misses a day."

"I do not doubt that, my dear Mrs. Poindexter," he assured her with a paternalistic chuckle. "His playing is technically far advanced. He has a gift, a talent. He could be a virtuoso. But something is lacking. Is the boy unhappy?"

"I don't know. He doesn't say."

"He is at a difficult age," Dr. Frischauer pointed out consolingly. "The coming of manhood is a time of introspection, melancholy brooding, doubt. Maybe he should go out more, mix more with boys and girls of his own age; have some fun. He has the special problems of being an only child, you know."

She frowned and bit her lower lip.

"May I make a suggestion?" he asked.

"Please do."

"A friend of mine runs a school of music in the Garden District."

"You don't mean you want to drop Alan, do you?"

"Certainly not. I'm sure that one day I'll be very proud he has been a pupil of mine. But this friend presents concerts. Soloists, chamber music, even a symphony orchestra. The standards are high. I could arrange something for Alan. I know the challenge would stimulate him. And he would make friendships with other young musicians. He would not feel isolated. Good idea?"

"Oh, yes, Dr. Frischauer! Would you speak with Alan about it? I know that if I did he'd have nothing to do with the idea."

"Alan's no great admirer of mine," Dr. Frischauer said with a rueful smile. "But I'm willing to do my best. As things are his talent could be wasted. We mustn't let that happen."

Dr. Frischauer went off to find out what might be done to further Alan's musical education and musical experience.

In the meantime, Alan distracted his mother from all consideration of music by announcing that his head felt kind of funny and his eyes ached. After testing his forehead with the gentle palm of her hand, she got a thermometer. His temperature was normal, but she put him to bed. He went quietly, without protest, though his bedroom was still bright with sunshine, until she carefully drew the curtains.

"I'll send for the doctor right away," she promised, patting her son's cheek. She smiled happily, relieved that he really had nothing wrong with him, except that he was ill. Now she could nurse him.

"Is there anything I can do for you?" she said.

"Only one thing," he murmured in the small voice of someone making a last request.

"What is it?"

"Promise?"

"Anything I can do," she said.

"Will you take me to the Waifs' Home, to see Mo?"

She thoughtfully chewed her lower lip, but only for a moment.

"Of course, darling," she said.

Alan eagerly raised his head.

"You will?"

"Yes, Alan." She leaned forward and kissed the top of his head. which he lowered to the pillow, as he knew he should. He closed his eyes and bravely smiled.

SEVEN

Louis Armstrong had been an inmate of the Colored Waifs' Home since the first day of the year. He was arrested in the street on New Year's Eve, when he was twelve years of age. His thirteenth birthday was on July 4.

"I didn't do nothing *bad*," Louis recounted to Moses. "They told the judge I was shooting up some other kid. That was a lie. I wouldn't do that. We were having fun. I borrowed my step-father's gun. I shot it up in the air. Only those blanks. How could they hurt? Some of us had been singing for the folks in the street late that night – you know, singing and dancing and passing the hat. It was at Rampart and Perdido. Close to home. *Everybody* was having fun. It was New Year's *Eve*. Nothing wrong in firing off a few blanks on New Year's Eve. But they grabbed me. Scared me half to death, those po-lice. I knew I was in bad trouble. But then it wasn't all that bad when they brought me here. Pops – that's Captain Jones – treats you real nice if you don't get out of line. After a while, he let Professor Davis give me music lessons. I like Professor Davis. He's *fine*."

Everybody in those days used to call Louis "Little Louis," because he was short. Sometimes they called him "Dippermouth" or "Dipper": he had a mouth as big as a cup. It was full of teeth as white as china and he flashed them a lot. He was short but strong and he knew his way around and the other boys liked him.

"Do you think the professor would give me lessons?" Moses wanted to know. "I play banjo."

"All you have to do is show them your best behavior. It's worth it. Don't give them no hard time, they'll go easy on you."

"I have my own banjo at home," Moses said. "They could bring it to me. It's a new, full-size banjo."

Louis shook his head

"No place here for a banjo. We have a brass band. We play marches. Sousa. You know? And church music."

"I like jazz."

Louis regarded the new boy with speculative interest.

"They started me off on tambourine and drums," Louis said. "But soon they let me try alto horn. Then bugle. You could blow yourself inside out blowing bugle. Professor Davis could see I was giving it everything. He promoted me to cornet. That is it. The valves make a big difference. There's a whole heap of music in a cornet."

"I've never played a cornet," Moses said contemplatively. He was speaking half to himself. Louis grinned.

"If you got the air and a big old powerful pair of lips – I *know* you got the time – I can show you how."

"Would you?"

"Professor Davis can even teach you how to *read* music. He knows all that stuff. If you work hard at the first things he'll soon move you on up to something better. And if you make out in the band this is home, sweet home."

After the hour in vocational-training woodwork, Moses happened to encounter Professor Davis in the corridor. Louis had pointed him out in assembly.

"Professor Davis," Moses said.

"Yes?"

"Please, Professor Davis. Will you teach me to play the cornet?"

Professor Davis smiled.

"I saw Louis and you having a talk. You aren't wasting any time."

"Will you, Professor Davis? Please, will you?"

"Trouble is, everybody in the band wants to play cornet."

"Can I be in the band?"

"What's your name, son?"

"Moses. Moses Decatur."

"Well, that's a good enough *name*. Maybe after a while. I'll watch out for you. We'll see how well you settle in."

"Thank you, Professor Davis. It wouldn't have to be the cornet. Not at first."

"Oh, it wouldn't? That's right cooperative, Moses. If I think of something I'll let you know."

Professor Davis recognized yearning ambition when he saw it. It was not in every boy's face. He did not keep Moses waiting long.

When Mrs. Poindexter wrote to Mr. Joseph Jones, Director of the Colored Waif's Home, to ask him when Moses would be allowed to receive her son and herself as visitors, Captain Jones consulted his assistant, the warden.

"Peter, how about Moses Decatur? How's he coming on? Would you say he's due for some privileges?"

"Moses?" said Professor Davis. "From what he tells me, I'd guess he's overdue."

So Captain Jones wrote back to say that Mrs. Poindexter and her son would be welcome to visit the home. He suggested three o'clock in the afternoon of the third Saturday in October, when the band would be giving a concert in aid of the home's athletic fund. He enclosed two tickets. For her guidance, he let her know the goal, the total sum of the benefactions so far, and the balance still being sought. It was quite considerable, almost as much as she customarily spent on a Mardi Gras ball-gown. However, she wrote a check for the full amount. Chesley never questioned her checks in support of good causes. The family had a public reputation for philanthropic generosity; and contributions to charity, of course, were tax-exempt. She felt a comforting glow of virtue as she sealed the envelope.

On the afternoon of the concert, Captain Jones welcomed Mrs. Poindexter and Alan as if they were royalty. He seated them next to his own place in the middle of the top plank of the temporary bleachers that had been erected in the shade of a dormitory, an institutionally plain gray barracks, overlooking the asphalt playground.

The bleachers were nearly full. There was an audience of perhaps forty or fifty, including a few rather selfconscious whites. There were more women than men. Almost all of them, black and white, male and female, appeared as though they had devoted several long decades to being devoutly, self-sacrificingly bored for the sake of the community. They wore suits and dresses of dim, crepuscular, ecclesiastical fuscousness as dull as doctoral theses in sociology. The women's somber, amorphous hats, or anti-hats, were declarations of self-abnegation, and the few clerical collars were not so much emblems of faith as admissions of resignation to the martyrdom of spiritual drudgery. The audience looked like an academic conference, glancing meekly, without hope, from their mimeographed programs to the empty playground.

"You have a beautiful afternoon for it," Mrs. Poindexter said with a gracious smile, as if complimenting Captain Jones on his own, personal good fortune, on having the same bright autumn sunshine and fresh air as the Poindexters had on Beauregard Street. "This is always my favorite season of the year. You couldn't get any nicer weather in California, could you?" Mrs. Poindexter had a cousin in Pasadena, which was socially quite acceptable.

"Yes, Mrs. Poindexter, this is very nice," agreed Captain Jones, who had never travelled farther west than Baton Rouge, Louisiana. He extracted a large silver Ingersoll railroad timepiece from a pocket of his dark-gray tropical worsted waistcoat. "It's just three. They should be starting now."

A loud blaring and banging of military musical instruments attested to the accuracy of the director's watch and to the punctuality, discipline and general good order of the home. The boys of the band, like midget chauffeurs in their black caps and black uniforms, marched in a compact squad, four abreast, around a corner of the building and onto the rectangle of asphalt. They carried with them a glorious dazzle of sunlight mirrored by polished metal. The band was marching and countermarching, back and forth across the playground, with gymnastic vigor, and playing at a peppy tempo with fervent raucousness.

Alan immediately spotted Moses. He was marching in the rearmost rank, but he was marching with an upright swagger, with his head high, adding more than his quota to the brassy pandemonium by repeatedly bringing together a pair of outsize cymbals with a sizzling clash. Alan felt a thrill of love and vicarious pride and a sharp pang of envy.

Moses, in turn, spotted Alan, sitting up there at the top of the bleachers, Captain Jones' guest of honor. The friends' eyes met. Moses gave Alan a broad smile, and Alan waved.

The liveliness of the spectacle and the music had a marvellous effect on the audience. It suddenly made them seem younger.

Alan thought he recognized the tune. He looked at the beginning of his program : "The Stars and Stripes Forever," composed by John Philip Sousa. Of course !

But something strange was happening to it. The short, stocky boy in the front rank, the boy playing the cornet, was breaking up phrases and bending some of the notes and altering the time. He was turning the march into jazz.

EIGHT

Captain Jones smiled and led the applause as the band, still playing, marched off the playground and returned to where they had come from.

"Such energy! Such enthusiasm!" Mrs. Poindexter politely exclaimed, offering her host the only praise that she was able honestly to utter. She felt sure she had never before heard such strident music. She was glad Chesley had not been present. He would have made no allowance for the children's ages. She could imagine the sort of comment he would have made: "What do you expect from jungle bunnies?" She applauded as long as any of the others in the audience and longer than some of them, though her white gloves unfortunately rendered her clapping almost silent.

The last rank marched around the corner of the dormitory building and the applause ceased. There was a murmurous babble of benign comments as the visitors slowly descended the steep steps of the bleachers.

"The boys seemed to be having a lovely time, didn't they?" Mrs. Poindexter said brightly. "Oh, my, children can be so funny, can't they? Bless them."

"We take the band seriously," Captain Jones said. "It gives all of us a sense of pride in the home."

"Of course," she earnestly assured him.

"Being chosen to play in the band is an honor."

"I'm sure it is."

She was glad she had not said a single flippant word about the eccentric musicianship. Why hurt the poor man's feelings?

"Moses was good, wasn't he?" Alan said.

"Which was he? I couldn't tell."

"He was playing the cymbals."

"The boys all looked the same in those caps. I thought the uniforms were adorable, Captain Jones."

"Thank you, Mrs. Poindexter."

"The cymbals were very loud, weren't they, Alan? Moses must have had a wonderful time."

"They're supposed to be loud," Alan said, knowing what all her comments meant.

Some of the senior waifs guided small groups of visitors around the home. The tour ended in the dining hall, a large, low-ceilinged room that smelled of floor polish and cooking fat. On this special occasion, there were bunches of yellow chrysanthemums in glass pots on the long refectory tables. Mrs. Poindexter and Alan were shown to the smaller table used by the staff.

Captain Jones made a speech of welcome and appreciation for the visitors' donations to the athletic fund and there was some more applause. Coffee and lemonade and cookies were served. After these formalities there was a period of what was listed in the program as "Get-Acquainted Socializing," during which the benefactors and beneficiaries of the home were given an opportunity to meet and chat about any interests that they might prove to have in common. Captain Jones invited Mrs. Poindexter and Alan to remain seated. He sent one of his assistants to fetch Moses. The other members of the faculty excused themselves from the table.

"Here's Moses!" Captain Jones said, getting up and genially waving Moses to a chair. "I must leave you folks for a while. I know you must have a lot to talk about. Moses has fifteen minutes."

Alan had expected Moses to have shrunk in captivity, but he did not appear to have changed at all; he looked as fit and cheery as ever. His easy, casual smile somehow seemed to diminish the importance of the visit. Alan could not have explained why, even to himself, but he felt slightly irritated by his friend's appearance of happy-go-lucky wellbeing.

"Thank you for coming, Mrs. Poindexter," Moses said. "How do you like our band, Alan?"

Alan's admiration for the music overcame his momentary misgiving.

"Swell!" he said. "You were really beating those cymbals."

"It isn't what I really want. But it's a beginning. Even Louis had to start on tambourine. He's only been here nine months, and look at him now! He's the cornet player. He's the leader. Cornet! That's what I want to play in the band. I'd give anything to do that. Louis is teaching me. I think I can do it. I told Professor Davis the band would be better with another cornet. He said he'll think about it."

42

"Yeah?" Alan said, wincing inside.

"What did you think of Louis?"

"He blows hard," Alan had to concede.

Mrs. Poindexter thought the cornet had been especially awful. The boy evidently could not keep proper time and he kept deviating from the proper tunes. Even so, she thought it was wrong of Alan to speak so rudely to his former playmate.

"I'm sure the boy is doing his best," she said tactfully. She poured more lemonade into the boys' glasses. "It must be very difficult to play a cornet."

"Oh, it is, Mrs. Poindexter. Very difficult. And Louis sings, too. He's really something! He's funny. He often forgets the words. But that doesn't stop him. He just keeps right on, singing made-up words. They aren't real words. They're better than the real ones. He sang that way the other day in front of Professor Davis. We all thought, 'Oh-oh! Here's trouble!' But you know what? Professor Davis liked it."

"Mo, Dr. Frischauer says I'm good enough now to play piano with the Garden District Junior Symphony."

"Good," Moses said. "And another thing Louis does is make up his own songs. He can make up melodies that nobody else ever thought of before."

"Dr. Frischauer said I could conduct the orchestra one day if I like."

Mrs. Poindexter decided the time had come to change the subject.

"Please give Benjamin and Sarah our very best wishes the next time you see them," she said to Moses.

The smile faded from his face. He looked puzzled.

"The next time? There hasn't been no first time. I was going to give *you* a message to give *them*."

That was how Moses learned that his foster father and foster mother had left the Poindexter household and that there had been no word from them and that their whereabouts were unknown.

Moses did not cry. He bowed his head and stared at the table. There was no more conversation, though Mrs. Poindexter made one or two tries. She was most embarrassed. Alan wanted to comfort Moses but could not think of a way. When Captain Jones returned to the table he found them sitting in gloomy silence.

"Time to say goodbye, Moses!" he said jovially. "Maybe Mrs. Poindexter and Alan will be able to come and visit you again some time."

Captain Jones dismissed Moses and escorted his visitors toward the front door.

"He seemed kind of subdued," the director said to Mrs. Poindexter. "Probably tired. The boys were all very excited about today."

"He said he doesn't like playing the cymbals," she reported with a merry little laugh. "If you ask me, I don't think Moses will be satisfied until he takes over from Louis!"

"Moses said that?"

"He's *determined* to play the cornet. You know, Captain Jones, I'd like to do something for him. He has an unfortunate background. Why not let him play the cornet? Would you do that? Of course, I'd be willing to pay for the instrument."

Later, when Captain Jones and Professor Davis were alone, Captain Jones told him what Mrs. Poindexter had said.

"I'm surprised at Moses, complaining like that to an outsider," Professor Davis said. "I thought Louis and Moses were friends. Louis has helped him. Maybe I misjudged Moses. That's too bad."

"You don't think we should let Mrs. Poindexter buy him a cornet?"

"I thought I was ready to gives Moses a chance to play second cornet, but now I think I'm going to have to make him wait. That Mrs. Poindexter can buy him a *gold-plated* cornet if she wants. But she can't buy the band."

Thus Alan's and Moses' musical apprenticeships progressed in their different ways, at their different speeds.

And in a maximum-security isolation cell in the wing for disturbed inmates of the East Louisiana State Hospital the legendary Buddy Bolden sat on the floor patiently counting his fingers. He moved them like the fingers on the valves of a cornet. He kept coming up with a different total and he kept counting again.

He had forgotten about the women of New Orleans and all the music and musicians.

Buddy Bolden had the blues so bad he didn't even know the word for them.

NINE

The late Dr. Frischauer would have been pleased with Alan's
progress at the Henri Mercier Conservatory of Music, in
the Garden District. The old man would have been less pleased
with Alan's secret progress at the grand piano in the Poindexters'
music room. A fellow student with a strong left hand showed Alan
how to play in the manner of Jelly Roll Morton and Alan worked
dilligently to master the style.

He attended the school three afternoons a week after Dr.
Frischauer died. As well as polishing his keyboard technique, Alan
began taking instruction in composition and harmony. Whenever
he got an opportunity to play for his own pleasure he turned from
the classics to jazz. He was developing marked musical schizo-
phrenia.

The school occupied a large red-brick mansion with high white
pillars in the style of an antebellum plantation house. It was surrounded by magnolia trees and azalea bushes set far back from the
live oaks of St. Charles Avenue. Although Alan's father was
merely indifferent to music on his better days, and on the rare
occasions when he was expected to listen to it he was bored and
then fretfully impatient, when he saw the school's splendid
traditional premises he felt sure that the establishment could do
his son no harm.

In this case, as in so many others, A. Chesley Poindexter III was
wrong. It was here that Alan made the acquaintance of Louise
Mercier, the principal's daughter. She was to have a profoundly
disturbing effect on his life.

She certainly did not seem at first to be potentially harmful.
He was sixteen and she was fifteen when they met in the school
library. It was summertime, in the first oppressive heat wave of
the year, but she looked fresh and cool in a pale blue cotton dress
with a demure white collar. She had long, straight, shiny black
hair, parted in the center like a ballerina's, fine black eyebrows
and wide-set eyes of an extraordinary light gray with thick curly
black lashes. Her nose was short and neat and she had a well-
rounded little chin. She was very, very pretty. But she was hum-

45

ming the musical score she was reading at the table where Alan was trying to read the score of something else.

"Do you have to do that?" he asked.

She stopped humming and looked at him with eyes opened wider than ever.

"Do what?" she said.

"Humming."

"Was I?"

"Yes. It's hard to read music when someone's sitting near you humming something different. And humming some of it wrong."

Soon they were arguing about Puccini, until the librarian, an arid spinster, irritably hushed them.

"Come on," Alan said. "Let's go. It's almost quitting time. I'll get you a lemonade and explain exactly what *con brio* means."

"I know what *con brio* means, but I'll take the lemonade."

The teenagers' conversational mating ritual continued with mock antagonism and sly allure in a vigorous and brisk manner. They got bottles of lemonade from the cooler in the cafeteria and sat by a window looking out over the garden. Before the lemonade was finished he had off-handedly suggested, and she had casually agreed to, a date to swim in the lake on Saturday afternoon.

On Saturday she was even prettier. She wore a short-sleeved cream linen dress with a matching silk headband. Her smooth, tawny complexion glowed peach in the sunlight. As he followed her into a streetcar he noticed tiny golden hairs glinting on her forearm. The car was crowded and they stood so close together that he could smell her warm hair, the mingled scents of jasmine and something as pure and wholesome and innocent as fresh-baked bread – herself. He inhaled her fragrance and his heart seemed to throb like a salmon leaping over rapids.

They went swimming. They walked in the park. They rode back in another streetcar. He took her to an ice-cream parlor. They had banana splits with everything on them. He looked at her lips. The cold made them as pink as raspberry sherbet.

He took her home. They paused in the shade of the portico and she made no move to ring the bell. He was suffering the sweet agony of desire and there was nothing he could do about it. In that long-ago era it was not unusual for sixteen-year-old boys and fifteen-year-old girls to be chaste. Alan had not very often kissed a girl. He felt awkward, and afraid that if he moved forward to kiss Louise she might reject him. They stood there for a long time making small talk about the afternoon.

At last, she kissed him.

The kiss was a light one, on his cheek, but it was a major event. He was elated.

"I love you," he said.

He had never spoken the words to a girl before. They seemed new and solemn and important.

"I'm a Creole," Louise said.

"I don't care what you are. I love you."

Louise smiled and gently touched his mouth with a warm hand.

"But I care," she said. "And so does my family. We're proud of what we are."

Alan told his mother about the wonderful Louise Mercier. His mother mentioned to Chesley that their son seemed to be head over heels with his first real girl friend. Chesley checked on the Merciers.

"A touch of the tar-brush there," he told his wife.

In the fall, he sent Alan away to Bull Run Military Academy. Many of the prep school's alumni went on to Virginia Military Institute.

"Bull Run will make a man of him," Chesley said. This time, in an unexpected way, he was right.

TEN

Bull Run, Virginia, 1916

Anthropologists, given the slightest encouragement, will tell you of primitive tribes in primitive countries whose rites of passage from boyhood to manhood are painfully severe. Typically they involve harsh tests of courage, strength and stamina. Sometimes, if the geography is convenient, the boy who applies to join the men is required to sally forth alone to hunt and kill a lion or some other wild beast. He may have to prove his willingness and ability to endure pain by submitting to ordeals by fire, the whip and the knife. There are frightening, hazardous and messy ceremonies of circumcision and sexual initiation. Tribal elders take the applicant into the bush and confidentially instruct him in the alarming facts of life and death, the methods, customs and ethics of combat and marriage. Blood is shed. Permanent scars are formed.

No anthropologist, however broad his experience and scholarship, can tell you of a place where the metamorphosis from Boy to Man is more arduous than at Bull Run Military Academy. Back in 1916, among American professional soldiers, of both North and South, the name of the academy was a by-word, a symbol of Spartan austerity and obedience enforced by discipline of crushing forcefulness.

Most of the inmates began their terms of servitude at the age of twelve. The academy conditioned every phase of their adolescence, forming their beliefs and opinions and the style of their behavior. The academy had the average student in its power for approximately six years before passing him on to his higher education. Six years were quite enough. After six years of physical and psychological training, a Bull Run man was a Bull Run man for ever. By the time the processing was complete, he could be counted on to act in unison with his comrades in response to any challenge, any stimulation. Bull Run men all shared the same sense of honor, duty and privilege. They were unshakably loyal to their alma mater and their fellow alumni. They reacted as one man to any threat of deviation from their articles of faith, which had long since been pronounced perfect and immutable. As one man, they laughed at the same jokes.

One of the jokes they always laughed at with a special harsh glee was a novice who was inducted into the student body late in his prep-school career and seemed on arrival to believe that he was as good as they were.

The day Alan arrived he was pleasantly surprised to be reminded of home. The neo-Colonial red-brick buildings, the oak trees and box hedges and the well-trimmed shrubberies and lawns reminded him of the part of New Orleans that he knew best.

The receptionist in the registrar's office was formally courteous. His manner implied approval of Alan's personal and scholastic credentials. It seemed that the paper work and the financial red tape were in good order.

A junior member of the faculty gave Alan a quick guided tour of the campus. The commentary emphasized the academy's traditions of valor in sport and war, calling his attention particularly to cadets at practice on the football field and to several dignified bronze statues of men in Confederate uniforms, larger than life and green with age, Bull Run graduates who had gone on to distinguish themselves, most of them fatally, in some of the great unsuccessful battles of the War Between the States.

Everything Alan saw gave him an impression of stability and order and the collective self-esteem of an institution of long-established integrity and masculine virtue. He felt secure.

This comfortable illusion was shattered during his first night of residence in Jefferson Hall. Exhausted by travel and novelty, Alan went to bed as early as possible. The narrow bed was as hard as a monastic pallet and the gray blankets and off-white sheets were coarse and smelled of institutional disinfectant, but Alan immediately fell asleep.

He was shocked awake by the white glare of a flashlight held close to his eyes. For a moment he did not know where he was. He did not know the time. The light was so bright that he did not see anything else at first.

"Time for your trial, Poindexter," said an invisible boy. "Get up."

Alan got out of bed. He was wearing an elegant new pair of dark blue sea island cotton pajamas. His mother had bought them and a lot of other things and she had done the packing.

In a dazzling circle of flashlights, he was tried by a kangaroo court of the boys of his dormitory. When he could make out the shadowy figures beyond the lights, he became aware that he was the only boy dressed in pajamas. The others wore their underwear and handkerchief masks.

One of the judges – they were all judges and jurors and executioners – whistled as a man might whistle at an attractive girl.

"Cute pajamas!"

"Take them off!' another judge decreed.

"What's the penalty for cute pajamas?"

"The gauntlet!"

"Down on your knees, Poindexter!"

"The faster you crawl, the easier for you."

Alan was shoved and kicked as he crawled over the waxed linoleum, between two files of torch-bearers. Some of them flogged him with knotted wet towels. They hurt.

"Stand against the wall," he was told. He stood against the wall. He was breathing hard. The flashlight beams examined him thoroughly from head to foot and back part way to focus on his genitals.

"It isn't very big!"

He covered himself with his right hand.

"No hiding! Let's see it!"

"How long is it, Poindexter?"

"How long is it? Speak when you're spoken to."

"We know you've measured it, you dirty little boy. How long is it?"

He looked down at himself. His penis, shrunken by fear and shame, had almost disappeared.

A hand slapped his face.

"Answer the question!"

"I don't know," Alan said.

"He says he doesn't know."

"Every red-blooded American boy knows how long his own prick is, for Pete's sake."

"What's the penalty for lying?"

"The razor."

"Prepare the prisoner for the razor."

Several powerful hands seized Alan in grips he could not struggle out of. They forced him down to the floor, to lie on his back, spread-eagled, vulnerable, helpless. Hands held his ankles and wrists far apart. Hands held his ears and the hair of his head.

Now they could do anything they wanted and he could not stop them.

"The razor!"

"No!" Alan protested in a voice hoarse with horror. "Don't!"

"I always heard tell these New Orleans kids were supposed to have fancy manners. He brought fancy pajamas. How come he forgot his manners? Why doesn't he say 'please'?"

"Please, fellows! Please!"

"He doesn't even say 'sir'!"

"Please, sir!"

"Too late. Appeal dismissed. Proceed with hazing."

He saw a hand holding an open cut-throat razor, silhouetted against the lights. He saw a masked face descending over him.

"For God's sake!" he shrilly cried.

He made a desperate effort to free his hands and feet, but he could not move them. He strained to lift his head, and the hands punished him by tugging his ears and his hair.

The razor was sharp. The boy wielding it was not altogether unskillful. But he did not use soap and water. When he shaved Alan's head, the cuts were few and superficial, but his scalp seemed to be on fire.

That was really all there was to it. The worst part of the experience had been imagining what they might do to him if they chose to.

They released him without any further comment. The lights moved away and soon went out in different parts of the long room. He lay where they had left him, motionless, quietly, bitterly sobbing. He would never forgive his father. Never.

Alan slowly got to his feet. He groped his way back to his bed.

In the morning, he found his pajamas on the floor. Someone had ripped the legs asunder.

There was much comradely laughter in the shower room. One of the more demonstratively extrovert members of the group gave an exhibition of masturbation, using a handful of soapsuds. He was cheered for being very fast.

At breakfast one of Alan's classmates winked at him, and, without being asked, passed him the sugar for his porridge. The porridge was lukewarm and lumpy.

Alan went to the quartermaster's stores and was issued uniforms. The headgear included a tall Confederate-gray shako with a black patent-leather visor and a black plume, suitable for an old-fashioned Ruritanian operetta.

He had three hours of lessons. The subjects were trigonometry, military history and calisthenics. They were representative samples of a curriculum that might have been specially designed to inculcate in Alan a smoldering contemptuous resentment of the System and all its works.

The entire Brigade of Cadets assembled in the parade ground at noon for drill and roll-call, before marching to the dining hall for chow. These toy-soldier exercises were accompanied by a brass band. The band played like a machine. The extreme contrast with the band of the Colored Waifs' Home reminded Alan of Moses. This was the first time he had thought about Moses for a long time.

ELEVEN

By exerting himself as little and as obviously grudgingly as possible in the classroom and as strenuously as he was able on the football field, Alan soon gained acceptance by his classmates. He did not value it, but it made existence in the unnatural confinement of a military school less difficult to endure.

The camaraderie of common suffering, the mystique of shared misery, did not inspire him at all. There are boy-men of all ages who feel ennobled by belonging to a cruelly oppressed all-male microcosm rigorously deprived of all civilized amenities. Alan felt otherwise. His fellow cadets evidently believed that there was merit in mortification, that getting up at dawn, bathing under cold showers, eating what they themselves always called pig-slop (said to be heavily dosed with saltpeter), memorizing boring facts about martial technology, exerting themselves monotonously in the gym and on the parade ground, running long distances across rough country in foul weather, competing violently intramurally and against the athletes of other schools, and submitting to the sadistically whimsical rules and regulations of upperclassmen were acts of heroism which would be rewarded one day in the distant future by the conferral of the gold bars of a second lieutenancy, an exalted state close to apotheosis. Right from the beginning of his term of captivity at Bull Run, Alan was quite sure that such a destiny was not for him. He had no desire to commit himself to any organization of any kind, military or civil, whatsoever.

Instructors in military history described, analyzed and criticized battles as if they had been works of art. The dispositions and movements of armies were demonstrated on maps, sand-tables and on the local terrain. The cadets were taken on trips to nearby Civil War battlefields as reverently as pilgrims are escorted to holy shrines. Alan went on field trips as far north as Gettysburg, as far south as Mechanicsville, Virginia. He was shown where Stonewall Jackson led his men to victories at McDowell, Fort Royal, Winchester, Cross Keys and Port Republic. And there were briefer visits to other historic sites where things had not gone quite so well.

"Do you think the Great War will go on long enough for us to get into it?" one of the more bellicose cadets anxiously asked Alan. "Us" meant the United States, the Commonwealth of Virginia, Bull Run's Class of 1918.

"The war's gone on a whole lot too long already, hasn't it?" Alan said, and his classmate flinched as though Alan had uttered a blasphemy. To most of the boys of the academy, Mars seemed to be the most possessive and demanding of the gods. None of Alan's classmates seemed to pay much attention to any of the goddesses, and least of all to Venus. These young apprentice soldiers had been banished from the world of civilian love before they had been able to come under her influence. Alan, having been a late arrival at the school, was an exception. Her continuing effect on him was one of the peculiarities that set him apart.

Alan had loved Louise during the short time he had spent in her company in New Orleans. As his body grew in strength and potency, his imagination became more luxuriantly fecund. Her reality faded in his mind; instead of remembered reality, a beautiful ideal magically burgeoned. He loved her more and more the longer he stayed away.

Every evening in study hall he wrote pages of the epic love letter of which he mailed a bulky installment once a week. He purloined a bottle of purple ink from Geography, so that the color of his romantically cursive handwriting could match his emotions and his prose style. His theme was simple; the variations proliferated extravagantly. He told her repeatedly in innumerable ways how much he loved her hair and her eyes and her lips, the grace of her movements and the sound of her voice. He declared at great length that he loved her body and soul and that he always would, until death and infinitely far beyond.

He progressed from love of Louise to love of the idea of Louise, to love of love, to love of the idea of love, to love of the expression of his perception of an abstraction. As his ardor intensified, his letters became increasingly vaguely poetic. When Louise showed some of the more advanced letters to one of her close girl friends it was apparent that she was favorably impressed. Louise, of course, was pleased. In her next short note to Alan she wrote that she was looking forward to seeing him again.

Her encouraging response thrilled him to the marrow. He was elated. He loved and he was loved. He began impatiently counting the days to the Christmas vacation.

54

In the meantime, the quality of his academic work deteriorated.

He sought solace at the piano in the recreation room. When he played jazz, the faculty supervisor stopped him. When he played a Bach fugue he was stopped by the jeers and catcalls of his fellow cadets. Everyone was delighted when he stuck to the lighter works of Stephen Foster.

The commandant summoned Alan and notified him that until his grades were satisfactory the recreation room was off limits to him.

Alan wrote a letter to his mother, a cry from the heart, complaining of the barbarity of life in a military academy. He listed only a few of the things that were wrong.

She wrote back to let him know that she had persuaded his father to take them to spend the Christmas vacation in Bermuda. In fact, he had already leased a marvellous house with a private beach and its own jetty. Wouldn't that be a lovely change? Alan wouldn't even have to come down to New Orleans. They would collect him in Washington on the way to the steamer.

That was when Alan ran away.

TWELVE

A lan told a dormitory buddy in sworn secrecy that he was heading for New York. Alan was confident that this intelligence would reach the authorities as soon as his absence was noticed, so they would alert the police along the railroad to the north-east.

"How will you get there, Alan?"

"I'll take the train."

"What'll you do there?"

"I don't know. I don't care. I'll get some kind of job. Anything you don't have to do in a uniform. Maybe I'll go to sea. Sail around the world."

"Gee. You've got some nerve."

"Any place would be better than this dump."

"Yeah. I wish I could come with you."

"Well, you can't. It's safer alone. I don't want to be caught and dragged back."

"No. But I still wish I could. How are you fixed for money?"

"I've been saving my allowance," Alan lied.

"How much have you saved?" his buddy persisted.

"I don't know. Enough. What difference does it make?"

"I could let you have some. I could let you have ten dollars."

"That's all right. But thanks."

Alan thought for a moment.

"It'd help," he admitted. "As soon as I get a job I'll pay you back. I'll mail it to you."

"You don't have to do that. I want to give it to you. We're classmates."

"Not any more."

"We're friends."

Alan raised his eyebrows. That was a concept that had not occurred to him. He felt embarrassed. Then he thought : perhaps his "secret" was too safe.

The other boy produced a wallet from his hip-pocket and gave Alan two five-dollar bills.

"Thanks a lot," Alan said, with feeling. "Look, will you do me another favor?"

"Sure."

"After I've gone, would you let it leak out, that I'm going to New York? I want people to know."

The boy smiled.

"When are you going?"

"Tonight. When it's dark. Late."

"O.K., Alan. Just tell me one thing. Where are you really going?"

"I said I'm going to New York."

"O.K., Alan. That's what I'll tell them, if that's what you want. Good luck, Alan. I'll be thinking of you."

Alan felt himself blushing

He went to bed in the dormitory as usual, but he did not sleep. He lay on his back staring into the darkness, thinking about what he was going to do. He was determined but nervous. At three o'clock by the luminous dial of his wristwatch, a going-away present from his mother, he stealthily got out of bed.

The night was almost black.

He was aware of the rows of sleeping bodies but he could not see them.

He felt for his locker and got out his civilian clothes and quickly dressed. He abandoned most of his few possessions. He considered doing something outrageous, like an outlaw, making a defiant gesture of his disesteem for the establishment. He had once heard of the burglars' practice of shitting on the carpet of houses they had broken into. He thought of shitting in his shako. He almost giggled aloud but he controlled himself. No, he decided, he must not impair the dignity and drama of his escape.

All he took was a small canvas grip containing his toilet kit, a couple of shirts, some underwear and socks and so on, and a thin sheaf of envelopes secured with an elastic band, Louise's letters.

At the door of the dormitory, he paused for a moment, looking back into the silent, obscure room.

"Very well, gentlemen," he murmured softly, mimicking the manner of the commandant addressing the assembled brigade. "In your hats!"

This inaudible declaration of contempt did little to fortify him as he tip-toed down the stone stairs, let himself out of the building, and hurried quietly across the lawns to one of the lesser exits to freedom. The December night was chill and clear. There was a half moon low in the sky. An owl hooted spookily and Alan shivered. As he passed through the gateway, he thought of his warm bed in the safety of regimentation.

"To hell with them!" he said aloud, stepping out along the side of the road and swinging his right arm as the drill instructor had taught him.

He was heading south-west, of course, in the direction of New Orleans. It was not easy to get rides in the middle of the night, but by day-break he was in Charlottesville, and as the sun came up he suddenly felt happy.

In a roadside café, he had a breakfast of fried eggs and sausages and grits, a stack of flapjacks and syrup and two glasses of buttermilk. It was the best meal he had had since he had left home. He was free and well fed and strong and optimistic. He strode energetically down the Lynchburg highway, enjoying breathing the cool winter air in the sunshine. He noticed that he was whistling Sousa's "Washington Post" march, and enjoying that, too.

A lot of cars passed him by, but some of them stopped and he made steady progress in a series of short lifts, through Lovingston, Amherst, Monroe, Lynchburg, Montvale, Roanoke, Christiansburg, Dublin, Pulaski, Max Meadows, Marion, Glade Spring and Abingdon, Virginia. He got a bed for the night in a rooming house behind a garage near Bluff City, Tennessee. He had made good time but he was exhausted. He meant to make an early start the next morning but he slept right through until nearly ten o'clock. The woman of the house gave him a thick ham steak and scrambled eggs and a mug of white coffee with plenty of sugar, and she didn't ask him any questions about where he was from and where he was going. Her hospitality was well worth a dollar.

He went a bit off course, via Spruce Pine, Old Fort and Swannanoa, to Ashville, North Carolina, where he stopped for the second night.

The landlady said she did not provide meals but she directed him to a hotel not very far down the street. He had another hearty breakfast. This one was expensive. He began worrying about money.

When he was only about half a mile beyond Ashville there was a heavy rainstorm and none of the drivers would stop. Then, by the time he was soaked, a big truck pulled over.

"Chattanooga?" Alan asked.

"Memphis."

When you are hitchhiking, a long ride in a slightly wrong direction is always more attractive than a short ride, no matter how much more direct. And it was still raining.

"Even better," Alan said, climbing up into the driver's cab.

The driver looked quite old – thirty or forty, Alan thought, or even more. He had a bald patch and a big moustache.

"Cigarette?" the driver said, offering a pack.

Alan was flattered. But he held up a hand in refusal.

"No, thanks,' he said. "Not now." He tried to sound casual about it, but resolute, as if he had been in the habit of smoking a lot but had given it up.

"You're smart. That's the worst thing you can do, smoke cigarettes." He laughed humourlessly. "One of the worst. I guess the worst is driving a truck. Staying awake, that's the tough part. Can you drive a truck?"

"No," Alan admitted.

"Too bad. What are you? Are you in the Army?"

"No," Alan replied emphatically, though he was gratified by the suggestion that he looked old enough.

"I thought maybe with that short haircut. . . . The Army, I thought, or you've been doing time in the pen." The driver laughed to show he was only kidding. "And you look too healthy for a jailbird. What are you then? Some kind of ballplayer?"

Conversation is the currency in which a hitchhiker is expected to pay his fare, so Alan felt obliged to make an effort, but he did not want to admit he was nothing more than a teenage runaway from prep school. His benefactor had certainly offered some broad openings into fantasy. However, Alan's answer emerged spontaneously from his subconsciousness, surprising him with its convincing rightness.

"I play piano," he said.

THIRTEEN

Memphis, 1916

Alan arrived in Memphis in the afternoon of his fourth day from Bull Run. The truck driver dropped him at a warehouse close to the Mississippi waterfront.

"There's the quay down the street there," the driver said, laughing and coughing through the cloud of blue smoke that floated around his head. "You could sail down to your girl in style." Over mugs of coffee in an all-night café, Alan had told the driver about Louise. The driver had pressed him for all sorts of physical details that he couldn't even imagine.

"That'd be swell," Alan agreed. He had three dollars and seventy cents in his pocket. He knew the exact amount because he had nervously counted it in the last gas-station men's room.

"It doesn't cost much," the driver added, having correctly interpreted Alan's doubtful frown. "It beats traveling by road."

They shook hands as if they were old friends. At the end of the block, Alan turned to wave, but, of course, the friendship was already over. The driver was intent on maneuvering his truck through the warehouse doors.

In a scruffy old street of bars and flophouses, Alan found what he needed.

The pawnbroker expertly opened the back of Alan's wristwatch and peered through a jeweller's eyepiece into the works. Alan anxiously appraised the process of appraisal. The pawnbroker's thin, parchment-colored face offered no clues, except that the pokerface blankness of it suggested that there was no danger that he would give way to any extravagant charitable impulse. He closed the watch and removed his eyepiece and regarded Alan with ineffable unexcitement.

"I can let you have fifty dollars," he said.

"I said I want to *sell* it," Alan said. "I'm leaving town."

"I know you want to sell it. That's what I'm talking."

"But fifty dollars. It's a gold watch."

"Take it or leave it."

Alan took it.

He bought a one-way ticket to New Orleans. The steamship agent didn't even ask whether Alan wanted a stateroom.

"There you are, son," the man said, sliding over the ticket and change. "The *Governor Claiborne*. Six-forty is the time."

While he was waiting, Alan went to a drugstore lunch counter. He was hungry but he was being careful to make his money stretch as far as possible. He supposed he would be able to find some kind of work in New Orleans but he had no idea what or how easily. There might be some lean days ahead. He had a glass of milk and a hot-dog that tasted of old grease. The glass was not large. On the way out he splurged on a chocolate bar. He remembered the abundant and delicious food and drink of home with a qualm of nostalgia.

Sitting on a bench looking across the great brown river, at six o'clock he heard the *Governor Claiborne*'s calliope steamily hooting "Dixie," to proclaim the ship's arrival at the quay. She was the flagship of the old Pelican Navigation Line, a splendid sternwheeler with three enclosed decks, a towering white superstructure with three tall red and black funnels gleaming in the amber light of the setting sun. The calliope was up on the sun-deck, behind the bridge. A musician uniformed like a naval officer stood at the keyboard that controlled the battery of shiny copper organ-pipes and whistles. The calliope reminded Alan of the carnival merry-go-rounds he had ridden on as a child. He imagined the music could be heard all over Memphis. It could. To people who loved the river, the sound was a sweetly seductive siren-song.

Alan climbed the gangway and went aboard. There was an almost full complement of passengers and there was a pleasant bustle of activity on the promenade decks, up and down ladders and stairways and in the spacious, ornate saloons. The décor was elaborately ornamental – Marine Rococo : there was much gilt, brass, varnish, lacquer, mirror and frosted glass.

He felt the deep tremor of the engines. The calliope became silent. A series of vibrant blasts on the hooter announced the ship's imminent departure. The sternwheel heavily rumbled. With slow dignity, the *Governor Claiborne* swung away from the quay and moved under way.

Leaning against the stern rail, gazing down into the pale khaki maelstrom of the wake, Alan was keenly aware of the momentousness of the beginning of his voyage into independence. He

61

thought of all the times he had watched the Mississippi steamers at New Orleans and had wondered what it would be like to sail in one of them.

As the ship gained a little speed, heading downriver in the main channel, Alan walked forward on the top deck and felt the cool breeze against his face. In the blue dusk, the yellow half-moon brightened. He went below.

Of all the public rooms, the most extravagantly theatrical in decoration and furnishings was the Grand Lounge, where passengers could eat and drink and dance. Mirrors multiplied the Tiffany lamps, the red-velvet draperies, the potted palms and the circular white marble tables and magnified the long bars and the dance floor. Almost all the tables were occupied and many men were standing at the bars. Black stewards hurried to and fro. Early in the evening, there were few dancers. A trio, piano, cello and violin, were playing waltzes. Alan stood unobtrusively against the wall near one of the entrances and watched and listened.

The music revolved as monotonously as the paddlewheel at the stern. The trio was a machine. The musicians were only cogs, automatic parts of the musical clockwork. Alan involuntarily counted the ponderous gyrations. He seemed to hear the voice of Dr. Frischauer: "Oom-pah-pah-*pah*, pah-*pah*, pah-*pah*; oom-pah-pah-*pah*, pah-*pah*, pah-*pah*. . . ."

At last the listless old alien music came to a stop. There was a perfunctory flutter of hand-clapping from some of the dancers as they separated and returned, slightly subdued, to their tables.

The pianist, who had oily black hair brushed as smooth as patent leather, nodded and smiled, as though gratefully acknowledging praise. The violinist, a fat man of middle age, took a handkerchief from a pocket of his tail-suit and mopped his pink round face. The cellist, gaunt and sallow, eased his stiff white wing-collar with a forefinger. Apparently, after all, the musicians were human.

The pianist stood up.

"That's it for now, folks," he said with a smile that was intended to be ingratiating. "Don't you-all go away. Me and the boys'll be right back after we take a little break."

The passengers ignored him. They were busy talking with the waiters and with each other.

The pianist closed the grand piano. The violinist gently laid his violin to rest in its case, like a baby in a coffin. The cellist propped his cello upright in the grip of a low metal tripod. Alan watched them diminish in stature as they left the back of the stand. They disappeared through a doorway behind two palms.

The Grand Lounge was quiet but for the sounds of the people dining and talking and the continuous low rhythmical throb of the engines.

Alan strolled over to the deserted stand.

The piano was a nice one, a Steinway.

He opened it.

He looked at the keys as a prospector might look at ore. The simple beauty of the keys of a piano! The neat blackness and whiteness! The inscrutability! The potential!

He lightly stroked the keys with the fingertips of his left hand, with a caress of extreme voluptuousness and awe.

If anybody happened to be watching him at that moment, he did not know or care. He was oblivious of everything but the piano.

He sat down.

His face was expressionless. He appeared to be looking into the far distance of the night.

He raised his hands, his distended fingers, over the keyboard, and hesitated, listening for some secret harmony in a remote silence.

And then he began to play.

Softly at first, tentatively, he searched for the notes, the runs and clusters of notes, the chords that meant what he felt about going back to New Orleans.

He bowed his head and closed his eyes and frowned and licked his lower lip. His movements gradually became stronger and more complicated. Inside his head, intricate, brilliant, abstract patterns of light shimmered and crystallized and dissolved and formed again in new shapes. Ideas beyond words glittered like electric jewels in the pounding darkness. Rockets soared and softly exploded, radiating drops of weeping fire. Alan was at the other end of the universe. He was making love.

When he stopped and sat back, he became aware of loud, prolonged applause, and realized it was for him – for his music. The music had moved him, too, so he felt no false modesty about the acclaim.

But then he noticed through the palms that the trio were

returning, led by the pianist. Alan's face flushed. He stood up.

"I hope you don't mind," he said, "I was just looking and then.... You know?"

The pianist must have heard the passengers' enthusiastic response but he did not seem resentful.

"What's the name of that piece?" he asked.

Alan grinned awkwardly

"It doesn't have a name. I mean, I was only kind of doodling around. I was thinking, 'Crescent City, here I come!' – something like that. I was feeling good. Well, thanks."

He backed away from the piano stool, giving way to its rightful occupant. The pianist sat down. The violinist and cellist took their places. The poor little violin was resurrected, the cello awakened from its zombie trance.

"I'd like for you to play some more," the pianist said to Alan. "But you know how it is. The folks are waiting to dance."

"Yes, sir. Of course."

The pianist put on his spectacles and turned some pages of the sheet music in front of him.

"That's some technique you have there, kid. I bet if you applied yourself you could play some real music."

"Thank you."

"Really. I'm not just saying that. You have a nice touch. That sounded real good, some of it. For nigger music."

Alan's polite smile sank without trace.

"Yes," he said. "Good night."

He left the stand and was heading for the doorway that led to the fantail when he felt a light tug at his sleeve.

FOURTEEN

Alan turned to face a man whose bearing and style reminded him of his father. The man was middle-aged and massive, with short brown hair and full sideburns and a neatly trimmed moustache, small eyes with a penetrating insistent glare, luxuriantly ruddy plump cheeks and a double chin, a cream silk shirt, a gray silk tie and a banker's-gray tropical worsted suit, with a red carnation in the buttonhole and a cream silk handkerchief drooping in elegant disarray from the breast pocket. His expression was cheerfully arrogant, confidently authoritative. His voice was the same as Alan's father's, old New Orleans modified somewhat by the University of Virginia; it was a voice of aristocratic charm and power. He even smelled the same – a rich blend of cologne, cigars and bourbon.

"Not so fast, young man!" he exclaimed, cordially baring both rows of teeth. "Won't you come and join me." The invitation was an order rather than a question. "I like the way you play. I want to buy you a drink."

Alan recognized the familiar sickening sensation of being dominated and he resisted.

"That's very kind of you, sir. But I don't drink."

"Time you learned then! Come on, young man. There's something I want to discuss with you."

"I was going out on deck to get some air."

"There's plenty of time for that. But I have an idea I think may be to your advantage. Come on."

No adult ever before had spoken to Alan so beguilingly. He was curious.

"I *am* kind of thirsty," he conceded.

"Good!" the man said.

Alan followed him to a small round table in a corner. From it they could survey the whole lounge. The trio was playing something slow, with the regularity of a metronome. Blue filters – electric moonlight – had turned the dancers into slowly shuffling ghosts.

A steward hurried to the table.

"The usual, Mr. Brewster, sir?"

"No. I'll have a bottle of Bollinger."

"Yes, *sir*!"

"Two glasses, Homer."

"No, thank you, sir," Alan said.

"I said bring two champagne glasses."

"Yes, sir. Coming right up."

Alan felt his will strengthen.

"Thank you, sir. But I mean it. I'd prefer sarsaparilla, please."

Mr. Brewster shrewdly appraised Alan's expression.

"And one sarsaparilla."

The steward grinned at Alan.

"And one sarsaparilla. Yes, sir, Mr. Brewster."

"You're a determined young man," Mr. Brewster said, smiling, offering his hand. "My name's Huntington Brewster. Hunt Brewster."

Alan had often seen the name in *The Times-Picayune*. One of *the* Brewsters – shipping, cotton, race horses, the usual clubs, and, of course, the State Legislature.

"I'm . . . Alan Dexter."

"No connection with A. Chesley Poindexter?" Mr. Brewster said with a knowing smile.

Alan flinched inside but looked straight into Mr. Brewster's small, clever eyes.

"No. No connection."

"All right," Mr. Brewster agreed tolerantly. "My mistake. You reminded me of the son of an old classmate of mine. Good-looking boy, very much like you. Clean cut. Auburn hair. Like his daddy used to be long ago, before he got heavy. But I haven't seen the kid for quite a while."

There did not seem to be much to say to that. Alan felt slightly uncomfortable. Mr. Brewster's attention was diverted by the return of the steward. On the tray were a bottle of champagne in a silver ice-bucket, two champagne glasses, a bottle of sarsaparilla and another glass. A tactful compromise.

The steward and Mr. Brewster quickly performed the ritual mime of offering and accepting the wine – the deferential display of the label, the brief scrutiny, the nod of approval, the pouring,

66

the tasting, the grunt of satisfaction, the gesture to go on pouring. Alan did not have much time for thought.

"Are you sure you won't join me?" Mr. Brewster murmured cajolingly.

"Quite sure, thank you."

"It's good stuff, this Bollinger. 'Gather ye rosebuds. . . .' You'll be in uniform almost before you know it. This war may take longer than Wilson says. But I won't *force* champagne on you. Let me know if you change your mind."

Alan wondered why the old fart wouldn't take no for an answer. Why did people presume that seniority gave them the right to be domineering? Alan drank some of the ice-cold pop. Its insipid sweetness reminded him of the trio, who were plinking and plunking and sawing away at some apparently indestructible old favorite whose title he could not remember, and had no wish to. Something about magnolias and satin and lace and hearts so true, no doubt. He wondered about Louise. He had been away for what seemed like a long time. He thought about Louise's eyes and lips. He wondered how much she loved him.

"I suppose you're wondering what I have to say to you," the smooth, plump Mr. Brewster said complacently.

"Yes."

"Well," he said, admiring his polished fingernails as he lifted his glass to his lips, "it happens that I know something about music. I mean the sort of music you were playing. I'm talking about what they call 'jazz.' I'm on a couple of Mardi Gras committees." He paused to enjoy Alan's raised eyebrows. "Surprised, eh? We oldsters may not be quite as senile as you young fellows imagine. Confidentially, Alan, thirty-nine isn't all that ancient. There's life in the old dog yet. Strictly between you and me, Alan" – Mr. Brewster leaned forward with an expression of mock solemnity – "it's not entirely impossible for men of your father's and my generation. . . ." He leaned even farther forward, half-way across the table, and looked even more playfully solemn. "We still have our . . . moments. Oh, yes, I assure you. We certainly do. I could tell you a thing or two about that father of yours."

"I – "

Mr. Brewster abruptly sat up straight and raised a forefinger like a miniature flag of truce.

"No need to protest!" he genially interrupted. "There is no

cause for alarm. I have no intention of being indiscreet. I am a Solon, as the headline-writers say. I merely wished to point out that we old fogeys in our later thirties may be more savvy, more closely in touch with what's going on, than you, in the full flower of your youth, may give us credit for."

"I – "

"Hush, dear boy. Desist. Hear me out."

Alan now realized that his host was not sober. He recognized the symptoms, the moist, rubescent complexion, the grandiloquence, only too easily. Mr. Brewster reminded Alan of his father after dinner.

"I was only going to say – "

"By the way," Mr. Brewster said curtly, "I am not tight."

Alan recognized the startling clairvoyance of the drunk. One had to be careful not to offend them. They were often more sharply observant than one thought.

"I didn't mean to – "

"Say no more about it," Mr. Brewster said, waving aside the apology.

"How old are you?" he suddenly asked.

Alan hesitated.

"Seventeen," he said. He would be seventeen in February.

"Seventeen," Mr. Brewster repeated speculatively. "Hmm. I don't suppose that matters these days."

"What doesn't matter?"

"You're a very well developed seventeen," Mr. Brewster said. There was a glitter in his eyes. "A mature seventeen. You'd do all right. If you're available, that is. Are you?"

"What do you mean?"

"But aren't you in school? What are you doing, aboard this boat, in schooltime? Playing hooky? Am I right?" Mr. Brewster gave Alan a smile of sweet intimacy. "I know. I was seventeen myself once upon a time." He sympathetically patted the back of Alan's hand on the table. Alan withdrew his hand as if it had been burnt.

Alan stood up.

"I don't mean to seem rude, Mr. Brewster, but – "

"Sit down, sit down," Mr. Brewster said in a commanding voice that Alan automatically obeyed. Mr. Brewster sighed and gently smiled. "I'm not prying into your private affairs, if that's what you're afraid of. But if you *are* available, I know a place that could use piano-playing like yours. I'm only trying to help. A very elegant place it is, too. Perhaps the most elegant."

Alan was hooked.

"You do?" he said.

"I do. That makes a difference, doesn't it?" Mr. Brewster paused, meditatively, slowly twirling his glass by its stem. He craftily smiled. "How do you and your daddy get along together?"

Alan was silent, attempting to contrive an answer.

"I see," Mr. Brewster said, with a judicious nod and a contented smirk. "It's like that."

Unable to defend himself, Alan looked down at the table.

"Don't feel bad," Mr. Brewster said. "It's the most usual thing in the world, at your age. Discontent, protest, rebellion. Chesley always was a stuffed shirt. In fact, a hypocrite. He's no angel, but he insists on very high standards for other people."

"I don't want to hear anything against my father."

"Then you do acknowledge that he's your daddy. You recognize the description as well as the name. Your loyalty is touching, Mr. . . . Dexter. I'll call you Alan. Now the question is : do you want a job or don't you?"

"Maybe. What is it exactly?"

"Playing piano. The way you did tonight. You know some of the popular tunes, don't you?"

"Of course."

"Can you read music?"

"Certainly. And I've studied composition and harmony."

"Then you're all set. The money's good."

"The job's in New Orleans?"

"In New Orleans. 'The birthplace of jazz.' What do you say?"

"Playing where?"

"The New Alhambra. You've heard of the New Alhambra."

Alan hadn't and his face was blank.

"No?" Mr. Brewster said, and the notion seemed to give him pleasure. "That's kind of like someone in Agra not having heard of the Taj Mahal. How charming! Here : I'll write down the name of the place and the person to see."

He took a slender gold pen and a card from his pocket and scribbled a few words.

"Give them this," he said grandly. "Everything will be taken care of."

"Thank you," Alan said, cautiously accepting the card. "But why are you doing this?"

"Why not? I'm a patron of the arts, a lover of beauty. Why are the young of today so suspicious?"

"I'm sorry if I seem that way. I appreciate your help, Mr. Brewster. I really need a job, and that's the truth."

Mr. Brewster smiled and smiled.

"You've got it. Now you'll join me in a glass of champagne. A glass of champagne never did anyone any harm."

Mr. Brewster lifted the bottle from the ice-bucket and filled both champagne glasses to the brim. Alan felt that he would have been churlish to refuse. He did not want to seem like a stuffed shirt.

The champagne was delicious. The bubbles tickled his nose and rose in his brain like bubbles of optimism.

Later he began giggling. The trio was so bad it was funny. He felt bubbles of wonderful music.

Later he felt giddy.

There was an arm around him, supporting him, guiding him. Out on deck the air was cooler.

"Dear boy," a man's voice said. "I'll take you down to your stateroom."

"Don't have a stateroom."

"You can stay in mine. It's a double. There's plenty of space."

Walking unsteadily along the deck, Alan felt a wet kiss on his cheek. He was shocked, frightened and indignant. He wrenched himself free.

"All right, Alan," Mr. Brewster said soothingly. "There's no need for a melodramatic scene."

Alan stumbled away in an angry stupor.

Mr. Brewster was disappointed for only a moment. He was something of a philosopher. As he went alone to his stateroom, he consoled himself with thoughts of the near future.

"That goddamn Chesley's going to be sorry," he muttered.

When Alan awoke on a bench on the promenade deck the next morning he felt awful. He felt guilty, but he did not know what for. In the men's room, he stripped to the waist and washed in cold water and brushed his teeth until his gums were sore, but he still felt guilty. He put on his last clean shirt, but that did not help much. Later, he found Mr. Brewster having breakfast in the saloon and went over to apologise.

Mr. Brewster couldn't have been nicer about the whole thing. "These things happen," he said. "It was probably my fault. Perhaps I gave you a little bit too much champagne."

He insisted that Alan sit down at his table and eat a hearty breakfast.

Alan felt better.

When the *Governor Claiborne* eventually approached the quay in New Orleans, Mr. Brewster shook Alan by the hand and wished him luck.

FIFTEEN

New Orleans, 1916

Alan walked at a brisk pace from the steamboat, down from the levee and across Jackson Square, in Christmas weather. The gray clouds sagged like a wet awning almost as low as the three steeples of St. Louis Cathedral and there was a steady downpour of cool rain. But he was glad to be back. Andrew Jackson sat on his rearing horse, waving his hat. Alan waved back as he passed close by the plinth and startled a pigeon from its perch on the general's head.

It seemed strange to be in New Orleans and not to be going home. His home – his father's house – was only a few blocks away. Alan turned down Chartres instead. He went into the Tchoupitoulas Café, a small, inexpensive place that smelled of French coffee, fragrantly bitter with chicory, warm bread, and the cigarettes of the men and women dressed as artists who were lounging at the small tables talking about working.

I'm an artist, too, Alan thought. He ordered *café au lait* and a couple of *beignets*, the sugary, stodgy French doughnuts without holes. Sipping coffee and looking around the room, he vowed that he must take up smoking. A cigarette in the hand seemed to give gestures extra emphasis and significance, an appearance of worldly sophistication, a suggestion of living life to the full. It was too bad that the only time Moses and he had tried smoking cigarettes they had both admitted the experience made them feel sick. Maybe one got used to them.

"And a pack of cigarettes, please," he told the elderly black waitress.

"What kind?"

"Oh, any kind," Alan said, as casually as possible. "The best." She gave him a rather skeptical look but brought him a pack. "Anything else?"

He started to raise his wrist but remembered he was not wearing a watch.

"No, thanks. I don't have time. I have an appointment. Just the check, please."

She wrote it and put it face down on the table.

"Thank you," he said. "There is one thing. Would you tell me where I can find the New Alhambra?"

She looked astonished.

"I certainly would *not*," she said. "Even if I knew, I mean." She went away, crossly mumbling to herself.

The rain had stopped and there were more people walking by when Alan emerged from the café. He accosted the first person who came along. His appearance suggested that he might have been a successful salesman.

"Excuse me, sir," Alan said. "Would you tell me the time?"

"Sure, kid. Eleven-forty."

"I wonder if you can help me, sir. I'm looking for a place called the New Alhambra. Do you know it?"

The man grinned.

"I wouldn't say I know it. But I know where it is. It's in The District. Near the corner of Basin and Bienville. Big new house there."

The man walked on, shaking his head, much amused.

The District! No wonder the waitress had disapproved. The District was at the hot center of the sexual mythology of Alan's adolescence, of the adolescence of every boy in New Orleans. The District was somewhere on the borderline between bliss and damnation. It was only a few blocks from the Poindexter mansion but it might as well have been a million miles away. The District was Storyville, the only legal red-light district in the entire United States.

SIXTEEN

In New Orleans in the late 1890's it was almost impossible to discern where virtue ended and vice began. They overlapped and the edges were blurred. Confusion and ambiguity made it difficult for churchmen to determine which citizens were good and which were bad, difficult for the police to know whom to arrest and to whom to apply for their bribes.

It was Alderman Sidney Story, successful broker and never-to-be-forgotten eponym, who devised the scheme for clarifying and simplifying the city's moral and administrative geography. He devised it after exhaustive research, conducted in person, at the expense, it may be assumed, of the tax-payers. He went over to Europe on a pioneer political fact-finding tour, to see for himself how the authorities there controlled prostitution. Like many other great legislative innovations, his plan for New Orleans was simple. If people were breaking the law, the law should be altered to accommodate their illegal activities.

On his return he introduced the legislation that established in effect, as intended, a ghetto for commercial sex, The District, Storyville. It was the tenderloin of tenderloins, the juiciest cut of all – a term applied to red-light districts because police officers fortunate enough to be assigned to them could be sure of eating the best.

Storyville was defined in negative terms; the City Council could not publicly give the impression that it was actively sponsoring vice. The law only delineated the area in which prostitutes might *not* legally engage in their trade.

Alderman Story proposed, and his colleagues agreed, that it should be "unlawful for any prostitute or woman notoriously abandoned to lewdness to occupy, inhabit, live or sleep in any house, room or closet, situated without the following limits. . . ." He then set forth the limits, clearly enough to guide the simplest hackney carriage driver. The large prohibited zone left a conveniently situated rectangular gap of thirty-eight blocks in the western corner of the French Quarter, from Customhouse Street (later Iberville) eastward to St. Louis Street and from Robertson

Street down to Basin Street. The street at the very heart of the grid was Liberty. About two thousand prostitutes took the hint and moved in, ready for business by October 1, 1897.

Right from the beginning, Storyville consisted of nothing but bars, dance-halls, cribs and brothels, a church and two cemeteries. Storyville provided all the necessary facilities for copulation and death. For men and women wavering in between, St. James Methodist Church offered first aid and hospitalization, in St. James Infirmary.

The houses of pleasure and the people who ran them and worked in them became legendary, known from coast to coast and, because of the comings and goings of amorous sailors, around the world. Fewclothes Cabaret, The Pig Ankle, The Terminal Saloon, Lulu White's Mahogany Hall, French Emma's House of All Nations and Countess Willie V. Piazza's Sporting Palace were among the names to conjure with. The street names of Storyville soon achieved the awful fame of the battle honors on a regimental flag – Villere, Marais, Franklin, Conai, Bienville, Basin. . . .

In Storyville, love for sale was more than an industry; it was a way of life. It was a way of life in which jazz played an important role. Storyville was sex and sex jazz and jazz was Storyville. The madames' circular syllogism was simplistic, perhaps, but there was no doubt that jazz was an aphrodisiac that helped to move the customers up the stairs. During Alan's boyhood, the names of the madames and the jazzmen of Storyville were linked together as an essential part of the culture of New Orleans.

Alan unknowingly applied for admittance into that historic cultural movement when he rang the front doorbell of the New Alhambra.

SEVENTEEN

The New Alhambra was the newest, biggest, most lavish house on Basin Street, a three-storey brick building with pink-washed stucco like the icing of a ceremonial cake. There were two balconies enclosed in black wrought-iron lace-work trellises. The black-lacquered double doors of the front entrance, fortified with black metal studs, would have been big enough to drive a horse and carriage through. The doors were closed. Within one of them, there was a small single door. This was where Alan stood, waiting.

He rang again.

At last, the door opened part way. A black man with the powerful physique of a heavyweight prize-fighter, wearing a collarless white shirt and the gold-striped maroon trousers of a doorman's livery, scowled out at him.

"Yes?" the man said. "What do you want?"

"My name's Alan Dexter. May I see Madame Robichaux?"

"Do you have an appointment?"

"No."

"Then you can't see her."

The door closed in Alan's face.

He rang the bell.

The door opened almost immediately.

"Listen, you," the man said. "Get away from here, or you'll wish you had. It ain't even midday yet."

"I was told to give Madame Robichaux this," Alan said, presenting the card. The doorman reluctantly scrutinized it. His face changed.

"Oh, a friend of Mr. Brewster's!" he said. "That's different." He opened the door wider and stood aside to let Alan in.

"An acquaintance."

"Yes, sir. Follow me."

The doorman led Alan across a small, dim patio, paved with cobblestones. In the middle, a green copper nymph held up an electric flambeau. The dense green foliage of the surrounding garden, like a miniature Rousseau jungle, smelled sweet and rotten, like gardenias and damp leaf-mold.

The doorman opened a pair of french windows. Alan was admitted to a formal foyer – a chandelier, Louis XIV mirrors in gilded frames, white roses in white urns, pastel-blue and gold furniture and a dove-gray carpet. And a curved stairway leading up to a closed white door.

"Please wait here," the doorman said, indicating a sofa. "I'll let Miss Fleur know you're here."

Alan sat down carefully on velvet and the doorman mounted the stairs. He shut the door silently behind him.

There was a large black-leather-bound album on a small table beside the sofa. The cover was inscribed *THE NEW ALHAMBRA*, in letters of gold. Alan took the book onto his lap and idly flipped the pages. What he saw gripped his attention.

The full-page sepia photographs were romantic "art studies" of naked women posing like classical statues. They were as voluptuously beautiful as the women in erotic dreams, dimpled Ingres houris in a heavenly Turkish bagnio. Their smiles were coyly flirtatious. The pictures were captioned with erotic kewpie-doll names, Mimi, Fifi, Yvette, Claudie. . . .

Fleur Robichaux had descended more than half-way down the stairs before Alan became aware of her presence. She made no sound but he sensed a disturbing aura, an electric radiance, a warmth, a perfume, that made him look up.

He stared slack-jawed.

She moved slowly in the regal manner of a great prima donna. She was not a tall woman but she seemed tall. Of course, this impression was enhanced by the fact that she was up there and he was down here. She had evidently already been in the hands of her hairdresser : her shiny black hair was not merely hair; it was a creation, swept up from her temples and the nape of her neck to form a preposterous structure of curls on top of her head. She had the face of an octoroon angel and the body of a belly dancer, but this, at the moment, a little before noon, was swathed from neck to ankles in the fluffy white feathers and white silk of an unusually dramatic dressing gown. As she came to the last stair, her expression was one of calm pride, almost haughtiness. In her late thirties, she was enjoying the realization of the full ripeness of her womanhood, her professional good fortune and her social power. She was formidable. But then her lips parted in a bright smile.

Awkwardly fumbling, Alan put the album down on the table and got to his feet. Madame Robichaux nodded toward the album approvingly.

"The most beautiful young ladies in New Orleans," she said. "Everyone agrees. The most beautiful in the whole *world*."

Alan gulped. She smiled.

"Sit down," she said.

He sat down. She sat beside him. He breathed in the warm, musky scent. He moved sideways to give her more room. She smiled.

"A shy professor!" she exclaimed. "That'd be a novelty. How old are you, Alan?" He wished people wouldn't always ask that. "Mr. Brewster phoned. He said you're one of the best piano players he ever heard."

"Eighteen," Alan said. With his right hand, he cracked the knuckle of his left forefinger.

"Don't break it," Madame Robichaux said with a playful pretence of severity. "Can't play good piano with no busted left hand."

"Going on eighteen," he said with a wry grimace of resignation.

"That's all right. Don't matter to me what your age is, not if you're good." She patted his knee with a slender, exquisitely manicured hand that was heavy with diamond rings. "I was curious, that's all. You look like a man to me. But kind of shy. Well, that's all right, too. The main man we got, he ain't near shy enough. That's one reason we got to get him out of here. That and because he drinks like a fool. When he's on the sauce, and that's almost all the time, he can't even *see* the piano. In this job, there can't be no messing. You understand? No getting loaded and no playing games with the young ladies."

"Of course."

" 'Of course.' Easy to say 'of course.' But they come on strong sometimes. Most of them don't even like men; they like *teasing* men. They can't tease the patrons, so they might pick on you. And I know some of them who would make a genuine pass at a good-looking fellow like you. All nice and clean and neat, and young. If I hire you to play piano, that is *all* you play."

"I understand."

"You better had. This is a fine position. Big tips. If the people like you, the sky's the limit. Plenty of musicians would give anything to play at the New Alhambra. This is the most expensive, most de luxe, most refined establishment in The District."

"Yes, ma'am."

"In the New Alhambra everything got to be *right*. We get some important visitors. Very important. You'd be surprised. Do you know I paid thirty-five thousand dollars just for the mirrors? We have furniture in the boudoirs from Paris, France. Wait till you see the oil paintings in the parlor – the reception lounge. That's where your piano is at, if you stay. A pink piano, with silver trim and genuine mother-of-pearl inlay, and hand-painted panels of young ladies, all custom-made. So-called Countess Piazza was always bragging about her white piano. She don't any more. A pianola is what it really was. It cost a dollar a time to play it. She's a chiseler. Jelly Roll said my piano's the best he ever played; looks best and sounds best. He knew what he was talking about, in the piano department at least. Patrons have offered me a fortune for the paintings, though I don't know where they'd put them. Not at home, where their old ladies would see them, that's for sure! The paintings are very sophisticated."

"Wouldn't you like to give me an audition?" Alan asked. "You haven't heard me play."

Like many other neophytes, he imagined that the main purpose of a job interview was to determine whether the applicant was qualified or at least had some potential aptitude for the job.

"We'll have to dress you up real sharp," Madame Robichaux said, holding her head back and half shutting her eyes as she considered his appearance and what should be done about it. "That suit you have on may be a good suit but it ain't fancy. You aren't signing up to play for one of those no-account bands that play for nickels and dimes on street corners. This is the big time. In my place everybody got to wear nothing but high fashion. I want you to wear a light-gray derby and an embroidered silk brocade waistcoat and those pretty arm garters. Did you ever see Tony Jackson before he left town?"

"No," Alan said with sincere regret, though Tony Jackson was reputed to suffer from certain defects. A black, alcoholic, epileptic, homosexual piano player in a brothel in the Deep South was not without problems in those days. But still at one time he was said to be the greatest jazz pianist in New Orleans. "I know some of his music. He wrote 'Pretty Baby,' didn't he?"

"He sometimes worked for me, in my other places. He was one sweet guy. It's a shame he started drinking so much. What is it with you musicians? On top of the world and then get all mixed up with gambling, booze, dope, love. I gave Tony a diamond ring for his pinky. He brought in a lot of business in the beginning. The stone was this big." She held the tips of a finger and thumb about an inch apart. "And it was real. And so are these." She held up her ring-bearing fingers for his inspection. "Don't believe anyone who tells you different. Everything about Fleur Robichaux is real, I guarantee. Oh, that Tony Jackson – such beautiful manners! Everybody used to like him, the young ladies *and* the gentlemen. He got more tips than he knew what to do with."

"I'll be careful," Alan promised. "If you want to try me. But don't you want me to show you how I play?"

"Honey, to tell you the truth, I don't care how you play that thing, as long as you know enough popular songs and you dress right and act right and don't make the music too loud."

"You don't care about my style?"

She smiled.

"Your style suits me fine."

"I mean – "

"As far as the music goes, I'll take Mr. Brewster's word on that. I always do."

"Mr. Brewster only heard me play one piece."

He wanted to play for her; he wanted to demonstrate how well he played.

"What you trying to do, boy? Talk yourself out of a job?"

"No, Madame Robichaux."

"All right then."

"But I wanted to make sure we agreed about the music."

"You act right and I'll leave the music up to you. That's what you'll be paid for. Now and then you can play my favorite number."

"What's that?"

She smiled and put her hand on his knee again and gave him a friendly squeeze.

" 'Meet Me Tonight In Dreamland,' "

Then her manner became businesslike.

"You can start this evening," she said. "Do you have a place to stay?"

"Not yet. I arrived this morning."

"Oh, yes. I'll call someone who can rent you a nice clean room not far from here. Be here at eight this evening and be ready to work till all hours. Get here on time. I don't care what you do in your own time but on my time I want you here *all* the time. Do you understand?"

"Yes, Madame Robichaux."

"Now you wait here a while. I'll phone the tailor. He's over on Canal. Only a few blocks. I have an account. He'll fix you up while you wait. Everything you need. I'll tell him. Charlie can give you all the necessary directions. O.K., professor? Is that a deal?"

She had not spelled out any of the financial details, but Alan did not dare to ask her for them. He did not dare ask her anything. He would be independent and he would be free to play music his way; those were the main things.

"Yes, Madame Robichaux."

"O.K., Al. See you tonight."

A. Chesley Poindexter IV was now Al Dexter.

"Thank you, Madame Robichaux."

She stood and he stood.

"And Madame Robichaux. . . ."

"Yes?"

"Don't worry about the young ladies. I have a girl."

EIGHTEEN

Right from the beginning jazz musicians had to work anywhere they could, at any price. Alan, or Al as he had become, was one of the rare lucky ones: at a tender age, without any previous professional experience, he had found employment in a *superior* whorehouse. Fleur Robichaux was not exaggerating when she told him that plenty of musicians would have given anything for his opportunity to play at the New Alhambra. No other establishment in the city provided a piano player such a sumptuous setting for his music, such big money, such an elegant gray bowler hat.

When Al went to collect his costume from the tailor on Canal Street, one Ludwig Mankowitz, the wizened old man with a bald head and a gray goat's beard made no attempt to conceal his curiosity.

"Miss Fleur took a shine to you – is that the situation?" Mr. Mankowitz said, as his young assistant read Al's measurements from an expertly manipulated tape.

"She hired me to play the piano," Al said.

"A young man like you? Where did you play before? Tell me that."

"Around."

"You played around? That's a good qualification. Where exactly, may I ask?"

"I played in Virginia," Al said defiantly. "I played on a riverboat, the *Governor Claiborne*."

"All right. Take it easy. Who's doubting? Why shouldn't she give you the job? It's a free country. She can hire anybody she wants. She must have her reasons. And don't worry; when I get through, at least you're going to look the part."

"Inside leg, thirty-three," the assistant said, speaking in the objective monotone of a lab technician.

"Mm, that's nice," Mr. Mankowitz commented with a suggestive leer. "A nice big boy. In the music business, looks are half the battle." The old man's brownish-mauve lips were twisted in a humorless smile. "The question is: is half the battle enough?"

Al confronted his triple reflection, a three-man tribunal examining him in the full-length triptych mirrors. Was there anything wrong with accepting Mr. Brewster's help and Madame Robichaux's offer? It was not as if he were not a competent pianist.

"I *can* play the piano," he said defensively. "I've been studying piano since I was a kid. I'm not bad."

"At the New Alhambra you're going to play piano because you're not bad? That's a good one. Do you know what class piano players have played before you in The District? Have you ever heard of Albert Carroll, Lorenzo Staub, Jelly Roll Morton, Tony Jackson? Some big names, some big talents. I've dressed them all. Players like those are going to take some living up to."

"I suppose so."

"You better suppose so. You won't be able to get by with chopsticks however much you smile. Those pianists could play anything and everything. If they didn't know it, they could fake it. They could make their own music. What can you play? Do you know all the dances – the bunny hug, the alligator, the barnyard strut? The Dixieland one-step, the slow drag? Do you?"

"Not all of them maybe. I can soon learn them."

"You can? What'll you do if you get requests for some of the comedy numbers? How about that one of Tony Jackson's – 'I've Got Elgin Movements In My Hips, With Twenty Years' Guarantee'? Can you play 'Rampart Street Hustle'? 'The Suicide Blues'?"

"Twenty-eight waist," the assistant reported, and Mr. Mankowitz automatically made a note of it.

"Nice waist," he said. "But what about the music?"

"If you really want to know," Al admitted, "I'm scared. Good and scared. Is that what you want?"

The tailor placed a finger and thumb against his closed eyelids and rubbed them deep inside their sockets, as if he were remembering something in his own past. He thoughtfully pinched the bridge of his nose. He relented.

"Frankly," he said, "in your position I'd be scared too. The District eats musicians alive and spits them out into the garbage. But don't take what I say too hard. I'm only jealous. I wish I were your age, with everything in front of me. You have the background; I can tell. But I don't know how much good that will do you. You'll have to have a talent, and you'll have to be tough. Are you tough? You don't look tough. But let me do you a favor: let me give you some advice. I'm doing some quick alterations on one outfit for you to wear this evening. In the meantime, this is what you should do: you should hurry around to Faber and Meyers – that's the best music store in New Orleans – and get yourself the sheet music of all the latest hits. Can you read music?"

Al nodded.

"Good. Like I say, get all the music, and play the hell out of it. Play it so hard and so well, the suckers won't have a chance to ask for any special requests. In the next few days you can get to work on filling in some of the gaps in your repertoire. The public isn't so smart. You can do it. You can do it, believe me."

Mr. Mankowitz had somehow miraculously turned into the sort of father Al wished he had.

"Thanks a lot," he said. "The only trouble is Madame Robichaux hasn't paid me anything yet."

The old man smiled.

"That's not a trouble."

He produced a thick roll of bills secured with a rubber band. He gave Al a twenty.

"There. That'll be enough to impress them tonight. Give them some hot numbers and some sweet numbers and some clever, fancy numbers – you know, with all those extra frills. That'll do the trick. You'll get more than this in tips. You can pay me back at the end of the week."

"This is very kind of you, Mr. ...."

"Mr. Mankowitz. Ludwig Mankowitz. Like Beethoven."

"I appreciate your advice, Mr. Mankowitz."

"Chest, forty-two," the assistant said.

"Think nothing of it, kid," the tailor said. "I want you to go over there and play your heart out. Give them the works. Remember: you'll be wearing my clothing."

When Al left to go to Faber and Meyers, Mr. Mankowitz added another item to Madame Robichaux's bill. Under "Alterations," he added the sum of thirty dollars.

NINETEEN

Carrying his grip and the bandbox from Mankowitz Custom Tailoring, with a cardboard portfolio of sheet music under one arm, Al walked to Burgundy Street near Bienville. The rooming house recommended by Madame Robichaux was a traditional French Quarter two-storey red-brick building with the usual balcony embellished with black lace-work wrought iron. The house had one unusual feature : the white paint on the door and shutters and the rest of the woodwork was fresh.

The lady of the house was an elderly, plump party with theatrical makeup and hair that was mostly as yellow as daffodils. She was expecting him. When he began nervously to explain his financial situation, she dismissed the problem with a wave of a long cigarette holder like a magic wand.

"You can pay the rent one week in advance starting next Monday," she said. "Miss Fleur explained. We're old friends. The first week's taken care of. Follow me. I'll show you your room. It's a nice clean room. This is a respectable residential hotel. All the guests stay by the week or month – no short time."

The room *was* clean. No efforts could have been spared in furnishing and decorating it. Major efforts must have been exerted to squeeze in the dark mahogany wardrobe, which covered half one wall and almost reached the ceiling. This monumental piece of nineteenth-century craftsmanship appeared to be much bigger than the doorway. Al imagined the removal of the front wall and the use of cranes. The bed was undoubtedly designed for single occupancy; it was narrow; but it was high, and the mahogany headboard was as bulky as a gravestone. There was a mahogany chest of drawers with a large oval mirror above it. The single armchair was covered in chintz of a bold floral design in purple, red and pink, matching the curtains and the bedspread. The red was almost the same shade as the red of a circular hooked rug that concealed part of the dark brown floor-boards. A reproduction of Millais' "Bubbles" brightened one brown wall, while on another wall a framed embroidered sampler warned the inmate that "God is Everywhere".

"No cooking in the rooms, of course. I'm sure you wouldn't want to be offended by cooking odors from the other guests. The bed-linen is changed every Monday. And the towel. It would be appreciated if the towel is used only for its proper intended purpose. There have been abuses. There is a small charge for laundry service. Absolutely no pets of any kind whatsoever, *please*. No visitors of the opposite sex are permitted at any time, except, by arrangement, in the downstairs parlor, up until ten o'clock. You may use the bathroom at the end of the hall. Please do not waste hot water, and always leave the bathtub et cetera in the condition you would hope to find them in. Do you have any questions?"

"No."

"With the guests' cooperation, we try to make the hotel a home from home," she said. "A gracious place of comfort and peace."

"Yes," he promised.

"So you're the New Alhambra's new professor."

"I'm starting tonight."

The landlady nibbled the end of her empty cigarette holder.

"My, my," she said. "That Fleur sure can pick 'em ! She always could."

TWENTY

In the bathtub and while he was shaving, Al thought about the loveliness of Louise Mercier. During their time of separation she had become an abstract ideal; he yearned for her reality. He was longing to see her, to hear her voice, to kiss her, to feel her warmth. His imagination faltered, in spite of all the talk at night in the dormitory at Bull Run.

Although he was impatient for a reunion, he decided not to communicate with her for a few days. He wanted to return to her in triumph. Soon he would have some money. He would be able to show her that he was doing well. Perhaps he would be allowed to take her out to lunch. He imagined them in conversation, their heads close together, over a table at Antoine's. His father had taken him and his mother to the restaurant on a few special occasions. This time Al would be the one giving the orders. At the end of the meal, as Louise and he sipped coffee, he would ask her formally to consider herself to be his. She would prettily blush and lower her eyes. That would be the moment to produce the tiny dark-red jewel box, a miniature treasure chest, and ask her to open it. There on the dark-red velvet would repose a ring bearing a single small, perfect stone – not a diamond maybe; maybe something more personal; he could find out what her birthstone was. When she saw it she would gasp in surprise, admiration and eternal devotion.

Back in his room, Al opened the bandbox to get out his clothes for the evening. On top of the tissue paper that enwrapped them there was a small blue book. Its title, appropriately, was *The Blue Book*. Al wondered why Mr. Mankowitz had sent it to him. He soon discovered why. The book was a guide to the sporting houses of Storyville. Two scraps of paper served as bookmarks to direct Al's attention to pages that Mr. Mankowitz apparently regarded as pertinent. One of them was a full-page advertisement for Mankowitz Custom Tailoring; the other carried several advertisements for several houses, including the New Alhambra.

"The New Alhambra, kept by Madame Fleur Robichaux, Bienville and Basin Streets, is the most de luxe, most refined establishment in all of New Orleans. Madame Robichaux's young ladies are universally acknowledged to be the most charming, most intelligent and most entertaining group of octoroon beauties ever assembled under one roof. In palatial grandeur that recalls the hey-day of Madame Pompadour, the most discriminating gentlemen may be sure of a discreet welcome and a swell time. Words cannot do justice to the splendor of the setting and the glamor and liveliness of Madame Robichaux's retinue of good-time gals.

"The high-life connoisseurs of New Orleans society all agree that until you have socialized with Madame Robichaux's bevy of red-hot beauties you have not lived. These pert princesses of pulchritude really know the score when it comes to making a man feel like a man. Why do you think the New Alhambra boasts the world's costliest collection of mirrors? Seeing is believing! Patrons may relax and enjoy some of the finer things in life secure in the knowledge that all necessary arrangements have been made to ensure their safety and comfort in every respect. Regular inspections are conducted on the premises by a distinguished, fully qualified member of the Medical Profession. First-class refreshments and the latest jazz music at all hours."

There it was, spelled out for him in plain language in black and white, the place of jazz in the social hierarchy, right at the bottom.

Al dressed in the costume provided. The black jacket and the black-and-gray-pin-striped trousers were rather like a banker's; unlike a banker's, however, the trousers were cut tight around the buttocks and under the crotch, and the legs were straight and very narrow. The high, white collar of the shirt was stiff with starch. He tied the red silk cravat several times before he thought it was knotted just right. The multicolored embroidery of the waistcoat was worthy of a prosperous Chinese bookie. As Madame Robichaux had said he must be, Al was dressed real sharp. His status could not be altogether unimportant.

Finally, standing in front of the oval mirror, he put on the pale-gray derby. It was very sharp indeed. He tilted it forward and a bit to one side and opened his mouth in a big grin and held out his hands as though acknowledging applause. The grin faded. He did not really convince himself. He felt like an impostor. He looked like a boy impersonating a grown-up. Should he grow a moustache? *Could* he grow a moustache? Surreptitiously comparing himself with other cadets in the communal shower-room at Bull Run, he had observed that he was as hairy as most of his contemporaries, but that was not saying a whole lot; the development of their pubic hair was quite manly but the hair on their chests still left a good deal to be desired. Anyway, he could not grow much of a moustache between now and eight o'clock. How could he face the people he would have to face? Would they expect too much of a piano player wearing such an advanced hat? He asked himself whether, on the other hand, the disguise wouldn't help to prove his right to be there. He hoped it would.

Clutching his cardboard portfolio, with his last few dollars in his pocket, Al quietly left the house. In the street, he felt that all the passersby were staring at him. He walked past two little black boys pitching pennies against a wall. He heard them chatter behind his back, and laugh, and he felt that they knew that he did not play well enough to dress like a whorehouse professor.

He checked the time in a café and found that he was too early to go to work. He ordered a muffuletta at the lunch counter. The bread was bulging with spicy Italian ham, salami, cheese and olive salad. Muffulettas were his favorite sandwiches. He took one bite. He could eat no more. He asked for a glass of milk.

"Something wrong with it?" the counterman demanded incredulously.

"No. It's fine."

"Something wrong with *you*? You look kind of green about the gills."

"I'll be all right."

"Want me to fix you a bromo?"

"No, thanks."

"Maybe all you need's a hair of the dog."

The suggestion made Al feel more confident.

"Yeah," he said. "Maybe that'll do the trick."

He left a larger tip than he could afford.

"Take care!" the counterman said, as Al left with an attempt at a swagger.

To kill time, he walked several blocks without paying attention to where he was going.

Suddenly he became aware of some wonderful sounds, coming from the next block. His musical antennae quivered with a thrill of appreciation and he quickened his pace. As he crossed the street, almost running, he could distinguish the classic New Orleans instrumental configuration – cornet, trombone and clarinet backed up by piano, banjo, bass and drums. He did not know who they were and he did not know what they were playing. He only knew that they were going at it hard and well and that the music was the most exciting he had ever heard. He felt it in his viscera, in his heart and in his brain. He felt it in his blood and in his bones. He felt like shouting to the band that he could hear them and he was on his way.

A small group of listeners was standing on the sidewalk around an open doorway. They were old men, middle-aged men, young men and a couple of boys, all shabbily dressed, standing around the doorway and staring in with expressions of hungry rapture, like those of new converts during a service in church.

Al stood at the back of the semi-circle and looked over shoulders and between heads. He saw a crowded bar-room, with a bandstand at the back. The audience was white and the musicians were black. They were all equally galvanized by the powerful vibrations, the strong beat and the shrill metallic howls and screams of the glorious musical din.

When it reached an insurmountable, terminal climax, there was an instant of silence and then there was a storm of handclapping and cheers.

Al was astonished and exalted by joy. He was inwardly seething with a happiness that he could not wholly contain. He found that he was slapping the back of the man in front of him. The man looked around unreproachfully.

"Excuse me!" Al said, restraining himself. "I couldn't help it."

The man sympathetically beamed.

"I know what you mean," he said. "That's what they do. They 'most carry you away."

Another man looked round and noticed Al's fancy costume.

"Move aside," he said, doing so himself. "Let the man in."

There was a general stirring of the small sidewalk audience as they made way for Al. When he realized what they thought, he gave them an apologetic smile.

"I'm not going in," he said. "I just heard the music and stopped for a minute."

"Thought you wanted to sit in and blow."

"I wish I could," Al said. "That's some band. Who are they? What was that they were playing?"

His question swivelled some more heads. He was subjected to the sort of scrutiny that he might have expected if had just arrived from the Moon. One of the older men took pity on him.

"That's Kid Ory's outfit," he said kindly. "They were playing King Oliver's composition, 'Bienville Breakdown'. That's Joe Oliver on cornet."

There were some amused smiles.

"Oh," Al said. "Thanks, mister. Thanks a lot."

He felt very ignorant. He got away as fast as he was able.

He arrived at the New Alhambra at twenty to eight. Charlie, the doorman, opened the front door. He was in full uniform, with a peaked cap. A long, black wooden truncheon dangled from his belt, for he was also a stickman, authorized by the police to carry this weapon and to use it, if necessary, to maintain the order and tranquillity of which Madame Robichaux was so proud. Now his smile was friendly.

"Evening, professor," he said. "Looking good!"

"I think I'm early," Al said. "I wanted to kind of get the feel of the piano a little bit ahead of time."

"Sure."

Charlie led the way to the parlor.

"Is Madame Robichaux here?" Al asked.

"She ain't back from the cemetery yet."

"A funeral?"

"No. She goes over to St. Louis Cemetery Number One every evening, to put flowers by Marie Laveau's tomb."

Marie Laveau was the most powerful queen of voodoo in New Orleans of all time. As the pioneer Spanish priests mollified their converts in the New World by admitting Indian gods into the Catholic Church, so Marie Laveau, a quadroon believed to have some Indian blood, in turn recruited Catholic saints to increase the local influence of voodoo.

There was some doubt that her ashes actually reposed in the Storyville tomb generally recognized as hers. Perhaps they did, though the tomb, strictly speaking, belonged to her daughter, Marie Legendre, née Maria Glapion, sometimes known as Marie Laveau II. Marie the Second was a prostitute in the Maison Blanche, a lakefront brothel that provided quadroons for white

91

men, until she moved down to the French Quarter and set herself up as a successful professional practitioner of voodoo.

Whatever it contained, the remains of the mother or the daughter or both, the tomb still inspired many people with a feeling of fearful respect. There were still some who believed that if you rubbed your right foot against the base of the tomb three times, made an X-mark on it with a red brick, placed your hand over the X and made a wish, the spirit of Marie Laveau would grant it. Al remembered that when he misbehaved as a young child Sarah sometimes crossly warned him that she would report him to Marie Laveau if he didn't shape up.

"Madame Robichaux goes over there every evening?" Al said.

"Yes, she does. I'm not saying she *believes*. I don't know about all that stuff. Me, I'm a Baptist myself. But she does always take a few flowers. Always plenty of flowers at the New Alhambra. We have to throw flowers away. The johns send them by the car-load. Miss Fleur says she likes to walk to the cemetery, she likes to get some fresh air before the night begins. She says maybe the flowers don't do no good, but they sure ain't going to do nobody no *harm*. Well, there's the piano. Help yourself. It's all yours. Good luck."

Alone in the ornate pink, cream and golden parlor, Al spun the pink velvet-covered top of the piano stool until its height was right. He got out his sheet music. He sat down. He opened the piano. He squeezed one hand and then the other and exercised his fingers in the manner of a concert pianist before a performance. He wondered what to play. He sounded a few speculative random chords and ran his right forefinger from one end of the keyboard to the other and back again. He sat quietly listening to the silence. He heard a melody that made him smile, and he began to play it. Simply, at first.

As well as he could remember it, which was very well indeed, he played King Oliver's "Bienville Breakdown". He played it straight, the way he had heard Kid Ory's band play it. Then he played his own variations. He played it as a rag, as a march, as a stomp and as a blues. He was playing it as a Bach fugue when one of the inner doors opened and a young woman came in. Al stopped in the middle of a phrase and awkwardly stood up.

She was really only a girl. She couldn't have been any older than Al but she had big breasts. The tight, low-cut bodice of her red silk dress temptingly displayed them like two ripe fruit. She had black hair and big brown eyes and big red lips. Only her voice was little. Inside the body lived a tiny soprano.

"What kind of crap is that?" she said. "How about playing something good? How about 'Mighty Like A Rose'?"

TWENTY-ONE

Soon there were half a dozen young ladies in the parlor. Three of them sat in armchairs in one corner, engaging in an animated discussion in low voices. The first arrival, whose name proved to be Celeste, and two others, Dee-Dee and Michele, stood around the piano, submitting Al to a close examination and candid analysis.

The young ladies were gorgeous. Their coiffures were gorgeous. Their makeup was gorgeous. Their dresses were gorgeous. Their perfumes were overwhelmingly gorgeous, at once aphrodisiac and narcotic. Al felt quite dizzy with desire and fear.

While he played up-to-date hit songs from the printed scores, to prove that he could, they peppered him with questions and comments.

"What's your name, Red?"

"Where do you come from?"

"Look at them blue eyes, will you?"

"Green is what they are."

"Are you married?"

"Are you going steady?"

"Are you getting much?"

"Are you cherry?"

"How old are you?"

"If they're big enough they're old enough."

"He's big enough."

"What do you weigh, Al?"

"How tall are you?"

"Are you an easy rider?"

"What's Miss Fleur paying you?"

"What did Ludwig charge for the vest?"

"It's a cute vest."

"It's the cat's whiskers!"

"The bee's knees!"

"The elephant's pajamas!"

"So's he."

"Hands off!" said Celeste. "I saw him first. Didn't I, Al?"

"He don't want you, you dumb bitch."

"You want a woman with an educated grind, right, Al?"

"Looks to me like he's got enough for the whole gang of us. That's what *I* say."

There was a minor playful skirmish, a little pushing and pinching and girlish high-pitched laughter. The New Alhambra evidently was not always an establishment of refinement. But Al stoically kept on playing.

Two more gorgeous young ladies joined his audience, Minnie and Jeanette. Like their colleagues, they were brunettes of luxuriously shapely embonpoint.

"Give us something with some pep in it," Jeannette impatiently urged him. "Show us how fast you can make it."

"Please would you play one for me?" Minnie asked in a long-drawn-out coaxing whine. She was devoting her career to impersonation of a traditional Southern belle. There was a steady demand for it. "Would you-all play a real *slow* . . . pretty . . . *sad* song? Would you, huh?"

The young ladies thus quickly gave Al a clear and comprehensive introductory lesson in public taste. Would there ever be any reason to modify this initial assessment?

As he was playing Minnie a tearfully sentimental ballad about unrequited love and loneliness and heart-ache, with what Mr. Mankowitz had called "all those extra frills", Celeste leaned across the piano, exhibiting the shady depth of her cleavage, and said:

"Got a cigarette, Al?"

"Concentrate, Alan!" admonished an echo of the voice of Dr. Frischauer in the back of Al's mind "Gon-zen-drate!"

Al did his best to keep his eyes on the music.

Madame Robichaux entered the parlor at precisely eight o'clock and the chatter was suddenly hushed. When Al looked at her his fingers stopped moving.

She was wearing a low-necked long black silk gown with a heavy fringe of black ermine at the hem. The richly gleaming blackness made the young ladies' bright colors seem frivolously juvenile. And, as if to ensure that there could be no uncertainty about her superiority, she was glittering with diamonds – diamond rings, diamond bracelets, a diamond necklace and a diamond tiara. It was a tiara fit for an empress on a state occasion on which she wished particularly to impress the neighbors. It used to be said in New Orleans that when Lulu White came down the stairs of Mahogany Hall arrayed in all her jewelry she looked like the St. Louis Exhibition lit up at night. When Fleur Robichaux had been in Lulu White's employ she had visually taken inventory of the celebrated madame's jewels with the accuracy of intense envy. As soon as possible after achieving independence and establishing a house of her own, Madame Robichaux had outshone her former employer by the simple expedient of estimating the number of her carats and doubling it. Madame Robichaux's jewelry must have been worth a sizable fortune.

"That sounded real pretty, Al," she said with a sweet smile. "Don't let me interrupt. Continue right on."

Al complied. He felt confident. He already knew what sort of playing they most admired. He added frills to the frills.

"Michele," Madame Robichaux said. "Here a minute."

Michele dutifully went there.

"Colonel Howell sent word he's going to try to get over from Baton Rouge. Are you well? Are you completely well?"

"Yes, Miss Fleur."

"If you say so, you better had be. The colonel's very fussy."

"I know, Miss Fleur. I remember that time."

"He asked for you."

"Thank you, Miss Fleur."

"All right then. You'll take him to the Japanese room. The Venetian room will be occupied." Madame Robichaux laughed. "Make him feel Japanese."

Michele laughed in response, pleased to see that Miss Fleur was in a good mood.

"Minnie," Madame Robichaux said briskly.

Minnie reluctantly turned away from the piano and her reverie of falling leaves.

"Miss Fleur?"

"You haven't forgotten it's Thursday."

"No, Miss Fleur. The senator."

"He said he has to go to the opera, but he'll get here as soon as he can after supper."

Al played a free and easy adaptation of an impressionistic Debussy tone poem, like a pink sunrise on a misty morning, while secretly he thought about the dirty sliding growl of a trombone.

A black girl dressed like a maid in a French farce – a white lace cap, an extremely short black dress with a white collar and a small white apron, black net stockings and black shoes with extra-high heels – came in through the front door of the parlor to announce the first visitors of the evening, the first johns.

There were four of them, in evening dress. They wore red roses in their buttonholes and big circular cardboard name badges above their breast pockets. They were delegates to the annual national convention of the Loyal Order of Moose. Evidently the formalities of the day's program were over. They were drunk.

Madame Robichaux said a few words in the maid's ear and the maid hurried away to comply.

"Welcome, boys!" said Madame Robichaux. "Take the weight off your feet. Make yourselves comfortable. The drinks will be right here."

"Now you're talking!" one of the boys declared. Madame Robichaux pretended to be interested in his badge.

"O.K., Stu! Put it down."

Then the diplomacy of the accomplished hostess demanded that she pay equally close attention to Cy, Hank and Elwood. Al went on playing music as unobtrusive as wall-paper.

Two girls in simple short white dresses brought in trays bearing four bottles of champagne, which they put on the small service bar across the room from the piano.

"Bubbly, everyone?" Madame Robichaux suggested in a shrill mad-cap party voice.

"How much does that cost a bottle?" asked Hank with shrewd, suspicious, half-closed eyes.

"Dear Lordy!" Madame Robichaux protested at this crass vulgarity and placed a genteel hand on her naked chest as though to calm a fluttering heart. "No gentleman is ever *obliged* to take a drink at the New Alhambra, specially if he don't feel sure he can afford it."

"Don't be a slob," Elwood told his good old buddy.

"I want to know how much it costs, that's all. What's wrong with wanting to know that?"

"Hey, cut it out you guys," Cy remonstrated, fearing without due cause that his devil-may-care group of adventurers, the Four Musketeers, might be in danger of relapsing into sobriety. "We don't come to New Orleans every day."

"Open up the wine!" said Stu. "To hell with money!"

With a subtle motion of her head, Madame Robichaux signalled to a black bartender who had somehow materialized, like a genie, behind the bar, and he opened the first bottle. It exploded with a loud pop and an orgasmic gush of foam.

"Ooh, Stu! Goody, goody!" Jeannette exclaimed, complimenting the brave big spender, slipping an arm around one of his and squeezing it excitedly. "I *love* champagne!"

The others apparently shared her iodiosyncrasy: everybody in the room, except Al, of course, moved closer to the bar. Glasses were quickly passed and there were more pops.

"How much is it?" Hank stubbornly insisted. He was ignored almost entirely, but not quite. Madame Robichaux got close to him and gave him one of her most charming smiles.

"Let *me* get *you* a drink, Hank," she said. "What'll it be? If you don't like that imported foreign wine, I bet a bourbon and branch water would hit the spot!"

Without waiting for a reply, she went and got a highball and came back and put it into his hand. For longer than necessary, her fingers lingered against his.

"There you go, Hank. The others'll take care of the champagne."

He took a long drink.

"As a matter of interest though," he said in a tolerant manner. "How much *does* it cost?"

"Same as at any of the high-class places," she told him. She was standing confidentially close to him. "Twenty-five dollars a bottle. It's highway robbery, isn't it?"

Hank laughed happily.

"I knew it would be something like that," he said. "Serves the goddamn fools right!" He finished his whiskey and held out his glass for more.

"I bet you been around, Hank. You so *smart.* I bet nobody never puts one over on you."

He complacently pinched her bottom as she headed back toward the bar with his glass, and she gave the bartender the sign that caused him to make the next highball a Mickey Finn. Hank did no more questioning and no more pinching that night. Charlie led him and dragged him and finally carried him to a small back room, more liked a padded cell than an ordinary bedroom, where patrons who drank and behaved injudiciously could

98

be kept until they recovered their faculties and their sense of decorum.

His companions did not miss him.

Al reverted to jazz, to "Bienville Breakdown" as a low-down blues in a slow tempo. Stu and Jeannette began dancing. That is to say that they stood close together, cheek to cheek, with his arms around her waist, while she worked her pelvis against his in time with the music. Somebody had turned off the ceiling lights, leaving only pink lights glowing through pink shades. Stu and Jeannette were the first couple to leave the parlor to go upstairs. At the doorway, he looked back over his shoulder and winked at the others.

Elwood and Cy uneasily winked back. They had somehow found themselves paired off with Dee-Dee and Celeste but were still busily anaesthetizing their small-town consciences and trying to build up sufficient bravado to follow their leader.

Al wondered what it would be like to go up to a bedroom with one of Madame Robichaux's young ladies, to go to bed naked with a naked woman. Would she know that he had never done it before? Would the general notion of sexual pleasure be reduced to an embarrassing ordeal by an intimate personal encounter with an individual stranger? Couldn't he close his eyes and keep her mind out of his mind and enjoy his flesh in the warmth of her flesh? Would she speak? Would she ask questions? Would she criticize? Anyway, Madame Robichaux had emphatically warned him that her young ladies were off limits. He remembered Louise. She was a young lady. Her clothes were different but she was the same underneath. He felt excited, and ashamed. Elwood and Cy roared with fraternal laughter, like Bull Run laughter, as if they knew what he wanted and that he could not have it.

He brusquely stepped up the tempo of the music as he segued into "Bill Bailey". The effect was almost the same as if he had brightened the lights. Madame Robichaux frowned. However, the unsexiness of the music gave Elwood the courage to ask Dee-Dee to dance. It did not take her long to encourage him to proceed further. She enabled him to feel devilish and strong and that he was taking the initiative. He whispered into her ear and she smiled and led him away. He went as meekly as a lamb to the slaughter. Madame Robichaux's benign smile indicated that all was well in the best of all possible houses.

99

Cy drank. His friends had all deserted him. He sagged morosely in his chair. He had lulled his conscience but he had lulled everything else, too. Celeste stopped nibbling the lobe of his ear and stroking his thigh. There were lovers and drinkers. She had observed that at least half the delegates to conventions were, first and last, only drinkers. Cy was a drinker. She ordered another bottle of champagne, because she was paid commission on that as well. She wanted him to buy as much drink as possible, short of running amok or throwing up or passing out. It was necessary to maintain a nice balance.

"Let's have a chicken sandwich," she suggested. She got thirty-three and a third per cent of the menu price. "Cy, honey, can we have a sandwich? I'm starving."

The maid notified Madame Robichaux that a special guest had arrived and she left the parlor to arrange his reception in a private room.

Cy tottered over to the piano.

"Hey, old buddy," he said. "What's that tune supposed to be?"

" 'My Gal Sal,' " Al said. "Don't you like it?"

"Terrible. This is a terrible town. Bunch of parasites. It's nearly Christmas. You ought to be playing Christmas songs. 'Oh, Come All Ye Faithful' and all that."

"I don't think – "

"Nobody asked you to think! Play a Christmas song."

Al looked over at Celeste for guidance. She shrugged her shoulders and looked away. He started playing "Silent Night".

"That's it," Cy said. His pink eyes and creased jowls made him look as lugubrious as a bloodhound. "Happy Christmas, everybody!"

Nobody responded. He returned unsteadily to his armchair and slumped into it and closed his eyes, holding his half-full champagne glass at a precarious angle. Celeste impatiently straightened it and filled it.

"Happy Christmas, Cy!" she said in a loud voice close to his ear. He started and opened his eyes. "Drink up!" she told him. "Your sandwich is here. Don't forget to tip the girl." He looked unenthusiastically with unfocused eyes at a dish piled high with small triangular sandwiches. He fumbled in his pocket and pulled out a bill and Celeste snatched it from his fingers as adroitly as a chameleon's tongue taking an insect.

Elwood and Dee-Dee were the first back downstairs. He seemed strangely sober.

"Bartender!" he said. "Give me one of those Sazerac cocktails! God damn it, this place is dead. What the hell are you playing, piano man? What is this, a church, for chrissake? Play something hot. Cy, what are *you* doing? Going to sleep? What's the matter with you? Don't waste time, drinking any more of that champagne. It'll rot your guts. Have a real drink! Have a Sazerac! Bartender, make a whole big batch of those things! Cy, God damn it, this is a *party*! We're in New Orleans. Let's get drunk!"

"Damn right, Elwood, old pal," Cy agreed, speaking half-consciously, like the Dormouse. Cy was as sporting as the next man. "Gimme a goddamn – gimme a drink!" Sazerac is a difficult name for a convention delegate to pronounce in the evening if he's a drinker rather than a lover.

The bartender dispensed drinks and Elwood and Cy drank them. The young ladies asked the bartender for special drinks.

Stu and Jeannette came back into the parlor. He was obviously in a state of extreme euphoria. Her hair was tied at the back in a simple knot.

"Let's have some drinks!" he shouted. "Listen to that music!" He took Jeannette to the piano. "You're all right!" he told Al. "That's a lot of music! D'you know 'Maple Leaf Rag'?"

That was before Al's time but he came up with a rough approximation of it and Stu didn't know the difference.

"This kiddo is red-hot!" Stu told the world. "Keep it going! Speed it up! Bartender, a drink for the piano player! Don't quit now! I'm stompin' tonight!"

The bartender looked at Al and Al nodded. Madame Robichaux had explained that the bartender would make Al toy drinks and charge the customer for real ones. If he saved the swizzle sticks, he, too, could claim a commission at the end of the night. In some respects he and the young ladies were performing the same function.

He beat the piano hard and sweated. He was thinking about the music when Stu grabbed the pale-gray derby. Al tried to grab it back but Stu nimbly danced backward beyond Al's reach. Al jumped to his feet. Jeannette quickly got between him and the triumphantly crowing Stu.

"Don't be crazy, boy!" she said with her hands against Al's

chest, and he saw that she was really concerned. "Get back to the piano. Plenty more hats where that one came from."

Al obeyed her. With grimly compressed lips, he went on playing. Stu and Elwood played a game of catch, skimming the hat to and fro across the room. Dee-Dee, entering into the spirit of the game, tried to intervene. Stu hugged the hat to his chest, like a football player hugging the ball, and fell on it, just as Madame Robichaux entered the room. Her majestic presence silenced the action and froze it.

"Having fun, gentlemen?" she asked.

"We sure are, ma'am," Stu said, grinning and scrambling to his feet.

"Have you finished with that derby?"

Stu looked down at its remains in his hand. The crown was crushed almost flat. He grinned again.

"Yeah, ma'am. I'd say everybody's finished with it." He held the brim firmly and punched the crown into shape, more or less.

"May I have it, please?"

He handed it over.

She smiled.

"Yes," she said to Stu. "I'd say you're right." She placed it on the piano, crown down. "But it'll be good for putting your tips in. You do appreciate Al's music, don't you? Al, play something nice. I'm sure these gentlemen will show their appreciation."

The giant figure of Charlie appeared at the door.

"Everything O.K., Miss Fleur?" he asked.

"Everything's just fine, Charlie. I'll call you if I need you."

He disappeared and the door closed.

"Now, bartender," she said brightly. "Drinks all round. Come on, boys. Drink up. These are on the house."

Madame Robichaux was completely in charge. The moment of tension was over. Drinks were served. Madame Robichaux raised her glass to Al as the music-lovers filled the ruined hat with crumpled bills of various denominations.

The job was a nerve-racking one but the money certainly was excellent.

Al looked through the sheet music and played "I'll See You In My Dreams".

TWENTY-TWO

By the end of the week Al had enough money to give Mr. Mankowitz his twenty dollars, pay a week's rent and put down the first installment on a ring. The small red stone was supposed to be Louise's birth-stone, a garnet. Mr. Mankowitz had recommended the jeweller, an old friend, so Al believed him. Whatever the stone was, it was a pretty color.

Al telephoned the Mercier home. Louise sounded surprised and pleased. She said he was lucky to go to a school that gave him such a long Christmas vacation. She could not see him immediately. There were unbreakable family engagements that weekend and exams all week. Her mother gave her permission to have lunch with him the following Saturday. He said he couldn't imagine how he'd get through all those days of waiting. He really couldn't.

In fact, his routine did not leave much spare time. Having played piano all night, he never got back to his room before the first light of dawn, and he got into the habit of sleeping until early afternoon. After going out for brunch in a neighborhood café, it was soon time to get ready for another night.

He was loneliest when he played piano best, surrounded by indifferent women and drunken men. He did not play for people; he played for tips. When they made requests he made sure that they did not overlook his upside-down derby. His new hat was a begging bowl. The men tipped competitively, to impress the women, and the beggar prospered. He became good at laughing at even the unfunniest jokers; it seemed to him that the laughs were on them. And in the early hours of the morning, when most of the clientele had gone upstairs or to their homes and only two or three somnolent drunks lingered in the parlor, Al played the slow, sad songs for himself.

On Monday, the quietest night of the week, another piano player took Al's place. It was his night off.

Dressed in his own inconspicuous clothes, he walked all over The District, through streets that the police patrolled only in twos. Even in the cool drizzle, the gutters stank. A rat, foraging in spilled garbage between ramshackle wooden houses, scuttled away into obscurity. Young black whores called to him from the windows and doorways of their one-room cribs.

"Here it is, baby ! I got something to show you !"

"Good time, mister ? Want a good time ?"

"Twenty-five cents – any way you want !"

When he ignored them, some of them shouted abuse.

He had only one aim, to go from bar to bar where there was jazz. There were plenty of them. Most of them were open to the street, so that the music stopped people and enticed some of them inside.

At his first few stops he stayed on the outside looking in. But he was getting wet and cold. He wanted to get close to a bandstand, to get right into the music and to see how the musicians were making it. He came to the entrance of a bar in North Rampart Street, a honky-tonk teeming and roiling with life. The lights glowed warmly through a haze of smoke and the music was fast and loud. The enticement was irresistible.

He entered rather hesitantly, hoping that nobody would stop him to ask his age. The bouncer gave him only a perfunctory glance and asked nothing. Al eased his way through the animated crowd to the end of the bar, as close as he could get to the stand. He bought a nickel schooner of draft beer. All along the bar there were bowls of free pretzels and peanuts. He drank the beer slowly while he listened to, and felt, the music.

The drummer was beating his drums furiously, as if trying to make them go faster. He was like a jockey booting and whipping his horse into the home stretch. The other musicians were racing by different routes to a common destination whose whereabouts had not yet been defined. The music moved Al's right foot and rattled his eardrums, and he loved it.

He listened so hard that he forgot to drink. Nobody pestered him to drink up and drink more. He stayed till the band took a break. Then he finished his beer and left. After that it was easy for him to go in anywhere.

In Henry Matranga's saloon on Perdido Street Al got a beer and slowly worked his way to a place near the stand and looked up, and there was Moses. He was standing right in the middle of the front line of a seven-piece band, leading the way, blowing his cornet like a declaration of war.

It had been three years and a bit more since the last time Al had seen him, at the Waifs' Home. Moses was a few inches taller, a few pounds heavier, than he had been then. He was still lean and lanky, built like a basketball player, and he stood in a deceptively relaxed slouch – loose but ready. As he played, his face looked more serious than the face that Al remembered. Moses was frowning and his eyes were tight shut and his cheeks and neck were bulging, as if the music required an effort that was causing him pain. But then, at last, the melodic lines were all interwoven neatly and pulled close together and tied in a satisfactory conclusive knot, the audience yelled and stamped in approval, and Moses was fooling around the same as ever, doing a few tricky dance steps and laughing.

"Mo!" Al shouted, waving his free hand.

Moses bent forward, shielding his eyes against the spotlights, and raised his eyebrows in surprise and howled.

"Alan!" He immediately leaped off the stand, a jump four or five feet down, and landed lightly on his toes in front of his friend.

"Is that really you?" Moses said, delightedly shaking Al's hand. "Son of a gun! Am I glad to see you!" Moses turned to the band. "Fellas! I got to take some time out. Found my boy here. Louis said he wants to sit in."

A short, stocky black boy was already mounting the steps at the side of the bandstand with a cornet and a broad grin. He muttered a few words to the piano player and to the others and tapped his foot a couple of times and the music started again.

"Let's go next door and grab us a cup of coffee," Moses said. "I want to know all about everything."

They sat at a table in a booth with thick white mugs of *café au lait* and compared their memories of the past three years.

"Sarah never did come to see me and she never wrote no letters while I was at the home," Moses said in a calm, matter-of-fact way. "But she wasn't my real mother. Captain Jones explained. He said it's often like that. When kids get into trouble and end up in the home the folks that used to look out for them feel kind of embarrassed, like it was their fault, what happened. I know it wasn't Sarah's fault. She was always good to me – you know that. But she and Benjamin disappeared. Maybe they split up. When I got out of the home I asked around. I asked everyone I could think of. I went to your mammy. She didn't know nothing. She was nice to me but she said it would be better if I didn't go there no more. I wrote you a letter but then I changed my mind, so I didn't mail it. I wondered how you were getting on."

"I missed you, Mo," Al said apologetically. He felt a bit guilty for not having made any effective effort to visit Moses again, after that one time.

"That's the way it goes," Moses assured him. Moses' philosophy had always been simple and unreproachfully fatalistic. What would be, would be; sufficient unto the day, and so on.

"When did you leave the home?"

"I was there a year. I got out soon after my fourteenth birthday, a little more than two years ago. It seems longer. A lot's happened. Me and Louis, we got out together. He helped me with my music in the home, helped me a whole lot. When we got out he helped me some more. When we were in the home we felt like we were in jail. We were always talking about what we'd do when we got out. But then when it was time to go we both felt kind of blue about leaving. Captain Jones and Professor Davis – they were good guys. They were like family. When I left I didn't have no place to go. I guess Sarah and Benjamin went and found work in another town. Maybe they headed up north. Anyway, Louis had his problems, too. An aunt took him in at first. He called her his aunt. She let me stay with them for a while, but she didn't have much and I had to go. But Louis and I kept in touch."

"I wish *we* had," Al said fretfully. "I could have got you some money somehow."

"That's all right, Alan."

"Al. I have a new name. I'm Al Dexter now."

"Al Dexter! That's a good name. It'd look good in lights."

They laughed.

Al told about Louise and how his father had sent him to Bull Run and how he had hated it and run away and how Mr. Brewster had heard him playing piano aboard the steamboat and introduced him to Madame Robichaux and –

"You're not playing piano for *her*?" Moses said.

"Sure. Why not? I get top money."

"Yeah. I bet. They say the New Alhambra's the highest-priced house on Basin Street. But is that all you think about – money?"

"Tony Jackson played on Basin Street, at Mahogany Hall. So did Jelly Roll Morton."

"I know. Even Papa Joe put some time in there when he had to. But he got away as soon as he could."

"Papa Joe?"

"That's what Louis calls him. I mean Joe Oliver. King Oliver."

"I heard him play. He's good."

"Only the best in the world. He's taught Louis a lot, and Louis always passes it on to me. Papa Joe even gave Louis a horn he was through with. Well, I'm glad you're playing piano. I didn't hardly dare ask. I thought your father would ship you off to college and the next thing you'd be stuck in his business and that would be that. Won't he still try to get you into line?"

Al smiled.

"He'd have to find me first. He doesn't even know I'm in town. You don't think I could live at home and play piano in The District, do you?"

"How about your ma? How do you think she feels if she doesn't know where you are?"

"Of course I've thought about that. Of course I'd like to see her. But if I tried to she'd turn me over to my father. I can't let her do that. I'm on my own now, and I'm going to stay on my own. No father, no school, none of that being ordered around, no more bullshit. I can play piano anywhere I like and look after myself."

"That's strange, isn't it?" Moses said thoughtfully. "Me looking for my family and you running away. You playing because you want to stay away from your family. Me playing because when I'm playing in a band that's my family. You playing to be free and me playing so's I *belong*. Isn't that strange?"

"We're both free," Al said doubtfully. "And we both have the music."

"Maybe neither one of us is free. I don't have the music; the music has me. And you may have your freedom from your daddy, but how free do you call playing piano at the beck and call of a whorehouse madame?"

"She lets me play the way I want," Al retorted.

"All the time?" Moses asked with a skeptical smile. Al scowled.

"Are you telling me that if you want to play this way and a rich customer says for you to play that way you say, 'Sorry, mister. This is how I like it and this is how I'm going to play?' Do you expect me to believe that?"

"Yes. You've got to eat," Al said.

"You don't have to eat shit."

"When you have a job you have to go along with the customers' ideas, the boss's ideas."

"Not if you are a true jazzman," Moses said. He spoke like an evangelist and emphasized his words with a clenched fist on the marble table. Al had never before seen Moses so stern. "When you're sad you should play sad. When you're happy you should play happy. Trouble with you, you playing sad when *they* sad; you playing happy when *they* happy. If you are a true jazzman you only play the truth."

"Amen," Al said sarcastically. "But really, Moses. Be honest about it. What if the owner of the saloon you're playing in – "

"The manager. Henry Matranga. He's O.K."

"The manager then. Even more so. What if an important customer told him he wanted to hear some old, old ragtime tune you didn't want to waste time on? What then?"

"Henry would have to tell him to try some place else. He don't own us."

"He pays you, doesn't he?"

"Not much. He pay us so little he knows he can't push us any way we don't want to go."

"What if he threatened to fire the whole band? Wouldn't you play the way he wanted?"

"No. He couldn't afford to threaten us because we have too little to lose, and because we're too good. A lot of folks come to listen. We've had Jimmy Noone playing with us. Cow Cow Davenport. Zue Robertson. Buddy Petit. Harry Zeno. The top men come and go. Anyway, he can't fire the band because it *ain't* a band. It's just a pickup group that changes from night to night. A bunch of guys that drop by and play."

"Doesn't that worry you, having no regular work?"

"Maybe it would worry me if I didn't. But I do. Louis and me. We work *very* regular. We work days on a coal-cart, delivering coal. That's the most regular kind of work you can do. When you work at carrying coal, you *know* you doing regular work. Your muscles tell you. And you know something? One of the places we deliver to is the New Alhambra. We ain't proud. We'll sell coal to *anyone*. But when we get off of that coal-cart we can play music any way we like."

TWENTY-THREE

Al and Louise took the St. Charles Avenue streetcar to Canal Street and walked to St. Louis Street. Antoine's was the oldest restaurant in the United States, established in 1840, and looked it. Like a superior bourgeois restaurant in a provincial town in France, it was almost arrogant in the stolidity of its plainness. This was long before the days of large-scale tourism, but at lunchtime on Saturday the place was quietly busy. Al had briefly considered and had rejected the idea of using his father's name, which was well known. They were not kept waiting long, but they were escorted to a table in the front room rather than in the dimly lighted inner sanctum at the back, which was reserved for favored regular patrons.

"This is lovely," Louise said, as they sat down. The napery was immaculately white; the silver and crystal glittered.

"*You* are lovely," Al said with debonair gallantry, surprising himself.

The waiter, a formal but rumpled, grandfatherly Cajun, with the strong, bony features of a Daumier lawyer, gave them menus and left them alone to peruse them.

"You're even lovelier than I remembered," Al added.

"I've never been here before," Louise said. "Would you order for me?"

Al's father had always ordered for him on his previous visits and he didn't know the meanings of the French names of most of the dishes.

"Would you like to start with some oysters?" he asked her.

"If you would," she said.

Al pointed to oysters *à la* something-or-other on the menu and the waiter silently nodded and eventually brought them some grilled oysters in a thick creamy sauce that tasted of garlic.

"Some wine, monsieur?" the waiter asked doubtfully. Al and Louise looked at each other for a decision. "Or perhaps the fruit punch?" the waiter kindly suggested.

"That sounds good," Louise said, obviously relieved.

"No," Al said boldly. "Let's have some wine. This is a special occasion, after all." He knew that you were supposed to have white wine with seafood but he couldn't remember the names. At home the butler always used to serve the wine from decanters. "What do you recommend with these oysters?" Al asked the waiter.

"I'll send you the sommelier," the waiter said.

"Yes, of course," Al said gravely. Ordering lunch at a restaurant like Antoine's wasn't a procedure that you could undertake by instinct alone.

The wine waiter tactfully intimated that a Chablis might prove to be more satisfactory than a sauterne with the oysters and Al gratefully accepted the hint.

"Is there any good fish today?" he asked the waiter, causing a minor muscular spasm in the old man's jaw. Was there any good fish at Antoine's? The old mind boggled, but he kept calm.

"The *pompano en papillote* is usually appreciated."

"Yes," Al said. "Would that be all right?" he asked Louise.

"Thank you, yes. That would be very nice."

"We'll both have that then."

"Tell me," Louise said when they were alone again, "is your school really as awful as you said in your letters?"

"Worse. I'm glad that's over."

"What do you mean, 'over?' How much vacation do you get?"

"I couldn't stand being separated any longer. I ran away."

He smiled triumphantly, awaiting her praise.

"You ran *away*! Isn't your daddy hopping mad at you?"

"I don't care if he is. He shouldn't have sent me there, should he? It's barbaric. He only did it to get me away from you. Well, he lost out, didn't he? Because here we are."

"You can't just quit school."

"I just did."

"What did your mother say? If I quit school – not that I would want to – my mother would *kill* me."

"They didn't send you away, did they? It's different for you. The commandant at Bull Run wouldn't even let me play the *piano*, for heaven's sake. You know that's what I care about more than anything else – after you, that is."

"I'm surprised your father let you get away with it. Is he still taking you to Bermuda for Christmas? There was an item in the society column, with his picture. We'll be separated over the vacation, won't we? But Bermuda isn't Bull Run, is it? I suppose if you go away to Bermuda that doesn't count."

Al enjoyed her perplexity and her jealousy.

"Shall we have baked Alaska for dessert?" he asked. "I know that's good."

"And then what? They'll send you to another prep school, won't they? I imagine they still plan for you to go on to the University of Virginia."

"No, they won't. No more prep school. No university. I'm staying right here. I love you, Louise."

"That's all very well. I'm fond of you, too. But what are you talking about? Have you gone crazy? How can you not go to university? How do you expect to prepare yourself to take over your father's brokerage when the time comes?"

"Simple. I don't expect to. I play piano."

"Of course. Daddy says you play it very well. Music will always give you pleasure, I'm sure. But you aren't going to make it a career, are you? You have family responsibilities."

"Family responsibilities? You mean I owe it to my father to spend the rest of my life buying and selling cotton – pieces of paper that *represent* cotton on some remote plantation? He can find plenty of eager-beaver young men in New Orleans who would jump at the chance to do that. I'm not one of them. I couldn't work for him anyway, not at anything. He's a tyrant. I refuse. You don't know what he's like."

"He's highly respected. You can't defy him. He's your father."

"Yes, I can. That's what I'm doing. I thought you'd be pleased that I'm standing on my own two feet."

"How do you figure that? You're still under his roof. He's still supporting you. He provided the clothes you're wearing – this food we're eating, and very delicious it is. You should be grateful. You owe him something. He brought you into the world."

"He wasn't doing me a favor," Al said bitterly. Although he had been relishing her ignorance of the true state of affairs, the conversation was not going as he had anticipated. He decided that he had better give her the good news in clearer terms.

"I'm not under his roof. He's not supporting me. I've left home for ever and I have a place of my own. I earned the money for this lunch."

"You've left home!" Louise exclaimed, appalled. Her beautiful face was marred by an ugly expression. She put down her knife and fork and stared at him as if he had started frothing at the mouth. "How could you do such a thing? That's *terrible*!"

"It was easy and I'm glad. I've never felt better. I'm my own man. I said I love you, Louise. I want to marry you."

"You're insane!" she protested. "How will you get your degree?"

"Let's have some baked Alaska and coffee," Al said soothingly, though inside he felt the mounting indignation of injured innocence. "I know the baked Alaska's good," he repeated.

"How can you talk about baked Alaska? You're throwing away your whole heritage and your whole future. Why don't you go to your daddy and ask him to forgive you? I'm sure it's not too late. You can blame everything on Bull Run – it was too strict; it was too much of an adjustment. He'd understand. There's so much at stake."

"Would you marry me if I graduated from college and settled down as a highly respected cotton broker?"

"Alan, dear! You sound so funny when you put it like that."

"Would you marry me as I am and as I'm going to be, a piano player who plays jazz?"

"Please, Alan. Now you're being silly. You know I couldn't possibly do that."

She enjoyed the baked Alaska, but the conversation deteriorated beyond redemption.

There never was an opportune moment for Al to produce the garnet ring. It stayed in its box in his pocket.

Outside the restaurant, Louise offered Al her hand. At first he could not believe that she expected him to shake it.

"I'm going to take you home," he said.

"No, Alan. I think it would be better if we parted here. I would prefer to go back on my own."

"But, Louise – "

"I'm sorry it had to turn out this way," she said, as if reciting the lines of a melodrama. "I hope, for your sake, that you change your mind. If you do I'd be pleased to hear from you. If not, this is goodbye."

Al was speechless.

Louise turned and walked briskly toward Royal Street. Al stood still, watching her go.

TWENTY-FOUR

The first thing that Al did was to take the ring back to the jeweller. Because of the connection with the New Alhambra, he allowed Al a partial refund of the first instalment, on condition that the credit was used to buy a wristwatch. The second thing that Al did was to go to Matranga's saloon. It was too early in the afternoon for the band, but not too early to drink beer. He drank more than one.

"Is Moses around?" he asked the bartender.

"Who's he?"

"Moses Decatur. Tall colored boy who plays the horn."

"I don't keep track of the musicians. They're always changing. The band will get together later."

Al had another beer.

"Would it be O.K. if I played the piano?" he asked.

"O.K. with me. Ask Mr. Matranga."

"Sure, kid," the manager said. "Go ahead."

Al put his beer-mug on top of the rickety upright piano and began playing. He played the blues. The wine and the beer did not help his accuracy but he played with feeling. When he finished the beer he returned to the bar.

"You can come in and play any time you want," Mr. Matranga said. "Have a drink. On the house."

"Want a short one?" the bartender said.

"Yeah. Why not?" To hell with Louise, he thought. He'd have a hundred drinks. A thousand.

"What'll it be? A bourbon?"

"Yeah. A bourbon."

Drinking was an act of defiance – defiance of Louise, defiance of his family, defiance of society, defiance of all authority. Drinking was like playing the piano his own way, for nobody but himself. To hell with everybody.

"Same again," he said, using the tough-guy voice he had heard others use and throwing a ten-dollar bill on the bar. He had got the ten as a tip. It wasn't real money. To hell with it, too. Easy come, easy go.

The bartender refilled the shot glass. There was no need to pour any more water. Al had not touched the chaser.

He began to feel glad to be rid of Louise. He didn't need her. She had never expressed any warm affection for him as a person. All she wanted was his family, the prestige of its name and money and security. She could go to hell. The world was full of girls – full of women. What made her think she was so precious?

He felt befuddled.

"Another?" the bartender asked.

"Next time," Al said. He stood up and for a moment the bar revolved like a Ferris wheel. He rubbed his eyes and it stopped. "Tell Mo I was asking for him. Tell him I got rid of that rotten little bitch Louise."

The bartender held up the nine dollars and change that Al had left on the bar but he did not seem to notice. As he slowly walked away toward the door, the bartender prudently refrained from saying more than "Thank you."

"Come and see us again," Mr. Matranga said. "We often have a place for a good piano man."

Al wandered the streets, occasionally stopping at bars. He had never before had so much to drink in such a short time. He went into the old Absinthe House, on Bourbon Street.

"What's yours?" the bartender asked.

"If it's an absinthe house, I'd better have absinthe," Al said.

He left several dollars on the bar there, as well. Al was a big tipper.

He did not see it happen but the sun dropped out of sight and a lopsided yellow moon appeared through a gap in the low scud. The night was fine.

He looked at his watch. The time was nearly seven-thirty. He should go back to his room to change for the evening. To hell with changing. He thought of the New Alhambra. He thought of Madame Robichaux. Seven-thirty! It was about the time when she took flowers to the tomb of Marie Laveau. Madame Robichaux! He must go to her, immediately. She appreciated him. She didn't criticize like Moses and Louise. Madame Robichaux did not hold it against him that he played the piano for her.

Hobbling along with quick, erratic, lurching steps, as though he did not know the exact length of his legs (it seemed to vary) and he was not sure when each foot would reach the sidewalk, he hurried in the direction of St. Louis Cemetery Number One, on Basin Street. The cemetery was conveniently close to the New Alhambra. He was smiling as eagerly as a Transylvanian insomniac on Walpurgis Night.

New Orleans was built at sea level, the annual rainfall is almost Amazonian, and the water table is very close to the surface of the ground. New Orleanians preferred not to bury their dead, on account of the possibility of dislodgement and disfigurement by flooding. People who might have accepted with equanimity the prospect of worms and decay in the earth baulked at the idea of the instability of a watery grave. If one floated about, one would not know where one was or where one might end up. A mobile coffin might make death seem insecure. Consequently, the people of New Orleans generally opted for cremation and immurement in tombs above the ground. St. Louis No. 1 looked like a miniature town, a necropolis of midgets. Inside the high wall, the grid of narrow streets was lined with the small dwellings of the dead. Some of them were not much bigger than dolls' houses. There were a few relatively large structures, the mausoleums of burial societies, whose members' remains, after years of payments of weekly dues, were sheltered close together in row upon row of identical cubicles, like the residents of apartment houses. The ashes of Marie Laveau (if they really were her ashes) reposed in a stately home, by mortuary standards, a mansion of a tomb, a château. It befitted her status and stature when she was alive. The building was about twice the height of Al.

Everything was yellow with moonlight or black with shadow. The white-washed stone façade of the tomb was moonlit; the side was black. The figure of a woman, bent over the flowers she was arranging in a stone urn, was back-lighted, so that her front was inscrutably obscure. When she heard Al's heavy footsteps unevenly crunching the gravel, she looked up. As he approached closer, she could see his face but he could not see hers. She stood upright.

"Is that you?" he asked.

"Al," she said. She did not sound alarmed or even surprised.

Somehow – afterward, he could never remember how it happened – he was kissing her. She did not seem to have a face. She had no identity. She was only thick, soft, warm, moist lips. She was an open mouth, a wet, slippery darkness that swallowed him. He sunk deeper and deeper into a warm, dark, spicy scent of garlic, wine, carnations and musk.

TWENTY-FIVE

The sweet scent of musk permeated the pillow. His eyelids gradually opened: black, dark red, light red, orange and – he winced – the dazzling white of day. A shaft of sunshine leaned in between the jalousies and stabbed his eyes.

He looked around, through the metal bars of a cage between him and the window. But he was not inside the cage. A gaudy macaw with a large curved gray beak stood motionless on a tiny trapeze, balefully looking back at him. The bird's red, green, blue and yellow plumage was so discordant that it hurt. He looked away.

Al (he knew who he was) lay alone in a wide four-poster bed. It had a scarlet satin canopy. The curtains were parted and elegantly draped and tied against the posts with scarlet ribbons. The scarlet satin quilt, the pink mohair blankets and the pink silk sheets appeared to have been disturbed by the explosion of a bomb of medium size. One pillow, dented, apparently by a head, was in the orthodox position, beside his own. There was one pillow at the foot of the bed, and another on the floor.

Al had a headache. Until then, he had not realized that a headache could be a tragic experience that actually altered the nature of the universe. Some great gyroscope, without whose orderly function the solar system was unable to maintain its balance, had evidently tumbled. The harmonious music of the spheres had become a harshly strident cacophony. He wished he were somebody else, in a different place at another time.

He rolled slowly from his side to his back to his other side, groaning. His arms and legs and back felt as sore as if he had been engaged in an all-night game of exceptionally vicious championship professional football, on the losing side. He cautiously moved back to the supine attitude of total surrender.

What had happened? Of course, he knew. The evidence unfortunately was all circumstantial but there could be only one verdict. There was one large body of testimony he would have liked to examine but it seemed to be wholly inaccessible. One of the two key witnesses, himself, claimed to know nothing. Apparently, he had just undergone one of the most momentous experiences of his life, and he had missed it. They said you never forgot the first time you made love. He had forgotten something he had never known. He felt no guilt, only a profound post-coital gloom.

The other witness had been more attentive.

Madame Robichaux came into the room wearing her dressing gown of white feathers and silk and a reminiscent smile.

"Coffee, Al!" she announced, placing a cup on the table at his side of the bed. "But first give me a little kiss." She sat heavily on the bed and leaned over him, with her breasts softly pressing his chest, and took his head firmly between her hands and voraciously kissed his lips. Her open mouth tasted of mint.

"My God!" she exclaimed, sitting up. "Whew, Al! Ain't you something?"

He struggled up onto one elbow, weakly smiling, like a brave convalescent the day after a major operation.

"I knew it would happen," she said. "It was only a question of when. I don't know why – I thought it'd be nice if you made the move. But I cheated a little. I asked Marie Laveau to help."

"She did."

"Was that the truth you told me last night?" she asked in a casual, chatty way. "It wasn't really your first time, was it? Your first *times*."

He replied obliquely.

"I'm not a child, you know. Mozart was only sixteen when he composed his *divertimenti* for strings." He paused to let the significance of the statement sink in. "In 1772," he added.

"I know you're not a child," she assured him.

"Well, then," he said, making an enigmatic grimace, suggesting that he had proved a point of some kind and that there was more to him than met the eye. He reached for the coffee. It was black and strong, and aromatic and laced with cognac. A few minutes earlier he had thought he would never again touch a drop of alcohol. But its warmth in his blood gave him a sensation of new vigor.

He held her and kissed her as fiercely as she had kissed him. She compliantly submitted but disengaged herself, at last, like a wrestler desperately breaking for a rest, panting hard.

"More?" she protested admiringly. "Wait a minute, Al, honey. Let me get the door."

She quickly went and locked it. On the way back to the bed, she undid the belt of her dressing gown and shrugged herself out of it and it fell to the floor.

This was the first time he ever saw a woman's body – consciously. He stared intently at her big dark nipples to fix them in his memory for all time. Her navel. The triangle of black fur. Her most exciting feature was her face, the look in her eyes.

He threw aside the entangled blankets and sheet, displaying his renewed readiness. Her expression as she came close to him was one of sweetly lustful devotion.

Murmurously she told him what she was going to do to him. And then she did exactly that; slowly, excruciatingly slowly.

Al placidly submitted himself to pleasure with a low moan of delight. The universe moved properly again in the infinitely intricate complexity of all its interlocking orbits. The spheres slowly circled against each other, smoothly, suavely.

The tense, pulsating silence was suddenly shattered by the raucous shrieks of the macaw.

"I'm coming!" it screamed. "I'm coming!"

The hysterical outcry was followed by howls of laughter, in which all three of them joined.

Fleur restored silence by getting off the bed and draping a dark-green cloth over the cage. Then she got back onto the bed and draped the sheet and blankets over Al and herself.

She grunted contentedly and soon slept. Al stayed awake for a long time, with one arm around her, looking up at the canopy and thinking quite pleasant thoughts.

He was adaptable.

TWENTY-SIX

A. Chesley Poindexter III got home late in the afternoon.
"Mrs. Poindexter said she doesn't want to be disturbed,"
the butler told him in the hushed, solemn tones in which a black
servant was expected to report the ailments of a wealthy white
hypochondriac. "She said she doesn't feel well."

Chesley nodded irritably and went upstairs. He opened the door
with exaggerated care, even though if by any chance she should
be asleep he intended to awake her. The room was dim and it
was obvious that the windows were closed. The air was stale and
heavy with a sweet scent of flowers. He felt that he was paying
his formal respects to an important corpse.

"Elizabeth?" he said in a whisper that was meant to express
respect for suffering. "Is it very bad?"

"Don't worry about me," the invalid said in a subdued voice
in which reproach was subtly disguised as pain. "I'll be all right,
after a while."

She had one of her migraine headaches, which so far had
proved not to be susceptible to medical diagnosis and treatment.

"I'm sorry, my dear," he said. "Is there anything you want?
Anything I can do?"

He expected no answer that would require any action by him.
The questions were part of an established routine. They both
knew it well.

"Nothing, thank you, Chesley. Dr. Symington came by. I have
taken my medicine. He said I should rest quietly and try not to
let anything upset me. He'll come to see me again tomorrow. Is
there any news of Alan?"

Chesley ground his molars together and silently counted up to
ten.

"No, Elizabeth. You know, there's no need to ask me that every
day. As soon as I hear anything I'll let you know right away.
The authorities are doing everything possible. Nothing can have
happened to him. If something had, you may be sure there would
have been an official report."

"I still think that private detectives . . ." Her voice faded hopelessly.

"There's no necessity for private detectives."

"He could be here, for all we know. Why won't you go to see Mr. Mercier? I'm sure Alan must have been in touch with Louise. Trying to keep them apart is what caused all the trouble. They're in *love*, Chesley. Don't you understand? Why must you be so stubborn? If you won't see Mr. Mercier, can't you write him a letter?"

"I've told you time and time again. The Mercier family is unsuitable. I don't wish to confide in them. You don't want a scandal, do you? Anyway, the school said Alan said he was going up to New York. The police are doing all they can."

"It has been a long time, Chesley. I'm afraid Alan needs our help. He's so proud."

"Don't worry. When he needs help he'll ask for it. And I'll give it – you know that. I've always given him too much, and so have you. We spoiled him."

"Does that matter now? He may be *hungry*. Don't you think it's natural that I should be concerned? I'm his mother. He's my only son."

"I'm well aware of that. You may recall that he's mine, too."

"Oh, Chesley," she said sorrowfully. "Why must you always resort to sarcasm? Dr. Symington said – "

"Yes, my dear. Yes, I know. I'm sorry. Do you want me to get you some ice-water or anything?"

"He said it's bad for me to be emotionally disturbed."

Chesley gritted his teeth and took a deep breath.

"Yes. I know I upset you. You have a nice rest now."

"I can imagine what this must be like for you, Chesley. The anxiety, the strain. If you don't want to eat dinner in the dining room, why don't you have it served in the library?"

He did not wish to eat dinner alone, and he knew that she knew that he didn't. He wondered what made her think that eating alone in the library was preferable to eating alone in the dining room. Was she genuinely that obtuse? She had ruined Christmas and New Year's Eve in Bermuda. She had ruined Mardi Gras. He would be damned if she was going to ruin his whole life. He made a serious effort to keep calm and to seem solicitous.

"Thank you, dear," he said. "But I think I'll get something at the club. You should try to sleep. Take one of your pills. I hope you'll feel better tomorrow. I won't disturb you tonight when I come in."

He tip-toed to her bed, acting the part of the considerate husband, and touched her cool forehead with his compressed, dry lips, as though kissing her. She closed her eyes, bestowing upon his retreating back her dying-martyr smile. He silently closed her bedroom door behind him.

It was good to breathe some oxygen. In the hall, he took the gold watch from his waistcoat pocket and glanced at it, not that the time made any difference. The sooner the better. He walked rapidly down the stairs, two at a time, collected his hat, coat, gloves and cane from the stand in the vestibule, and let himself out of the house.

The evening air of early Spring was soft and balmy. It made him feel alive. He enjoyed walking for a couple of blocks, but he was impatient. At the corner of Royal and Toulouse, he raised his cane to hail a Surrey.

"Good evening, sir," the driver said. "Nice evening."

"Yes," Chesley said, settling back comfortably against the leather upholstery. "Very nice. The New Alhambra, please."

TWENTY-SEVEN

A little later in the evening, Al was sitting at the piano in the parlor, playing for the women of the house and their clients. He was playing a wide variety of numbers, including the usual fatuous requests; but he was playing everything with a more marked jazz inflection than before and in a more individualistic style. He had stripped it of many of its extraneous furbelows. It was simpler, firmer, chunkier and more substantial. Although some of the listeners missed the embellishments, there were no overt complaints. His obviously close relationship with Madame Robichaux raised him above criticism.

During the past three months or so, Al had heard a lot of jazz. He sat in many times with Moses and Louis and the others at Matranga's. Al listened and played in some of the barrelhouses in Gretna and Algiers, across the river. One of them, Jay Schwartz's Horseshoe, off Lafayette Street, was so tough that the bandstand was enclosed by a screen of chicken wire, to protect the musicians against thrown bottles. Jack Lamont asked Al to help out at a dance over in Metairie one evening, when the band's regular pianist was missing, presumed drunk. Johnny Dodds, in a spontaneous afternoon session at Pete Lala's Cabaret, turned and pointed his clarinet at Al, and, for a whole chorus of "Louisiana Lament", seemed to play a duet with him, within the looser collaboration of the ensemble, and, at the end, nodded and told him he was "all right" – a rare tribute from a performer of Johnny Dodds' virtuosity.

In New York, on February 26, the Original Dixieland Jass Band, five white New Orleans musicians led by Nick LaRocca on cornet, had made the first jazz record. The historic record, "The Dixieland Jass Band One-Step" and "Livery Stable Blues", was released on March 7, and Moses bought a copy of it the following week. He invited Al over to hear it. In Moses' small room in a house on St. Philip Street, they sat on the unmade bed and listened to the record, both sides, over and over again, on a tinny phonograph that they took turns to wind up.

"That ain't *bad* horn," Moses commented grudgingly. "But it's small and thin compared with Papa Joe's. I'm going to play better than Nick LaRocca."

"What do you think of the piano?" Al asked anxiously.

"Pianola. That's what *Mister* Henry Ragas sounds like to me."

"He's fast," Al had to concede.

"They probably have to wind him up, like this Victrola. You could cut him any day."

"Do you really think so?"

"I never say nothing I don't mean."

"Let's play 'Livery Stable Blues' once more. The piano *wasn't* all that marvellous. I'll wind."

"That's barnyard music," Moses said. "Listen to that trombone, hee-hawing like a donkey. Reminds me of the minstrels at that picnic. Do you remember the time we went to the picnic? That's not music. He's a comedian, not a musician. Ain't it a shame that the first jazz record ain't the real thing? Listen to that cornet!"

"You play much better than that."

"I heard Freddie Keppard could have been first. A Creole. A company offered him the chance. He turned it down, said he wasn't going to put none of his music on no record so anyone who wanted could steal his ideas. Freddie Keppard plays real pretty cornet. And it's jazz cornet."

"But the Original Dixieland Jass Band got in there and did it, Mo. They're the first. Nobody can take that away. Think how they must feel. People will buy thousands of copies of their records – maybe millions. People will listen to them all over America. Everyone will start playing jazz. I'd give anything to have done what the Original Dixieland Jass Band has done. Think of the money they must be making!"

"What's stopping you?" Moses demanded in a sudden blaze of zeal. "Alan! – Al, I mean. Why don't you and me get together and start a band of our own? We could show them."

"It *would* be fun."

"Fun? It would be a lot more than that. Let's do it. We could."

"Maybe one day. It would take capital. Right now, I have a job to do. I'd better be getting along."

The moment had passed.

Now Al was sitting in the parlor, playing "Livery Stable Blues".

Madame Robichaux, wearing a green satin sheath the color of

crème de menthe, sashayed sinuously across the room, causing one man to spill his drink. She smiled at Al and he thought : she is coming to me. She enlivened his playing.

"How do you like it?" he said. " 'Livery Stable Blues'. It's the latest thing from New York, but it's really from New Orleans."

"Hot stuff."

She moved close to his side and spoke so that only he could hear her.

"You won't be able to have supper with me tonight, Al. Sorry about that."

"That's O.K., Fleur. I can get a quick bite around the corner. I like the dress."

"Yeah."

"Do you feel all right?" he asked. "There's nothing wrong, is there?"

"No, nothing wrong. Just business."

Al's face stiffened.

"Oh," he said. "You mean upstairs business?"

The question irritated her.

"That's right. Upstairs business. That's the line of business I'm in."

"I'm sorry, Fleur. Don't get mad."

"I ain't mad at you. It's you I'd like to be with. I'll try to get rid of him. I'll get rid of him as soon as I can."

"Why don't you get rid of him right now? Couldn't one of the girls . . . ?"

"He always wants to talk. He drinks like a fool and has to tell me all his troubles. He's one of *those* kind. It's my ear he has to bend – won't settle for no substitute. I'll give him some strong drinks, maybe hurry things. Can't make them too strong, though. Make them too strong and it'll be an all-night trick."

"You don't love him, do you?"

Fleur laughed and playfully tousled Al's hair.

"Love him? Oh, Lawd have *mercy*! If you could see him, specially after a while. He likes to wear my black suspender belt. Love him? No, Al. You don't have nothing to feel jealous about. He's a *pig*. And he's a cry-baby. When he gets real good and drunk he talks baby talk and wants to be treated like a baby."

"You don't have to put up with that stuff!" Al said. He stopped playing.

"Play that thing," Fleur said. He played.

"I can get rid of him for you. I'll throw him out."

"Thanks, honey. That ain't the problem. If there was any throwing out to be done, Charlie could do it. *I* could do it. I have a cute little twenty-two in my purse, with those dum-dum bullets that go in small and come out big. Blow the back of a man's head off. It's called self-defence. But that wouldn't solve nothing."

"Have I seen him?"

"No, honey. He don't come through this way. He's a *privilege* man. He has his own key to the back."

"I still say I ought to throw him out."

"But I don't want you to. He's important, honey. He spends a heap of money. And he's an old friend of Mr. Brewster's. Used to be a close friend. I think they maybe kind of broke up somehow; I'm not sure. I'm playing it safe; Mr. Brewster's *strange*."

"Does Mr. Brewster spend a lot here?"

"Hey, you really are jealous, ain't you, Al? I like that. No. Mr. Brewster don't spend nothing here. He don't go for our kind of amusement. He has other interests in the love department. He just *owns* the joint."

"Brewster! So that's why you hired me!"

"That was one reason."

"Can't you make some kind of excuse tonight?" Al said unhappily.

"No, honey. Don't worry. It's nothing personal with me. I have to go now. He must be wondering why I've been so long. You go and have a nice supper, hear? Not just a sandwich. Take your time. I'll pay."

"But Fleur – "

The inner door of the parlor burst open.

"What the hell's going on?" A. Chesley Poindexter III demanded. "Fleur! You said you'd be right back!"

Al stared in disbelief. His father had always been in command, in a position of unassailable superiority – in command of the situation, in command of his family, in command of his employees, and, above all, in command of himself. Now he seemed to have lost all control. Frustration, impatience, suspicion and anger had turned him into a grotesque caricature of himself, a snarling, rabid Mr. Hyde. His sparse, sandy-colored hair was in wild disorder, his face was bloated, inflamed and sweaty with bourbon and rage.

His jacket was open, his necktie was awry, his collar was open : he gave an overall impression of difficulties with buttons.

Fleur looked alarmed, for an instant; Madame Robichaux resolutely crossed the room to deal with the crisis. The onlookers were fascinated, mildly amused and absolutely quiet.

"Damn it, Fleur," Chesley said. "I've been waiting."

"Go on back up, honey," she said, trying to restrain him with a gentle hand against his chest. "I'll be right with you."

Al was on his feet, behind the piano. His heart was thumping (like a double bass) and he was breathing stertorously, but he was not afraid. He was ashamed, but not of himself. He was disgusted and angry. He *was* jealous. The adrenalin was gushing. He instinctively clenched his fists.

"Got someone else down here, have you?" Chesley said with a wolfish grin. It was a mad, distorted exaggeration of the sarcastic smile that Al remembered from many a painful dinner-table interrogation. "One man not enough?" Chesley violently cast aside her hand and pushed past and stood swaying slightly in the center of the room, glaring around with eyes like marbles. "We'll see about that!"

Moving like a blind cripple, he staggered toward the piano. Al wondered whether his father was capable of recognizing him.

They looked into each other's eyes with terrible intimacy. Al felt sick, hollow, literally gutless.

"For Christ's sake, go away!" Al said. "Why don't you go home?"

Al's father glowered silently for a moment and then guffawed. He roared with laughter. He wept. His mirth was threatening. The noise abruptly stopped. He came closer. His tan reddened and his face appeared to swell. He looked close to a heart attack or a murder. He came closer still and loomed bigger. He spoke in a hoarse, vicious whisper, which was more intense and more menacing than a shout. He hissed so vehemently that he spattered saliva.

"Mother's little genius! So this is where your music got you! Do you know what you've done to your mother? You . . . lousy . . . little . . . *shit*!"

Al's father seemed to move in slow motion, like a monstrous figure in a nightmare, slowly winding up a roundhouse right and slowly swinging a big fist at the end of a long arm in a wide arc in the general direction of Al's head. Al moved clear long before the fist's arrival. His father lurched off balance and plunged forward. With an angry whimper, Al punched his father's blubbery cheek. His father fell to his hands and knees, clumsily attempted to climb to his feet, and collapsed heavily on his face.

The moment of triumph was immediately followed by an overwhelming feeling of remorse. Al was bending over, attempting to arouse the unconscious body, when Fleur seized his arm.

"Leave him alone, you idiot!" she said.

Fleur was wearing her executive-madame expression.

"But he's my – "

"He's a powerful man," she said angrily. "He has all kinds of influence at City Hall."

"Yes, I know. He's my father!"

She was not impressed. Business was business.

"Then why the hell couldn't you play along with him?" she demanded. "Couldn't you see he's been drinking?"

"Yes, I could."

"You'd better get out of here – fast. Or you'll be in bad trouble. He could come to at any minute."

"I can't leave him lying on the floor."

"Get out. I mean it. You can send Charlie in. We'll get things straightened out."

Al hesitated.

"If you say so," he said. "I'll see you tomorrow then."

"Go on."

He lingered to ask one question.

"You don't have to call him 'honey', do you?"

Fleur frowned, then smiled.

"Don't be silly," she said. "That don't mean nothing. That's what I call everybody."

TWENTY-EIGHT

A l slept fitfully, disturbed by bad dreams of being pursued, caught, punished and jeered at. He finally awoke with a headache and smarting eyes, feeling frightened and defiled. He was greatly relieved to find himself surrounded by the hideous dark mahogany furniture of the rooming house and not, as he had subconsciously feared, by the immemorial furniture of the bedroom of his childhood, at home. Now, his father would never dare to try to force Al to go back. If Mr. Brewster had got him the job to humiliate his father to settle some old score, what would the retaliation be?

While Al was dressing in clothes fresh from the laundry and the cleaner's, he wondered what his father had meant when he had asked Al whether he knew what he had done to his mother. Was that accusative question only drunken, spiteful raving? Was it bluff? Or was his mother dead or dying, grief-stricken by his defection and disappearance? Surely not. And surely she would not expect him to kowtow to the bullies of Bull Run and to his bullying father. She must understand that Al had grown up and that he had to assert his manhood.

He could not go to her now; but one day, when he was a success, when he was a man of substance and reputation, he would go home, if only for a day. Al would be nationally famous. He would be celebrated as Al Dexter, the rich, popular bandleader, admired and imitated by other musicians, worshipped by the fans and adored by beautiful women; Al Dexter, the prolific, best-selling recording star; Al Dexter, immortal composer. His name would be up in lights on the marquees of the most illustrious theaters from coast to coast. His face would smile from the front pages of newspapers and from the covers of magazines and millions of copies of sheet music. But he would never boast nor gloat. He would be magnanimous. He would be praised and loved for his humanely democratic ways. There would be a new element of respect in his mother's adulation. He would respond to her with modesty and warmth. His father, having seen the error of his ways, would be contrite and, in a subdued and diffident manner, eager to make amends. Al's dealings with him would be coolly punctilious at first, and then – well, then they would see.

Standing before the oval mirror in his bedroom, Al was not displeased by what he saw. He was no longer the raw, gawky, boy-next-door type. Although still in his teens, he no longer looked like the traditional teenager. His hair had grown back and a Basin Street barber, recommended by Fleur, had skillfully repaired the razor's depredation. The color of Al's hair no longer suggested carrots. It had darkened naturally to the color of rust, and he darkened it further by dousing it with mauve brilliantine from a large bottle that Fleur had given him. The lotion had a luxuriously oily, expensive scent of violets, and under its unctuous discipline neither upstart cowlick nor languorous forelock could defy the comb. His freckles had faded. He carefully adjusted the dimple below the knot of his new silk tie, blue with white polka dots, another present from Fleur, who had assured him that it was "a gentleman's tie."

Like most other whores, Fleur set great store by emblems of gentility. But her petty snobbishness was entirely ingenuous and easily disregarded; even she did not take it too seriously. She put it on as capriciously as a flower in her hair. And if she did not have the legendary whore's heart of gold, Fleur's heart was of an alloy that contained at least a noticeable, significant percentage of some precious metal, which was more than most people could justly lay claim to.

The thought of Fleur made Al smile fondly. He had once believed that he loved Louise, but he had loved only an abstraction, the idea of being in love. Fleur was real. Hot damn, was she ever! *She* was no narrow-minded, selfish little nit. Fleur was a real woman. She was a natural, spontaneous, straight-forward, outspoken, impulsively emotional, passionately hot-blooded woman. As advertised in *The Blue Book*, she had helped him to know what it was to be a man. She had taught him the elaborate technology of erotic bliss, and she had taught him a lot more. She had taught him the right mental attitude to enable him to experience pleasure by giving it.

In her sensible, direct way, Fleur was generously romantic, and totally unsentimental. When she was with Al in her bed, she attacked sex ardently, with gusto, without any quibbles or reservations. She did not make love; she fucked. She did so with

zealous, uncalculated abandon and boisterous good humor, energetically working herself up into shuddering, grimacing, biting,
scratching, howling seizures of ecstasy. Her orgasms were awesome,
cataclysmic, transcendental.

The madame known as French Emma was quite different. She
had gained renown by challenging men sexually and defeating
them. She promised that any man who could get into her and prolong coition for more than a minute without being compelled to
ejaculate would be rewarded by having the experience free of
charge; no man had ever won. Fleur's approach to Al was always
more benign. Her bountiful physique, her resourcefulness and
skill raised him to hitherto unimaginable heights of sensual enjoyment and kept him there, on and on, beyond awareness of time.
With Fleur, sex was not a conflict; it was an alliance. Her compli-
ments and caresses gave him such great confidence that he felt
himself become bigger and better. Fleur inspired Al to grow.

Having passed his own appreciative inspection in the mirror,
he went out for a late lunch of shrimps and rice, and the world
seemed to be a pleasant place.

After lunch, just to pass the time, he strolled over to Jackson
Square. The grass was green and there was a soft, mild breeze
from the river. He whistled a bit of "The Bucket's Got A Hole
In It", a cheerfully resigned song about a tragic subject. A per-
forated bucket was a sobering disadvantage during an epoch when
rushing the growler, hurrying with your own container, was the
customary method of carrying beer away from a saloon. There
have been sadder songs about less poignant sorrows. The simple
melody and the easy tempo provided a sound basis and an ample
opportunity for improvisation. He fooled around with it absent-
mindedly, until he noticed, rather irritably, that he was exactly
reproducing one of Little Louis' flashy cornet breaks. Louis was
good, all right; Al did not dispute the fact. He only wished that
Moses wouldn't keep saying so, so often and at such length.
Louis was only the same age as they were; he couldn't possibly be
as far ahead musically as Moses said. Whistling another chorus,
Al deliberately repeated the break, considering each note. There
really wasn't very much to it. He stopped whistling.

Al crossed Decatur Street to the sidewalk café on the corner and
ordered a coffee. Someone had left the morning paper on the table.
Al idly glanced through it while he waited. A Washington poli-

tician had made a speech demanding that "our boys" should go over and settle the Kaiser's hash once and for all. To hell with that, Al thought. The politician's boys would have to get along without him. He wasn't interested in the Kaiser's hash. Al was not going to let a remote foreign war spoil his life in New Orleans.

When he rang the bell at the New Alhambra that evening, Charlie greeted him at the door, as usual, but not with his usual grin. He stood in Al's way.

"I hate to tell you," Charlie said, "but Miss Fleur said for me not to let you in. She told me to give you this."

He handed Al an envelope.

"What do you mean?" Al said. "Why would she say a thing like that? Is this some kind of gag?"

"Ain't no gag, Al. She said she has to let you go."

"I don't believe it. Let me in, Charlie. I want to talk with her."

Al put a hand on Charlie's arm, as if to ease him aside. Charlie grabbed Al's arm in a grip of iron.

"Don't mess with me, Al," the doorman said, with a pained and pleading look. "That's orders. Read the letter, why don't you? Don't want no trouble. I know Miss Fleur feels bad about it, too. But that's the way things are."

Al opened the envelope. The letter was pencilled in a childish scrawl on a sheet of ruled notepaper. Fleur's concern with the emblems of gentility did not extend to correspondence. She wasn't much of a letter-writer. She had written to say that Al must never go around there no more for any reason and it wasn't no use writing or calling on the phone because she could not see him no matter what and she was sorry and she had fixed up for him to play piano over at Dolores Bolivar's Golden Frolics on Liberty near Conti and she knew he would always make out and she wished him luck and she would light a candle and ask Marie Laveau to look out for him and she signed the letter with love and several X's and her full name, Madame Fleur Robichaux. She enclosed some money – fifty dollars.

Al's eyes felt hot. His vision blurred. He had to blink quickly.

"So you see?" Charlie said uncomfortably.

"Yes, I see."

He saw A. Chesley Poindexter III had taken his revenge.

"No hard feelings, Al," Charlie said, sticking out a big gloved hand. Al weakly smiled and shook it. He turned and slowly walked away.

"Sure like the way you play that piano!" Charlie called after him.

TWENTY-NINE

The Golden Frolics was not a high-class establishment. It was quite different from the New Alhambra. While Fleur Robichaux prided herself on offering top-quality divertissements at top prices to a restricted clientele, her friend Dolores Bolivar believed in a large and rapid turnover at cut rates. Her house was said to provide the fastest service in Storyville. At the lower end of the scale, there were five-minute tricks with girls who kept their shoes on. Dolores's slogan was "Come one, come all". No customers and no holds were barred.

A portly muscular black woman, no longer young, with a handsome but scarred face like an African mask that had been carved in ebony with verve and a blunt axe, she claimed direct descent from Simon Bolivar, the great South American liberator. Nobody who gave the claim any serious thought believed it, because there was such a strong doubt about the identity of a more immediate ancestor, her father. She liked to think he was a traveller by the name of Joe Bolivar, reputed to have taken it on the lam from Haiti, who had paused in passing through New Orleans just long enough to beget her.

Dolories herself was certainly a liberarian; and, up to the time of her recent voluntary retirement from active professional service upstairs, she had been a libertine of outstanding profligacy. Her *laisser-faire* policy in running her business afforded hospitality to rakeshells, stumblebums and seafaring men of all nationalities, some of whom otherwise might have been at a loss to find companionship even in this liberal city. Her place was wide open and everyone who entered it was deemed innocent until actually detected pulling a knife or purposely breaking a bottle as if preparing to use it as a weapon or in any other way obviously contemplating making a disturbance of the peace. Dolores was tolerance itself up to a point. Beyond that point she was a veritable pillar of wrath. Then she caused things to happen with determination and despatch. She dealt with malefactors severely. After her staff was through with them, there was rarely any necessity for the police to take any further action. She had long since come to a friendly understanding with the numerous police officers on her payrool.

The entrance to The Golden Frolics was by way of a commodious saloon on Liberty Street. Early in the evening the bar was already packed. Many of its patrons never bothered to try to penetrate any farther.

Al asked one of the bartenders where he could find Madame Bolivar. He jerked his thumb in the direction of the big black woman sitting on a stool beside the cash register behind the bar. She was puffing a long black stogie. The smoke made her keep her eyes half shut.

He introduced himself. She didn't attempt to speak to him in the loud babble of the bar. She pointed to a door at the end of the bar, slid heavily off the stool and waddled away to a back room, where he found her. She was cordial enough but the interview was succinct.

"Piano, right?" she said.

"Yes."

"Good. Need a piano man in the circus."

"In the what?"

"In the circus. Didn't Fleur tell you?"

"No, she just sent me over."

"We have a voodoo circus. Twice a night. In the ballroom. It's our specialty. It's an extra, tickets at the door; always a good crowd. Two shows, only an hour each. There's a quartet, if you can call it a quartet with three guys in it. See Art. Art Lefevre. He should be back there now, changing into his costume. He's supposed to be the leader. He'll give you something to wear." She chuckled at some private joke. "Art'll tell you all you need to know."

"What sort of music do they play?"

She looked slightly surprised.

"It's regular music music."

"Oh."

She studied him silently for a while.

"Fleur thinks a lot of you," she said. "Maybe you could do more than play piano."

He waited for her to say more.

"You could earn more if you want to perform in the circus. Do you want to?"

"Doing what?"
She laughed. His naiveté amused her.
"You can decide later," she said.

THIRTY

The ballroom, at the back of the building, was a large, dingy hall of curiously disparate functions. It was a voodoo chapel on Sundays. During the rest of the week it was used for the voodoo circus, a travesty of religious ritual. At the front of the hall there were an altar, a bandstand and a dance-floor; at the back there were rows of shabbily upholstered pews and a bar.

Primitive murals, daubed in splashes and streaks of tropical colors, depicted a hectic imagination's fantasy of Haiti – jungles gaudy with birds and flowers and writhing with snakes and erupting volcanic fire. A human skeleton lolled against each end of the altar. The top of it was decorated with human and animal skulls and, as if to compensate for the prospect of death, with voluptuously vulviform pink conch shells and a central towering erect serpent, made of *papier mâché*, painted black.

Al found the ballroom empty. It smelled sweet and musty. He eyed the small bandstand with some misgivings : an upright piano with peeling dull brown varnish was almost entirely concealed by an extensive battery of drums of various shapes and sizes, including a pair of exceptionally tall bongos. What did *they* mean ?

There were two doors, both closed, at the opposite ends of the altar. The first one he tried gave onto a cobbled alley and stables. He opened the other door and got a shock that made him catch his breath. He was face to face with a savage.

He was a tall, powerfully built brown man wearing only a leopard skin fastened over one shoulder and a headdress of ostrich feathers. But the most alarming feature of his appearance was his face. It was covered with zig-zag broad stripes of black, red and yellow paint that gave him an expression of fierce belligerence.

His voice was not at all war-like.

"Hello there, kid. What's on your mind ?"

"Excuse me. I'm looking for Mr. Lefevre."

"You got him. In person. Are you the one that's going to play piano ?"

"Yes."

"Starting now, I hope?"

"Madame Bolivar said in the circus. Is that what you're dressed for?"

Art Lefevre looked down at his leopard skin.

"No, I always go around like this. These are my street clothes. In a minute I'm going to change into my work clothes."

Al smiled awkwardly.

"She did say there was a special costume, but I didn't expect anything like this."

"This is show business. You got to give the people what they want. You'll get used to it. Can you read music?"

"Sure. And write it."

"Reading's all you need. There's one piece you have to learn. It's a catchy tune."

"Only one?"

"Only one. It's entitled 'The Voodoo Love Song'. It's my own composition. We play it over and over, all through the show. Only the tempo changes. We gradually hot it up. All you have to do is follow me. Don't worry about it."

"What do you play?"

"What do *I* play? I'm Art Lefevre."

"Yes."

"Maybe you're new in town. I'm on drums. All you have to do is back me up. The piano, bass and banjo are strictly background."

Al's heart was sinking.

"You'll soon catch on," Art said. "Do exactly what I say and I know you can handle it."

He went over to a closet and produced a small, plain brown piece, not much more than a swatch, of imitation fur. It was thin and limp and bald in patches and tattered around the edges. Al took it and examined it doubtfully.

"How am I supposed to put this on?"

"Like a diaper. Haven't you ever changed a baby's diaper? You know, you fold it under the crotch and pin it at the sides. There should be some safety pins over there somewhere, on the table."

"Is that all I wear?"

"That's it."

"No leopard skin or anything?"

"No leopard skin. I'm the leader. You won't be cold. It gets plenty warm out there when it fills up."

Art went to the dressing table and opened a drawer.

"I almost forgot your headdress."

He pulled out a single drooping gray ostrich feather attached to an off-white elastic headband.

"Stick this on your head," he said.

"Am I supposed to paint my face like yours?"

"No. Like I said, I'm the leader. You get only two stripes, straight ones, one black and one yellow. No red. The whole quartet is built around the drums. It's more artistic this way."

Art showed Al how to apply the greasepaint.

"You get it off after with cold cream and soap and water. It isn't very hard to get off. And if a little stays on it impresses the people you meet. They know you're in show business."

Al nervously undressed. When he put on his costume he still felt naked. It was only slightly larger than a jock-strap but it did not feel as secure.

"Are you sure I can go on like this?" he asked.

"Why not? Who cares? You'll be sitting in the back there, at the piano. Nobody's going to look at you. Frankly, between you and me, we don't even really need a piano player for this act. I told Dolores, but she thinks it'd be a waste to have a piano with nobody playing it."

Al felt self-conscious as he smeared the black and yellow greasepaint across his cheeks and nose. But when the other two members of the quartet, Bo Harris, the bass player, and Herbie Fox, banjo, slouched into the dressing room a few minutes before show time they did not give him a second glance.

"Are you guys drunk?" Art asked them.

"Hell, no!" Herbie said. "Just had a beer. Didn't we, Bo?"

"That's right," Bo said. "Just a couple of beers is all."

"Dolores says there isn't going to be another warning. If you ever play around like a couple of drunk cowboys like you did the other night that'll be it."

"We didn't do the donkey any harm," Herbie said.

"They way I heard it," Art said, "the donkey didn't agree. You could have ruined it, and that's an expensive donkey. That donkey has been trained."

"We won't lay a finger on it," Bo promised. "So help me." He crossed his heart and laughed. Art glanced at him briefly and ineffectually and said no more.

"The thing is, Al," he said solemnly, "you have to make your mind up : either you're a musician or you're a *performer*. If you're a musician you stay on the stand and don't go interfering on the floor. In a show like this there's no place for ad libbing. Things could get out of hand."

An inner door opened and a face appeared.

"Five minutes!" the man said.

"Let's go, Al," Art said. "I'll show you the music. I like to get limbered up. You two – get the lead out! Let's all get out there and do it right."

Five minutes were plenty of time for Al to master the score.

Most of the pews were occupied. The audience consisted entirely of men. They looked like the sort of men whose hobby might have been attending lynchings, or the sort of men that the police might have called upon to make up an identification line-up in the case of a particularly nasty assault behind a warehouse on the waterfront. They were men who appeared unlikely to have any fixed abode or any admissible gainful occupation. Many of them wore the clothing, such as threadbare pea jackets, scuffed leather windbreakers and faded denims, of former merchant seamen who had been on the beach longer than had been good for them. There were some who frequented downtown sidewalks as panhandlers or muggers, according to the conditions of the day or night and the urgency of their requirements. There were others who specialized in peddling drugs of shady provenance and questionable purity. There were a few who depended to an unhealthy extent upon selling pints of their blood, diluted in the veins with California port and muscatel, to commercial blood collection agencies. There were thick ears and Neanderthal brows and bent, flattened noses. There were bruises and the odd red eye. When mouths opened wide in uproarious discourse and laughter, as they often did, there were unwished-for glimpses of incomplete sets of imperfect teeth.

This was his public, Al thought disconsolately as he looked around from the piano stool, the people for whom he was obliged soon to play Art Lefevre's composition, "The Voodoo Love Song".

Al dilated his nostrils. The sweet mustiness he had sniffed on first entering the hall had suddenly become stronger. He saw why. Two buxom young black women, wearing red turbans, abbreviated red sarongs as transparent as gossamer, and garlands of artificial bougainvillea, like Hawaiian leis, that hung from their necks and almost concealed their breasts, were kneeling at the altar, lighting joss sticks, sending up columns of blue smoke that spread and drifted slowly in the stagnant, warm air. The incense was perfumed with jasmine. It may not be generally realized that the old number usually known as "Jazz Me Blues", an erotic play on words, was originally entitled "Jasmine Blues".

The master of ceremonies took his place in front of the bandstand. A middle-aged black man of imposing height and girth, he was dressed in the battered black top hat and tails of the dreaded Baron Samedi, haunter of graveyards and implacable taskmaster of the walking dead. But this was Baron Samedi on one of his more playful nights.

"Folks!" he proclaimed in a loud, gravelly voice that called the audience to order. "Here's what you-all been waiting for. Yeah! Madame Bolivar and The Gold Frolics proudly present the most glamorous [laughter], most edu-*cational* [louder laughter] cabaret in The District – Madame Bolivar's one and only . . . Voo-doo circus! O.K., folks. Let's hear it now! Bring them on with a nice, big hand!"

There was an outbreak of clapping, cheering, whooping and whistling and the thunderous stamping of many boots.

Art Lefevre swung a mallet and bashed a large gong, whose shivering, brazen boom, with its suggestion of mysterious oriental foul play and feeding time, was the signal for the quartet to begin the music and for the performers to begin to assemble on the dance-floor.

Art dominated the music from the start, playing only the bongos. He stood near the front of the stand and played them with his hands, stroking them, lightly pitter-pattering with his fingertips, slapping, beating and chopping the taut drumheads and the drums' shiny, lacquered wooden sides with the palms and the heels of his hands and his hands' hard edges. Art's bongos were not African talking drums but the gist of what he was trying to suggest was clear enough. He had been correct when he told Al there really was no need for a pianist. But Al stoically did his duty, repeating the calls and responses of the simple, ancient theme that Art had taken and transcribed as his own. Very soon Al was free to think of other things, such as the dance of the voodoo queen.

As the star of the show, and in keeping with the name of the establishment, she wore a golden turban and a golden sarong, and she set the tone of the whole program. She made her entrance wearing a snake coiled around her waist and draped around her shoulders.

The snake was a boa (*Constrictor constrictor*), a handsome, sleek, young creature. Light brown with dark brown markings, it was thicker than her arm and nearly seven feet long. It seemed drowsy at first. But when it did move, with a smooth ripple, its head sliding down the soft furrow of her spine, sliding around her side and sliding up between her big, pale-brown breasts, it was obvious that the snake was more than an ornament: it was a symbol of maleness; it was a giant phallus, and it was alive. It was her lover. She grasped its firm circumference in both hands and lifted its blunt head close to her open lips and tenderly, passionately adored it.

The audience was silent.

Art softly pounded the bongos at the speed of an excited human pulse.

She held the snake up horizontal with her hands wide apart and high above her head, displaying the snake, triumphantly brandishing it.

She took away one hand and the snake hung vertically, swinging from side to side. With the free hand, she released a catch at the back of her sarong and it fell from her body. She was naked. Al gasped.

She danced with her head thrown back, with her eyes closed and her mouth partly open. She danced with her shoulders and her breasts and her belly and her pelvis. She whirled the snake around with both hands, turning her back to the audience, and she danced with the big, soft muscles of her round hips and buttocks. She turned back again.

Art gradually increased the tempo and the loudness of the drumbeats, and the queen danced faster and faster, shaking her head, shaking her breasts, shaking all over, in a realistic facsimile of frenzy. She was dancing with the snake. She seemed to be dancing *for* the snake.

Al hammered the keys of the piano in time with the drums, bass and banjo. He was sweating profusely. So was she. Her body was wet. He imagined its heat, its slipperiness.

Baron Samedi led the other performers into the hall, five young mulatto women in red turbans and red sarongs and five young mulatto men in red loincloths. They were trudging with the slow, heavy, automatic tread of zombies. The wicked baron abandoned them. They lined up lethargically in pairs in a semicircle in front of the voodoo queen.

She danced frenetically back and forth along the line, shaking herself and the snake in their apparently oblivious faces. This was the part of the performance that demonstrated the dancers' acting talent.

The queen's treatment of the snake became more explicit. With its tail securely coiled around her waist, she guided its head between her thighs. Holding the snake with both hands, she pulled it closer, thrusting herself forward and squealing as though experiencing paroxysms of delight.

She aroused the zombies. Without any further theatrical preliminaries, they stripped off their clothes and set to with fervour and gymnastic agility, joining their bodies together in a variety of permutations that proved that they were phenomenally flexible and greedily alive. They changed positions and connections, with different partners and groups, with the bounces and twists and contortions of acrobats.

The music now attained the steady, hard-driving rhythm of advanced copulation. The audience enthusiastically reinforced the beat by clapping their hands in time with it, like the congregation at a down-home holy-roller sing-song.

Baron Samedi, with an evil leer, brought on the clowns – two spider monkeys, about three feet tall, with black hairy wiry long arms and legs. Manifestly in a state of extreme excitement, they cavorted, scurried and leaped about among the twosomes and threesomes, inquisitively examining at close quarters the anatomy and behavior of humans in rut and eagerly offering assistance and otherwise interfering at every opportunity. The audience hilariously applauded every outrage, and the applause seemed to incite the participants to more daring, more bizarre activities. One of the monkeys, the male, jumped astride a momentarily disengaged woman and she opened her legs to him. The other monkey, female, used her long prehensile tail as a lasso, wrapping it around a man's thigh and pulling him closer so that she could conveniently lick him.

The music moved onward and upward in crescendo.

Baron Samedi led by a rope halter the voodoo queen's co-star, a dark-gray donkey about seven hands high.

The female monkey, being fickle and having a limited attention span, immediately left her human playmate for this greater challenge and greater thrill. While four sturdy roustabouts in navy-blue sweaters and blue denims, pulling on an ingenious rig of blocks and tackle, hoisted the donkey into a rampant stance, up on its hind legs with its forelegs extended, the monkey titillated it behind as the queen titillated it below. The effect of their seductive ministrations was like the opening of a telescope, the unreeling of a black rubber hose.

No, Al thought, it isn't possible. She can't.

But it was. She could. She did.

The donkey was not permitted unlimited access to her. It wore a wooden disc, like a disc fitted part-way up a ship's hawser to prevent rats from climbing aboard. However, the donkey got quite far enough, and the queen, presenting herself to him on her hands and knees on a red-velvet-covered pedestal, was evidently pleasing. His movements rapidly accelerated, to the frantic accompaniment of Art Lefevre, on drums; Bo Harris, bass; Herbie Fox, banjo, and Al Dexter, piano.

Suddenly, the donkey's haunches quivered and twitched in spasms and its jaws opened wide and uttered the loud, inane braying of a Dixieland trombone. Nature was imitating art. The donkey was imitating Eddie Edwards, of The Original Dixieland Jass Band.

And Art was imitating nature. He achieved a veritable orgasm of drumming and then climactically beat the gong. The performers, animal and human, followed the master of ceremonies out of the hall; the audience stomped and yelled and laughed and dispersed and headed for the bars : the night's first performance was over.

A member of the audience, with a two-day stubble on his chin and a scrofulous complexion, detained Al on his way down from the stand.

"Do you mind if I ask you a question about the show?" the man asked.

"Go ahead," Al replied resignedly. He did not feel inclined to discuss what he had witnessed with some perverted voodoo fanatic.

"Who's on banjo? He's *good*."

THIRTY-ONE

A l removed his breech-clout and had a shower and awaited his turn at the washbasin.

Herbie Fox, standing ahead of him, was scrubbing the make-up off his face with a washcloth and cursing. Though incompletely successful, he soon gave up, and moved aside for Al.

"I don't know why I even bother to try," Herbie said. 'It'll soon be midnight, time for the second show."

Al told Herbie about the compliment from one of the fans.

"Someone said that? I wonder who that could have been. What did he look like?"

"Nice-looking guy," Al said, not wishing to invalidate the praise.

"You'd think he could've told me, if he had something to say about the way I play," Herbie said sourly, but he could not help looking gratified. "I'll buy you a drink, Al. When you're all through prettying up your hair, that is. Join me at the back bar."

Pleased to be accepted by a senior, Al soon followed him.

"What's got you down?" Herbie asked. "Got the booze blues?"

"The what blues?"

"A hangover. You look kind of low."

"No, I don't drink much." Al remembered how recently he had been able to say he did not drink, period.

"Anyway, have a little shot now. It'll set you up."

"What are you drinking?"

"Rye."

"I'll try one of those."

Herbie smiled and conveyed the request to the bartender.

"People often get depressed after the first time they play a show here. You'll get used to it."

"I did feel kind of stupid out there. Dressed that way, and with that make-up and all."

"And playing in a combination butcher's shop and zoo. I know."

"Some of those women are really good-looking though," Al said politely.

"Yeah. They're all right, if you go for the type that fucks with snakes and monkeys and donkeys. But if you think it's bad now, you should have been here before."

"What happened then?"

"Well, one thing we used to have was a geek. That wasn't very nice."

"A *geek*? What kind of animal is that?"

"A geek is a guy, the dregs of a carnival sideshow. One of those carny freaks that bite off the heads of live chickens and drink their blood. Only this is a sex show, so this geek had to do more."

"I'm glad I missed that."

"It wasn't all bad. The consolation was that I had an arrangement with him. At the end of the night he used to get rid of the chickens, what was left of them. I had first option. He used to sell them cheap."

"He was a vegetarian, I suppose. No wonder!"

"No, he wasn't a vegetarian. It was only these particular chickens he couldn't eat. He said he felt a kind of yen for them. He was very sentimental, in his way."

"It's difficult to think about what you're playing in a place like this, isn't it?" Al said.

"It ain't easy. But it used to be worse, before I got rid of that damned parrot. You played piano at the New Alhambra before you came to us, didn't you?"

"Yes."

"Fleur has the parrot in her bedroom."

Al's face flushed.

"A macaw," he said flatly.

"A parrot, a macaw. What's the difference? Anyway, you know the bird I mean. Congratulations. But what I was going to tell you about that parrot – that macaw. I'm the one who persuaded Dolores to give it to Fleur. Fleur comes here Sundays for the service and she always has Charlie bring over a whole lot of flowers for the hall. I knew Dolores wanted to do something for her and it was hard to think of something Fleur didn't already have. Jesus! Was I glad to see the back of that bird."

"I think I know what you mean," Al said. "It's noisy."

"That's putting it mild. It used to be part of the show. A gimmick. Funny, if you weren't playing in the band. But you know what that bird used to do? It always used to scream in C-Minor, when we were playing in F."

"You really care about music, don't you?" Al said. He had already forgiven Herbie for knowing about Fleur's bedroom. He knew he had to accept the fact that there had been many other men there before him, and that there would be many others after him. "Doesn't it get you down playing that same number, that 'Voodoo Love Song', over and over?"

"Naturally it gets me down. Or it did get me down. I hardly hear it any more. And we play some other things between shows. In fact, we're due on the stand in ten minutes. If you're a performer in the show you only do two hours a night. Who could do more? But musicians are expected to put out *all* night. It's a hard grind, but it helps save us from going crazy with 'The Voodoo Love Song'."

"Have you ever played in other towns?"

"I've played all over. New Orleans isn't the only place. Have you heard James P. Johnson on piano rolls, those fine Q.R.S. piano rolls?"

"I have. They're marvelous."

"I thought so. I noticed that strong left hand you got there."

"Thanks. I'm trying to develop it."

"That's the foundation. But you got to keep a balance. You can over-do the left hand. Like Cow Cow Davenport. Have you ever heard that running ground bass of his? Quadruple time, eight notes to the bar. I don't suppose that'll ever catch on. He pays so much mind to his left hand, his right hand gets real lonely."

"He couldn't beat James P. Johnson."

"Those piano rolls have gone all over the country. You can hear people playing like that 'way out in Texas. Up in St. Louis and Kansas City and Chicago. Even over in the East, in Washington and Baltimore. Up in Philly. And New York, of course. And now with the jazz phonograph records, too, jazz will soon be everywhere."

"Do you like playing with Art Lefevre?"

"Ask me if I like paying the rent. Ask if I like to eat."

"This place must bring in a lot of money."

"A *lot* of money. It's mighty comforting to get a piece of it every Friday."

"Yes, sure," Al said hesitantly. "But don't you sometimes wish you could get away from this – the circus, I mean – and play nothing but good jazz with good musicians?"

"Sometimes I think about it," Herbie said, signalling for another drink. "And then I remember what it's like playing one-night stands. I'm getting old. I like working steady. What's your excuse?"

"My excuse?" Al said, forcing a laugh. "I guess my excuse is that I'm young."

THIRTY-TWO

Moses kept asking Al when he was going to quit The Golden Frolics so that he could spend every night playing "real jazz".

"What d'you mean, 'real jazz'?" Al once irritably replied. "You're always going on about this 'real jazz'. Do you think you own it? All right then, define it."

"I don't know the words for it," Moses admitted. "If I could say what it means maybe I wouldn't have to play it. I didn't have your schooling. But I know jazz when I hear it, and so do you. Not exactly sure how to make it, maybe. But while I'm finding the way I sure as hell know what it *ain't*. And so do you. And one of the things it ain't is that lousy 'Voodoo Love Song' you whistle all the time."

"I do?"

Al looked as abashed as if Moses had told him he had bad breath. Moses slapped his thigh and laughed.

"Yeah, you better had look ashamed. 'The Voodoo Love Song' ain't music – it's a disease. Like you got a dose of clap over there at The Golden Frolics. Maybe you did: maybe you got the kind of clap that eats away your common sense. Why don't you *quit*? I could get you some gigs to start you off. You know some of the guys; you could take it from there. A man who can play piano like you ain't never going to *starve*. Why don't you stop wasting time?"

"You don't have to go on saying that. You've said it a thousand times. As a matter of fact, I have been thinking about quitting."

"When?"

"I don't know exactly *when*. But soon. I'd have to move to a cheaper room. It'd be quite a job to get my things packed. I've bought a lot of clothes and things. Books – music books."

"That's no big deal. I'll help you."

"That isn't all. There are a few more payments to make on the Victrola. And I still owe Ludwig Mankowitz quite a bit."

"Sell the Victrola! Sell the books! They're nice to have, but what's more important – other people's music or your own? Sell some of the clothes if you have to. Clothes don't matter."

"Maybe you're right."

"So when are you going to quit?"

"Soon, Moses. Soon."

Spring passed and the hot, humid days of summer weighed heavily on the city. Al could not imagine undertaking any major change. It was so hot that it was difficult to sleep at any time of the day or night. He bought a big electric fan for his room. It was an expensive fan but he had to get some sleep. He needed summer clothes. Ludwig Mankowitz talked him into buying two good-looking, impractical white linen suits. Then Al found that after each wearing they were wrinkled and soiled and had to be cleaned, so he had to buy two seersucker suits as well. How could he possibly get through the summer without such things? He decided that he had better stay at The Golden Frolics till autumn. Moses continued to goad him, and, as a result, he began to see less and less of Moses. Al felt that the hot weather and his own conscience were discomforts enough; he did not need the harassment of Moses' sermons.

By midsummer Al was playing only what he was obliged to play to earn a living. He consoled himself by telling himself that the quartet had its moments. Art used up a great deal of energy on drums during the shows and his listlessness during the sessions in between undoubtedly improved the chances of the other three to make some reasonable music. But summertime was a thirsty season. Herbie and Bo cared more for juleps than for jazz. For Al, the music late at night was often an ordeal.

Dolores Bolivar seemed to be quite satisfied. She never complained. She never seriously suggested that Al should forsake the piano to join the circus troupe, although she sometimes mentioned the idea, especially when he appeared to need cheering up.

"We'll make a hoochy-coochy dancer out of you yet," she used to say, pointing her stogie at him and chuckling and gurgling deep within her fat.

She also had a disconcerting habit of suddenly asking him questions.

"How's your love life?" was one she asked quite often, and he was not sure whether she expected a straight answer. The question embarrassed him mainly because at the time he had nothing that could have been described even loosely as a love life. Playing piano for a sex exhibition in a brothel, he was as celibate as a monk.

Workers in chocolate factories are said to be put off chocolates.

"Fleur asked after you," Dolores said one Sunday evening.

"She did?" Al said eagerly.

"Down, boy. She has a real soft spot for you, but that's all past history. She said you should forget about her."

"Yes."

"Don't you have eyes for nobody new? Young man your age! You ought to get yourself a bottle of those love-drops. Take some of those and even the monkeys would look good."

One evening she summoned him to her place beside the cash register and said:

"You ain't a government man, are you, Al?"

"Of course not, Madame Bolivar. What kind of government man?"

"There's a lot of rumors going around. Ever since that crazy Carrie Nation woman butted in at Tom Anderson's place, telling the customers that Jesus didn't want them to drink, there's been talk about outsiders causing trouble. Jesus liked his wine – says so right in the Bible. The world is full of spoilers, specially in Washington."

"Carrie Nation doesn't have anything to do with the government, though, does she?"

"I'm talking about all kinds of outsiders."

"I was born right here in New Orleans."

"That's O.K., Al. I just wanted to hear you say you didn't work for the government. Your word's good enough. But you can't blame me for wondering. Any newcomer to The District could turn out to be something strange. Didn't you hear about the Secret Service agents?"

Al hadn't.

"Damned if they didn't set up as whores in the dollar-a-trick cribs, over on Rampart. They were out to catch those poor young foreign whores who've been coming in from the Caribbean without the right papers. Haitian girls, some of them – lovely girls, *believers*. Can you imagine how a john would feel, goes to a crib in good faith to get his ashes hauled and the whore gets him started, gets his pants off, then whips off the wig and flashes a Secret Service badge and starts asking damn-fool questions about the girls? That kind of thing could rub off on all of us, give us all a bad name."

"But if the Secret Service is working the cribs under cover to look for illegal immigrants, wouldn't they go in as customers?"

"Even worse!" Dolores exclaimed indignantly. "A girl could serve a man and not find out till too late she'd been had by a Secret Service agent. Think of that! She'd never be able to forgive herself."

Dolores Bolivar's concern was one of the first omens of the trouble that was soon to afflict all Storyville.

When the United States entered World War One, some unthinking madames rejoiced. Who could be better customers than young servicemen on leave with their pockets full of money?

Being a great port, New Orleans had more than its share of Navy personnel. It wasn't long before the bars and brothels of The District were crowded with young sailors in their crisp white summer uniforms.

The Golden Frolics welcomed them and it soon became the Navy's favorite establishment. Many of the sailors were innocent young lads, new recruits from some of the less worldly regions of the country; the Navy has always attracted a disproportionately large number of natives of the rustic hinterland, far from the sea. The sailors seemed to bring with them the fresh air of remote farms. The voodoo circus was precisely what they were in search of.

The sailors thronged the front bar and the so-called ballroom, often carelessly jostling the established civilian clientele. Dolores beamed as she listened to the quickening ringing of the cash register. She had extra pews installed for the enlarged audiences. The front row was very close to the performers on the diminished dance-floor. Al noticed without any premonition of disaster that the boyish grins and scrubbed pink faces of the sailors were almost as numerous as the rogues'-gallery mugs of the familiar patrons.

Nobody could subsequently tell the magistrate and the officers of the court martial exactly how the riot broke out. In retrospect, it was obvious to all concerned that the sailors and civilians, crowded close together, disinhibited by alcohol and stimulated by sex, constituted a dangerously volatile mixture. It did not matter much what particular frictional spark caused the flare-up that set off the explosion. The fatal chain-reaction might have been initiated by a sailor rebuking a civilian for bad language, by a civilian suggesting that a sailor should shove off and go chase a U-boat, by a sailor enquiring why a civilian was not in uniform, or by some more serious provocation, such as by an elbow jogging a glass. The witnesses were not in agreement, except on one strikingly evident matter of fact : all hell broke loose.

The fight was much worse than an ordinary saloon brawl, because it was bigger, more complicated and more confused. Nobody knew what had happened or even what was happening, but everybody seemed to feel an urgent need to clobber everybody else within reach. Fists thudded against jaws in the orthodox fashion. Knees and boots caused bodies to double up and collapse and slide across the floor wherever there was space for them to do so. In general, sailors tended to hit civilians and civilians tended to hit sailors, but there was no strict discrimination; there was no clear division of antagonists and therefore there could be no victory or defeat. The muddled situation was exacerbated by the involvement of the voodoo circus, whose members were quick to take advantage of this chance to indicate what they felt about voyeurs. Angrily screaming naked women pulled out men's hair by the handfuls and raked men's faces with sharp talons. The spider monkeys, excitedly chattering and snickering, leaped and swung from head to head. The donkey tore itself free from the encumbrance of its harness of ropes and pulleys, bolted into the center of the *mêlée* and kicked out in all directions, scattering contestants like ten-pins.

The noise ! – the asinine hee-hawing, the heavy clattering and scraping of hobnails on floorboards, the roars and shrieks of fury and pain, the music ! In the *Titanic* tradition, the Art Lefevre quartet continued to play "The Voodoo Love Song" throughout the disturbance.

Dolores Bolivar reacted swiftly, but, for once, even her gang of thugs was unable to subdue the outbreak. To the contrary, by joining the conflict they prolonged and intensified it.

With the utmost reluctance, she called for the police. Before very long, several black patrol wagons, with squealing tires, convened at Liberty and Conti, and a swarm of police officers, their night-sticks raised, bulled their way through the bar, hardly able to believe that they were permitted on this occasion – invited ! – to have their way with the customers.

But the police had cracked only a few skulls before the arrival of competition. A Navy wagon unloaded a squad of Shore Patrolmen, big men, whose whites were fortified with leggings,

153

broad belts and holsters containing forty-fives. Unspoiled by the soft life of the police of The District, the S.P.s were fighting fit and they made up with dedication and vigor for their short service and lack of practice with night-sticks. They soon equalled and surpassed the civilian officers' score in fractured heads. There was a sudden consensus in the room that enough was enough.

"Quiet, you guys!" a police lieutenant shouted at the quartet. "Give us a rest!"

The room was silent.

The men of the New Orleans Police Department and the Shore Patrol of the United States Navy worked together in a temporary truce to sort out the heap of bodies in the middle of the dance-floor, consigning each category to the appropriate custody.

After all that violence, there were many grievous injuries but only one man was dead. The bottommost man of all was a young sailor mortally crushed in the embrace of the snake. The naval authorities were not in any way appeased by the fact that he had died wearing a smile.

THIRTY-THREE

There were other incidents in which sailors visiting Storyville came to harm. Robberies, beatings, stabbings, shootings and venereal infections were reducing the efficiency of the Navy's war effort. Washington ran out of patience.

The War Department and the Navy Department late in August sent an emissary to inspect Storyville. After the inspection, the Secretary of War, Newton D. Baker, issued an order prohibiting prostitution within five miles of any military installation. The ban meant that Storyville must close down.

The Mayor of New Orleans, Martin Behrman, was shocked. The Federal Government was threatening to undermine the foundation of the city's social structure and seriously to reduce his income.

Mayor Behrman journeyed to Washington in September, but Secretary Baker and the Secretary of the Navy, Josephus Daniels, refused to meet him. When he returned to New Orleans Mayor Behrman received an ultimatum.

"Close the red-light district," Secretary Daniels warned, "or the armed forces will."

The Mayor ignored the ultimatum. On October 1, Secretary Daniels sent the Mayor a final warning.

The next day, to avert martial interference in his municipal administration, Mayor Behrman called a meeting of the City Council and presented an ordinance to disestablish Storyville. After much acrimonious debate, the City Council enacted a law to do so on November 12.

The principal fire-insurance companies declared in the middle of October that policies covering Storyville properties were no longer valid. There were no cases of arson; the madames had left it too late. The Police Department sent most of its men to Storyville two days before the end, to be prepared to curb civil disorders. Storyville was gloomily peaceful.

"Sorry, folks," Dolores Bolivar said, "it's been real nice having you."

The last of the one-room cribs was closed and the girl evicted from it took her bed and walked.

When he collected his last week's pay, Al swallowed his pride and walked around to Matranga's to see Moses. Al realized he hadn't gone there for months.

"Moses left town," someone said. "No, he didn't leave no forwarding address. He didn't say where he was going."

There were wet leaves in the gutters around Jackson Square. Al felt cold.

THIRTY-FOUR

S tately, plump Louis Armstrong walked solemnly along the railroad platform, hoping that dignity would conceal his fear. He was twenty-two years old – no beginner – and he weighed two hundred and twenty-six pounds, representing a lot of chitlins and turnip greens; but he felt younger and smaller. He made an effort to walk tall.

The train from New Orleans had arrived at Illinois Central Station on time, but he did not expect anyone to meet him. This was not his first journey away from his home-town. He had played his cornet aboard the riverboats. But this time he did not know whether he would ever return. He felt like going back right now, in the next train, but he managed to overcome the impulse.

He was wearing a new white boater with a black silk ribbon; a new ginger-brown suit with square shoulders and wide lapels and a belt in the back, and shiny new yellow-brown high-buttoned shoes with narrow, pointed toes. The salesman at Krauss's Department Store at Canal and Basin had assured him that everything was the latest style. But was it the latest style in the nation's second city, up North?

Louis looked doubtfully at the other passengers confidently hurrying past him. He licked his dry lips and tightened his grip on the handles of his new brown imitation-leather suitcase and the black imitation-leather case containing his cornet. He reminded himself that he had good news in his pocket, a telegram from his teacher and benefactor, Papa Joe, King Oliver, summoning him to play second cornet in the famous Creole Jazz Band. King Oliver would make Little Louis big, if he could deliver the goods. There couldn't be any if; he had to. He gulped and manfully lengthened his stride.

He stopped at the barrier and put down his cases and felt in his pocket for his ticket. He couldn't find it. He fumbled nervously in other pockets.

"Move to one side," the uniformed white ticket-collector told him. "You're holding up the works."

Louis eventually found the ticket, which he had somehow missed in the first pocket.

"Here it is!" he said, handing it over and grinning. "Say, mister, would you tell me where I can find the Lincoln Gardens Café?"

"Ask a cop," the ticket-collector said, collecting tickets.

Louis popped his eyes and turned down his big mouth in a grimace of mock bafflement and chagrin, behind the man's back, picked up the cases and went on. He was wandering uncertainly through the station, looking for a sign that might give him some sort of clue, when he heard a familiar, cheerful voice hail him.

"Dipper!"

Louis' face brightened.

"Moses! Am I glad to see you, you rascal you!"

Moses was wearing a wide-brimmed white fedora and a light-tan sharkskin suit and two-tone shoes, brown and white.

He and Louis hugged each other, showing a lot of teeth. They stood back from each other and beamed and did some powerful hand-shaking.

"Welcome to Chicago, goddamn it!"

"Now I *feel* welcome. Easy on the hand, Mo. Leave some fingers for the horn!"

Moses grabbed Louis' suitcase.

"What you got here, man? Cases full of beans and rice?"

"It ain't money, that's for sure! Charge you the earth to travel on their railroad!"

"Don't fret about money. This town's *full* of money. Nobody has time to count the money. Like the song says, this is a toddlin' town."

"How did you know I was coming?" Louis asked, walking briskly to keep up with Moses.

"They all been talking about that second chair – Honoré, Johnny, little old Baby Dodds: all of them. The Creole Jazz Band is just about the best band in town – "

" 'Just about'?"

"O.K., the best. So a bunch of us from the other places always go over to the Lincoln Gardens every chance we get. Sometimes seems there's more musicians hanging out there than regular public, and it's a big room. A big, *big* room. The King asked me to sit in last night. To tell you the truth, Louis, there was a time

I thought maybe he'd take me in the band, seeing as I was already here and you were down yonder. But he won't have nobody but you."

"Papa Joe! He's my man."

"Yeah, that he is. Anyway, I was wailing along pretty good in there last night. We tore the music apart and put it back together again. I was keeping the chair warm for you."

"There should be *three* cornets."

"With you two on the stand? Wouldn't be room to fit in one more note."

Late in the August afternoon, the sun was still hot. Louis took a large white handkerchief out of his breast pocket and mopped his face and neck. Moses laughed.

"Still the sweatingest man around!" he said.

"I thought it would be cool up here near the North Pole," Louis protested.

"You'll feel like an Eskimo in the winter, I guarantee. Hot in the summer, cold in the winter. Everything here's in extremes. Let's cross the street. I know a place in the back there where we can get you a nice welcome-to-Chicago drink."

"Lead on, friend! I'm with *you*."

They cut between two buildings, along a narrow alley. Moses knocked on an unmarked door. A small section of it slid open to disclose a peep-hole at eye-level.

"Oh, it's you," a voice said approvingly. They heard the rattle of a chain and the sliding of a bolt and the door opened just wide enough to let them in. The doorman closed the door behind them and locked it and opened an inner door to a crowded, dimly lighted bar.

Moses ordered two bottles of beer.

"That's good beer," Louis said, after a long swallow. He was not called Dippermouth for nothing. His mouth was ideally suited to everything that mouths were designed for. The amply cushioned protuberances of his lips facilitated the arrangement of a jutting embouchure that readily fitted beermugs, brass musical instruments and other mouths. "Is it easy to get good booze in Chicago?"

"Chicago is booze headquarters, man. They import the best, from Europe, Canada, everywhere. And they make the stuff here. Half the town's a distillery and there's a speakeasy in every other building. There are more drinkers drinking more drinks in more bars in Chicago now than there ever were before the beginning of Prohibition. I'm telling you, Louis : this town is *booming*. You ain't never seen nothing like it. The town's full of money, full of booze, full of music. There's jobs aplenty."

Louis flashed a wide, white smile.

"Is that so? Now ain't that bodacious? And where do you hang your hat in this fine town, Mo? Can you tell me the best section to look for a room, not too far from the Lincoln Gardens?"

"You can stay in my place tonight," Moses said. "I can show you around tomorrow."

"That's swell. I got to go check in with my man. That's the first thing I got to do."

"It's no palace, Louis, where I live. There's plenty of money around but prices are high. Most of us live on the South Side. You'll see a lot of folks from down home. Thousands and thousands came up during the war and after, to work in the factories. Too many, maybe. The rents went sky-high. People had to double up, sleep in shifts : some beds *never* got a chance to cool off. We have fun, though – that Saturday night function."

"How far are you from here?"

"Not far. It's only a few blocks down to the Lincoln Gardens; that's near the lake. It's a few blocks from there to where I'm playing, the Dreamland Café. Hey, how's Al doing? Al Dexter. Where's he playing now?"

"Around town. He's playing real nice piano, but he don't never stay long with one group. Things ain't what they used to be, you know, and they never was all that easy, remember? Some of the guys are kind of hungry and I think Al's one of them. I told him the last time I seen him – he was mooching along the street there, just the other day – I told him I'm heading for Chicago, and I said he ought to do the same. But you know the way he feels about New Orleans, the way he talks. Maybe, he said. He said he was thinking about it. Some day maybe. What do you care so much about him for?"

"He's my friend."

Moses never remained too serious for too long. He did not immediately change the subject but he altered it.

"He plays good enough to make it here," he said. "But there's some mighty sharp piano players in this town. There's a girl on piano at the Dreamland. She is sen-*sational*. Name's Lil, Lil

Hardin. She studied up a lot on it, same as Al. She went to a school called Fisk."

"A woman piano player!" Louis exclaimed disgustedly.

"What's wrong with a woman piano player?"

"Ain't nothin' wrong with a woman *piano player*. I don't have nothin' against women as piano players – only against women as women."

Moses smiled quizzically.

"That's something new," he said. "Since when?"

"Since a short time after you left New Orleans. I got married."

"You did? Well, well, well! Where is she? Is she going to follow? Who is it? Is it Hester?"

"Her name was Daisy. From over in Gretna. I say was. We was married but we ain't no more. We almost killed each other, one way and another. It was hello and goodbye. Never again, daddy-o!"

"That's too bad. Have another beer."

"It's my turn."

"Your first day in Chicago, you don't have no turn. Wait till you're on the payroll."

"Give me a lemonade then."

The bartender looked slightly pained by this outlandish request but he made allowances for the outlandish cut of the man's suit and complied.

"I've cut down on the drinking," Louis explained to Moses. "Don't do your chops no good, and it can make people do crazy things. When Daisy was boozed up she used to reach for a knife, and that ain't healthy. I don't need women and I don't need drinking. I got my horn. That's what counts. How about you? Don't tell me *you're* married."

"There's been some near misses. But when you tell them you're a musician they lose interest. Gangster, O.K.; musician, no."

"Well, I'd better get moving. Where do you live?"

"A few more blocks on down from the Dreamland. Near the Union Stockyards. We only get the bad smell when the wind's from the west."

"Which way does the wind usually blow?"

"From the west."

THIRTY-FIVE

The bedsprings were rhythmically creaking in the warm summer night.

Sweat was dripping from Moses onto the obscure face of the woman bouncing and writhing beneath him. She seized the hard clenching, soft unclenching, hard clenching muscles of his laboring buttocks. He was panting like a runner near the end of a marathon. She was groaning and mewling.

"Don't stop!" Lil cried. "Don't stop! Don't ever stop! Oh, my darling! My darling, darling, *darling*!"

He moved faster.

She squealed.

"Oh, yes! Now! Oh, now, Louis!"

He immediately stopped and straightened his arms, pushing himself up, disengaging himself from her body.

"My name is Moses," he said.

She rolled over to face the wall, with her back to him, and said nothing.

She felt his weight press and release the edge of the mattress as he got up.

She heard the shower's muffled hiss.

Shucks! she thought. Let him go. He doesn't own me. She turned onto her back. She was relaxed all the way down to her toes; they felt warm and soft. She felt like purring.

The bathroom door opened, fanning a bright yellow beam of light across the floor and the bed. She raised a forearm to shield her eyes. He switched off the light. She heard the other door-knob turn and the door open, brushing the carpet.

To hell with him then, she thought.

She heard kitchen sounds: water gushed into a kettle; china clinked against china.

She smelled coffee.

She felt his weight depress the side of the mattress.

"Here you are," he said gently. "Have some coffee."

She pretended to awake and to be surprised.

"Oh," she said. "Thanks." She sat up and switched on a bedside light and accepted the steaming cup. "I thought you'd gone back to your place."

"I'm sorry, Lil," he said. "But Jesus."

"It didn't mean anything," she said, smiling blithely. "I'm Lil Hardin; you're Moses Decatur; he's Louis Armstrong. There's no case of mistaken identities. You couldn't be anybody but you. There isn't anybody else in the world like you. You know how I feel about you, don't you? Can't you tell, when we're together, in each other's arms, making love?"

"I suppose so."

"I should hope so. It's never been like that with anybody else. Not for me at least. Perhaps for you."

"No, it's never been like that for me."

"There you are then. You see? It was only a slip of the tongue. You can't imagine me and Louis together like that, can you?"

Moses put his cup on the floor and sat a little closer to her and looked at her. She put her cup beside the lamp on the bedside table and turned back and held out her arms to him. She smiled. He held her hands but moved no closer.

"Moses? You can't, can you?"

"I don't want to."

"So why are you sitting 'way over there? Come to me. Isn't there something you didn't quite finish?"

Moses frowned and stayed where he was. He said:

"You've been going over to the Lincoln Gardens every night since the first time Joe Oliver introduced you to Louis."

"So have you. We've always gone over a lot. Even between sets. And after hours, too, with Joe and the boys to the Pekin."

"But not every night."

"All right, so now we go every night. What's wrong with that? They're playing some marvellous music. It's better than ever since Louis joined. You think so as well. You said so yourself."

"But are you sure it's only the music?"

"What is this. Some kind of third degree? What's the charge?"

"If it's Louis you want, not me, why don't you say so?"

"I like the way he plays that cornet. I happen to be a musician, too, just as much as you, in case you've forgotten."

"No need to get mad. I was only saying – "

"Well, don't. I don't have to make excuses for going to the Lincoln Gardens or anywhere else. I like the Lincoln Gardens.

I like Joe Oliver. I like Honoré Dutrey. I like Johnny Dodds. I like – "

"You don't have to go through them all. I know the names. I've known them longer than you have. I've known them from New Orleans days. You don't have to – "

"And I like Louis Armstrong. He's kind of a hick. He doesn't know how to dress. He eats too much. He has the voice of a bull with laryngitis. But right from the first night he blew that horn. . . . Mmm-*mmm*! He can really blow!"

"So you think he plays better than me. Is that what you're saying?"

Lil chose to ignore this suggestion.

"There is one thing he's got that I think you should try to cultivate."

"Yeah?" Moses said sulkily. "What's that?"

"Louis takes jazz very seriously. Louis has ambition. He has what it takes to get to the top."

Moses released her hands.

"And I have no ambition. Is that it?"

She smiled almost tenderly. She was still invitingly holding out her arms.

"Come here, Moses."

"But no ambition, right?"

"Let's say you live for today."

"Every day's today. Ain't no other day."

"Moses, come here. You have one kind of ambition that makes up for a lot."

"Is that so."

"You have a lot of ambition in bed. Let's go on from where I interrupted."

He would have liked to remain aloof, but he couldn't.

As he leaned closer, she reached for the bath towel which was fastened at his waist and unfastened it. She reached down and stroked him. He stiffened in her hand.

He sighed.

She whispered in his ear.

"Lie on your back, Moses, sweetheart. I'm going to make you happy."

Moses lay down and closed his eyes.

Psychoanalysts have said that whenever a man and woman

go to bed together there are at least three persons present, often four, sometimes more.

Moses wondered for only an instant whether Lil was thinking about Louis.

Lil did not wonder what Moses was wondering about. She was too busy.

THIRTY-SIX

Chicago, 1924

L ouis Armstrong and Lillian Hardin were married in a brief
civil ceremony on February 5.

Moses Decatur was one of the witnesses.

Louis Armstrong was still playing second cornet in King
Oliver's Creole Jazz Band. The ingenious harmony of the secretly
planned spontaneity of the Oliver–Armstrong cornet breaks was
a wonder and an inspiration to all the musicians who heard
them. Oliver had given Lil a job in the band. She played the
piano. Louis thought he was on top of the world.

But Lil told Louis that King Oliver was holding him back,
because King Oliver was afraid that otherwise Louis might
surpass him. She tried to persuade Louis to quit. By June, she
succeeded.

Louis worked for a while with Moses, in Ollie Powers' band, at
the Dreamland Café.

In September, Louis got his big chance. Fletcher Henderson
asked him to join the Henderson band in New York. Louis went.

Lil stayed in Chicago.

THIRTY-SEVEN

Al had left New Orleans reluctantly, without having achieved any success big enough to enable him to try to effect a reconciliation with his family. A cautious adventurer, he moved northward gradually, with long stays in Memphis, St. Louis and Kansas City, and some short side-trips to small towns, on his way to Chicago.

As he went along, he took any jobs he could get. He played in dance-halls, speakeasies and even in motion-picture theaters. He was always as quick as a chameleon to adjust to suit local conditions. He was not musically doctrinaire; he was a pragmatist. His technique, of course, was constant; but his style was eclectic and readily variable.

On request, he would reach back for the old Joplinesque rags and for the so-called "blues" of W. C. Handy, especially that curious tango mutant, "The St. Louis Blues"; Al would play Jelly Roll Morton's popular recent compositions, such as "Grandpa's Spells", "Milenburg Joys" and "Wolverine Blues"; Al would accurately reproduce some of the latest records by the new Harlem school of piano players. James P. Johnson's pioneer work was being carried forward by many admirers, including Willie (The Lion) Smith and Fats Waller. In short, Al would give the customers whatever they asked for or seemed to want. He would play anything in any way for a buck. When he arrived in Chicago, in November, he was ready for anything and open to suggestions.

He walked from the railroad station. His suitcase was heavy. In the blue evening twilight, a freezing wind nipped his ears and made his eyes water. He sniffed and pulled up the collar of his coat and pulled down the brim of his hat. He had nowhere special to go to. He wondered whether he would ever get used to the bleak melancholy of arriving alone in a strange town.

A gust of wind whipped up a cold swirl of grit. Immediately, he felt a piece of it in his right eye. He rubbed the eyelid and picked at the corners of his eye with his right forefinger, opening his mouth, as one sometimes does, for some reason, when trying to get something out of one's eye. He failed and made his eye sore.

In the next block, he came to a small drugstore and went in.

A plain young brunette with bobbed hair and a fringe and glasses was sitting behind the counter reading *True Romances* and chewing gum. She was wearing a white coat that was possibly supposed to make her look hygienic and efficient. If his eye had not hurt, he might have felt sorry for her. Even though he was preoccupied, he automatically flirted a little.

"This is the scene when they meet," he said, smiling. "He has something in his eye and she's sweetly sympathetic."

"No she isn't. She's bored. She yawns in his face."

"Wouldn't you have a look?" he said, tilting his face and spreading his eyelids wide open with a finger and thumb close to a light over the counter. "It feels so big, I'm sure you'll be able to see it."

"This isn't a first-aid station. You want to buy an eye-bath?"

"Aw, please, babe. I need your help."

"Don't give me that 'please, babe.' Save your sob story for my husband. He's in the back – the great scientist, busy turning gold into lead."

Al sighed dispiritedly.

"O.K. Give me an eye-bath then," he said.

Her face did not appear to soften but she turned it toward a frosted glass door inscribed *PHARMACY*.

"Morris!" she shouted, and the pharmacist emerged, frowning and blinking, as if he had been in the dark for a long time, waiting for her call. "Man says he has something in his eye."

"Yes, dear," he said. "Please step this way, will you? and we'll see what we can do." He indicated a goose-necked lamp with a green glass shade near the end of the counter.

"How do you like the medical 'we'?" she asked, smiling but not improving her expression. "Dr. Pasteur is on the job."

"Please, dear," he protested mildly. He peered closely with doe-like brown eyes as he manipulated Al's upper lid and delicately probed his eye with an orange-stick swab like a tiny doll's mop.

"Ah!" the pharmacist sighed with satisfaction. "Here we are." He displayed the foreign body under the light – an almost invisible black speck on the cotton wool.

Al felt instant relief. For a moment, he felt less lonely.

"Thanks a lot," he said, reaching for his wallet. "What do I owe you?"

"That's all right. Glad to help you out."

"Are you sure? Well, while I'm here . . . Let me have some Gillette blades. A pack of ten."

"There's no need," the pharmacist assured him, "unless you really want them."

"Oh, no, no need at all," his wife said. "This isn't a business; it's a vocation."

"I do need some blades," Al told the pharmacist. "And some shaving cream. A big tube of Gillette shaving cream."

The woman turned to her magazine, ostentatiously ignoring them.

"Visiting Chicago?" the man said, as he taped the paper bag. His wife found it impossible not to comment.

"No, he's visiting San Francisco," she said.

Now Al felt that he had to prolong the conversation at least sufficiently to ignore her.

"I'm not sure how long I'll be staying," he said. "It depends. Could you recommend a hotel around here? Nothing too special."

"Well," the pharmacist said hesitantly, trying to make an assessment. Al's dark-gray suit was shabbily respectable but he was wearing a rather flashy red and silver-gray silk tie.

"Something reasonably central," Al suggested. "I want to catch some music, without a lot of long-distance cab rides."

"Well, there's the Loop Hotel. That's near. It's a medium-price hotel and I understand they'll give you a weekly rate."

Al looked pleased.

"You mean we're near The Loop?"

The woman groaned. The idea that someone did not know the location of The Loop was too much for her.

"Yes," the pharmacist said. "There's plenty of first-class entertainment. If you tell me what sort of music you like, maybe I can help."

"Is the Lincoln Gardens in The Loop?"

"No. You wouldn't like the Lincoln Gardens."

"Isn't that one of the best places for jazz?"

"Do you like jazz?" the woman asked, putting down the magazine.

"If that's what you like," the pharmacist said, "the best jazz is uptown."

"I thought King Oliver played at the Lincoln Gardens," Al said.

"Take my tip. Go uptown."

"Isn't King Oliver there any more?"

"You sound like you're from the South. Aren't you?"

"Yes, I – "

"Didn't you know King Oliver's a jigaboo? His band just came down from out of the trees. The white bands play uptown."

"King Oliver plays great cornet," Al said.

The pharmacist looked at his watch.

"I have things to do," he said abruptly. He returned to his room at the back.

His wife leaned forward and spoke to Al in a confidential voice.

"King Oliver's still there," she said. "It's a perfectly safe place. You'll be amazed: he's even better in person than he is on his records."

THIRTY-EIGHT

Walking north up State Street, Al was tiring of the suitcase when he saw the flashing blue neon sign of the Loop Hotel. The pharmacist's remark about King Oliver had been dumb, Al thought, but that was no reason that he should inconvenience himself by walking any farther than he had to. Boycotting the hotel would not have done King Oliver any good.

The desk clerk checked a board indicating occupancy and said he could let Al have a single with shower. The room could be rented for seven days for the price of six and the price was moderate.

"Is that all your baggage?" the clerk asked.

"Yeah."

"The rent's payable by cash in advance."

Al had stayed in many worse hotels in the past few years and such rules did not offend him. He paid and registered and the clerk gave him a key attached to a rectangle of plywood about a foot long.

"Your room's on the second floor," the clerk said. "The elevator operator will take you up. He should be there. Don't try to operate the elevator yourself."

As Al had never yearned to operate one, he accepted the prohibition without any demur. Anyway, the operator was at his post. He was a short black youth in a uniform a couple of sizes too large, chocolate-brown with tarnished gold frogging and gold buttons (one missing) and *Loop Hotel* embroidered in gold above his breast pocket. His hair evidently had been straightened electrically and heavily greased and brushed down as flat as paint. He was leaning against an elevator door jamb, picking his teeth unenthusiastically with a cardboard match. Two of his teeth were of gold much brighter than the braid on his uniform. He stood up straight, ushered Al into the small cubicle, which smelled of stale cigarette smoke, followed him in, closed the steel trellis door with a clang, eased over a lever that caused the elevator to shudder slowly upward and said :

"Want to get laid, mister?"

"Not right now," Al said.

The operator moved the lever back and the elevator jerked to a halt.

"Watch the step," the operator said. Only the least observant of passengers could have failed to notice the extensive gap between the floors of the elevator and the corridor.

"This way," the youth said, switching roles from that of elevator operator to that of porter, though not to the extent of actually offering to carry Al's bag.

Al waited while his guide found the right master key on his key-ring and led the way into the room. There was only just enough floor-space for both of them to stand beside the bed but he seemed to feel that he was expected to show Al all the amenities.

"There's the shower in there," he said, with a quick double swish of a shower curtain made of grayish towelling.

"Telephone," he said, pointing to the telephone on the desk.

"Radiator. No use fooling with it though. The super sets the thermostat down in the basement."

He opened the wardrobe and flipped a row of wire hangers into motion on a wooden rail.

"Plenty of hangers," he pointed out.

"O.K.," Al said. The performance was beginning to bore him. "Is there a key to the wardrobe?"

"No. There's a safe in the office."

"I don't need that. I have nothing of much value," Al emphasized, thinking of the youth's skeleton key.

"Suit yourself. Do you want a bottle?"

"No, thanks."

"Any time you want one, ask me. If you call the desk they'll charge more. I'll give you a good deal."

"I'll remember."

The elevator operator/procurer/porter/bootlegger persisted.

"How about a shoe-shine?" he said. "If you're going out, you could use one."

Al looked down at his shoes. The journey had dulled them.

"You win," he said. "I'll have a shine."

"The things are downstairs. Give me your shoes."

"No, I'll be down in a few minutes." Al felt in a trouser pocket. "Here," he said, depositing two small coins in the outstretched white glove. "I'll take care of you later."

172

"O.K., mister. I trust you."

People who make declarations of trust are likely to be untrusting and untrustworthy, but Al charitably nodded.

The door closed.

His room was in the front of the building, overlooking State Street. The traffic was noisy. The hotel's neon sign intermittently glowed blue through the window. He pulled down the blind. It had a strong spring. When he released the cord, the blind shot up. He pulled it down again; again it shot up. Impatiently, he pulled it down so hard that he detached the roller at the top and the whole contraption fell on the window-sill with a clatter.

Al sat on the edge of the bed and held his head in his hands. The circumstances were certainly dreary. He was saddened by the thought of unsuccessful attempts at cosmetic self-improvement, the straightened hair and gold teeth. On reflection, he supposed he should feel fortunate. He could play the piano. What must it have been like to be a hustler without anything to hustle?

He had a shower and dressed. The elevator operator took Al down to the ground-floor; the shoe-shine boy shined Al's shoes. Al stood with one shoe resting on the home-made wooden pedestal of a packing-case shoe-shine stand and looked down on the neatly shaven central parting of the short black hair. The syncopated shoe-shine rag was snapping and popping as dynamically as a tap-dancer's steel-tipped toes and heels. It reminded him of the improvised rhythm section of a spasm band long ago.

"What's your name?" Al asked.

"Dipper. That ain't my right baptism name, you understand. But that's what I like to be called."

"That's funny. I used to know someone called Dipper. He played fine cornet."

"You talking now about Louis Armstrong. That's where I get the name. I named myself after him. That's what I'd like to do, play like him."

"He learned to play cornet in a waifs' home, down in New Orleans."

"Is that right? He was lucky. They didn't teach me *nothin'* in my school." Dipper looked up and grinned. "I wouldn't hold still long enough. I quit when I was twelve. Meat-market delivery boy. We had plenty of steak to eat till they fired me."

Dipper lightly tapped the side of Al's shoe to indicate that it was finished. Al put up the other shoe and Dipper went energetically to work on it.

"Some people teach themselves to play," Al said encouragingly. "It's possible."

"First you have to get your hands on a horn. Even in a hock shop, a horn costs money."

"But you seem to be in all kinds of business," Al said.

"I'm keeping my folks. My daddy can't work."

The reply did not seem reproachful but it stung.

After a silence, Al tried again.

"I was hoping to see Louis – Dipper – the other Dipper – to-night. Maybe you could tell me how to get to the Lincoln Gardens."

"Sure, I'll tell you how to get there," Dipper said, as he finished the second shoe and stood up. "It's at Thirty-First and Cottage Grove. But you left it kind of late. He left the Lincoln Gardens last summer. And he left Chicago two months ago."

"I hadn't heard. Is anything wrong?"

"He went to New York, to play with Smack Henderson."

"But King Oliver's still here, isn't he?"

"Doesn't sound to me like these jazzmen are real *close* friends of yours," Dipper said with a slyly malicious smile.

Al was annoyed. He didn't see why he should be on the defensive, but in some way it seemed that he was.

"It isn't easy to have any close friends when you're always travelling around, playing all over."

"You're a jazz musician?" Dipper asked respectfully.

"Yes, I am," Al said with dignity.

"What do you play?"

"Piano."

There was a pause.

Dipper smiled kindly.

"*Everybody* can't play horn," he pointed out.

Al gave him a dollar but as he hailed a cab on State Street he still felt put down.

THIRTY-NINE

His very first night in Chicago, Al met Moses at the Lincoln Gardens.

Moses was sitting with two other men at a table near the bandstand. The band was playing "Yellow Dog Blues", and he was not paying close attention. He saw Al before Al saw him. Moses was able to arrange his face in a calm smile, the way he used to control his breathing when he had raced Al home from school, to give the impression that getting there first had been easy.

"Hey, there, slowpoke!" he greeted Al. "What kept you?"

But Moses never was able, and never wanted, to conceal his true spontaneous feelings. He laughed delightedly and jumped up and seized Al's hand and thumped him on the back.

Al was glad to see him but he felt somewhat embarrassed about the way he had allowed their friendship to lapse in New Orleans. He disguised this feeling in a manner of playful accusation.

"So this is where you've been hiding!" he said. "I often wondered what happened to you."

"How are you?" Moses asked, eagerly searching Al's face. "How's everything?"

"Pretty good. And you?"

"Terrific. I'm at the Dreamland. What you doing?"

"I just got in."

"It's been a long time, Al."

"Seven years."

"That long?" Moses said, smiling and shaking his head incredulously. "No kidding!" He looked up at the band. The cornet, clarinet and trombone seemed to be struggling for supremacy; the cornet was winning. "Let's go down the street. I know a quiet little place. We can come back later."

Moses rang a side-street door-bell in a special way and they were eventually admitted into a bar and grill. They sat at a small table with a red-and-white checkered cloth. There was a painting of the Bay of Naples on the wall beside them. Al picked up a matchbook from a Cinzano ashtray next to a chrome dispenser of

paper napkins. The place was called the *Ristorante Vesuvio*.
Moses ordered drinks.

"The veal's good," he said. "And so's the spaghetti, if you like
spaghetti."

"I'm not eating," Al said, trying to appear indifferent as he
scanned the prices on the menu. "I had something in the train."

"I think I'll have a steak, Julie," Moses told the waitress. "Give
me a nice, big T-bone – "

"Medium?"

"Yeah, Julie. With everything – french fries, onions, mushrooms,
tomatoes, string beans and a salad."

"With lots of Thousand Island dressing."

"With lots of Thousand Island dressing. Yeah!" He turned
happily to Al. "Come on, Al. How about you? They put out a
fine T-bone."

Al sipped his drink and shook his head. The waitress went away.

"They seem to know you well," Al said.

"They should. Come here 'most every night. This is one of the
places that'll serve *anyone*. The man has a thing about musicians.
Papa Joe eats here a lot. And some of the white guys. It's kind of
nice that way."

Al sipped his drink. Moses thoughtfully examined him before
speaking again.

"What did you have in the train?" Moses asked casually.

"Oh, you know. A sandwich."

"Where did you come from?"

"Today? Only Springfield."

"When did you get in?"

"About six."

Moses looked straight into Al's eyes.

"It's past nine."

"So?"

"So I know you have to be hungry. I'm your friend, Al, for
God's sake, not someone you just met for the first time. Have a
steak."

"Maybe I'll have a hamburger," Al said. "To keep you company."

Moses raised a hand and the waitress came over.

"Make that two steaks," he said. "Medium?" he asked Al.

"Medium-rare."

"One medium-rare. Two of everything."

"French dressing, please," Al said. Specifying a different way of cooking the steak and a different salad dressing somehow helped him to feel that he was saving face.

"French dressing," Moses confirmed. He looked at Al's glass. "And two more drinks, Julie." She went to the bar. "Old Volcano, a blend," he told Al. "They make it in the basement. Take care not to spill any on your shoes."

"Thank you, Mo," Al said with feeling.

"Aw, shucks, Al. It ain't nothing. You'd do the same. I know what it's like. I was *there*. And don't forget : I owe you; I lived in your house."

"Not my house."

Moses disregarded the quibble.

"Remember the pies we used to share?" he said, grinning. "I mean, when I didn't get to them behind your back."

"Sarah was a wonderful cook," Al recalled mournfully.

"Seems to me you could use some wonderful cooking right now," Moses said. He raised his new drink. "I can tell you this, Al : you've come to the right town. There's all kinds of action here. Knowing all the piano you know, you could make it here if you only had one hand. Don't worry, Al. You'll soon be in the money. Get yourself all duded up, play that fine music, and you'll be riding high !"

"I hope you're right. I've had some ups and downs, Moses. It's murder, playing in some of those small towns. Do you remember that time, back in New Orleans, you said you and I should get together and organize a band of our own?"

Moses nodded and smiled nostalgically.

"Yeah, I remember. I sure was wet behind the ears, saying a thing like that. But it was a beautiful thought."

"I didn't dare give up my job at the New Alhambra, and then I had to. I didn't even have the nerve to quit the Golden Frolics, and then I had to. I'm sorry, Moses. I was foolish not to get away from those places before. But I've been around since then. Why don't we get together now?"

Moses looked mildly surprised.

"You say you've been around? Where've you been? Haven't you noticed a little something called the color bar? It's stricter up here than it ever was in New Orleans. You never see colored and white musicians playing together up here. Never in public."

"I hear there's a lot of new white jazz in this town. The white jazz is really getting somewhere."

"Some of those guys are good. Bunch of kids from the West Side. Haven't you heard of the Austin High School gang? They're a bit rough at the edges but they full of the spirit. Jimmy McPartland, Frank Teschemacher, Bud Freeman, Dave Tough – they're always coming down here to listen and pick up ideas. And you got to give them credit: they have some ideas of their own, too. Joe Sullivan and Jess Stacy – they're a couple of piano men you'd like. Some of them are real young. There's a boy by the name of Benny Goodman. He's only fifteen but he plays a whole lot of clarinet – maybe too much. He always seems to be trying to prove how many notes he can fit in. But if he loosens up he might turn out all right. And there are some nice cornets – Muggsy Spanier, Bix Beiderbecke, though I'm not sure about him; he may be in Ohio. Yes, the white jazz is a new kind of jazz. More breaks, more solos. You know? But the main difference is that it's white. It sounds white. It feels white."

The waitress served their steaks and there was a conversational lull. The food and drink gave Al a growing sensation of well-being and optimism.

"Of course, the whites are getting paid more, I suppose?"

"Of course. The whites have the booking agencies and the record companies that count. They control the union. They own the big theaters and the fashionable cabarets. They get the best jobs. All we have is the best music."

"What are we waiting for?" Al said. "You don't have to let the color bar bother you. You could go any way you like."

"I already am where I want to be."

"But what I mean . . . if you wanted . . . you could – "

" '*Passeblanc*' is the word we used to use back home. Is that what you're trying to say?"

"Well, why not? If that's where the money is. . . . You *could* pass. I've always thought that. There are whites with tan complexions. Your skin isn't very dark."

"I used to think the Louisiana law was very unfair," Moses said calmly. "You know: it said if a man had any colored blood at all that made him colored. He was legally colored. When I was very young I sometimes used to look at myself in the mirror and pinch my nostrils together and try to make my lips smaller – kind of tuck them in – and half close my eyes and try to imagine what it would be like to be really white. I'd look at Sarah and Benjamin when we were out together and I'd feel ashamed. Now, when I think about it, I'm ashamed I was ashamed."

"You don't have to think about all that," Al said. "Just be practical. You'd be better off if you passed."

"If you even think of passing for white," Moses patiently explained, "that means you can't be white. I don't know how much Negro blood I have and how much white blood. All I do know is the Negro blood must be mighty strong blood. Because I feel I'm a Negro, and when I play the horn I *know* I'm a Negro."

"Don't take it personally," Al said. "Maybe I shouldn't have mentioned it. I was only trying to help."

Moses smiled.

"How's the steak?" he asked.

FORTY

Chicago, 1928

Things were going well. Al was playing music he liked and he was earning good money.

There had been difficult days at first. He joined Dave Hanley's Slaughterhouse Seven, when Red Gander lost his paternity suit and his legal counsel advised him to leave town. But Dave was a compulsive poker player for high stakes and he could not abide a pianist who refused to gamble. There was a profitable but short-lasting engagement with Wayne Charlton's Pyramid Club Foot-warmers, in place of handsome, young Vic Charlton, who could not resist an offer to go out to Hollywood. Wayne let Al go because of what the temperamental maestro called "a clash of personal-ities". Al subsequently felt vindicated when he heard on the musicians' grapevine that Wayne had an acute bile-duct pro-lem, but of course the explanation did not get Al's job back. Al spent a few happy months with Dick Kilian and His Calumet Rhythm Kings, until the band's tax accountant did something very wrong and the band had to disperse.

All sorts of vicissitudes cast shadows on the jazz scene, but many of the passing clouds had silver linings. One man's trouble was likely to provide another man's opportunity. When internecine strife suddenly devastated the morale of The Club Michigan Sophisticates (there had been a dispute over the key in which it would be best to play "I've Found a New Baby"), Al got a lucky break. Controversies of that nature often radically influence musical careers. He had built up something of a local reputation for being a good deal more than merely competent at the piano, but he was surprised when he received a call to take over and reorganize the band.

When Al's appointment became known, several members of the band tendered their resignations, giving him a welcome chance to hire the most suitable musicians, his friends. He was able imme-diately to rescue Dick Kilian from despondent withdrawal in a neighborhood speakeasy in Calumet Park. Al was confident that Kilian, with discipline, would rank with George Wettling and

Gene Krupa as one of the major Chicago drummers of the late nineteen-twenties.

"That's great, Al!" Kilian said, when Al found him and told him he was wanted. "I've worked out a swell arrangement of 'Sugar' I can let you have. You're going to love it. Get this: the stand is dark. Then there's a baby pink spot, on the drums. I start alone, with a slow press roll. It gets louder and louder – then *bam*! I slash the ride cymbal, and you and the rest of the boys come in – with all the lights now – and we're off to the races! With a double paradiddle and a ratamascue!" He demonstrated what he meant with a knife and fork on his sandwich plate, a beer bottle and a glass on the bar.

"Yeah, Dickie, right, I like it," Al said, wondering whether he had made a wise decision. "Let's go now though. We have a lot of work to do."

"Sure, Al," Kilian amiably agreed. "Whatever you say." And he turned out fine. It was easy to forget about the pink baby spot.

The rest of the line-up that Al assembled was as good as that of any other band in town. He got John Anstey and Alex Low on trumpets. Like many of their contemporaries, they had switched from the blunt sonorities of the cornet to the keener, more piercing clarity of the trumpet. John could produce long, high notes like white-hot tungsten wires, when he was in the mood. The rest of the personnel were George Gale, on a threateningly growling trombone; Steve Barber, clarinet, who was renowned for his mellow tone in the lower register and for his thrillingly shrill vibrato in the upper; Phil Wallace, a rare combination of romantic lyricism and academic pedantry on tenor saxophone; Jackson (Big J.) Kroll, persuasively eloquent on guitar and subtly introspective in his vocals; and old Hank Fairley, whose plodding, absolutely reliable bass had a way of making the wildest jazz seem secure and somehow *honest*.

Now, half-way through the second set, shortly before twelve o'clock on Saturday night, Al was leading the band through a solidly chugging rendition of "Nobody's Sweetheart". The elegant Club Michigan, in a converted turn-of-the-century brownstone mansion catercorner across the square from the Garfield House, was pleasantly crowded with young men in black dinner jackets and young women in long necklaces and short silk evening dresses, and everybody seemed to be having a good time.

Al took a solo, which was not the interruption that many piano solos are; his indirect restatement of the melody wound it up to a higher level, in preparation for the solos to come. George Gale's trombone was briskly laborious, like a saw rasping through an oak log. Steve Barber's clarinet slithered upward in convulsive gyrations like an excited electric eel. Phil Wallace was so wrought up that his saxophone, in an uncharacteristic tizzy, honked like a startled goose warning a citadel. Alex Low's trumpet heroically screamed, like a bugle calling the band to unite for the victorious charge of the final chorus. When it came to an end, the white-tuxedoed musicians sat back with heated red faces and beamed at each other in mutual high esteem. Furthermore, there was also some hearty applause from the customers.

None of them applauded with a greater show of enthusiasm than a pretty young brunette in black silk and pearls who was sitting alone at a table for four close to the piano. She had a glass of champagne in front of her and a black Turkish cigarette in a green jade holder. But while the band played its strenuous up-tempo version of "China Boy" she did not touch her drink and her cigarette holder lay propped against an ash-tray. She sat quite motionless, with her chin cupped in her long, white fingers, and stared intently at Al.

When she applauded this time, Al felt that she was applauding him personally.

During the next number, "Friar's Point Shuffle", he noticed her in consultation with a waiter. Al wondered if she had lost interest. She had not. The waiter soon handed him a folded slip of paper.

"Thank you, ladies and gentlemen," Al said, silencing the applause with a modest smile and an upraised hand. "I've had a special request for a lovely new piece. Some of you may have heard it in broadcasts from the New York Cotton Club. This'll give most of the boys in the band a chance to take it easy for a while. We haven't yet had time to work this one out. Ladies and gentlemen," he said, looking at the young woman, "I'd like to play you the latest Duke Ellington composition, 'Creole Love Call'. I hope you like it."

He smiled at the young woman. She continued to gaze steadily at him, waiting for him to play, but she did not smile back. Feeling somewhat disconcerted, he looked around for support from the guitar, bass and drums, muttered a few words of guidance, tapped his foot to establish the time, and began.

He played the eerie melody slowly and simply. The second time around, he added some variations of his own. They were entirely faithful to the spirit of the original work, for which he felt great respect, admiration and sympathy. Duke Ellington was from Washington, D.C., but it seemed to Al that the music conveyed a deep emotional sense of the sweet, melancholy passion of Louisiana. As Duke wrote it and Al played it, "Creole Love Call", with its funereally somber repetitiveness and its high keening wails of amorous lamentation and desire, was a song of survival. The female cry of love was strong. It overcame death.

When the music finished, Al remained immersed in it for a moment, looking down at his hands resting on the keys. There was not much applause. It was not the sort of music to which applause seemed appropriate. But the spell was broken by an outburst of laughter at a table where a birthday was being celebrated, and again there was a normal cheerful babble of nightclub conversation. Al looked at the table beside him to see the young woman's reaction to what he had played for her.

The table was empty.

FORTY-ONE

The young woman's discourteous departure was surprising and rather disappointing but Al did not give it much thought. He knew that it would be foolish to let the behavior of the public upset him.

He announced "There'll Be Some Changes Made". The band played this number at an ambiguous medium pace, not as brightly as most other bands usually rendered it. Big J.'s interpretation of the ostensibly optimistic words always amused Al. Big J. sang all lyrics to his guitar as if trying to pacify an unhappy babe in arms, while at the same time managing to accentuate every possible neurotic innuendo and every hint of imminent misadventure and grief. He sang "Changes", in a low, mournful voice intimating that every change was bound to be a change for the worse. His anxious frown and hesitant manner suggested that the prospective change in the weather would bring thunder and lightning and that when he changed the way he strutted his stuff it would be because an incurable injury would have reduced him to a wretched stumbling limp. This performance came as close as Al ever allowed the band to come to comedy. Jazz was always joyful, he believed; even the saddest blues implied its opposite; but he believed that jazz should never be ludicrous.

During the outchorus the *maître d'* led a man to the table that the young woman had abandoned. He wasn't Al Capone but he looked rather like him – a meaty Napoleonic figure in a well-cut midnight-blue dinner jacket, with receding wavy black hair, heavy black eyebrows and smiling thick red lips that held a large cigar. His plump face had the talcumed, massaged, freshly shaven pinkness of an expensively embalmed corpse. He might have been only about thirty years of age but his massiveness, the spring in his step and the arrogant complacence of his smile gave an impression of greater seniority. A tip of major significance obviously had already changed hands. When the newcomer sat down and dismissed the *maître d'* with a casual gesture he bowed with cringing obsequiousness before hurrying away to give an order to a waiter. The newcomer confidently looked around and then looked at Al as if to say that everyone in the room was now permitted to proceed.

"Your champagne, Mr. Perino," a waiter said, smoothing an imaginary wrinkle from the tablecloth.

Mr. Perino grunted in acknowledgment. He puffed ineffectually at his cigar, which had gone out. The waiter, like a conjuror, produced a match that was magically already alight. Mr. Perino waved it aside and lit the cigar with a large, plain gold lighter.

"Tell Al Dexter I want to talk to him," he said.

"Yes, Mr. Perino."

"There's no rush," Mr. Perino added tolerantly. "Tell him that when he's finished the set is soon enough."

"Yes, Mr. Perino. Thank you, sir."

Though the table was so close that Al, without leaving the piano-stool, could have reached over and shaken Mr. Perino's hand, the waiter walked as if on a diplomatic mission to the back of the stand and delivered the message there. Dick Kilian passed it to Al and Al passed back his reply.

The number they were still playing was really the last one of the set but Al got the band to play another, to assert his right to delay his response to the summons. He did not like Mr. Perino's face. However, it had the unmistakable appearance of money and power, which, as Al knew only too well from earliest childhood, were one and the same thing.

"O.K., fellas," he said. "Take fifteen."

Lighting a cigarette on the way, he walked around to Mr. Perino.

"Good evening, Mr. Perino," he said. "You wanted to say something?"

"Sit down, Mr. Dexter," Mr. Perino said with a wide smile. "What are you drinking?"

"An orange juice, please," Al said, sitting opposite his host.

Without turning his head, Mr. Perino raised an arm and snapped the finger and thumb of a small, plump hand. The waiter immediately materialized, like a genie. Mr. Perino tersely made his wish known and the waiter went to make it come true.

"This is a nice room," Mr. Perino said blandly.

"Yes," Al said. "We like it."

"Nice crowd you got here."

"Yes."

"Is it like this every night?"

"People don't dress up quite so much on week-nights."

"But you always play to a full house?"

"Yes."

"That's nice. You have a nice band."

"Thank you."

"And Fran was right. You look real nice at the piano."

Gratified but slightly embarrassed, Al laughed.

"Thanks," he said. "Who's Fran?"

"Didn't you notice her? She said she was sitting right here. At the table by the piano. She 'phoned me. They kept the table for me."

"Oh, yes. I wondered what happened to her."

"Nothing happened to her. She just 'phoned me. That's all."

"I mean I wondered why she left like that. She made a request and left while we were playing it."

"Are you making a complaint?" Mr. Perino asked calmly, removing the cigar from his smile.

"No, of course not. I only wondered. She seemed to be enjoying our music and then she suddenly left. What's her name? I don't think I've seen her here before."

"Fran DiPaola. You haven't seen her here before on account of she hasn't been here before. She left suddenly because she suddenly got an idea. She gets a lot of ideas."

"Fran DiPaola.... Is she any relation to –"

"Right. Frank DiPaola's her father."

"Oh," Al said. Francis X. DiPaola was a celebrity. He was one of the best-known men in Chicago. The newspapers often ran stories about Frank (The Spray) DiPaola. It was not certain whether his nickname referred to the thoroughness of his technique with a Thompson submachine gun during the days when he was getting established in his chosen profession or to the small red rubber gadget whose nozzle he stuck in his nose during asthma attacks. Now he was one of Al Capone's senior henchmen, to whom important administrative duties were often delegated during his boss's visits to Florida.

"She's a very charming young lady," Mr Perino said emphatically.

"Yes, I'm sure she is," Al said politely. "She certainly looked it."

"She looks exactly like her late mother when she was young. Fran is the only child. Frank adores her."

"Yes," Al said, wondering what the conversation could be leading to. He couldn't think why but Mr. Perino's account of Frank DiPaola's devotion to his daughter seemed vaguely ominous. Al drank some orange juice. "She seemed to enjoy jazz."

"She's very musically orientated," Mr. Perino said. He sucked his cigar and the ash glowed red. He blew out a cloud of smoke. Al was interested to see how closely Mr. Perino's pursed lips resembled a dog's anus.

"Who's your manager?" Mr. Perino asked.

"My manager?" Al asked. "I don't have a manager."

"Who books you?"

"I don't really need a manager."

"Everybody in the entertainment business needs a manager."

"But I'm all set. Everything's fine."

"I'll be your manager," Mr. Perino said.

Al smiled uneasily.

"I appreciate your offer," he said. "But no thanks. I have a very good contract here."

"Ah, you see, a contract!" Mr. Perino said. "You'll need a manager to get you out of it, so you can move."

"I don't want to move. Why should I want to move?"

"I think you'll be moving. I'll only charge you thirty per cent. It's a bargain."

"I'm sorry, Mr. Perino," Al said curtly. Mr. Perino was strangely obtuse. Al forgot to be nervous about Mr. Perino's connections. "That's out of the question. I've never had a manager. I don't need one now. Why should I pay anyone a commission at this stage?"

"I don't have time to discuss the situation any further tonight," Mr. Perino said, standing and casually tossing a couple of high-denomination bills on the table. "Believe me, though, you need a manager. With me as your manager, you won't have anything to worry about. I'll be in touch Tuesday."

"Please don't bother," Al said. "I won't change my mind. The management here is perfectly satisfied. I don't have anything to worry about."

Mr. Perino's smile widened. He removed his cigar and slowly extinguished it by squashing it into the ash-tray.

"By Tuesday," he said, "you'll have something to worry about. I guarantee."

FORTY-TWO

On Monday morning, while he was still lying (alone) in bed in his apartment, considering the possibility of getting up to make the day's first cup of coffee, Al's telephone rang. He looked at his watch: nine-thirty – a hell of a time to call a nightclub musician, especially on a Monday, after all the exertions of the weekend. Al coughed to clear his throat.

"Yeah?" he said unwelcomingly.

"Mr. Dexter?" a woman asked.

"This is Al Dexter. Do you know what time it is?"

"I'm sorry, Mr. Dexter. Mr. Lombardi told me to be sure to call before you went out."

"*Sam* Lombardi?"

"Yes, Mr. Dexter. He – "

"He knows better than to call at a time like this."

Sam Lombardi was the executive secretary of the local office of the Musicians' Union. He had never previously telephoned Al at home.

"Mr. Lombardi will be here at ten-thirty. He said for you to come in and see him then."

"What about?"

"He didn't say. He just said for you to come in. He said don't be late, Mr. Dexter. He said it's important."

Irritated and apprehensive, Al shaved badly, nicking the difficult place immediately beneath the center of his nose. The cut was minimal but it spoiled the shave. His mood was improved only a little by dressing in a new Glen Urquhart plaid suit, gray and dark blue. Four years of increasing success in Chicago had enlarged and smartened his wardrobe. He put on a camel's hair coat and a dark-brown soft felt hat and went out. The December sky was the color of lead and there was a sharp Canadian wind that felt like snow. The wind chilled his face during the short walk from the blue awning of the apartment house to the coffee shop on the corner.

He sat at the counter and read the *Tribune* while he had scrambled eggs and black coffee for breakfast. There wasn't any news of importance. The only gang killing of the past twenty-four hours, noted in a brief report on page 6, was a routine execution in Little Sicily. Two unidentified gunmen had entered a barbershop while Rocky Amato reclined under a hot towel and had blasted his brains all over the mirror and basin. Al idly wondered what sort of irrational death-wish impelled so many gangsters to offer themselves as sitting targets by regularly and frequently patronising the same barbers. Then he turned the pages to the comic strips.

He rode in a black-and-white cab to the union office. He arrived on time. The receptionist asked him to take a seat. He sat and read *Variety* and smoked cigarettes. Sam Lombardi kept him waiting for nearly forty minutes. By the time the girl told Al to go in he was indignant and agitated.

"What's the idea, Sam?" he said as he went through the doorway to the inner office. "You have me waked up at dawn, I come hurrying over, and then you keep me waiting all this time – what's up?"

Sam Lombardi looked like a well-taken-care-of ward heeler. He was fat and flashy, with a card-sharp's blank face and shrewd eyes, sitting back in a swivel chair behind a large desk. He had the cold white light of the window behind him, giving him an advantage.

"Don't get your bowels in an uproar," he mildly chided Al. "Have a chair and listen. You're in trouble. I'm doing you a favor."

Al obediently sat down. What could be wrong? He had heard of all kinds of union hassles in the early days of the jazz musicians' migration from New Orleans to Chicago, ten years ago and more. The Chicago musicians had resented the Southerners and had succeeded at first in keeping them out of the union. But the invasion had done more good than harm; it had stimulated the public's appetite for jazz; soon there were more than enough jobs to go around, for all musicians with even rudimentary skill. Al had joined the union in Chicago without any difficulty, before he had looked for his first job there. He had never got involved in union politics; he had no ambition to gain any union office or to exert any influence on the union's policies and activities; he attended membership meetings only on the rare occasions when they were obligatory. He always paid his dues. So what could be the matter?

Sam seemed to be enjoying watch Al squirm. But Sam was not

one to waste words. He got to the point with brutal directness.

"It looks like you could lose your card," he said. He paused to let the idea sink in. It did not take long. Al looked aghast. If the local lifted his membership card it would be impossible for The Club Michigan to keep him on as the leader of The Sophisticates. The management's regard, if any, for the quality of his musicianship could not save him if he were discredited by the union. If the club tried to employ a scab musician there would certainly be pickets; the club's waiters and kitchen staff were all union labor, who would, of course, refuse to cross a picket line.

"I've paid my dues," Al said.

"Yes. Your record is clean in that respect. I checked it out. I could bring that fact to the attention of the disciplinary committee next time we meet, but I don't think that would do your case much good."

"My case? What case?"

"What does the name Joe Tulane mean to you?"

"Joe Tulane?" Al repeated, puzzled.

"Yes, Joe Tulane," Sam said impatiently. "I understand that someone called Joe Tulane played trumpet with your band during your recent recording session for Okeh."

"Oh, yes," Al said, smiling, "Joe Tulane. I'd forgotten him for a minute there. I know who you mean. He filled in on a couple of numbers the day Alex was unavailable."

"Six sides, to be exact?"

"Was it that many? Maybe."

"There's no maybe about it. And there's no maybe about Joe Tulane. There's no union man by that name. Is it possible his real name is Moses Decatur? And is that Moses Decatur the high yaller who usually plays with Louis Armstrong and Carroll Dickerson at the Savoy Ballroom? That's one of the best colored bands in town. That's a good job Moses Decatur has. It'd be tough if he lost it because of you. He's a man who does belong to the union. But he has an exclusive recording contract with Black Orchid."

"Who told you all that?"

"Never mind who told me all that. But those are the facts, aren't they? There's no use arguing. I have someone who's willing to swear to them. He's one of your men, and he was there."

Al's mind quickly flicked through a memory-bank card-index of the names of the members of the band, all good friends of his, or so he believed. It was inconceivable that any of them would have betrayed him – unless, perhaps, one of them had succumbed to some unbearable secret coercive pressure.

"Surely you aren't going to make a case out of a little thing like that, are you?" Al said, with a feeble conciliatory smile.

"We surely are."

"But, Sam! It happens all the time. You know that. It's common knowledge. Men under contract to one record company often record under phoney names for another company. Sometimes, early in their careers, musicians get stuck with very unfair contracts that pay peanuts. The union turns a blind eye."

"You admit that Moses Decatur played trumpet for you during your Okeh session last month, don't you?"

"I didn't say I admitted it. But what if he did? What if he was doing me a favor?"

"That was strictly un-kosher, and you know it. If a record company notifies us that a member of the union has cheated on his contract like that, we are obliged to take action."

"Okeh didn't complain, did they? The studio was booked. If we hadn't had a second trumpet we'd have had to cancel. It was in Okeh's interest for us to have – to have a substitute. Black Orchid didn't complain, did they? How would they have known anything about it?"

"All I'm saying at this time is that this breach of contract has been brought to our attention."

"And you're seriously considering lifting my card?"

Al could feel sweat trickling down from his armpits.

"Yours and Moses Decatur's."

"Oh, Sam, for Christ's sake! You wouldn't have to take *his*! I was responsible for that band."

Sam chuckled.

"There's no need for you to be a hero, Al," he said. "This is a friendly little advisory conference we're having here, just between you and I. What I really meant was: according to the book. I should bring this infraction before the disciplinary committee. The matter has not yet been formally listed on our agenda. I said I was doing you a favor. I'm warning you."

"What do you want me to do, Sam? You want me to make a donation to your favorite charity or something?"

Sam looked stern.

"That was a very foolish thing to suggest," he said piously. "Let's pretend you didn't say it."

"I was only kidding," Al said. It was hard to believe that all the rumors about Sam Lombardi were untrue and that a man with a face like his could not be bribed. "What do you really want me to do?"

"All you have to do is remember this conversation the next time you see Vince Perino."

FORTY-THREE

The next morning was Tuesday and Mr. Perino's guaranteed prophecy proved to be valid : Al did have something to worry about. He was worrying about it, wearing his innocent white terry-cloth bathrobe, sitting in his buttercup-yellow kitchenette, drinking black coffee and smoking a cigarette, when the telephone jangled like a fire alarm. The bell seemed to be connected directly with the innermost, most sensitive wiring of his central nervous system. He hurried to the telephone.

"Mr. Perino would like to see you in his office at twelve noon," a woman said.

"Where's his office?" Al asked.

"Where's Mr. Perino's *office*?" she said, as though he had asked her for the location of City Hall. "The Hawthorne Inn. Do you know where that is?"

"Yes," Al said in a dull voice of resignation. "I know where that is. I'll be there at twelve."

The Hawthorne Inn was the Capone syndicate's Cicero headquarters. Cicero, just west of the city's limits, was where Al Capone had his heaviest concentration of gambling establishments, nightclubs and saloons, next to his brothels in Stickney.

Al Dexter's taxi arrived at the hotel a few minutes before twelve. Steel shutters protected the windows and the front doors of the building. Inside the main entrance, a guard in plain clothes requested Al to raise his arms and thoroughly frisked him, quickly patting him all over, even between his legs right up to the crotch.

A woman at a reception desk sent Al into Mr. Perino's office without delay.

Mr. Perino's dark-gray suit, with a gold watch-chain looped from pocket to pocket across the convexity of his waistcoat; his black-and-gray-striped silk tie, his stiff white collar and the modestly displayed three white apexes of the folded handkerchief in his breast pocket; the gold-rimmed glasses through which he gravely scrutinized the papers on his desk; the dark-blue Persian rug on the parquet floor, the oak-panelled walls, the rows of leather-bound reference books, the eighteenth-century English hunting prints, the dark-brown leather-upholstered armchairs and the log fire in a fireplace of marble like aged Gorgonzola gave Al the impression that he had entered the presence of a senior officer of an exceptionally prosperous institution of high finance. And so, of course, Al had.

Mr. Perino looked up, removing his glasses, and his thick, red lips stretched and parted in a smile.

"Al Dexter!" he exclaimed. "How nice! Please sit down – no, not that chair; this other one's more comfortable. I was going to order some coffee. You'll join me, won't you?"

Mr. Perino's manner was so fulsomely gracious that Al was taken aback. Was this the irony of a sadist? Some sort of cat-and-mouse game?

"Perhaps a nice shot in the coffee?" Mr. Perino suggested. "You must be cold. It's as cold as a witch's tit out there."

That last sentence sounded genuine enough, Al thought, but he remained wary.

"No, thank you, Mr. Perino," he said.

"O.K., no coffee. But call me Vince."

"Let's get down to brass tacks," Al said grimly. "As you undoubtedly know, I saw Sam Lombardi yesterday. I don't know how you got to him – I can guess – but he made it very clear you have me over a barrel. So, here I am. You want to be my manager? With all this?" Al's gesture took in all the opulence of the room. "That's a laugh. There isn't much money involved with The Sophisticates, even if you took a hundred per cent of what I make. You – "

"Take it easy, Al. Relax. Wait till I tell you the deal I have for you. It's nothing but good news."

"I don't want a deal. I'm happy the way things are."

"Now you're being unrealistic, Al," Vince said with a hint of severity. "Things never stay the same. But let's talk over lunch. I've arranged a nice little lunch in the executives' dining room. I hope Frank will be able to eat with us."

Vince stood up and arranged the papers in a neat pile on his blotter and smiled. Aware that he had no choice, Al followed him out of the room, along a softly carpeted corridor, and into a dining room with scarlet-brocade-covered walls and a long mahogany table with three places set at one end. A white-jacketed steward looked in from the pantry.

"We'll wait for Mr. DiPaola," Vince told him. "Bring Mr. Dexter and me some wine."

Vince sat at the right-hand side of the head of the table and indicated that Al should sit opposite. The steward poured foaming Asti Spumante into large champagne glasses with gold rims.

"Your good health," Vince said.

"Yeah, sure," Al said ruefully.

The wine was very cold and rather sweet.

"First of all," Vince said, "let me tell you you're going to make a lot more money. Frank does everything with class."

"Why don't you simply lay it on the line?"

"All right. Why not? It's this: Frank's opening a new club, The Palermo, a restaurant-cabaret. It's kind of a twenty-first birthday present for Fran. As I told you, she's very interested in music. She's been looking around town for a suitable music director. She caught your act the other night. She liked your style. She wants you at the club. So naturally Frank wants you. So naturally you're going to be there. That means you'll come under my management. And that's really all there is to it. The club opens next week."

Al laughed.

"That's very flattering, I suppose," he said. "But that isn't the way the music business works."

"Yes, it is," Vince assured him.

"Well, it's not the way I work. I have a contract with The Club Michigan. I can't pull the band out just like that. Apart from the ethics of it, think of my reputation. Even if I didn't have a contract, there's the band to consider. Maybe they wouldn't want to make the move."

"Let me put your mind at ease," Vince said, with a smile that was meant to be charming. "First, the contract. You can forget about the contract. I've already taken care of that. Second, the band. The band won't be coming with you. We've already hired a band. We only want you. And don't worry about our piano player; we've got rid of him. Fran's very pleased about the whole deal. I ran a quick check on you already, and Frank is happy. That makes me happy. So, be happy, Al. You're in."

Vince reached forward with his foot and pressed a bell push beneath the table. The steward came and refilled the glasses.

"What do you mean, you ran a check on me?" Al asked.

"Security. Frank doesn't take any chances where his daughter's concerned. I got the police department to work on it and we have our private sources. They're fast. I just checked on your history a little. You've done well since you hit town, and no record, nothing messy. Very nice family background – Frank liked that. We'll keep quiet about your jobs in New Orleans. Let's keep that information between you and I. I don't want to spoil everything."

"What do you know about my family?"

"Be nice, Al," Vince said soothingly. "I don't like it when people talk to me in that tone of voice."

"I'm sorry. I wondered how you could find out about my family."

"Moses Decatur was very cooperative."

"Moses! What did he tell you?"

"Enough. All I wanted to know. He said nothing but good things, and I had them checked, and they were right. He was only trying to help you." Vince chuckled smugly. "He was real talkative when I explained if he didn't help you might take a dive into Lake Michigan."

"Sam threatened to lift Moses' union card."

"Yes, that's right," Vince said approvingly.

"He won't do that, will he?"

"Take it easy, Al. No, I don't see any reason he should have to do that. What would he have to do that for now? You and I have come to an agreement, haven't we? Certainly we have. Everything's working out to everyone's satisfaction."

"How did you contact Moses? How did you know he helped out with the Okeh recording session? Did one of my musicians talk?"

Vince smiled indulgently. It was the smile of a man who takes pride from the skillful practice of his craft.

"Doesn't everyone talk?" he said. "Everybody talks if it's better for them to talk. Everyone has a weakness. Everyone has something to hide. It's easy enough to find, if you know how and you try hard enough. But enough shop talk. Here comes Frank. He doesn't like shop talk at the table. It upsets his digestion."

Frank DiPaola was unusually small and fragile for a master gangster. His head was completely bald. He, too, was wearing the conservative clothes of a banker. He had a Florida sun-tan, deep brown with pink blotches on top of his head and on the backs of his hands, and impenetrably black sunglasses. He was obliged to attend frequent business conferences at Palm Island.

"Mr. Dexter," he said, enthusiastically hobbling across the room with his bony right hand extended. "You have made my Fran a very happy girl."

Mr. DiPaola took his place at the head of the table. He did not remove his sunglasses. When he said grace, Vince respectfully bowed his head a few inches but kept his eyes open. He was bowing to Mr. DiPaola, rather than to any authority whose power in Chicago was less clearly manifest than Mr. DiPaola's, and Vince's eyes remained open for Mr. DiPaola's sake. Grace was very nice but it was always better to be safe than sorry.

Vince and Al lunched on asparagus tips and prosciutto and Fettucine Alfredo and salad and red, white and green spumoni. Mr. DiPaola was always meticulous in observance of his allegiances. For lunch, he himself had a bowl of cottage cheese, garnished with grated carrot and raisins, and a glass of buttermilk. When he had finished, he carefully wiped his thin, pale lips with his napkin, produced a small medicine bottle from an inner pocket, poured a teaspoonful of white liquid into a glass of water, drank it, grimaced and shuddered, and the audience was over.

"Mr. Dexter," he said, as they walked slowly toward the door, "don't let me forget to give you the name of my stockbroker. He's a genius, and completely reliable."

FORTY-FOUR

Jazz musicians could never reasonably expect regard for friendship to hold a man back when he was offered an opportunity to move to a better job. A better job was any job that paid better. Questions of musical preference, affinity and ability, of course, always had to take second place to financial considerations. Paul Whiteman, the preposterously self-styled "King of Jazz", the proprietor of the biggest, most vulgarly commercial, unjazziest jazz orchestra of the era, was easily able to buy the aesthetically fastidious Bix Beiderbecke. Although well aware that at least one of The Sophisticates knew better, Al told his colleagues he was leaving them for the only forgivable reason, to make more money. To have said that he was leaving for the sake of playing better music, though obviously untrue, would have hurt his friends' feelings. To have admitted that he was leaving under duress, having been threatened by blackmailers and murderers, would have hurt his own feelings. He was too ashamed to discuss the matter with Moses. Of all people, Moses must have understood the situation best; for that very reason, Al stayed away from him.

He made much more money and he found that there were some considerable fringe benefits. The day he reported to The Palermo, in The Loop, for the first rehearsal of his new band, it became apparent that Mr. DiPaolo had issued instructions that Al was to enjoy privileged status. For example, when he asked for his check after lunch in the restaurant, the head waiter came over and said there wasn't one.

"Mr. DiPaolo said you have anything you want, only to sign, Mr. Dexter," he explained. "The osso buco – it was all right? You like it?"

"Yes, it was fine. What's the system then? Do I have a weekly account or what?"

"No, not at all, Mr. Dexter. Only sign. The veal was tender?"

"Very tender."

"Not too much garlic for you?"

"No. Perfect."

"Thank you, Mr. Dexter. If you like the cuisine and the service, please mention to Mr. DiPaolo. And if there's any special dishes you wish, only tell me and I'll arrange for you."

Fran was in a state of high excitement. Her brown eyes sparkled and her cheeks were pink as she gave urgent, complicated commands and countermands to the decorators, the lighting men, the sound men, the waiting staff and the rest of them, in preparation for the opening of the nightclub. She was all over the place and frantically busy but obviously delighted with the way things were taking shape. She was not too busy to talk to Al about the music. As he came away from the stand at the end of the rehearsal and the musicians dispersed, she brightly accosted him.

"Wonderful, Mr. Dexter!" she said. "You had them right in the palm of your hand."

"I did? Thanks. We were just feeling around to find out what we can do. I think we'll be all right."

"Of course you will! You'll be much better than all right. We'll have the best band in Chicago! I'd like to make some suggestions that will help. I have a minor carpet problem in the powder room, then let's have a conference. Would you order me some coffee in the bar?"

Al complied. Fran soon came and sat with him.

"Everything's going to be wonderful!" she said. "I can hardly wait. I *love* the way you play the piano!"

"Thank you very much."

"There's only one thing."

"What's that?"

"You don't mind if I criticize, do you?"

"No, of course not. Comments are always welcome," he lied.

"Well, I want you to change your style a little."

"Oh? In what way?"

"It would be better if you played *sweeter*."

"I play jazz," Al said.

"And it's great fun," Fran kindly conceded. "You're very good at it. I could understand how The Sophisticates appealed to the young college crowd that The Club Michigan caters to. But really, Mr. Dexter, sophisticated was one thing the band wasn't. I want to cater to the truly sophisticated Chicagoans. That means you must give them sophisticated *romance*. The minute I saw you, the way you wore your tux, I knew you could do it. That's what I hired you for. I want you to play less old-style jazz, more up-to-date ballads."

Al remained calm. He felt sure there must be a misunderstanding over terminology.

"On Saturday night you requested 'Creole Love Call'," he reminded her. "That's jazz."

"It was a romantic ballad," she said.

"It's a beautiful melody."

"That's what I mean. Play more tunes like that."

"They aren't so easy to come by," Al said with a smile. She was pretty. Even her frown was pretty. He wanted to help her. But he hoped she wasn't going to be a nuisance. Perhaps he should make it quite clear from the start that she could not interfere with the way he ran the band. "I'll do my best," he said. "I'll keep what you say in mind."

The lines of Fran's frown deepened, especially the vertical lines between her fine black eyebrows. She looked determined.

"I'm not a child," she said. "I know exactly what I want and I'm going to get it. What's his name, the man who composed 'Creole Love Call'?"

"Duke Ellington."

"Yes. Give him a call. Order a batch of ballads like 'Creole Love Call'. Tell him you're calling for Mr. Francis X. DiPaola of Chicago. Tell Mr. Ellington whatever his usual rates are we'll pay double. And tell him to hurry."

Al suddenly felt tired. He didn't feel like arguing.

"Yes, Miss DiPaola," he said.

She smiled. She had a lovely smile.

"As we're going to be working closely together," she said, "I think we should use first names. Al."

"Yes, Fran."

He asked the doorman to get him a taxi.

"Mr. DiPaola said for me to order you a limousine," the doorman said. "I'll call your chauffeur."

FORTY-FIVE

Chicago, 1929

January is usually a quiet month in nightclubs; but the economy was exceptionally buoyant, particularly in Chicago and most of all in The Palermo.

Frank DiPaola, operating unobtrusively behind the scenes, was largely responsible for his daughter's great success as a nightclub hostess. The Palermo was luxurious, the food and drink were excellent, the band was big and powerful and smooth, and, of course, everything was extremely expensive. Other nightclubs offered the same basic amenities, at equally obviously extreme expense. But The Palermo offered more. Frank DiPaola had friends in high places on the local newspapers and in the local radio stations. The Palermo became famous for being famous. To dine at a choice table of the front rank beside the dance-floor was a sure way of being noticed by the leg-men of Chicago's most distinguished and influential gossip columnists. The new rich, many of whom were millionaires many times over, at least on paper, jostled each other for primacy at the *maître d'hôtel's* red-velvet-covered rope and signalled for attention like rival bidders at a highly competitive auction. The Palermo was the hottest box in town.

Al derived little enjoyment from the music his band was required to play, but he enjoyed the illusion of success. His music might not be growing, but his musical reputation was – his reputation as a musician, the good-looking young man who led the band at The Palermo.

Frank DiPaola candidly confessed he was shocked when he learned from Al where he was living.

"You can't live in a crummy dump downtown," Mr. DiPaola protested. "What if *that* got in the papers? It's part of my philosophy: *you are your address*, the same as you're the clothing you wear and the car you ride in."

He persuaded Al to move to a penthouse suite at the top of a new twenty-storey apartment house on Lake Shore Drive. DiPaola Associates, Inc., a company that looked after many of Mr. DiPaola's legitimate business interests, was able to provide this superior accommodation at favorable terms without the formality of a lease.

"Who knows?" Mr. DiPaola said. "Maybe you'll only want it temporary. Maybe one day soon you'll be looking to secure something more substantial. A town house, maybe, and a weekend place in the country."

Suggestions of this sort caused Al to suspect that the ageing gangster might be grooming him for a role beyond the bandstand. The thought of such a possibility made Al somewhat nervous.

But Fran was awful cute. And she was so appreciative.

"When I see everyone clapping like mad, you make me feel so *proud* of you," she said, on more than one occasion.

He somehow got into the habit of taking Fran out on Monday evenings, when the club was closed. Away from the smart set, as she called her customers, she seemed even younger than she was. She wore red angora ear-muffs, embroidered woollen gloves, a shaggy raccoon coat, knee-length socks and white buckskin shoes with red rubber soles. Her idea of a perfect date was skating or bowling, cheeseburgers and chocolate malteds, and the movies, preferably a tragic love story or a custard-pie comedy. After that she liked to go on to a speakeasy where there were soft lights and sweet music, for a couple of nightcaps and a discussion of the film they had just seen.

After one tubercular heroine's protracted deathbed valedictory, Fran said:

"You don't look twenty-eight, Al. Anyway, twenty-eight isn't so old these days."

The first time Al kissed her, in the back of the limousine on the way back to her father's house, she surprised him by the passion of her response. She opened her lips and slipped the tip of her tongue into his mouth. There was a lot of squirming and panting and Al was encouraged to suggest that they should leave the limo and go back to his apartment.

"I'm sorry, Al, darling," she said, sitting up straight and moving away and fastening her coat and patting his cheek. "Nothing doing. I'm saving all that till I'm married."

So much for Flaming Youth in The Jazz Age, he thought. He took her to her front door and returned immediately to the waiting limousine, suffering from an ache he had not experienced since adolescence.

In his sumptuous, empty apartment, he fixed himself a strong sedative bourbon and soda, lit a cigarette and sat at his rented baby-grand Bechstein. He played the blues in the defiantly up-beat manner of Earl Hines.

The next day he awoke with a hangover. He drank a Bromo Seltzer and swore that he would not answer the telephone. Fran had got into the habit of calling him late every morning to discuss their plans for the day.

The telephone rang at eleven-thirty. He let it ring. After nearly half a minute, it stopped ringing. After a few seconds, it started ringing again. He picked it up.

"Hi, sugar!" Fran said. "Did I catch you in the tub?"

"No, you didn't."

"Oh-oh – grouchy! You're not embarrassed, are you?"

"No, I'm not embarrassed. Why should I be?"

"Well, you shouldn't be. There's no need to be. I know that's how men are built."

He was embarrassed.

"Al? Can you hear me?"

"Yes, I can hear you."

"I thought we'd been cut off. There's something funny about your 'phone this morning. Or something funny about you."

"There's nothing funny about me."

"I wish you didn't sound so *severe*. It's a beautiful, bright, sunny, cold February day. . . . Al!"

"Yes, O.K., I got that. Look, Fran. I have to hang up. There's someone at the door. I'll see you at the club."

"Don't you *dare* hang up! There's nobody at the door. And if there is, he can wait. Or she. Have you got a she waiting at your door, Al?"

"Fran, I'm not in a joking mood. I had a couple of highballs when I got home last night and I have a head."

"Oh, Al! I'm sorry. Did I drive you to drink? If it makes you feel any better, I couldn't get to sleep for just *hours*. I wanted you, too, you know. I, too, am human."

He uttered a hollow laugh.

"That's better!" Fran said, "Al, I have a terrific, overpowering desire for shish kebab. You know, on flaming swords and every-thing. So you have to take me to The Pump Room for lunch. Right?"

"I must?"

"Yes, you positively must. Because, one, I'm hungry; two, I love you; and, three – three, I love you some more. So how about one o'clock?"

There seemed to be a real and present danger of girlish cajolery. He had witnessed a coaxing of her father. Fran had even resorted to caressing his brown, bald pate; and his sickly, simpering smile had been awful to behold.

Al met her at The Pump Room.

The absurdly costumed waiters made an absurd production out of the service, but the shish kebab was very good. A middle-aged woman in an ermine cape came over to their table and asked Al to autograph her menu. He signed it. She thanked him. He thanked her. There were smiles.

"There, you see," Fran said, as though the incident had proved her right about something.

"I suppose I should thank you for that honor," he said, trying ineffectually to cover up his gratification.

After lunch, they walked arm-in-arm for a few blocks. Fran had been right about the weather. It was beautiful. The sky was clear, dark blue and the edges of the skyscrapers looked sharp.

Fran happily squeezed his arm and began singing, in a high, inaccurate voice:

"Oh-oh, say can you see, by the dawn's early light?"

It is a difficult song for the best of singers. Fran quickly foundered in high-spirited laughter and Al waved for a taxi.

He opened the taxi door for her. When she was sitting in it, he leaned in and said:

"I'll get another one for me. I'll see you later at the club."

"No, Al. You *must* take me home. I'm terribly tight. Really."

In the taxi, she snuggled close to him.

"Al, it was a lovely lunch. I loved it. I loved it when that woman asked for your autograph. You're a celebrity!"

She wasn't terribly tight. She was only a little bit tight. She had just wanted to make him stay with her longer. He was pleased.

"Al," she said. Her face was very near his

"Yes?"

"Papa insists on giving me a big, big wedding. In the Cathedral.

He has connections with the Church. There'll be hundreds of people. The cardinal, a couple of monsignors. Everyone."

"Oh, yes?"

"If Papa asks you anything about your religion, for God's sake don't double-cross me."

"How could I do that? In what way?"

Fran giggled.

"Well, I said you go to mass every Sunday, so don't tell him you're some strange sort of holy roller or something. Even if you are."

Al was in his dressing room at The Palermo between sets that evening when the telephone rang.

"Al Dexter," Al said.

"Hello, Al. This is Moses. How's everything?"

"Great. I've been meaning to get in touch. How's everything with you?"

"I'm down at The Paradise. We got a good group."

"Well, that's great. I certainly would like to see you."

"That's what I called about. Bessie's in town."

"Bessie Smith?"

"Is there another Bessie?"

"I guess not. How is she? I heard she's been hitting the bottle pretty hard."

"Bessie is Bessie. She still has the most powerful voice in the world. She's staying in the usual place, with Jimmy Yancey."

"The boogie woogie man."

"Yeah, Jimmy Yancey. We're having a party tonight – you know, nothing fancy. A few thousand drinks, a few numbers, a few laughs. We'd like you to drop by. Fatha Hines will probably make it."

"Funny, I was thinking about him last night."

"Well, Al, what do you say? Bring a jug. We'll expect you. Let me give you the address – "

"I wish I could, Mo. I really do. But I'm working."

"Sure you're working. I know you're working. I'm talking about after."

"We go on and on and on, Mo. Gee, Mo, I sure am sorry. It'd be great to see you. We must get together some time, real soon."

FORTY-SIX

A few evenings later, in the first week of February, Fran and Al were dining at their usual corner table at The Palermo. She had hired a trio to fill in between the band's first and second sets, so that Al was free every evening for a leisurely dinner with her, though "free" was possibly not the word he might have used to describe his state. The longer his engagement at the club continued, the less free he felt.

He recognized that the conditions of his employment could hardly have been any better financially. His pay was lavish, and Mr. DiPaola's own stockbroker, as a special favor, had planned and enacted for Al a program of investment in high-yield shares in companies known to Mr. DiPaola personally. The investments tied up a rather large percentage of Al's income, which was already reduced by Vince Perino's thirty per cent. But Al did not need much money for his current expenses; his rent was low, his transportation and most of his meals were complimentary, and his long hours at the club did not leave much time for outside activities. As Mr. DiPaola said, "It'd be a crime to leave surplus cash lay idle in the bank."

Al was not unappreciative of his material good fortune, but sometimes he could not help wishing that his employer was less possessive, less concerned with everything he did and even with everything he thought.

He looked at her, in her night-time black silk, busily dissecting a Dover sole. She was very pretty. Her downcast eyelashes looked innocent.

Feeling his appraisal, she looked up and smiled.

"What?" she asked.

"Nothing," he said.

"You looked as if you were going to say something."

"No, I was only looking at you."

"Is there anything wrong with your lobster imperial?"

"No. I'm not very hungry."

"I thought you liked lobster."

"I do. It's very good."

He loaded his fork and showed it to her and put it in his mouth to show goodwill.

"Are you happy about the band?" she asked.

"What do you mean?"

"Are you *satisfied* with it?"

"It's very smooth."

"That isn't enough for you, is it?"

"The customers like it."

"I have a feeling you're bored."

"Me? Bored?" he said with an unconvincing laugh. "Why should I be bored?"

"I watch your face when you're playing."

"I can't help my face."

"It's a lovely face, but bored."

The waiter brought them peaches and then coffee.

"I have an idea to cure your boredom," she said.

"I said I'm not bored. But what is it?"

"There isn't time now. You've got to get back for the second set."

"Is it an idea that takes a long time to tell about?"

"The best thing would be to go to your place, after we close."

"To *my* place? What about your father?"

"My father's out of town till tomorrow afternoon."

"That sounds like a good cure," Al said.

The rest of the night's work seemed long.

At last they reached his apartment. He unlocked the door and led the way in and switched on some discreet indirect lighting. He took her coat and draped it over the back of a chair and moved back to her with his arms outstretched.

"No," she said, evading his grasp. "Please fix us a nightcap."

Al restrained himself. After waiting all these weeks, he must be patient. Perhaps she was nervous. He went to his Hawaiian bar, made of yellow bamboo and thatch.

"Bourbon O.K.?" he said, getting an ice-tray from the refrigerator.

"Sure. Do you want to hear my idea?"

He nodded and smiled.

"Well," she said, "I think it would be good for you – and good for The Palermo – if we arranged a radio show. From the club, thirty minutes, once a week. Local at first; then, when it's a success, we can go network. And you should make some records. Network radio and records are the only ways for a band to win national renown. And that's what we want, isn't it?"

"That's the idea?"

"That isn't all," Fran said. She was saving the best part till last. "You're right about the band; it *is* very smooth; but I think you'll agree a band has to have an extra something for radio. You know what it needs?"

"We came over here to talk about the band?"

"The band needs a vocalist," she said.

This suggestion distracted him from his earlier expectations.

"I had a vocalist in my last band," he said. "He was quite funny in his way."

"I'm not talking about anything like that. I'm talking about a girl vocalist."

"What girl vocalist?"

Fran beamed.

"Me," she said.

"You!"

"Yes, me. Go sit at that piano I got you. I'm going to sing you something." She opened her handbag and gave him a folded sheet of music. "Play this."

So at four-twenty in the morning, heavy with fatigue and disappointment, Al played "Tea For Two". Fran sang the familiar words to a tune of her own devising that she seemed to make up as she went along.

She was awful.

FORTY-SEVEN

You can tell people, without much danger of offending them, that they are unsuited to diving off the cliffs at Acapulco or performing a surgical operation on the brain (unless, of course, they happen to be Mexican-Indian professional divers or brain surgeons); but there must be very few people, if any, who are prepared to acknowledge that they have no sense of humor or that they are tone-deaf.

The evening after the pre-dawn surprise audition, Fran persisted in presenting to Al her arguments in favor of her singing with the band. It was clearly apparent that all of them, in essence, were based on the fact that she *wanted* to sing with the band. In the circumstances, this was a fact that could not be disregarded, let alone dismissed; it was as massive and unoverturnable as the Great Pyramid of Gizeh.

Al did his best, for many hours, as diplomatically as he was able, to persuade Fran to change her mind. However, her mind was not something she was accustomed to changing once it was made up. Twenty-one years of being her father's daughter had invested her most casual whim with the authority of an imperial fiat, and her wish to sing with the band was much more than a casual whim.

"It's hard work, singing with a band," Al pointed out. "The public thinks that any good-looking girl can just get up there and smile and the music somehow takes care of itself. It doesn't."

"I'm not the public," she said. "I know there's a lot of work involved. I'm willing to work."

"All right. Why don't you go to a voice teacher? Learn about music. Learn how to sing. Give it a few months. Then see how you feel."

"You aren't telling me that all the popular band singers had conservatory training, are you?"

"No," he admitted cautiously. "A lot of them would sing a lot better if they had."

"Think of the jazz singers you like best," Fran said. She spoke in the sweetly modulated voice of rational civilized discourse.

"There are some naturals," he conceded.

She looked wide-eyed and waited for a compliment but none was forthcoming.

"You're not really *ready*," he said, hoping that if he could keep her off the stand for even a few weeks she might lose interest in the idea.

"I'm not insisting on broadcasting right away," she said. "To begin with, I'll only sing with the band for our club audience. I don't see how you could possibly object to that. You don't, do you?"

"I don't *object*," he said uncomfortably. He wished he could think of a gentler word that might appease her. "It's really that I'm *concerned*. I'm concerned about you, and I'm concerned about the band. I wouldn't want you to find you'd taken on more than you could handle. Everything feels very different when you're up there behind the microphone. It could be a painful experience. Music is highly technical. Wanting to make music is part of it, but wanting to isn't nearly enough."

"Thanks for telling me. But you needn't be all that concerned. I don't mind taking a risk, if there is one, which I doubt. Don't you have faith in me?"

"It isn't a matter of *faith*," Al said, as if splitting the finest of hairs.

"Well, what the hell is it a matter of?" Fran demanded. "Stop beating around the bush. Let's have it."

"You want my honest opinion?"

He still naively believed that there were times when people recognized the benefit of hearing the worst.

"Certainly I do," she said. "What else?"

"O.K., Fran. I hate to tell you this. But I think you should know." He hesitated.

"Spill it."

"Look, it's not your fault, Fran. Some people are born with perfect pitch. They're the fortunate few – or unfortunate sometimes; it depends on your point of view. Some others, with training and experience, learn to distinguish differences in musical pitch."

"Yes?"

"And then there are others who can never learn. They're tone-deaf. It's nothing to be ashamed of. It's no worse than being color-blind. Fran, you're tone-deaf."

There was no tearful appeal against his judgment. There was no temper tantrum. She spoke quite calmly.

"You arrogant son of a bitch," she said, and left him sitting at the table. He was sorry if he had hurt her feelings, but he was glad to have brought out into the open the reason she could not reasonably expect to sing with the band. He had made enough compromises; being at The Palermo had been a compromise from the word go; he had to draw the line somewhere.

There was no sign of Fran while he was playing the last set. For the first time for six weeks, there was no sign of her when the night's music was over. Poor Fran, he thought. He hoped she wasn't too upset. He felt sure she would feel better in the morning.

He was wearing pajamas and slippers when his doorbell rang. He smiled and thought, poor Fran. She shouldn't have bothered to come all this way at such an hour. But he was glad she had. He put his mug of cocoa on the kitchen table. As he was approaching the door, the bell rang again.

"O.K., O.K.," he said. "I'm coming."

He opened the door.

Two large men stood there. They were wearing the traditional black snap-brims and black topcoats with the collars up. One of them reminded Al of the guard who had frisked him at the entrance of the Hawthorne Inn; but the type was not unusual. The other one did the talking. He smiled with all the cordiality of a barracuda.

"Hello, Mr. Dexter. Hope we're not interrupting anything."

"No, you're not."

He spoke with more certainty than he felt.

"We want to talk to you a minute."

"I'm going to bed."

"I said we want to talk to you a minute, Mr. Dexter."

If they knew his name and where he lived, they must be Frank DiPaola's employees. Al reasoned; and, if they were, there was nothing to worry about.

"And I said I'm going to bed," he said. "It's late. What do you want?"

With a look of mock dismay, the spokesman turned to his companion and said:

"That don't sound like that famous Southern hospitality, does it, Tony?"

Tony frowned unhappily, and shook his head.

"No, Maxie."

Maxie showed his teeth in another barracuda smile.

"Tony agrees with me, so that makes it a majority. We don't think you're being very hospitable. I mean, I don't think *you-all* are being very hospitable," he added in a burlesque Southern drawl. In his own Chicago voice he tersely suggested: "Why don't you invite us in for a drink?"

They had to be DiPaola men, Al decided. They didn't seem drunk. They might be high on something else.

"Who are you?" he asked.

"We're music-lovers. Aren't we, Tony?"

"Yes, Maxie."

Al made a fast move to slam the door shut. He did not move as fast as one of Maxie's large, pointed black shoes.

"That's not only not very hospitable, Mr. Dexter," Maxie complained. "That's rude."

Tony thereupon abruptly pushed the door very hard and the two men entered the apartment. They pushed past Al and he followed them into the living room. Maxie looked around.

"Tony, the door. Mr. Dexter forgot to lock it."

Tony shut and bolted the door.

"Look, Tony!" Maxie exclaimed in a voice of simulated delight. "A piano! Isn't that wonderful? You're a lucky man, Mr. Dexter, to be able to play the piano."

Al was afraid. He had read somewhere that you must always look dangerous animals in the eye and never let them know of your fear. He imagined that the same advice applied to hoods. He tried to seem quite normally relaxed.

"Let's have a drink then," he said. "But do you mind if we make it short? I've had a long night at The Palermo – " he emphasized the name hopefully – "and I'm playing tomorrow. I have to get some sleep."

Maxie smiled.

"That's better. I'll have a large brandy and ice. Is that what you want, Tony?"

"Yes, Maxie."

"Two large brandies and ice," Maxie said.

Al went behind the bar. He poured their drinks and a bourbon and soda for himself. His hand was trembling.

"Nice place you have here," Maxie said sociably, as he accepted his drink. "That must be a good job, playing piano at The Palermo."

"Yes," Al said. "Now, would you please tell me what you want?"

"Yeah, sure," Maxie said. He raised his glass. "Here's looking at you, Tony. And you, too, Mr. Dexter." Maxie took a long gulp and sighed appreciatively. "Five-star."

"Yes, Maxie," Tony said. "Five-star."

Al looked at them, and they looked at him.

"Why don't you play something for us?" Maxie asked Al.

"Now?" Al asked stupidly.

"Yes, now. It would be a shame not to hear you play while we have the opportunity."

Al could tell that Maxie's request was to be complied with.

Al sat at the piano and opened it. Maxie brought his drink over and stood close to Al's left shoulder. Tony followed and stood at Al's right. Al could not feel their breath on the nape of his neck but he imagined it.

"What do you want to hear?" Al asked.

"Anything you like," Maxie said. "Play that music you got there on the piano."

Al played "Tea For Two".

"That's good," Maxie said. "Isn't it, Tony?"

"Yes, Maxie."

Maxie reached past Al and slammed the lid of the piano on Al's fingers – not very hard, not hard enough to break any bones, but quite hard enough to hurt.

"Jesus!" Al cried out.

Tony laughed.

Maxie grabbed Al's left arm.

"Get his right arm, Tony!" Maxie said.

"Yes, Maxie," Tony said.

Al could not move his hands from the keyboard.

Maxie raised the lid.

"A pianist has to be very careful of his fingers," Maxie solemnly remarked.

"You could have broken them," Al said.

"That's right, Mr. Dexter," Maxie agreed. "But I didn't. Of course, I still could break them. Or any other part of you, for that matter."

"I don't know what you think you're doing," Al said. "I don't keep much money here. You must be crazy."

Maxie gave Al a stinging slap on his left cheek.

"Watch it, Mr. Dexter! Nobody calls me crazy. You know, Tony, I don't think I like to keep company with musicians."

"Me neither," Tony said.

"Musicians stink."

Tony giggled.

"Yes, Maxie."

"So let's get this over with. Mr. Dexter, it's nothing complicated."

"What do you want?"

"All we want is your word. You have to give us your promise that you'll take on Miss DiPaola as the vocalist with your band and that you'll feature her prominently. Got that?"

For a moment, Al was too surprised to be frightened.

"Are you kidding?" he said.

"We are not kidding. Are we, Tony?"

"No, Maxie. We are not."

"This is ridiculous!" Al protested. "I can't believe it. What were Mr. DiPaola's exact words?"

"You're beginning to gripe me, Mr. Dexter," Maxie said. "The knife, Tony."

"Yes, Maxie!"

Tony reached into his hip pocket and produced a knife. He pressed a catch and an eight-inch switchblade emerged from the handle.

"Now, Mr. Dexter," Maxie said. "Here's the pitch. Give us your promise and everything's copacetic. We all finish our drinks. Tony and me take a powder and you can go bye-bye. Of course, if you break your promise, Tony and me can always make a return visit. The alternative: you refuse, and my colleague here cuts off one of your fingers. You keep refusing, he keeps cutting off fingers. You lose one or two fingers, maybe you have to change your piano style. You lose a lot of fingers – maybe you have to go into some other line of work. Any questions?"

214

"Mr. DiPaola wouldn't want anything like that to happen to me. You're bluffing!"

"Tut, tut, Mr. Dexter!" Maxie said. "You should never accuse a pro of bluffing. Tony doesn't hold with that kind of talk. Don't make Tony lose his temper. Tony has a sunny disposition, as they say, but when he gets mad he gets *mad*. Tony, convince him. Blood is a great convincer. Not a whole finger, Tony. Only a teentsy-weentsy slice. A sample."

"You wouldn't dare!" Al exclaimed, though now he knew that they would.

"The end of the right pinky," Maxie said.

"Sure, Maxie."

The blade was as sharp as a scalpel. For the first instant, Al hardly felt it. Then there was a quick, heavy crunch through the gristle and bone of the first joint of his little finger, and he felt a frightful fiery pain. The neat little fingernail and half an inch of finger lay apart from the rest of the finger, spurting scarlet blood over the white ivory.

"No!" he shouted.

He felt violated.

Maxie was perfectly calm.

"We're not kidding, Mr. Dexter. We're not bluffing. We *would* dare. Now you get another chance. Be sensible. You haven't lost much yet. You can go get this dressed in the nearest accident room and you won't be much worse off. Give the word."

Al promised that Fran could sing with the band.

Maxie and Tony finished their drinks and said goodnight and left.

Al went to a hospital and an intern took care of the injured finger.

"Ninety per cent of all accidents occur in the home," the young doctor said. "Anyway, you're lucky. It's a good, clean wound. Come in again tomorrow."

"Oh, you sad, stubborn darling!" Fran said when she saw the bandaged finger at the club the next evening. "That's terrible! And so unnecessary! I told them to try to avoid that sort of thing. Will you be all right to play by next weekend?"

FORTY-EIGHT

"Wouldn't you use your influence?" Al asked Frank DiPaola after a rehearsal with Fran and the band the next afternoon. "Fran insists she's going to make her singing début on Saturday night. I've told her she isn't going to be ready that soon but she won't listen to me."

"If she says she's going to make her début Saturday, that's what she's going to do," the bald little gangster said. "There's no way anyone in the world can stop her. She's a very determined young lady. She takes after her mother, God rest her. You'll have to go along with whatever Fran wants. If she wants to sing, she's going to sing. After all, it's her nightclub. Just make sure you show her how to sing, and present her right, so we can all be proud. Whatever she needs, whatever the band needs, whatever you need – get it. Money's no object. All I care about is results. I'm counting on you, my boy."

"I'll do my best, Mr. DiPaola."

"That's more like it. So my little girl wants to be a band singer. ... What type songs is she going to sing?"

"She's having posters printed – 'Frances Paul, the Queen of Jazz'."

" 'Frances Paul'? What's wrong with using her right name?"

"She's hired a publicity man. He says the public would think she had an unfair advantage if she used your name. And Fran wants to prove she can make it on her own."

"Yes, I can understand that. She would. But let's give her all the help we can. So, she's going to be 'The Queen of Jazz.' I suppose that means no opera, no Italian songs of any kind."

"I'm afraid so."

"Well, Al, that's a great compliment to you, isn't it? I hope you appreciate it. All the more reason you should give the project everything you've got."

"Yes, Mr. DiPaola."

"Al, who's the best woman jazz singer around today?"

"There are quite a few – Ma Rainey, Alberta Hunter, Ethel

Waters, Bessie Smith. Some people who know what they're talking about say Bessie Smith is still the best."

"Where is she?"

"She moves around a lot. But she's been visiting Chicago. She may be in town."

"Get her."

"Get her?"

"Get her over to The Palermo. She can give Fran a few lessons." Al smiled.

"I don't think Bessie Smith would be available for that sort of thing."

Mr. DiPaola frowned. His frown reminded Al of Fran's expression when she was crossed.

"Everybody's available," Mr. DiPaola said impatiently. "It's only a question of price. You can track her down, can't you? Vince can help you on that."

"I think I can."

"Get onto it right away then."

When Al stood to leave, Mr. DiPaola solicitously enquired: "What have you done to your hand?"

Al wondered momentarily but Mr. DiPaola's mien was quite ingenuous.

"Nothing serious," Al said. "Only a cut."

"The bachelor life!" Mr. DiPaola said with a sympathetic smile. "You need someone to take care of you."

Al telephoned The Paradise. The person who answered was able to give him Moses' telephone number, and Moses gave Al the number for Jimmy Yancey. Al explained why he was calling.

"It was nice of you to think of Bessie," Moses said. "She doesn't work all the time and I know she can use the money. Do you want me to speak with her? She doesn't always get on too well with . . . strangers."

"You mean with whites?"

"Yes, Al. You know how it is."

"Yes. I'd have asked you over to the club long before now if it wasn't segregated. Yes, please do tell her what we want. I'd be grateful. Tell her she can name her price, and the sooner she can start, the better. I'll be over at the club from four on."

"O.K., Al," Moses said. "Good luck on Saturday, hear? And let's get together soon."

"Yes," Al said, meaning it. "We really must do that."

When he got to The Palermo, he learned that Bessie Smith had already been in touch with Fran.

"You should have been here a half hour ago," Fran said. "You missed quite a scene. I can laugh about it now, but it wasn't funny at the time."

"What happened?"

"The celebrated Bessie Smith was here."

"Already? Wonderful! When will she be back?"

"I should say, she *claimed* to be Bessie Smith. Maybe she was. She was a big old fat drunk Negress in a beat-up hat and a shabby coat. She was the way her records sound (not that I've heard many of them) – crude and angry. She said she'd come to give me a singing lesson! Was that your gag? We don't have time to fool around. When I said there must be a mistake, I wasn't buying any, she turned nasty. She yelled at me, words I won't repeat. Two of the boys had to give her the bum's rush. Bessie Smith! She represents what we don't want from jazz. At The Palermo, we only want the happy side of jazz. The elegance."

Fran and her staff spared no efforts and no expense to ensure that her début would be an elegant one. She spent less time with Al and the band, to their heartfelt relief, than with her dressmaker, the chef, the *maître d'* and the publicity man, who was churning out press releases about the discovery of a great new talent, the birth of a star. Fran gave several newspaper and radio interviews on the story of her life, her political views, her theories on life after death, her wardrobe, her hobbies, her favorite dessert, and even her music.

" 'What kind of jazz do I like best?' said the pert, raven-haired songstress," according to the foremost feature-writer for one local rotogravure section. " 'I just love all kinds of jazz, so long as it's elegant.' " One of the captions identified her as "The Elegant Chanteuse." The photograph showed the elegant chanteuse, in the kitchen of her home on Lake Shore Drive, cooking angel food cake for her Chihuahua. Another photograph showed her singing, or posing as though singing, for "some of her young fans," a captive audience, immobile in the children's ward of a local hospital to which The Palermo had just contributed a sizeable donation. When she announced that the proceeds of her opening night would be given to the widows' and orphans' fund of the Police Benevolent

Association, a cause in which, she said, her family had always taken a special interest, the Mayor presented her with a key to the city and a good citizenship certificate in City Hall, and the photographers were there.

In a very short time, it became apparent that Fran's début was going to be a major social event. Admission was to be by ticket only. Some of the tickets were assigned to invited guests, including a select few of Mr. DiPaola's business associates and clients, some recognized socialites with gossip-column credits, a Cook County Congressman, and several members of the City Council whom Mr. DiPaola favored with his patronage. Most of the tickets were for sale. They were all snapped up the day they were first offered; and, during the few days that remained before the concert, as the prospective performance was now being called, the scalpers sold many of the tickets again. One of the purchasers, who willingly paid a small fortune for no fewer than sixteen of them, was Dr. Reinhart H. Schwimmer, an oculist and a crony of George Bugs Moran.

Diplomatic relations were uneasy at that time between the Capone syndicate and the old Dion O'Banion gang, which Bugs Moran had taken over following the untimely demise of Vincent The Schemer Drucci. A rough-cut racketeer of the North Side, where the Sicilian niceties of criminal protocol were not always faithfully observed, Bugs Moran had recently incurred Capone's disfavor by upsetting a long-standing commercial agreement between the two organizations. Moran had cancelled his regular order for Old Log Cabin whiskey, which Capone had been supplying. Moran, it was generally believed, had then obtained his supplies of the whiskey by hijacking Capone trucks that were bringing it into the city. For one bootlegger to hijack another bootlegger's whiskey was considered unethical. The belief that Moran was the mastermind behind the hijackings was founded on no more than suspicion, but it was a strong one and discomforting. Dr. Schwimmer bought the tickets for Bugs Moran and six of his henchmen and himself and eight women as a conciliatory gesture intended to help bring about renewed amity and cooperation between the two gangs. After consultation at the highest level, the Moran party was assigned a group of four of the best tables in the house. Frank DiPaola, too, being a practical man, preferred peace to war.

FORTY-NINE

There was an atmosphere of great excitement at The Palermo early on Saturday evening. A cavalcade of florists' vans delivered many thousands of dollars' worth of bouquets and floral wreaths to the club's side entrance, the way to the dressing rooms. Local connoisseurs of such measurements of esteem and homage estimated that Fran received as many flowers as Angelo Genna on the occasion of his funeral.

Flowers filled Fran's specially decorated suite and overflowed it. The surplus made the corridor smell like a greenhouse. Beside her door, which was emblazoned with a large gold star and inscribed with her professional name, *FRANCES PAUL*, in letters of gold, two overalled delivery men carefully propped up an eight-foot horseshoe of red, white and green carnations, *"FOR FRAN WITH LOVE FROM PAPA."* Under the ministrations of her hairdresser and makeup man, Fran sat in the bright glare of her dressing-table lights and smiled serenely, while her maid looked on in tears of pride and joy.

Al, wearing white tie and tails (by order), left his own small dressing room and made his way along the corridor like an explorer through an unfamiliar jungle. He knocked on Fran's door. Her shrill response was a command :

"Come in !"

"I just came by to wish you luck," he said.

She offered him her cheek for a showbiz ritual opening-night kiss.

"Don't muss me," she warned him.

He kissed her.

"Don't be nervous," he nervously urged her.

"Who's nervous?"

"The place is packed solid," he said.

"I should hope so. I'm glad you dropped in, Al. There's one thing I have to tell you. You know we were going to open with 'The St. Louis Blues' ?"

"Yes, of course. I'm sure it'll be all right, if you do what I told you yesterday at rehearsal."

"I've changed my mind. We ought to start with something with more life in it. We'll do 'Chicago'."

"But we haven't rehearsed it. You said – "

"Forget what I said. This is what I'm saying now. We open with 'Chicago'."

"Oh, Fran...."

"Don't give me that 'Oh, Fran' stuff. You know the music, don't you? The band knows the music?"

"Yes, but – "

"And I know the words. So we're in business. Please close the door. I have to get dressed."

Al decided that this would be a good time for a drink. He passed the bandstand, crossed the dance-floor, and hesitated, looking for the best way to the bar. Many extra tables had been squeezed into the room. He was confronted by an unusually long table, which had been made by pushing together four small tables. The sixteen people sitting around it, eight men and eight women, seemed already to be full of the fiesta spirit.

"You're Al Dexter!" proclaimed a young man in a tuxedo at one end of the table.

"Hi, Al!" said one of the women, fluttering her eyelashes and the fingers of an upraised hand. "Come and join us!"

"I'm Dr. Schwimmer," the young man said. "Dr. Reinhart H. Schwimmer. Have a drink!" He waved hospitably toward the long table, which was heavily laden with all sorts of bottles.

"Good evening, Dr. Schwimmer," Al said. "Thanks a lot, but it's almost show time."

"Always time for a drink," Dr. Schwimmer pointed out. "How about a highball? D'you like Old Log Cabin?" This suggestion made some of the other men laugh.

"Thanks," Al said. "That'd be fine." It was quicker and easier to agree. These days he seemed to be taking a lot of orders of one kind and another. Dr. Schwimmer handed him a brown whiskey and soda.

"Your good health," Dr. Schwimmer said. "Meet my friends. The good-looking man at the end there – " he indicated a brawny middle-aged man with the scarred, bent face of a veteran prize-fighter " – that's Bugs, Bugs Moran."

"Good evening, Mr. Moran," Al said, with a polite nod.

"That's Frank Gusenberg," Dr. Schwimmer went on, with

gestures along both sides of the table, "John May, Al Weinshank, James Clark, Adam Heyer, and Frank's brother, Peter. And les girls. You'll have to find out their names for yourself."

"Good evening," Al said, and there was a genial burble of greetings.

"Hey, Al," said Bugs Moran. "How about 'Danny Boy' when the band starts up?"

"Gee, Mr. Moran, I'm really sorry, I can't play any requests. Miss DiPaola's – Miss Paul's – program is all set. I can't change it.'

"You ain't anti-Irish, I hope?" Bugs Moran asked.

"Oh, no, Mr. Moran, not at all. I like Irish songs. Any other time I'd be glad to play 'Danny Boy'."

"But 'Danny Boy' ain't good enough for her royal highness, 'The Queen of Jazz' is that it?"

"No, it isn't that," Al earnestly assured him. Bugs Moran was noted for his quick temper. "Her father wanted her to sing Italian songs, and she isn't going to sing any of those either."

"You turned down Frank DiPaola?" Bugs Moran said with a wide grin. Al did not meet the question precisely head-on.

"Miss Paul has selected her own material," he said.

Bugs Moran looked around at his associates.

"That's rich – no Italian songs. Ain't that rich?"

There were appreciative murmurs of assent.

"That's a promise then?" he said to Al. "No Irish songs, but definitely also no Italian songs of any kind whatsoever."

"That's a promise," Al said.

"O.K., Al. Put it there, buddy." Bugs Moran crushingly shook Al's hand – his left hand. Al showed him his right hand, to explain the aberration. His little finger now wore a much smaller bandage but it was still extremely tender. "You're O.K., Al," the big man said. "I like the way you stand up for your rights and play only what you want to play. Good luck now."

Fran was welcomed with a standing ovation. The applause must have gone on for two minutes or more, as though in recognition of a splendid achievement. Her appearance was certainly splendid. She wore a small white orchid in her black hair. Her face was radiant. Her long, white gown was as simple as a Greek goddess's, and much more expensive.

Eventually, she raised a peremptory hand to silence the

audience. They settled down in their seats. After one or two coughs, the room became absolutely quiet and electric with anticipation.

Fran turned toward Al and gave him a nod of command and turned back to her microphone.

He played an unusually elaborate, protracted solo introduction, partly in recognition of the importance of the occasion, and partly in the hope that she might be able to gain from it some notion of the key that she should try to sing in.

He waved his wounded right hand with a conductor's flourish, down, across, up and down, and the rest of the band came in. Then it was her turn. He looked pleadingly at the back of her head and tried to will her into joining them at approximately the right time.

She did not jump onto the music as it went by, so, vamping steadily, he brought it around again, like a bareback rider's reliable horse. During the interim, she turned to him briefly and gave him a furious scowl. He clenched his teeth and smiled and encouragingly showed her the tempo with his right hand.

At the second opportunity, she plunged.

"Chi-ca-go . . ."

She got the word right.

Everything else was hopelessly, hideously wrong.

Fran's singing was not the sort that one could ignore. She sang very loud, very close to the microphone. The loudspeaker system screamed back at her but she overpowered it.

The sourness of the discord did not stop her. But she did not reach the end of the song. She was stopped by laughter.

Bugs Moran started it. He rocked back and forth, slapping his thigh, shaking his head from side to side in a frenzy of incredulous delight, guffawing, bellowing, bawling, hooting with laughter.

The others at his table soon laughed with him, and then the whole room was uproarious with uncontrolled mirth. There were only a few persons who did not laugh. Some of the waiters managed to restrain themselves. The band did not laugh. Al looked across the room at Frank DiPaola's table. Mr. DiPaola was not laughing. His face was as far from laughing as a face can get.

Fran abandoned the song in mid-lyric and ran to her dressing room.

Al kept the band going until the end of the chorus.

"Play it again !" he shouted as he got up from the piano. "Play it till I come back !"

In an attempt to give an impression of calmness, he left the room at a walk.

He knocked at Fran's door.

There was no reply.

He knocked louder.

No reply.

He hoped she wasn't doing anything rash. She was an emotional girl and she must feel terribly disappointed.

"Fran?" he said. "Fran!" he shouted. "It's me – Al! May I come in?"

There was still no response, so he tried the handle. The door was unlocked.

She was sitting at her dressing table. As he entered the room, she put down the telephone.

"Fran!" he said, relieved of his fear but still anxious. "I'm sorry, Fran. It'll be better next time."

"You lummox !" she said.

"We can go back after a while and try something else," he suggested doubtfully.

"You did that on purpose, didn't you?" she said.

"Did what?"

"You lousy schmuck ! You know that isn't the key I sing in !"

"But, Jesus, *Fran* ... !"

"Get the hell out of my room !" she said.

He thought of trying to reason with her, and then he thought again. He withdrew and gently closed her door. It was obviously better to leave her alone for the time being.

He was wondering whether he dared to show his face on the stand and whether he dared not to, when he heard the *clump-clump* of heavy footsteps rapidly approaching the right-angle bend of the corridor. Instinctively, he sought cover.

Al found concealment behind the eight-foot good-luck floral horseshoe, just as Maxie and Tony ran by, clumsily knocking over baskets of flowers to right and left in their haste.

They stopped at the door to Al's dressing room. He had left it locked. Maxie knocked, then pounded on the door, then hammered on it with both his ham-like fists.

"Open up !" he shouted.

"Maybe he didn't get back yet," Tony said, in a rare flash of lucidity.

"That's very good thinking, Tony. We'll give him a little surprise. Break the door down."

"Yes, Maxie."

Tony prepared his shoulder and used himself as a human battering ram. The door burst open first try. Tony and Maxie went inside and Maxie closed the door.

Tip-toeing fast, Al left the building.

He ran right into the arms of a man even larger than Maxie. The man had a companion. They were both wearing black snapbrims and black topcoats with the collars up. Al did not immediately remember where he had seen their ugly faces before.

"Easy does it," said the man Al had collided with. Al felt as if he had run into a brick wall. He realized there would be no point in trying to fight his way past them.

"Let's talk about this," he said.

"The car's around the corner," the second man said. "In the parking lot the other side of the front door."

"Look," Al said. "I know she's mad now, but she'll get over it. Can't we work something out?"

"We'd better get going," the first man said, putting his hand under Al's elbow and firmly guiding him forward.

"Act natural," the second man advised, "and we won't have any trouble."

The first man got in the driver's seat of the customary big, black Packard sedan; the second man held the rear door open for Al.

Al reluctantly got in. The second man followed him and slammed the door and the car leaped forward with a roar of the motor and a squeal of tires.

"Where are you taking me?" Al asked, not that he had any reason to believe that the destination mattered.

"Mr. Moran thought you'd probably like to get out of town," said Frank Gusenberg.

"He said you gave him the biggest laugh he's had in a long time, but Frank DiPaola didn't look too pleased," said Pete Gusenberg.

"When Mr. Moran seen Maxie and Tony follow you out, he

said to us 'Why should we let DiPaola have the satisfaction?' "
said Frank.

"So we headed for the dressing rooms, by the scenic route," said
Pete.

"We were going to give you a hand," Frank explained.

"But when we was heading in, you was heading out already,"
Pete added.

"So all's well that ends well," Frank said piously.

"There's a New York train at ten forty-five," said Pete.

"Why New York?" Al asked.

"It's the best place for you to get lost in for a while," said
Frank.

"It's the next train out," Pete said.

"But all my things!" Al protested.

"You should only thank God you got your head on your
shoulders," Frank pointed out.

FIFTY

Al arrived in New York on St. Valentine's Day.

Reading the *Daily News* in a coffee shop the next morning, he learned that the previous day there had been a massacre in a garage at 2122 Clark Street, Chicago, where the Bugs Moran gang used to store liquor. At ten-fifty a.m., a car had stopped there and unloaded five men. Three were in police uniform. The five of them lined up seven other men against a wall inside the garage, and shot them to death with machine guns. It was believed that the victims had agreed to the rendezvous after being offered a cut-rate consignment of Old Log Cabin whiskey.

Al was sorry to read the names of the casualties. He had met them all – Dr. Reinhart H. Schwimmer, Frank Gusenberg, John May, Al Weinshank, James Clark, Adam Heyer, and Frank's brother, Pete.

How had Bugs Moran avoided being included among the dead? Al read on; the explanation was simple : being of Irish descent, Bugs Moran had arrived late for the appointment.

FIFTY-ONE

In Transit, 1938

Al was asleep in the back of the bus, dreaming he was in a bus, when there was a minor explosion. The bus slowed down, pulled over and stopped. He opened one pink eye and warily peeped out from under the brim of his hat.

The poker game continued unabated. There was a heap of crumpled paper money on the black tarpaulin-covered case of the brass drum, which blocked the aisle. The smoke from the players' reefers was sweet and pungent. There were band chicks in every town, like sailors' girls in every port, but for musicians on the road there was nobody, there was nothing, as reliable as Mary Jane. With tea, who needed sympathy? Al did, for one, though he did not expect any.

Raising a hand to shield his face against the lights, he pressed his nose against the window. Black. He looked at his watch. Four-twenty – the worst time. He looked at the players.

"What happened?" he asked.

The second trombone looked up from the cards in his hand.

"It's alive," he said.

The first alto sax was more informative.

"We got a flat," he said.

"Oh, Jesus," Al said. "Where the hell are we?"

"Who knows?" said the second trombone.

"We just crossed the state line," the alto sax said.

"Into nowhere," said the second trombone.

"To be exact," said the alto sax, "we're somewhere between Baxter Springs, Kansas, and Commerce, Oklahoma."

" 'To be exact,' he says," said the second trombone. "What's exact about that?"

"It's only an hour to Tulsa," said the guitar, who was an optimist even when he wasn't high.

"Make that two hours," retorted a tenor, automatically disagreeing, as if setting up a bet.

"If we had wheels," the alto sax felt bound to point out.

"What are we doing here?" asked the second trombone, who was nearly eighty dollars down. "Playing poker or studying geography?"

Al looked beyond the game, past the sprawling legs of men who were pretending the seats were beds. Their leader was standing up front, leaning over the driver and gesticulating. They were having words.

"It's your charter," the driver said. "If you say we go, we go. At your own risk."

"What risk? You drive slowly. You find a diner. We wait. You change the wheel."

"It'll ruin the tire."

"What's to ruin? The tire's already ruined."

"In its present condition, the tire could be fixed."

"Let's you and I agree it couldn't."

"I'm the one that'd take the rap."

"The tire must have been ready to blow. The whole Goddamn bus is an antique."

"There's no need to get nasty. It ain't my fault."

Al could not hear the squabble but he could guess, only too easily, what it must be like. He could imagine its pettiness, its slowness, its increasing vehemence and its inevitable outcome; on this level, Steve's will-power always prevailed. Eventually, another obstacle would be overcome on the long, erratic, uncomfortable journey in pursuit of the razzle-dazzle of the Hit Parade, which was always discernible at the same distance far ahead, glimmering like the aurora borealis over the horizon. Ah! Al thought – the glamour and excitement of being the piano player and star arranger in a big swing band!

The motor started, the bus slowly moved forward, and he allowed his head to fall back against the soiled antimacassar.

Miami, Oklahoma, is one of the lesser Miami's but there was a brightly lighted all-night café beside the highway on the outskirts of town. The bus stopped on a cinder parking lot and most of the musicians got out, followed by the driver, who had the bitter, excommunicated look of a man who is about to change a wheel. Al was one of the few who remained in their seats.

During the past couple of years, there had been so many one-night stands, so many four-hundred-mile bus-rides between remote primitive dance-halls! (Visiting musician : "Any special problems with the acoustics in this room?" Local entrepreneur : "Certainly not. We don't have none of them new-fangled things.") There had been so many bad meals in flea-bag hotels, so much discomfort in such bad weather, so many mechanical breakdowns and temperamental upsets, so many greedy and dishonest promoters, so many vain and untalented musicians, so many demanding and obtuse fans!

Al had an aching head, a dry mouth, an acid stomach and an acute case of ennui. He was not in the mood for overdone Salisbury steak, soft french fries and mushy succotash and his colleagues' comments.

As a matter of fact, as he often had to remind himself, he had achieved some progress since his early days in New York.

Admittedly, right at the start, fate had kneed him in the groin, at a time when it kneed millions of others in the same place. On October 29, 1929, the Stock Market crash wiped out his Chicago investments. He lost only about two thousand dollars; but losing everything you have, on any scale, no matter how small, is depressing. However, in spite of the economic slump – to the contrary, partly because of it, he found that his musical skills were in demand. The public, being worse off financially than it had been during the 'twenties, wanted more cheerful entertainment than ever, especially bright, happy music.

When drinking alcohol became legal, after ratification of the Twenty-First Amendment on December 5, 1933, Americans went out less to drink; but radio and records had greatly increased popular interest in light music, and they went out to dance. Jazz always had been dance music. It became music for more and more people to dance to. For the first time, jazz became a universal part of American popular culture. The dance-halls and dance bands rapidly proliferated and grew in size. Big bands, unable to play extemporaneously with the ease of the small jazz bands of New Orleans and Chicago, needed to have the music written down. Al, one of the musically literate minority, became an arranger.

Always one to try to keep his eye on the buttery side of the bread, while quite sure that his first considerations were aesthetic, Al fashioned his work after the most advanced models that were admired by other musicians and, directly or indirectly, were successfully making their mark. Thus, naturally, he latched onto the orchestral modes and stylistic ideas of Don Redman of the Fletcher Henderson band, and those of Fletcher Henderson himself. Al was no innovator. Even his improvisation at the piano was derived from the best of the improvisations he had heard. But he was more than a mere imitator. Like a clever impresario or editor, Al was a shrewd spotter of trends; he was a developer and refiner. He composed no original melodies, but he was able to arrange other musicians' compositions so that they could be played better than they had been played ever before.

Al progressed alongside Fletcher Henderson, on a parallel course. Al admired Fletcher Henderson's organization of the band into sections of brass, reeds and rhythm (at least three trumpets, two trombones, four saxophones/clarinets, with piano, guitar, bass and drums), the call-and-response duality within a strong, all-encompassing unity, the orderly framework of harmony and counterpoint in which his virtuoso soloists were free to perform with daringly imaginative spontaneity, the juxtapositions of like and unlike voices – the powerful beat, the beautiful noise! And everything that Al admired he carefully analyzed and used. As a free-lance arranger in New York, he wrote and sold many scores. During this productive period he lived by himself most of the time, in a pleasant three-room apartment in a brownstone on East Thirty-Eighth Street, in Murray Hill.

There was a shock in 1934 when Fletcher Henderson's band foundered and the maestro went broke and Al was afraid that he had allowed himself to be influenced by a loser. But the alarm was false. Al was relieved to learn that Fletcher Henderson's failure had been caused by personal weakness in the administration of band discipline, not by any fundamental musical fault. Al felt he was vindicated when Fletcher Henderson succeeded in selling his whole book of arrangements to Benny Goodman, and Goodman's band, after its triumph at the Palomar Ballroom, in Hollywood, late in the summer of 1935, became the hottest swing band in the business. It was a big business and Benny Goodman was one of the smartest of businessmen. Al knew he was on a winner.

His arrangements were noted in the trade for their up-to-date style and their sound craftsmanship; they were well built; they were reliably functional, and (this was important), they arrived on time. Al was aware that his writing was somewhat skimpy when it came to emotional content. He contended that it was his task primarily to provide the form; most of the emotion should be supplied by the performers.

When Steve Barber managed to get the financial backing for

a band of his own, in 1936, he thought of Al. Though sentiment was only a minor factor in the recruiting process, the personnel of the new band already included one other veteran of The Sophisticates. Dick Kilian was on drums. Shortly after Al joined, Kilian told him that he had been the third choice, after Edgar Sampson and Jimmy Mundy. This information did not distress Al; he was accustomed to the mercilessness of musicians' shop-talk; the main thing was that he had the job.

The job was a good one. When they were on the road he was able to put a sizeable percentage of his pay in the bank and leave it there. But there were times, like now, waiting in a disabled bus somewhere in Oklahoma at five in the morning, when he wondered what he was doing and why. Were other musicians being paid better for more interesting work? If so, where were they and how had they got there? On the other hand, what had happened to all the musicians who had dropped out of sight, never to be heard of again? At such times, Al was assailed by misgivings: was he wrong not to try to effect a reconciliation with his father?

Travelling from town to town, Al usually had no time off. When the band did stay in one place for a while, there were days when he had plenty of time and very little to do. To kill a couple of hours in a main-street town in the afternoon, he would go to the movies. He preferred horror and comedy, or love stories that combined both; however, lolling drowsily in the back row, sipping lukewarm bourbon from a limp Dixie cup, he was not a severe critic. Occasionally, by chance, he saw something that surprised him.

He had recently seen a movie in Logansport, Indiana, that had made him sit up. Entitled "Blue Grass Blues", it was a musical romance about the handsome young heir to an old Kentucky home threatened by the machinations of a covetous neighbor. Being a gallant blue-grass blue-blood, the hero sportingly agreed to wager his homestead, his stud farm and the future of his faithful workers and his fiancée on the outcome of the Kentucky Derby. If the hero's beloved favorite thoroughbred won the race the villain would have to tear up the hero's mortgage; but if not. . . . The alternative was grim.

The hero and the movie were saved by the fact that the most faithful workers of all were played by Louis Armstrong and his band. Their elaborate production numbers were devised to raise the hero's stake money (the magic of love, the magic of jazz) and to provide relief from the dramatic tension. And the eyeball-rolling, rabbit's-foot-kissing, tap-dancing, trumpet-blowing stable-boy who finally rode the hero's horse to victory was none other than Moses Decatur.

Depression Kentucky had been transmogrified into Hollywood's traditional Dear Old Southland, where, beneath the constantly flowering old magnolias down the hill from the big house, Louis was forever swinging the spirituals and, in the everlasting sunset, a massed choir was devoutly crooning the songs of Stephen Foster. Louis blew so loud and high that a rheumatic, bearded gaffer gleefully leaped from his rocking chair and jitterbugged with a chortling, roly-poly, bandanna-wearing *Aunt Jemima,* while all the piccaninnies, sure enough, clapped their hands and flipped with delight, and the young bucks and the high-yaller lovelies did that old-time Savoy Ballroom Lindy Hop, choreographed by Hermes Pan.

There were not many scenes in which Moses played his trumpet. He did a lot of loosely relaxed clowning. Al remembered Mo's idealistic talk, his harangues, his sermons, about musical freedom and sincerity. Perhaps some of the sincere music had been silenced on the cutting-room floor. Al felt sorry for him.

After dozing for a short time, Al looked again at his watch. Five-thirty-five. The wheel must have been changed long ago. He was very bored. He decided to go and get some coffee.

The diner was not much but it seemed cheerful after the bus. On one side of the room there was a long red counter. Behind it, a plump man with a sallow face, dressed like a chef, stood at a blackened grill and prodded hamburgers with a spatula, making them sizzle. There was a row of chromium pedestals with thick, circular tops covered in red Leatherette, like giant artificial toad-stools. The bus driver sat on one of them. He was busily eating blueberry pie *à la mode*. On the other side of the room there were tables in booths. There were no customers in the place except the driver and Steve Barber and His Barberians. At the far end of the room several of the men of the band were lounging around a juke box.

It was a marvellous juke box, more ornate than necessary. It was an altar to swing. Illuminated bubbles, like aspirations, arose continually in streamlined bulbous columns of internally lighted red, amber and purple glass. It was a good example of 1938 Juke Box Baroque, the essential artifact of its age. For a nickel you could activate the machinery of dreams and pretend for three minutes that you were elsewhere.

Al recognized the hysterical tempo of Benny Goodman's aptly named "Madhouse", a Jimmy Mundy arrangement that had been recorded in Kansas City a few months earlier. Al had to admit that the writing for the sax section was better than average. What he really admired and envied, though, was Jess Stacy's piano solo. Steve, of course, had to speak right in the middle of it.

"Stacy must have bribed him," he said, meaning, presumably, Mundy. "Thirty-two bars – much too much. But once again the clarinet saves the day. Goodman catches the ball and runs for a touchdown. Oh, there you are Al. Come and listen to this! This is what I mean by giving the clarinet a bit of elbow-room, some room to breathe. This is what you should be doing for me, Al."

Al wished he had stayed in the bus.

"Put a nickel in, someone," Steve said. "Al, there's a record for you. Your old girl friend."

A woman quite competently sang a swing version of "Tea For Two".

"Who's that?" Al asked.

"Look at it," Steve said. "If you don't read it you won't believe it."

Al went over to the juke box and read the name aloud.

"Frances Paul," he said. He did a double take. "Frances Paul! That's impossible!"

"Ain't that a killer-diller?" Steve said. "A voice from the past."

"That isn't her voice!" Al said. "She must be about thirty now, but she couldn't have learned to sing like that in a million years."

"Money, Al," Steve pointed out. "Money. With money, you can buy yourself a voice. The record company does the rest. They're doing all kinds of things with music in the recording studios these days. But it takes more than money to get a mediocre record on all the juke boxes. This Frances Paul record has been on every juke box I've played this week."

"They say the mob's taken over most of the juke boxes," Al said. "This proves it."

234

"If that's true, the mob are the best song pluggers around. The juke boxes are the short cut to the Hit Parade." Steve sighed. "What use are you, Al? Why did you have to foul up at The Palermo?"

In the bus, Al told himself that Steve was only kidding. Or was he? Al pulled the brim of his hat down over his eyes. Half asleep, riding through limbo, he thought about money.

FIFTY-TWO

New York, 1940

Money definitely was not everything, Moses decided. He had enjoyed the few weeks of filming with Louis; he had not enjoyed Hollywood. It was much too far from Harlem, which was now his home. Even West Forty-Fourth Street was too far from Harlem. He had made the mistake of letting some musician friends, late one Saturday night, talk him into auditioning for a Broadway swing musical-comedy version of *Hamlet*.

To swing Shakespeare was a thriving industry at the time. The notion was evidently based on the theory that Shakespeare was solemnly respectable and swing was not and the contrast was automatically funny – an insult both to Shakespeare and to jazz. And the producers took the idea one stage further: they believed that using an all-Negro cast compounded the joke. What, they asked each other, could be as hilarious as a Negro jazzman reciting the high-falutin' Elizabethan blank verse with a hep twist? Nothing, they told each other, unless it could be the same man blasting a madrigal to musical smithereens.

"Hamlet" in swingtime was called " 'Murder!' He said." Moses showed up for the audition, in a theater near Forty-Fourth Street and Sixth Avenue, wearing a black hat with a low crown and a wide brim and a mauve zoot suit, with the jacket cut down to his baggy knees and cuffs cut so tight that his trouser-legs had to have zip-fasteners.

His appeareance delighted the white director.

"Perfect, darling!" he exclaimed. "If your trumpet-playing and singing are anywhere near as good as you look, you're in!"

"Nobody said anything about singing," Moses said.

"In this show, everybody sings. Gag it up! It's all strictly for laughs."

Moses was assigned the role of Second Grave-Digger, whose main contribution to the merriment of the production was to play and sing a number entitled, "Dig This Grave!" segueing into "Frolic With Yorick!"

Moses' performance was a show-stopper. It got an even bigger hand than Hamlet's big solo, "This Flesh Is Solid, Gate!"

Now Moses was sitting in a Sixth Avenue bar, not very far, but very different, from Sardi's, after the first night, waiting for the first editions of the morning papers. He felt uncharacteristically depressed. He was suffering from an uncomfortable sensation that he might be dishonoring his race, his music and himself. This was like Hollywood, but worse. When he had complained to Louis about the Stepin Fetchit aspects of the absurd characters they were portraying, Louis had grinned in his easy-going way and said :

"Don't give it a second thought, Mo. Stepin Fetchit rides around this town in a Cadillac a block long. Take their money and run."

It was the live, white audience that made the downtown Manhattan theater worse. Clowning around on the stage of the Apollo Theatre, up in Harlem, was something else. There the comedy was colored comedy, in the tradition of Butterbeans & Susie and Buck & Bubbles, for a colored audience. The clowning and the laughter were all in the family. Here the audience was laughing down at him. He knew that he should not sell them the right to do that.

Two more cups of coffee later, at last it was time to go to the corner to pick up the papers.

"I'll be right back," he told the anxious-looking woman who was with him. "Don't look like the world's coming to an end, honey. It isn't."

She gave him a rather queasy smile.

He returned in a few minutes and slapped the papers down on the table. They did not talk as they looked for the reviews.

It was when he was leafing through the bulk of *The New York Times* that Moses broke their silence.

"Poindexter !" he exclaimed. "What d'you know ?"

The woman looked over the top of *The Herald Tribune*.

"What's that ?" she said.

"The headline jumped right off the page at me. They've given him a big write-up. 'A. Chesley Poindexter III, New Orleans Philanthropist.' "

"What's that got to do with anything ?"

"He's dead. There's a long obituary."

"I thought we were looking for your reviews."

"Isn't that a coincidence though ? No, I guess not. The rest of the world goes on, even the night I open in a lousy musical. People go on dying."

"What we want to know is, did the *show* live or die? That's what we want to know."

"But A. Chesley Poindexter III, Mae, honey! It was his house I lived in when I was a kid, down in New Orleans. He was the father of Al Dexter, the arranger. Al's my old friend from 'way back. Maybe the article mentions him."

"Do you care about him, this guy who died?"

"No, I didn't *care* about him. But it's interesting, isn't it? It says he was sixty-four."

"That's a regular, ordinary dying age."

"It goes on about the Poindexter house on Beauregard Street. That's where I lived. 'The historic eighteenth-century mansion, with its Classical portico' – whatever that is – 'and its wrought-iron balconies, is one of the show-places of the city's old French Quarter.' It was a fabulous house, Mae."

"What did he leave you?"

"Don't be silly. My father was the butler. My foster father, I mean. Then the article goes on about Mr. Poindexter's ancestors and education and career et cetera. They're going to have the funeral in St. Louis Cathedral. Oh, Mrs. Poindexter died in nineteen-twenty-two. Al's the only survivor – 'A. Chesley Poindexter IV.' It sounds kind of strange after all this time. So now Al's really on his own, poor guy."

"Rich guy."

"I bet he feels bad."

"Let me see how bad," she said, taking the paper from him. She gave it a shake and straightened it out and found the place.

"Since early in the nineteenth century," she read aloud in a derisive burlesque of an upperclass accent, "the Poindexter family always has been prominent in the commercial, political and social life of Louisiana. The first A. Chesley Poindexter founded the brokerage company that bears his name. Blah, blah, blah. Now, here it is; 'Mr. Poindexter, a benefactor of many local charitable and cultural institutions, recently announced that he would leave his entire estate, estimated to be in excess of seven million dollars, to the A. Chesley Poindexter Foundation, a medical research organization devoted particularly to investigation of diseases of the liver.' It looks like Mr. Poindexter left everything in memory of himself, so your friend's out of luck."

"Al's the same age as me," Moses said, as though speaking to himself. "But it doesn't make any difference how old you are. When the time comes, it's tough to lose your mother and father."

"The reviews will cheer you up," Mae said.

The *News* critic began :

"Something is groovy in the state of Denmark."

The *Mirror* said :

"The Bard is a solid sender. The first-nighters at the Shubert Theater snapped their caps – "

"That's enough," Moses said.

"It's all like that."

"Ofay jive-talk gives me stomach cramps. Let's have a drink. What'll you have ?"

"These reviews are going to sell tickets. The show's going to be a smash."

"Can you imagine what it'll be like, going through that routine night after night, plus matinees for the matrons from West-chester ?"

"Beats walking the streets, Mo. It'll be nice for you to have some regular money coming in."

"Money . . ." Mo said. "It always comes down to that, doesn't it ?"

"You're tired, Mo. Let's have that drink. I'd like a Cuba libre."

Moses got the drinks. They both drank in thoughtful silence.

"Mo," she said.

"Yes ?"

"There's something I didn't want to mention, until I knew you were all set. But . . . well, I. . . ."

"What is it ?"

"It's that same old subject again. Money."

"Won't it keep till tomorrow ?"

"I've been holding back for a couple of weeks. I must tell you. I was hoping I wouldn't have to bother you. But I need some money. I'm pregnant."

"You are ?"

"Yes, Mo. There's no doubt about it. But don't worry, Mo. I know someone who knows someone. I can get it taken care of for a hundred dollars."

"Are you sure you're pregnant?"

"Yes, Mo. I'm sorry."

"I hope you don't mean that – I mean about being sorry. That's great! We'll get married."

Mae smiled sadly.

"No, Mo. I thought you might say that. But I'm not trying to trap you. I'll be all right. The operation's nothing, the way they do it now. It's quite safe."

"You're not going to let them do that to any child of mine," Moses said decisively. "And no child of mine is going to be without a father. So we'll have to get married, and that's all there is to it. If you're willing to marry a thirty-nine-year-old musician."

"You don't have to marry me."

"There's another good reason for getting married that maybe I should have mentioned before. I love you."

Small's Paradise hatcheck girls were not easy to break down, but Mo was too much.

She wept.

He held her hand and gently squeezed it.

"If they call us 'Mo and Mae,'" he said, "they can use the biggest letters on the marquee."

FIFTY-THREE

New York, 1941

Al was out of town throughout the long run of " 'Murder!' He Said," but he read in *Variety* about the success of the show and about Moses' success in it. When Al returned to New York he traced Moses through Local 802. Al was moved by friendship and by awareness of a new freedom. At last, jazz seemed to be growing interracial on a sound, public, commercial basis. He called Moses and they agreed to meet at the Hickory House, on Fifty-Second Street.

They ordered bottles of Ballantine's ale.

"I was sorry to hear about your father," Moses said.

"Thanks. It was too bad."

"You never did get together with him, did you?"

"No. He left everything to medicine. The house is some sort of museum."

Moses looked pained, so Al reassured him.

"It's all right, Mo. Life goes on. Let's talk of pleasanter things. Let's talk about the future."

Al outlined his idea of their forming a group – trumpet, trombone, alto sax, piano, guitar, bass and drums. He believed there was a good chance of getting into The Onyx Club or The Downbeat. They had a few more ales.

"The way I figure it," he said, "we ought to combine Duke Ellington's creative force, Jimmy Lunceford's drive, Count Basie's beat and Benny Carter's smooth, round tone."

"Why not throw in some Goodman, Dorsey and Shaw while we're at it?" Moses suggested with a grin. "We don't want to seem prejudiced. And maybe a smidgin of Bob Crosby. The Bobcats are sounding good."

"And John Kirby. We must have a big, thumping but precise bass."

"And some of this Joe Marsala sound would fit in nicely. The alto will have to be able to double on clarinet."

"You used to blow a little like Red Allen. Shall we have some of that?"

"This is still a septet we're talking about?" Moses asked.

"We'll make it the biggest septet on The Street," Al promised.

"I'll drink to that!" Moses said, doing so. "It's taken a quarter of a century to get our act together. We'd better do it right."

"So here's to Fletcher Henderson!" Al said.

"And Benny Goodman!" Moses responded courteously.

"Yes, he helped."

"Hiring Lionel Hampton was a break-through."

"And Teddy Wilson."

"That took nerve."

"And guts. And taste."

"I got a good one," Moses said. "Here's to Gene Krupa!"

"And to Gene Krupa's first trumpet!"

"Yeah, that's what I mean. Here's to Roy Eldridge! Roy and Anita O'Day are a gas! Did you catch 'Let Me Off Uptown'? Oh, man, what a horn!"

"Let's drink twice to him then. Little Jazz!"

"Roy *Big* Jazz Eldridge – that's what they should call him."

"But most of all," Al said, "here's to Moses Decatur!"

"Al Dexter!"

Joe Marsala put down his clarinet; his wife, Adele, covered her harp; they and the others left the stand.

"Time for some serious drinking," said Dave Tough, who was enjoying a drummer's thirst. Leo Watson and The Spirits of Rhythm prepared to take over. Joe Marsala was white; Leo Watson was black; the music was polychromatic.

After about ten minutes of Leo Watson's exhaustingly intricate, surrealistic scatting, Moses said :

"Let's take a walk down the street, see how Bean's doing."

The Fall evening was clear and crisp. There was a white crescent moon. The first stars were sparkling as coldly as diamonds. The warm electric signs glowed beckoningly – *The Famous Door, The Three Deuces, Jimmy Ryan's*. . . .

They found that Coleman Hawkins was doing fine.

So was Max Kaminsky.

So was Billie Holiday.

And so, in their own way, were Al and Moses, musicians as listeners, moving from bar to bar, from combo to combo, their hearts enlivened synchronously by the ubiquitous pulse of jazz.

"Duke Ellington said it well," Al remarked.

"Duke says everything well," Moses said. "How about that 'Baby, When You Ain't There'?"

"I was thinking about his show, 'Jump For Joy', in Los Angeles last summer – that number at the end of the first act: 'Uncle Tom's Cabin Is A Drive-In Now'. That's the new word."

"It's a beautiful thought," Moses said. "But it was only the end of the first act. They made him take one number out – 'I've Got A Passport From Georgia (And I'm Going To The U.S.A.)'."

But Moses was never discouraged for long.

"Can't win 'em all," he said. "But I'm game if you are. We'll start next week."

"Next week!" Al agreed.

"We'll slay 'em!" Moses said.

His optimism seemed at first to have been justified. The following week their septet was really wailing and Moses and Al were happy.

"I liked that riff you were playing there in the last chorus," Al said to Moses after a strenuous free-for-all based on "Ring Dem Bells". "That could be built up into a whole other number."

"Help yourself," Moses said. "It's all yours."

Al was serious. The next day he had it down on paper. The septet played it. They all liked it.

"That was a real inspiration," Al said.

"There's lots more where that came from," Moses assured him with a boyish smile.

"I'll tell you what I'll do," Al said. "When something like that comes along, I'll jot it down, and take it home and work on it. We'll look for a publisher. You could earn a fortune."

"Well, all reet, pops! We'll split anything we make fifty-fifty."

Al wrote several scores.

Unfortunately, however, within a month, the Japanese bombed Pearl Harbor and the United States was in the war.

"Are you going to join anything?" Al asked Moses late one night, when they were eating pastrami on rye in a delicatessen.

"Why should I?" Moses said. "I already belong to the best group in town."

"I was just wondering."

"Stop wondering then. You're forty years *old*, man. A lot too old for that gung-ho foolishness, if you were wondering about getting fitted out in a khaki suit."

243

"There are things a musician can do in the Army."

"Yeah, I know, especially if you aren't careful. Ford Lee Washington had the right idea. Did you hear 'Long Gone From Bowling Green'? He said: 'You don't think my legs are going to stand around and see my body *abused*, do you?' And Sonny Greer has the same philosophy. Sonny's motto is, 'Feet save ass, ass do feet a good turn some day.' Besides, Al, my Little Louis is only seven months old. What if something should happen to me? He's too young to take care of Mae. I want to make her a home in Sugar Hill before I'm through."

"I wasn't trying to talk you into anything," Al said. He wondered, with some amazement, whether his brief exposure to the martial virus of Bull Run had somehow infected him, after all.

"And not only that," Moses said, "Uncle Sam hasn't yet got the word on equality. If I enlisted they'd have me in some construction outfit. Or worse: they'd have me cleaning latrines all the way from here to Tokyo. No thanks, Al. I'll stay on the home front and boost civilian morale – mine."

"But this is war," Al said. "Think of the publicity."

Trying as usual to get in vogue, he joined the Army. It assigned him to the U.S.O. He played piano in camp shows all over the United States. Some of the singers he accompanied were so bad they reminded him of Fran. After strings were pulled, he finally reached the rank of buck sergeant.

FIFTY-FOUR

There had been some major changes in the Big Apple while Al
had been away in Sticksville, serving his country.

He stayed at the Biltmore while he was getting settled.

He was a sergeant when he checked in and went up to his
room. He came down a civilian, in a new light-blue gabardine
suit and a wide silk tie whose pattern of yellow and white sunbursts
on a ground of orange, someone in the garment industry had
prudently decided, was a bit too flamboyant for Miami beach
pajamas.

"Take my word for it," the Macy's salesman had said, "this is the
look this Fall."

After nearly four years in uniform, Al wanted to dress like everybody else.

"I don't want to be conspicuous," he said.

"Take it then," the salesman advised. "Without a tie like this
you'd stick out like a sore thumb."

The apartment rents in his old neighborhood in Murray Hill
had risen out of sight. A real estate agent, soon tiring of reasoning
with Al, sent him down to Greenwich Village.

Near Bleecker Street and Seventh Avenue, he found what a
classified advertisement in the *Times* called an "efficiency" apartment, up three flights of stairs in a building that would have
looked like a tenement if the landlord had not had the brick
façade painted dark gray and the front door yellow-ochre. The
gracious-living motif was accented with two antique-style coach-
lamps, one on each side of the entrance, and with a laurel bush in
a wooden tub that almost concealed the steep steps to the areaway
garbage cans. The building superintendent, a plump middle-aged
man in a gray cardigan and khaki pants, was as welcoming as a
night-shift turnkey at the Tombs. He wheezed and muttered to
himself as he led the way up the stairs.

"Anybody home?" he shouted, warning the cockroaches to hide,
as he opened the door. "There was a young lady," he explained to
Al. "She's gone already. She didn't pay the rent. I hope you'll

be staying a while. I have things to do apart from showing apart-
ments. You're lucky you're in the rear here. It's quieter."

Al surveyed the single room. The janitor stood waiting in one
corner, with the expression of a martyr assailed by doubts. The
room contained enough furniture to serve as a bedroom and a
sitting room. It had an old New York apartment's characteristic
faint odor of dry rot and cooking fat, but everything appeared to
be clean. There were a small bathroom and an even smaller
kitchen.

The rent was low.

"I'll take it," Al said.

They descended four flights to the janitor's basement lair,
which smelled of carbolic disinfectant and cats. Al paid a month's
rent and filled out a lease of the kind that people obtain from
drugstores if they don't want to commit themselves too profoundly,
and the janitor gave him a receipt. All that having been done, the
janitor seemed almost friendly.

"You can walk over to Washington Square from here," he said.
"It isn't far. It's nice on a warm evening."

"Thanks," Al said. "I'll move in tomorrow."

"Here's two keys. You want me to help with anything, press
the buzzer here. I'll take care of you, you take care of me, right?
You can do anything you like up there, you know what I mean?"
The janitor winked. "But it's a quiet house. We like to keep it
that way, fair enough?"

Al returned to the Biltmore and celebrated the solution of his
housing problem by having a dozen bluepoints on the half-shell
and a bottle of Pabst in the seafood bar. They were not as good
as Louisiana oysters but they gave him a hearty appetite. He had
the rest of his dinner in a Third Avenue steakhouse. Then, on his
first night back in New York, of course he had to go to hear some
jazz.

The musical bars of Fifty-Second Street looked more or less
the same as he remembered. They sounded very different from the
officers' club at Fort Bragg, North Carolina, where he had spent
most of the last year of his service career. Still a sergeant, he had
played piano there during "the cocktail hour", which usually
went on from five o'clock until after midnight. Homesick young
lieutenants, full of martinis, requested – ordered – "Sentimental
Journey" several times every evening. He must have played it a

thousand times in all. Visits to Fayetteville on evenings off provided only limited relief: there was a juke box on which Louis Jordan accompanied by his Tympani Five, sang "Knock Me A Kiss" and "Is You Is Or Is You Ain't My Baby?" He had heard rumors and inklings and faint reverberations of the bebop revolution that was said to be radically transforming jazz. He was not ready for the impact of the new music close up.

He first tried the Three Deuces. The Negro quintet – trumpet, alto, piano, bass and drums – wore black berets, black horn-rimmed sunglasses, small tufts of beard below their lower lips, and big, droopy bow ties. They looked like comic-strip caricatures of the artists of the Left Bank of Paris. Al wondered whether they were kidding. But the music did not sound as if they meant it to be funny. The music seemed hurried, nervous, twitchy and shrill, like St. Vitus dancing on broken glass.

The drummer, hunched over and gloatingly cackling like a mad scientist, laid down a rapid four-four beat on his bass drum, kept his cymbals continuously sizzling in two-four time, and frequently, irregularly attacked the rims of his snare-drums with explosive rattles of accents in a tempo so complex that it seemed to be no tempo at all. When Al adjusted to this turbulent time-keeping, he was suddenly thrown off balance by a sudden switch into more elaborate Afro-Cuban rhythms. It was hardly surprising that the trumpet and alto disengaged themselves from all this percussive turmoil and rose higher and higher, frantically squealing, each apparently seeking some private escape, perhaps into a supersonic harmony audible only to dogs, angels and junkies.

"Arpeggiate, man!" shouted a drinker standing beside Al at the bar. "Arpeggiate!"

Al observed that this enthusiast was wearing the same bebop accessories as the musicians on the stand. Whether his esoteric instruction to the pianist was sympathetically received or not, Al could not be sure. There was no immediate ripple of arpeggios, but the fan did not seem disappointed. Possibly he was one who shouted for the sake of shouting. Now he turned to Al.

" 'Oop Bop Sh'Bam'!" the man said.

"What did you say?" Al asked.

"Name of the new number. It ain't no 'Salt Peanuts', but it tells a story. It's wiggy. You dig?"

"It's interesting."

247

"Bam, rebop, boom, bam," the man commented.

"Is that Charlie Parker on alto sax?" Al asked. "I've been in the Army," he explained apologetically.

"You can catch Bird at the Spotlite. Then Bird and Dizzy are going out to The Coast. What do you think they want to do a crazy thing like that for? This is where it's at."

"I think I have a lot of listening to do," Al said. "I'm not tuned in yet."

"When you get there, you're going to wonder where you were before. Wait till they play 'The Street Beat'. That is *it*."

"The speed is one thing that makes it difficult to follow."

The man gave Al a baleful look.

"You going to have to change more than that tie, man."

"The tie's wrong, is it?"

"The tie is *wrong*."

"I suspected it might be."

Al took off the tie.

"That's better," the man said. "Give me some skin, man!"

Al offered his hand. The man ceremoniously stroked his palm against Al's.

"My name's Al Dexter," Al said. "Piano."

"Righteous! Mine's Voot O'Roony."

"Voot O'Roony?"

"Yeah. That's my this-week name."

"What do you play?"

"Horses mostly."

"What are you drinking?" Al asked. He was curious. Voot seemed enviably cheerful.

"Later maybe. I got to see a man. Back in a while."

The music stopped. The musicians left the stand. Voot followed them out of the room, through a door in the rear. He returned within five minutes.

"All right then!" he said. "Let me get it. Be my guest."

Voot insisted on buying.

"Did you hear about the two bopsters?" he asked.

"No."

"There's these two bopsters, you understand, they're walking along the avenue, and suddenly from out of nowhere a gigantic church bell — you know? — it falls out of the steeple and it falls and falls and it just misses them and lands right at their feet —

bam! – it shatters, I mean it just really *shatters*, man, and one bopster, he's real shook up, he grabs the other bopster's arm and he says 'Hey, man! What was *that*?' And the other bopster says : 'F Sharp.' "

Al politely laughed.

"Are you sure you didn't hear about that other time?" Voot asked. "Same two bopsters."

"No," Al said.

"That time these two bopsters, feeling good, you understand, they stepping across the street and an ambulance comes screaming along, siren going full blast, electric bells ringing, red lights spinning, it misses them by inches and goes screaming on, and one bopster says to the other bopster, 'Man, I thought he'd *never* leave!' "

"That's good," Al said.

The musicians were returning to the stand.

"Aren't you a user?" Voot asked.

"No," Al said. "Not if you mean what I think you mean. At one time I used to smoke a little tea."

"I thought you couldn't be. If you want to dig this music, you got to shoot up. That's the only way you can stay with it. Think about it. If you ever need me, this is where I am."

Al finished his drink and left.

FIFTY-FIVE

Riverhead, New York, 1947

Moses met Al at the railroad station.

Moses' eagerness made him look younger than his age. So did his undergraduate clothes. He was in Ivy League summer dress, a gray and white seersucker jacket, a blue button-down shirt, a British regimental tie, with dark-red and dark-blue stripes, dark-gray flannel trousers, dark-blue socks and well polished old loafers.

Moses looked up and down the platform. At midday on a Saturday in August, not many people were getting off the train from the city. The sun was a fierce white glare in the hazy pale-blue sky. He did not see Al and felt a pang of disappointment. Perhaps he had been unable to make it, for some reason. But surely he would have telephoned, wouldn't he? It had been Al who had made the effort to get in touch after so many years. Nearly six.

A bop musician stumbled and steadied himself on the step down from a door in the coach section. Moses' attention had been focused mainly on the parlor cars. The bop musician, under the beret, the shades and the goatee, was white. He was wearing a crumpled light-gray business suit and scuffed purplish-brown cordovan shoes.

"Al!" Moses exclaimed. He hurried over and they shook hands.

"Great to see you, Mo. Now I know why they call it Long Island. The train took for ever."

"You're right on time."

"I've been up since dawn, it seems," Al said. "I wouldn't have missed this for anything," he added more tactfully. "You're looking great!"

Moses looked at Al and was unable to say as much. Al's face was thin and pale.

"The car's this way, out in front," Moses said. Al followed him to a three-year-old black Chevrolet two-door sedan.

"Safer with only two doors," Moses said. "Lou's almost six and a half. He's at that very active age."

Al wondered how he was supposed to know what that meant.

"I have no use for an automobile in the city," he said, as if

Moses had never lived there. "In the city an automobile's more trouble than it's worth. I haven't had an automobile since Fort Bragg. I had to have one there, out in the sticks."

"Riverhead's a nice little old town," Moses said.

"What made you choose Riverhead?"

"Mae has some family here. You know, an uncle, some cousins. It's nice to have family living near. They've been very kind to us. We see a lot of them."

"Yeah. Can we stop for a minute on the way to your place?"

"You mean for a drink?"

"Yes, for a drink. This heat. . . ."

"Sure," Moses said, stopping the car by the bar that Al had noticed. They got out.

"Averages ten degrees cooler than the city at this time of the year," Moses said. "That's the advantage of living near the water. We're right next to Great Peconic Bay, and close to the Sound – "

"I know where you are on the map."

" – and not too far from the Atlantic Ocean," Moses concluded, holding the barroom door open for his guest. "Maybe they'll desegregate some of those good South Shore beaches one of these days."

Al sat at the bar, waiting expectantly, and Moses ordered the drinks. Al's was a shot of bourbon with a water chaser. He didn't touch the chaser. Moses wondered why Al had bothered to try to give the impression that he was thirsty because of the heat.

"I didn't recognize you at first," Moses said, gesturing toward Al's beret. "You make me feel like a rube, a hayseed."

"A Brooks Brothers hayseed, of course," Al said, smiling. "Sorry about this," he added, removing his beret and stuffing it into an inside pocket, where it made his jacket bulge. Moses saw that Al's rust-brown hair was streaked with gray over his ears. "I forgot I was in a respectable place. And these can go." Al took off his sunglasses and stuck them into another pocket. "That's better."

Moses noticed the dark shadows under Al's tired, bloodshot eyes.

"Have another drink," Moses said.

"Thanks."

"And then let's get back. I know Mae's impatient to meet you. I've told her a lot about you."

Al drank his shot of bourbon in one gulp.

"I'm looking forward to meeting her," he said. "I'm ready."

On the way, Moses reminisced about the old days in New Orleans. Al was not responsive. Moses reminisced about the not-so-old days, about the pleasures of the music of their short-lasting septet.

"Fifty-Second Street isn't the same now," Moses said.

"Music is always changing," Al pointed out. "It has to change."

"It has to grow," Moses said.

"It has to *change*," Al insisted. "Everything has to change or it atrophies."

"I suppose you're right," Moses conceded.

"You don't mean that, do you, Mo?"

"No, I don't," Moses said.

They were laughing in the old relaxed manner as they walked from the car along the short concrete path to a neat, two-storey white frame house, in a row of almost identical neat, two-storey white frame houses. There was a locust tree with meager foliage on the withered grass of the front yard. A red tricycle lay on its side by the front door.

"Lou doesn't think too much of this," Moses said, lifting the tricycle to one side and standing it upright. "He thinks it's time for a change, too. But Mae doesn't want to see him go on two wheels yet."

"You're not saying I'm too *young* for bop, are you?" Al said. They were still laughing when they went into the house.

FIFTY-SIX

Mae smiled at their laughter. She was a good-looking woman, in an advanced stage of pregnancy, wearing a pink smock.

"Perfect timing!" she said. "It's ready to go on the table whenever you wish. You'd like a drink first, wouldn't you?"

Moses looked impassively at Al.

"That's all right," Al said. "Unless *you* want one."

"Good," she said. "Mo, will you fix them?"

"What would you like?" Moses asked Al.

"Whatever you're having," Al replied airily. "Bourbon if there is any."

"With water?"

"That's right, Mo," Al said, pretending to be pleasantly surprised. "You remember!"

Moses said nothing to that. He mixed two long, pale highballs and a lemon Coke for Mae.

"Where's young Louis?" Al asked sociably, when he had his drink in his hand.

"He's over at Aunt Emma's," Mae said. "They're all going to a Walt Disney movie. We thought we'd have lunch in peace. He'll be back soon enough."

"Mae's cooked us a real down-home meal," Moses said. "Let's take our drinks to the table."

"There's no rush," Mae assured them. "But all right. Mo's always hungry," she told Al proudly.

"He always was," Al said. "Especially when there was a smell of pie in the air."

"You used to grab your share, I seem to recall," Moses said affectionately.

"Now, boys!" Mae said. "I think there's enough here for the both of you."

The dining-room table was as pretty as a color photograph in *Good Housekeeping*. The centerpiece was a white porcelain figurine of a Spanish dancing girl, decorated with two gardenias. Gardenia petals were floating in the glass fingerbowls.

"Very nice," Al said.

"Cordon bleu cook and a graduate of the parent-teacher association course in flower-arranging," Moses said.

"Oh, stop it, Mo!" Mae protested with girlish gratitude.

"Lou's a graduate of nursery school," Moses continued. "They even had their own commencement program, handed out diplomas. Everyone in this family's a graduate of something, except me."

Moses and Mae sat at opposite ends of the table and Mae placed Al in the middle, on her right.

The first course was dainty green and orange melon balls, honey-dew and cantaloupe, with a sprinkling of ginger and slices of lime, in fragile little glass dishes.

"I hope you like ginger," Mae said. "I should have asked you."

"I do," Al assured her.

He finished his drink. He looked over at Moses, but he did not seem to notice the signal.

"Good cantaloupe," Moses said. "Where did you get it?"

"From the farm stand. Over on the Aquebogue road."

"Oh, yeah. You can't beat it."

He's loyal even to local fruit and vegetables, Al thought.

"Moses," Mae said. "Al's glass is empty."

"Excuse me, Al," Moses said. "I was just going to fetch some ice tea. Would you like some of that? Or would you like another highball?"

"A highball would be good."

"Right."

"Easier on the water this time, please," Al said.

When Moses returned from the kitchen, his smile had a rather forced look. It became genuine when Mae brought in a deep platter piled high with a steaming heap of shrimp jambalaya.

"There!" she said. "I hope you like it, Al. Mo got me a Creole cook book. This is supposed to be an authentic New Orleans recipe."

"*Supposed* to be! It *is* authentic!" Moses zealously affirmed. "This is the most authentic shrimp jambalaya known to mankind. This is the recipe they use at Galatoire's."

Mae recited the names of the ingredients and described her method of preparation in some detail and Al's mind wandered indolently through the streets of the French Quarter.

". . . they say the okra's important," she said.

"The okra?" Al said. "Oh, yes. Very important."

"The best way to enjoy jambalaya," Moses suggested, "is to eat it. That's what I always say."

"Here you are, Al," Mae said, passing him a Gargantuan portion. "I'll let you add your own Tabasco sauce. It's too hot for me, but Mo loves it. He uses so much Tabasco it makes your eyelids sweat just to look at it."

Moses passed Al the small red bottle of liquid fire.

Al probed in the rice and speared a big shrimp.

"This looks wonderful!" he said.

He was about to raise his fork to his mouth, when Moses said:

"What's your story, morning glory? What's new in the big city?"

Mae's eyes followed Al's laden fork as he rested it on his plate.

"Charlie Parker is better than ever. He's a giant. He's the biggest jazz musician who ever lived."

"Aw, knock it off, Al. He may be good, I'm not denying that, but nobody's that good. Nobody has cornered the market in being good, not even Louis. Louis says no one man can begin to cover all the ground."

"You asked me a question. This is the answer: Bird is the *most*, the *greatest*, and positively *the living end*." Al declared with the solemn, dogmatic finality of an *ex cathedra* pronouncement: "Bird is Bird. There is no Bird but Bird. That's all there is to it. When Bird blows his axe it's something else. He makes all other alto men seem like beginners."

"Rabbit's no beginner. Nobody can swing prettier than him."

"Johnny Hodges was all right in his day. This is a new day. He's obsolete."

Moses was peeved.

"That's plain dumb," he said. "I've heard you say some dumb things, but that's the dumbest yet!"

"Mo!" his wife said. "Al's our guest."

"Al's no ordinary guest. Al's my old friend. If a friend of mine says something dumb it's my duty to straighten him out. Isn't that right, Al?"

Moses grinned disarmingly. Al grinned back.

"All right, old friend," he said. "If I'm a friend of yours you can fix my drink."

255

Moses made no attempt to conceal his chagrin. He exchanged a quick look with Mae, who almost imperceptibly shrugged, as if to say, "Why not?"

Al noticed their reactions and resorted to cunning.

"On second thoughts, Mo, forget it. I don't want to drink up all your booze."

Moses immediately got up and took Al's glass.

"When you're in my house, Al, you can drink as much as you like."

When Moses was seated again, Al ingratiatingly smiled.

"Sorry, Mo. I shouldn't have come on so strong. But Bird is so great. I can't help going overboard. You should go up to Minton's late some night when Bird and Dizzy and Monk and the rest of them are jamming. It's out of this world."

"Monk? Who's he?"

"You haven't heard Monk? Thelonious Monk?"

"I don't get into the city much."

"He's mostly a sort of man behind the scenes. But everyone will know him one day. He's the greatest piano man of all time."

Moses almost rose again to the challenge, but Mae frowned at him and he subsided. He merely said:

"I like Art Tatum."

Al ignored this. He had been drinking since breakfast time – the time when people eat breakfast if they eat breakfast.

"You ought to come in one night. We'll go over to the Roost – "

"The place on Broadway?"

"The Royal Roost. The Metropolitan Bopera House – "

That suddenly seemed extraordinarily witty, and Al laughed so hard that he had a fit of coughing. Moses moved around and slapped him on the back, perhaps a little harder than necessary.

"Sorry," Al said. "What was I saying?"

"About the Royal Roost," Moses said coolly.

"There's a young trumpet man there now," Al said. "Miles Davis. He's – "

" – the greatest trumpet man since the creation of the universe!" Mo put in.

Al gave him a small, chastened smile.

"O.K., Mo," he said. "I'm sorry. You know me. It's only because I so much admire the way you play that I want to tell you about the other things I like, so you'll like them, too. Miles is good, but he doesn't have your feeling for melody. His style isn't as hot as yours."

Moses was immediately appeased.

"It doesn't matter, Al. There's plenty of room in jazz for all kinds of opinions. Jazz is big enough for everybody. The group I'm with out here plays what you cats on The Street call 'moldy fig.' But it swings. A lot of people still like it. I think they always will. If it's still good enough for Satch, it must have something. I liked Charlie Parker's 'Meandering', but I must admit some of the new records leave me cold. Have you been doing any recording, Al? I don't even know where you're playing. Where *are* you playing?"

"Moldy fig is right," Al mumbled.

Mae was getting worried about the food.

"Al, won't you try the jambalaya? Would you like me to heat yours for you?"

"Excuse me," Al said, suddenly standing and pushing back his chair, which fell over backward. "Where's . . . toilet?"

"This way, Al," Moses said, gently taking him by the arm, as though leading a blind man.

"Excuse me," Al repeated carefully. He seemed to be speaking to the world in general. "Don't feel . . . too good."

Moses took him up to the bathroom and returned to the dining room.

"I'm very sorry, Mae," he said.

"Is he all right? His face was a terrible gray color."

"I think he was about to throw up. He's in bad shape. He was juiced when he got off the train. I've never seen him like this before. I really am sorry about the jambalaya."

"*That* doesn't matter. He was probably out on the town last night. He reminds me of the nights at Small's. Thank God we're out of all that. Maybe I'd better make up the bed in the guest room. He'll be O.K. if he has a good night's rest."

"You're a doll," Moses said. He went over to her and kissed her.

Moses and Mae tried to eat. They only picked at their food. They were listening for Al. There wasn't a sound from upstairs.

"Better go see if he's all right," she said after a while.

Moses was gone for only a few minutes.

"He sounds fine. He said he'll be down soon. He must feel embarrassed. Let's stay in this evening, sit around, take it easy, play cards or something like that – kind of smooth things over. I know you'd really like him if you got to know him in normal circumstances. He's a really nice guy."

"I'm sure he is."

When Al came down his face was as white as chalk, but he seemed quite composed.

"I hope you feel better," Mae said.

"Much better, thanks," Al said. "I'm sorry about that."

"Would you like something to eat? Maybe some soup . . . ?"

"No, thanks. Nothing. I feel fine. Would you give me a rain check on the jambalaya? That's my favorite dish."

"Sure," Mae said.

"And now, Mo," Al said, "if you could just run me to the station. . . ."

Moses and Mae put up only token opposition to this proposal.

"We thought you'd be staying overnight," she said without notable enthusiasm.

"Oh, no, thanks, I couldn't," Al said. "I have an appointment in the city. A business appointment. I've got to get back. Perhaps you'll give me a call when you're in the city? I'm in the book. I know a couple of places in the Village I think you'd like. Will you do that?"

"Sure, Al," Mae said. "We'd like to do that one day."

In the car, Al said :

"You're very lucky, Mo. She's lovely."

"Yes, she is."

"I envy you."

"You ought to try it. Every man ought to be married."

"I am married, Mo."

"You are?" Moses said, looking around at him. "Why didn't you tell me?"

"I'm married to a needle."

"So that's what you were doing up there. I was afraid it was something like that."

"I didn't leave a trace of anything. I opened the window."

"How long has this been going on?"

"Not long. You needn't look like that, Mo. There's no need to feel sorry for me. It has its moments, like nothing else. You get to hear some beautiful music."

"A lot of that music isn't there, Al."

258

"Music's what you think you hear. It's all in the mind. Try it one time, as an experiment. I can fix you up."

"No, thank you, Al. I wish you'd let me take you to see my doctor. He's very sympathetic. He understands about drugs. There wouldn't be any police problem."

Al smiled a lazy, beatific smile. He was now at peace with everyone, even people who criticized.

"Bird's a user," he said. "And Bud Powell. Everybody's on the big H."

"It'll kill you if you let it," Moses said. "It'll kill all of you."

Al smiled.

They reached the station.

"Moses," Al said, "I meant to tell you earlier. You remember when we had our group before the war?"

"Of course. That was a great group. I wish – "

"Remember I scored some of your melodic ideas?"

"Yeah. Some of those worked out real nice. What happened?"

"Norman Granz is a friend of mine," Al said.

"The man who organized Jazz At The Philharmonic?"

"The same. He gave me the name of a music publisher. You'll be getting some money."

"That'd be swell. We're saving to go into the bar and grill business. With music. Anything you come up with would be very welcome."

"In the meantime though, Mo, I need some cash. For the man I'm going to see in the city."

"Oh, I see. How much do you want?"

"A hundred."

"A hundred! Al, I don't carry that kind of money on me. I'm sorry. Maybe I could let you have twenty, twenty-five, something like that."

"Please, Mo. I've got to have a hundred. He's not the kind of man who takes no for an answer. If I don't come up with the cash tonight I'll be in serious trouble."

"Oh, Jesus, Al.... Why do you do this to yourself?"

"Can you get me a hundred dollars now? I mean *now*?"

"Come on. There's a restaurant that'll cash a check for me. Oh, Al. Goddamn it."

They drove to the restaurant and Moses gave Al the money.

"I'll pay you back as soon as I can," Al said, putting the cash in his pocket. "Don't worry about it."

"Al, you know and I know : that's a hundred bucks I'm going to have to write off. Take it. You know you're welcome to anything I have. But I don't have money to throw away. We need all I make – we need more. So don't call me again, unless you want me to introduce you to my doctor. I'd like to do that right now, if you'll say the word."

"Thanks, Mo. I have a train to catch. Thanks to Mae. And say hello to your boy for me. I'm sorry I didn't have a chance to meet him."

FIFTY-SEVEN

Moses had been busy earning money for their new daughter, their new house, their new restaurant. He told himself that he should never be too busy for the preservation of a friendship, even a difficult one – especially a difficult one. This feeling, usually at the back of his mind, strengthened as Christmas approached. Three Christmases had gone by, three unanswered Christmas cards, since Al's unfortunate visit to Long Island. Christmas cards obviously were not enough. Moses sent Al a registered letter, inviting him to spend a weekend with them. Moses mentioned the rumpus room, with a pool table and an upright piano. The letter was accepted and signed for, but there was no reply. Moses decided that life was too short to wait any longer. He drove into the city.

The house on Bleecker Street did not impress him favorably. The yellow door did not compensate sufficiently for the building's general dinginess. Along one wall of the cramped vestibule, there was a row of seven gray metal mailboxes. Beside it, there was a vertical row of bell-pushes and hand-written name-cards. There was Al – *Al Dexter (3b)*. The neatness of the writing somehow made the name look lonely and rather pathetic.

Moses rang. He rang again and again. There was no responsive buzz at the locked inner door. There was no small nasal metallic voice from the intercom. Moses pressed the bell labelled *Super (B)* and got no reply. He found the outside steps down to the basement and knocked on the door, good and loud. At last the door opened a few inches on a chain and a white man's face appeared.

"Sorry," he said. "No coloreds."

"Don't shut the door," Moses said. "I want to talk with you."

"I ain't buying any."

"It's this important," Moses said, holding up a dollar bill.

Wheezing and grouchily muttering, the janitor led the way up to the third floor. Moses banged on the door. There wasn't a sound.

"He's out," the janitor said.

"I'd like to make sure," Moses said. "Use your master key."

"I can't let you into a tenant's apartment."

Moses gave him five dollars.

"You can stay till I see if he's here," Moses said. The janitor produced his key-ring and opened the door.

Al, fully dressed, was lying face-down on the floor.

Moses went down on one knee beside him and gently turned him over. The janitor stayed in the hall, peering in.

"Is he dead?" he asked unexcitedly.

"No, I'm not," Al said, opening his eyes. "Moses!" he exclaimed weakly, closing them again.

"I don't bother him and he doesn't bother me," the janitor stubbornly insisted.

"Fuck off!" Moses said savagely.

The janitor retreated.

"It ain't my job to play nursemaid to drunks," he said, as he lumbered ponderously down the stairs.

Moses hauled Al across the floor and up onto the unmade bed. He loosened Al's necktie and undid the top button of his unclean white shirt.

"Jesus!" Moses protested. "Al, look at you!"

Al's faded auburn hair was dull and tangled. His face was thin and as pale as putty, with a faint yellowish tinge, and apparently had not been shaved for several days. His whiskers were more gray than red. He was wearing the same light-gray suit he had worn on his visit to Riverhead. Al and the suit looked more than three years older. They both looked worn out.

"Oh, Jesus!" Moses kept repeating fretfully, as he looked disgustedly around the disorderly room. "Why the hell did I leave it this long?"

Typically, his first reaction was a feeling of guilt. Typically, it lasted for only a moment. There were things that he had to do.

First, he made two telephone calls.

These having been taken care of, he returned to Al. He was lying on his side, facing the wall, with his head bent downward, his hands clasped and pressed between his thighs, and his knees drawn up, in the position of an embryo in the womb. He was shuddering and mumbling incoherently and incomprehensibly.

Moses turned him over onto his back. Al's face was wet with sweat, but his teeth were chattering as if he were freezing. His

262

eyes were wide open. He seemed to be staring through Moses and beyond the ceiling.

"Al," Moses said.

Al did not reply.

Moses touched Al's shoulder. Al's arms and legs convulsively jerked, as though Moses' hand had electrically galvanized the muscles.

"It's O.K., Al," Moses said. "I'm going to get you out of here."

"Go away," Al said. "Leave me alone."

"You're sick, Al."

"Thank you, Doctor Decatur, for that valuable diagnosis. I've been lying here wondering what was wrong, and now I know."

"How about a cup of coffee? I'll make some. Why don't you have a hot shower? I think that'd help."

Al seemed to make an effort to focus his eyes. He gazed at Moses with an expression of profound compassion.

"Mo, it's good to see you. I love you, Mo. But you're talking out of your ass."

"Let me help you up," Moses said in a voice of synthetic brightness. "Stand under the shower and soak. It'll make you feel better. Come on."

"That isn't what I need. As any fool could see, I need a fix. If you want to help, go and get me a fix. I'll tell you where to go. There's some money on the dresser."

"I'm not going to do that, Al."

"All right, God damn it, I'll have to get it myself."

Al managed to climb off the bed. He feebly pushed Moses aside and went over to the dresser, whose top was cluttered with dirty laundry, a plate with a congealed fried egg on it, an empty gin bottle and two glasses, half full, and a pile of musical manuscripts and printed song sheets. He searched through the chaos calmly, then agitatedly and frantically, taking things up and throwing them to one side or the other.

"It's gone!" he said. "Mo! What did you do with the money?"

"I didn't touch any money, Al. Sit down. Relax. I'll look."

"It was here!" Al said, slapping the top of the dresser accusatively. "It was right here! I know it was. There must have been fifty bucks – at least!"

"Sit down," Moses said, firmly easing Al toward the bed. "I'll take care of everything."

Al was suddenly totally unresistant. He sat down heavily and began quietly sobbing. Moses painfully winced and turned to the dresser.

Of course, he found no money there. Even in his present distressed state of mind, however, Moses, in accordance with years of habit, glanced through the song sheets. He had to make a deliberate effort to refrain from commenting on what he saw. The topmost sheet was headed "BAYOU BOUNCE, by Al Dexter and Moses Decatur"; the second, "GUMBO JUMBO, by Al Dexter and Moses Decatur"; and there were several more in the same format. Moses was particularly surprised and hurt by the copyright that all of them bore – "© Voot O'Roony Enterprises, Inc., 1946." These were publications that Moses had never heard of.

There was no point in saying anything then. He went to the kitchen. Now he knew what people meant when they said "more in sorrow than in anger."

The kitchen was bad. The sink was full of unwashed dishes and stagnant water. A half-submerged frying pan contained a puddle of filth, white globules of fat and cultures of hairy pale-green mold.

Moses violently raised a window and let in a draught of cold, fresh air.

He boiled some water and, having found two clean mugs and a jar of Nescafé, made two black coffees.

"Here," he said to Al, who was still sitting on the bed, with his head bowed, silently snivelling. "Drink this."

His tone had authority. Al slowly sipped the hot coffee.

"Do you have a suitcase?" Moses said.

"In the closet," Al replied in a low, subdued voice. "Over there."

"Is there anyone we ought to call before we go? Have you been playing for anyone who might wonder what's happened to you?"

Al was silent.

"No, I suppose not," Moses said unkindly. "You couldn't be playing piano anywhere like this."

"There's a lot of racial prejudice in the jazz world," Al remarked, making a strange noise that was part gasp, part snicker.

"What kind of excuse is that?"

"No more Jim Crow," Al said, speaking to the floor. "It's the other way around – Crow Jim. You have to be colored. Your people have jazz all locked up."

"Jazz is something nobody can monopolize," Moses retorted automatically. "It's time you wised up to yourself. One thing you could do is shave off that Goddamn little beard. On you it's ridiculous. Oh, for Christ's sake! Let's save the argument for some other time."

In spite of the bizarre circumstances, Moses smiled.

"It isn't fair of you to complain about racial prejudice when you have me at a disadvantage. That's a low blow, Al. All right now, you can skip the shower. It's time we got the show on the road."

"It's all a lousy hassle," Al said. "How can I make a living? Fuzz victimized me. That's what they did, Mo. They victimized me. They even took away my cabaret card."

Al sniffed and shuddered.

"If I don't get a fix soon," he said, "I'll jump out of my fucking skin."

"Come on, babe," Moses said. "Let's go."

FIFTY-EIGHT

Westhampton, New York, 1950

The Decatur family doctor took a quick look at Al and immediately referred him to Dr. Malcolm Wheeler, the proprietor and medical director of a small, private sanatorium well known in east-central Long Island for rehabilitating drug addicts.

Moses drove Al the short distance from Riverhead to Westhampton right away. They arrived there in time for a pale yellow and gray sunset. Out of season, there was little traffic in the town, even along the main street. They passed the shops ("Merry Christmas!") and turned onto the quiet residential road that leads toward the bridge and Westhampton Beach. Still a short distance inland from the bay and the Atlantic, they came to a high privet hedge, the stone pillars of a gateway, and a modest painted sign, black on white, that said: "Westhampton House". They drove along a semi-circular asphalt drive between a few blue spruce trees on snow-powdered lawns and stopped in front of a large nineteenth-century gray clapboard house with white shutters. The garden, darkening in the dusk, looked as cold as a gray monochrome photograph, but some of the windows of the house were lighted bright yellow.

The farewell scene was brief, as they both wanted it to be. Both of them were shyly laconic. Each of them, in his own way, for his own reasons, seemed to be relieved of responsibility when Moses delivered Al to the white-uniformed, matronly receptionist and hurried away.

Dr. Wheeler received Al in a small, formal, entirely unclinical, oak-panelled library with a log fire blazing in a large granite fireplace. The doctor was a stocky, barrel-chested, middle-aged man in a brown Shetland tweed jacket and a neatly knotted dark-blue and -brown paisley bow tie of dull Ancient Madder silk. It was the sort of tie you could trust. He had a big, firm, roundish, pink head with very short gray hair and bushy brown eyebrows and blue eyes that appeared to be astonished and delighted to find themselves alive on such an extraordinarily amusing planet.

"Welcome," he said briskly. "Sit down. Dr. Weindorf tells me that you're in a bit of a mess." He laughed cheerily and vigorously manipulated the lobe of his right ear. "Fear not. We can do something about that. He says you're sound enough, basically. I'll examine you tomorrow. I'm a pragmatist. Let me tell you what I mean by that : there won't be any sort of doctrinaire bullshit. No criticism; no systematic analysis – that's a bore; no absolution. All I can offer you is physical health. It's up to you to accept it. Then, as far as I'm concerned, you can do anything you like with it – it'll be yours. I'm not the slightest bit interested in your psyche or your philosophy of life or your plans for the future. Agreed? Good. Now, I expect you need a fix. Don't panic. You shall have one, without delay. I don't believe in cold-turkey withdrawal. Unnecessarily uncomfortable. You can get off the stuff gradually; it won't take long. Much better that way. That's the end of the speech. We'll knock you out tonight. Have a good, long, deep sleep. Then we can have a talk. Goodnight."

FIFTY-NINE

By the end of March, Al felt very well.

Early every morning he went for a long walk along the empty beach. He enjoyed the lukewarm Spring sunshine. He enjoyed the shade. He even enjoyed the rain. When it was not raining, he enjoyed sitting in the lee of a breakwater, watching the sandpipers running, in their quick, nimble, clockwork gait, across the wet, firm sand, inches ahead of the incoming foaming water at the edge of the sea. The gulls, soaring and swooping and gliding, conducted his gaze across the white turmoil of the rolling breakers, out over the shining dark-green, dark-gray waves, over the flat ocean, like a sheet of steel, to the sharp horizon and the immensity of white clouds in a light sky. The fresh, cool gusts of Atlantic air, smelling of salt and sea-weed, rinsed out his body and mind, making him feel clean and strong and ravenously eager to get back to the city.

In the sanatorium itself, the time began to drag. The only thing he had in common with the other inmates was that he and they were all there together. He did not play ping-pong or bridge or pencil-and-paper games. There was no piano. The main events of the day were the meals, which were plain, substantial and good. He read. Most of the books in the lounge were paperback novels about homicidal hide-and-seek in exotic foreign capitals and adultery and crises of identity in the suburbs. He watched television – all of it.

He looked through his own music, which he had brought in his luggage, thanks to Moses. There were complete compositions and incomplete compositions; there were many notes for compositions, mere fragments in wildly erratic manuscript that he could not remember having written. Reading much of this music was like reading the works of a stranger for the first time. Some of it, to his surprise, seemed original, lively and interesting, and he wished he had a piano to play it on. He experienced a growing desire to make music.

Moses kept in touch by telephone and sometimes came to see him. Moses was always cheerful. When he came in the afternoon of the first Saturday in April, Al had some good news for him. They drove over to the beach and went for a walk.

"He says I'm ready to go," Al said.

"That's great!" Moses said. "He told Dr. Weindorf you have the constitution of an ox."

"I can't tell you how grateful I am, Mo."

"Aw shucks, fella – 'tain't nothin'!" Moses said, turning a cartwheel that was less than wholly successful. He landed on his back on the sand, jumped up laughing and brushed his hands. "Out of practice."

"I haven't yet asked about my bill. Bills, I should say. There's Dr. Weindorf's as well, of course."

"Don't worry about a thing. Everything's under control. You're in good shape – that's what counts. Jazzmen have been dropping like flies, seems like."

"Listen now, Mo. Seriously. I've been through all that muddle of papers, and found my royalty statements, and I've figured out your share so far."

"That's fine. Before you go on though, let me say this: there's no rush. The business is going well and the group's been fully booked and it looks like we're going to make some records. Mae's quite a manager."

"Anyway, Mo. I've drawn up a kind of document, listing all I owe you. I'll complete it when I'm about to check out of here. It's the best way, I think. As soon as I start earning money I'll start paying you back."

"O.K., Al, O.K. That's cool. But until that happy day. . . . I recently applied to the bank for a loan. We're redecorating and enlarging the restaurant. It went through just like that. Our credit is tops. For the first time in my life, I seem to be making more than I need. But what about you? Do you have any plans? Do you know what you want to do? Maybe I can help some way."

"One thing kind of cramps my style: I don't have a cabaret card."

"I know. You told me. That's too bad."

"I did? Oh. Anyway, that means I can't play in the New York clubs. Maybe Dr. Wheeler can do something – maybe his testimony that I've straightened out. . . . I don't know. But to start with, I do have an idea."

"What's that?"

"Well, I was looking at some of my music. And I've been looking at TV. Some of the music for the commercials is quite good; but some of it's lousy. I know I could put a lot more oomph into some of those jingles if I introduced a subtle but strong jazz feeling. Those flatted fifths and sevenths could tickle the nerve-ends that inspire all those housewives to buy."

Moses almost said something but he saw that Al was speaking in earnest.

"Uh-huh," Moses said, as neutrally as possible.

"Have you noticed the Vita-Crunch commercials?" Al asked.

"No, can't say I have."

"No, you probably wouldn't see them. They're on in the mornings. They're obviously aimed at women. The message is short and to the point – 'Vita-Crunch is the Lovers' Lunch!' Only eight syllables, eight little notes. But they have the wrong notes."

Al sang the slogan.

"I see what you mean," Moses said.

"I found this sequence of mine jotted down – part of an unfinished opus. Listen to this!"

Al sang again.

"Crazy!" Moses said.

"It's a little different," Al said. "Only eight notes, but they're notes that could stick in Mrs. America's wig-box when she goes to the supermarket."

"Yes, they might at that. You got one note more to play around with than Pepsi-Cola, and look what they did!"

"This is music written on Cloud Nine, fitted to the words in the TV lounge of a sanatorium – how can it miss?"

"It's got everything going for it," Moses agreed, confirming his opinion with a cartwheel that went all the way.

The next morning, Dr. Wheeler sent for Al.

"It's been nice having you," the doctor said, toying with his ear, "and now I think you should go, if you feel able to face all those people out there. It's best to get out before there's any danger you might get to like it here. Is there anything you wish to ask me?"

"What about drinking?" Al asked.

"What about drinking?" Dr. Wheeler repeated.

"Would it be all right if I had a few drinks?"

"As your medical adviser, I can say only that there is no physical disability on your part. There is no medical reason that you should not drink. If you want my own, personal opinion, I would say, man to man, that anyone who lives in New York and doesn't drink must be out of his mind."

SIXTY

New York, 1951

With money that Moses had practically forced on him, Al took a small furnished apartment on West Seventy-Fifth Street, within half a block of Central Park.

"You can't write commercial jingles in a pig-sty," Moses had pointed out. "Who ever heard of a pig writing commercial jingles? Good ones, I mean."

In a local delicatessen, Al asked for a packet of Vita-Crunch.

"I only sell food here," the delicatessen owner said. "Try the supermarket."

Al stopped the girl at the check-out counter from putting the packet in a paper bag.

"Thanks," he said, "but I'm going to read it here."

"Another nut," the girl's weary nod seemed to say.

There was a long list of ingredients in fine print – the artificial flavorings, artificial colorings, emulsifiers, antioxidants and all the other stuff that made Vita-Crunch what it was. And beneath this list was the name of the manufacturer, in even finer print – American Nutrition, Inc., of Omaha, Nebraska. Al telephoned the company and eventually succeeded in eliciting from them the name of their advertising agency, the mighty Hudson, Rubicon & Meander, of New York. Remembering a Dale Carnegie precept from his subconscious store of folk mythology, he went to the agency's Madison Avenue office in person, which is always the best way to go anywhere. When he stepped from the taxi, the *Newsweek* building proclaimed that the time was eleven-fifty and the temperature was sixty-eight degrees.

The English woman at the reception desk said the Vita-Crunch account executive was unavailable, unattainable, unnameable. No, he was not in a meeting. No, there was no point in waiting. No, he wasn't there. Al gave her a direct person-to-person look that penetrated her contact lenses and pierced the very soul of her confidentiality. She impetuously disclosed that the account executive's name was Howard von Hagen and that he was on his way to P.J. Clarke's and Al was not to tell him she had said so.

Al entered the small, old red-brick saloon by its Third Avenue entrance and found himself in an Irish bar. At a few minutes after noon, it was not as yet crowded. The first thing he noticed was the music from the juke box, Bix Beiderbecke's wistful piano rendition of his own composition, "In A Mist". Al liked it. It was old hat, of course, but it was old hat of the finest quality.

He asked one of the grizzled barmen whether he knew a Mr. von Hagen. The barman pointed to a man in a group of half a dozen agency vice-presidents in their Springtime lightweight olive-green suits, blue shirts and black knit ties, who were zapping each other with zippy one-liners, while drinking cold Guinness from small glass tankards, even though none of them had the account.

Al introduced himself to Howard von Hagen, a man in his mid-thirties who wore his sparse black hair carefully arranged sideways across his scalp, like General MacArthur's, heavy, black horn-rims and the quizzical, ironic smile of one who had got through existential poetry unscathed only to discover that the real intellectual toughies of our time are all in communications and marketing. He did not receive Al with any warmth until he said :

"Good juke box. Not many bars would have 'In A Mist' on their juke box."

"You've been here before," von Hagen said.

"No."

"Then you're a Bix fan," von Hagen said approvingly. "That record's one reason I always try to get over here early. In half an hour you won't be able to get near the juke box, or, if you can, you won't be able to hear 'In A Mist'. They keep the sound 'way down. He was a fantastic musician. I like him on piano even better than on cornet."

"I only saw him play piano once," Al said. "Piano was something very private with him. He didn't like to play it in public."

"You *saw* him play piano? What do you mean, you saw him?"

"In Chicago, back in the twenties. That was when he was with the Wolverines. It was an after-hours joint, very late. He was stoned, of course. It was tantalizing. He passed out, with his forehead on the keys, right in the middle of something wonderful. He had a piano style of his own. He had that beautiful, melancholy purity that seems to mean more than it says and somehow makes you happy. My own piano didn't sound right for a week. He made me feel clumsy."

"Let me get this straight now," von Hagen said slowly. "You knew Bix?"

"I saw him. I met him. I don't suppose anyone ever really knew him."

"But Jesus!" von Hagen said clapping his hand around Al's shoulders. "You were there! You met him : you knew him. What did you say your name was?"

Howard turned to the others.

"Hey, you guys," he said, "Al here was a friend of Bix Beiderbecke's in Chicago!"

Howie later invited Al to Sunday brunch in the Village.

"It's open house," Howie said. "Come over whenever you surface. There'll be all kinds of people drifting in and out. Creative people, fun people. We'll have a ball. We always do."

Al was willing to do almost anything to get his music into a commercial for Vita-Crunch, so he said he would be there.

SIXTY-ONE

Like many other senior young advertising men, Howie savored the experientially most meaningful segments of his life at home on weekends. Sometimes under the pressure of a particularly rugged brain-storming session at the agency he would loosen his necktie; at home he often didn't wear one.

He lived in a stimulating, aware block of Sullivan Street, below Houston Street, in Little Italy. His bachelor pad, a studio apartment, consisted of one very large charcoal-gray room, functional and comfortable, with free-form furniture of natural light woods, aluminum, leather and glass, brightened here and there with artfully positioned what-the-hell little cushions in absolutely uncompromising primary red, yellow and blue. Ferns and ivy in hanging wire baskets screened the Pullman kitchen, which Howie called "the bar". There was a big, recognizably expensive abstraction, dark brown bisected by a zig-zag of light brown. He kept it on the wall even though he found it impossible to forget that one of his guests had once said the painting looked like an electrical storm in a vat of fudge. On another wall, to thwart attempts at classification, there was an eighteen-century Pennsylvania Dutch primitive oil painting of an infant girl whose formal dress gave her the appearance of a midget bride. The décor was completed by the naked black machinery of an elaborate do-it-yourself high-fidelity ensemble, a dark mahogany upright piano and some of the obligatory imitation Tiffany ceramic lampshades that are often cited in Greenwich Village as proof of the axiom that it doesn't matter what anything is or what you put it with as long as it's *good design*.

Al arrived at one-fifteen. Howie opened the door. He was wearing a Bloomingdale's "French Week" *matelot*'s T-shirt, with horizontal blue and white stripes, coarse off-white trousers tightly laced at one side, and Mexican *huarache* sandals. As Al crossed the threshold, Howie pressed into his hand a frosty pewter tankard.

"Booth's gin and Schweppes ginger beer with masses of ice and a couple of slices of cucumber," he said. "It's delicious! Or haven't you got a hangover? You can have something else, if you like."

"This is fine, thanks."

"I love the blazer," Howie said. "So marvellously prim and proper. Come and meet some of my friends."

He introduced Al to twelve or fourteen men and women. Some of them were standing and drinking and talking; some were talking and drinking and reclining, like contortionists at rest, cupped in chairs like giant canvas oyster-shells or giant leather doughnuts. They were all identified by brand-names with which they were associated in one way or another or by the media through which they enriched the cultural life of the city. In spite of his protestations, Al was established as someone who had been "very close to Bix."

Al forgot the names of most of the other guests almost immediately and he was willing to forget their faces. But there was one striking exception. There was an exceptionally good-looking blonde with dramatic brown eyes, a sun-tan and pale pink lips. She was wearing a turquoise suit of Thai silk, a pink coral bracelet and a gold wedding ring. She appeared to be of the age when many attractive women of energy and means are working on their second divorces.

"Ann Faraday," Howie said. "You remember her husband, Bob, of course." He looked solemn for a couple of seconds, paying his respects to the deceased, and then, as a dutiful host, brightened. "Al plays piano, too, Ann. Get him to tell you about his days with Bix Beiderbecke."

Al, like most other Americans, did remember Bob Faraday, a pianist known as "the witty, urbane Washington society bandleader." His plane had disappeared over the Sea of Japan last Christmas Eve. He had been on his way from Tokyo to Pusan, Korea, to join Irv Frank, the comedian, and his big Christmas show for the troops. During the past three months there had been a not altogether unsuccessful posthumous public-relations effort to make Bob Faraday the Glen Miller of the Korean War. Critical assessments of Bob Faraday's music, which one reviewer in *The Washington Post* had once accurately described as "marshmallow music," were upgraded after his death. The Bob Faraday Orchestra, under the uninspired and uninspiring leadership of Gil Merriam, the embarrassing tenor sax exhibitionist, was still a going concern; but even its most devout admirers were already noticing the paucity of new ideas. As he pulled a chair close to the lovely widow, Al hoped that she would not expect him to praise her late husband's declining band.

"Before you sit down," she said with a charming smile, "be an angel and get me a gin and tonic."

The normality of her request gave him hope that there would be no need for him to express his sympathy in the false terms of a memorial eulogy. He gave her the drink and sat down and spoke from the heart.

"That's a terrific tan. Where did you get it?"

She touched her cheek and smiled ruefully.

"I suppose it looks rather callous," she said. "Widows should be pale, shouldn't they? I was spending Christmas with friends at Lyford Quay when the Defense Department sent me word of Bob's death. They persuaded me to stay. I did most of my mourning in a bikini. That sounds awful, doesn't it?"

Al imagined her in a bikini.

"No," he said. "Not at all. It was probably the best thing to do. Where's Lyford Quay?"

"New Providence. The same island as Nassau. Bob and I spent our honeymoon in the Bahamas. We sailed with two other couples from Palm Beach to Eleuthera. It was a disaster. Bob was seasick all the way. He's no sailor. He *was* no sailor, I mean."

Al was irrationally jealous. A few minutes after having met her, he already minded her sentences that began "Bob and I" and "We". He was glad Bob had been sea-sick.

"I've never been down there," he said in a voice that he hoped implied he preferred to winter in the Swiss Alps.

"You should try it. I'm sure you'd like it."

"I'll keep it in mind," he promised ironically, considering his financial situation and prospects for the foreseeable future.

She lowered her eyes as she sipped her drink, and he yearningly admired her eyelashes.

"Eggs benedict soon, everyone!" Howie announced. "I hope all of you like them, because that's what we're having."

"How's the gin holding out?" somebody asked.

"Oodles," Howie said. "From now on, everyone has to help themselves."

The gaiety of the occasion seemed to have snicked into a higher gear.

"There ought to be some music," a woman said.

Al tried to make himself invisible. He needed not have felt any sense of danger that he might be put upon. Her suggestion was directed at a regular member of Howie's entourage, a young man in fawn corduroy slacks and a red shirt who looked like Truman Capote before his face changed.

"Play something, Terry!" Howie said. Terry needed no urging. He was already sitting down and opening the piano.

"He's supposed to be very good," Ann said, turning slightly, to face the piano.

Al felt another twinge of jealousy. This is ridiculous, he thought. He glanced at her profile, the straight, short nose, the curves of her lips, the brave line of her jaw, her long, slender neck. Her hair was up and the nape of her neck looked silky with light blonde down. He turned to Terry.

Quite unexpectedly, the music first pleased and then amused him. Terry was a clever pianist but not as clever as he thought. He was daring to the point of recklessness. He repeatedly got himself into difficulties which he usually managed to cover up with elaborately ornamental embroidery. But he made one error that seemed to Al so gross and so glaring that he groaned aloud in protest. He had not noticed that Howie was standing close beside him.

"What's the matter?" Howie asked. "Did our Terry make a boo-boo?" .

"It was nothing," Al said.

"Certainly it was something. Come and tell him. It's good for him. He's much too pleased with himself."

Howie, smiling maliciously, dragged Al over to the piano. Terry, having perceived extrasensorily that something was going on, something, perhaps, not a hundred per cent *comme il faut*, wound up the number and confronted them.

"Yes?" he said.

"I think Al has something to tell you about your playing," Howie said.

"No, I haven't," Al said. "Really. I thought it was very interesting."

" 'Very interesting' – oh, dear!" Terry exclaimed. "That's what one tells the producer when the play stinks. What did I do to deserve that? Didn't I play the way Bix would have liked?"

"It had nothing to do with Bix," Al said irritably.

" 'It' – then there *was* something wrong," Howie said coaxingly. "What?"

"All right," Al said. At this stage, he didn't care very much about Hudson, Rubicon & Meander and the lousy Vita-Crunch account. "A minor point. I'm sure nobody else cared or even noticed, but you got the bridge all wrong."

Terry clapped a hand over his forehead as though mortified. He turned to Howie.

"Goodness gracious me!" Terry said. "He says I got the bridge all wrong."

"What's the bridge?" Howie asked.

"The release," Al said impatiently. "The middle bit. I'm sorry I didn't keep quiet. Who cares? I really couldn't care less. Please go on, play something else."

"No, wait a minute," Terry said. "There's no hurry. What about the bridge? There was nothing wrong with the way I played the bridge."

"You mangled it," Al said coldly.

"Al's a pianist," Howie reminded his young friend. "There's nothing for anyone to get upset about."

"Oh, shut up!" Terry told Howie. "I know he's a pianist. At least, you already said so. But isn't he a rather *old* pianist?" He turned to Al again. "Perhaps what I was playing is a bit *avant garde* for your taste. A bit after your time."

"It isn't even very new," Al said, smiling now. His smile seemed to annoy Terry.

"Tell me more, smarty-pants," he said.

"It dates back to before the war."

"Wrong. Anything else?"

"Maybe you've heard Monk play it. He was playing it last year. He can make anything sound new."

"Oh, he's heard of Monk."

"O.K., Terry," Howie said. "That's enough. Why don't you play for us?"

"No, this is fascinating," Terry said nastily. "I always love meeting these old know-alls. There's one at every party – an old music bore who doesn't know what he's talking about."

"But I do know," Al said. "In this instance, at any rate. I happen to know that rather obscure piece that you tried and failed to play. It's called 'Gumbo Jumbo'."

Terry was silent.

"Well?" Howie asked him. "Is that what it's called?"

Terry ignored him. He got up from the piano.

"All right," he said to Al. "You say you know so much. Prove it. Let's hear you try."

Al's annoyance had completely dissipated his reluctance. He sat down. He played "Gumbo Jumbo" straight. He played it up and down, forwards and backwards, sideways and diagonally and inside out. He played it slowly and he played it fast, in every time signature known to Western man.

When he finished, everybody cheered – everybody including Terry.

"That was absolutely sensational!" he said. "Utterly brilliant. I take back everything I said. I take back everything I *thought*. If only the composer could have heard that!"

It was one of those moments of *Walter Mitty* triumph that people dream about.

"I am the composer," Al said.

SIXTY-TWO

"That was most satisfactory," Ann said.

"Thank you," Al said. "It was for me, too."

"Oh, yes, that was most satisfactory as well. Very obviously. I was talking about your prowess at the pianoforte."

"Thanks again. It was kind of fun, wasn't it?"

"Wonderful, wonderful fun."

"The whole day has been fun. I never imagined a day could be this much fun."

"Nor did I," she said.

They reviewed in their minds the day's events.

"I wish you'd seen the expression on that young man's face when you were playing and he realized how good you are. You slayed him."

"He took it very well really."

" 'Utterly brilliant!' he said. He was right. You are, Al. You are utterly, utterly brilliant."

"Right now, I'm utterly, utterly starving."

"So am I," she said, delighted that they had hunger, too in common.

"We'll go out and eat huge steaks," he promised. "Later. Are you really allergic to hollandaise sauce?"

"Me allergic to hollandaise? Of course not. I adore hollandaise. I dote on it."

"I'm glad. But it was very wicked of you then, telling Howie you couldn't eat his eggs benedict."

"It was the first excuse that came to mind. I didn't want to stay any longer. Did you?"

"No, not a minute longer. I was impatient to get back here."

"You're still glad we did, aren't you?"

"God, yes," he said. "Aren't you?"

"Yes, I am. Very."

"Howie couldn't have been too badly put out. He asked me to his office tomorrow. 'We'll talk jingle,' he said."

"Madison Avenue tycoons adore success. They dote on it."

"Like hollandaise."

"Exactly. Creamy success. Your performance today was a smash hit. He was very impressed."

"I hope you're right."

"I'm sure I'm right. Those were his very words. He said : 'I'm very impressed.' "

"Maybe he'll give me a contract for my Vita-Crunch music."

"Of course he will."

"I'm going to assign all the proceeds from my first jingle to Louis Decatur. There could be a lot of residuals."

"*Louis* Decatur?"

"Moses' son."

"You think a lot of Moses, don't you?"

"I do."

"But you won't mind moving down to Washington, will you?"

"No. I'm looking forward to it. I said I'd give it a whirl. I don't see why I shouldn't be able to do something for the band. I'll try. I've written plenty of arrangements. I've played with all sorts of groups of various sizes."

"I don't doubt your ability, Al. I know you'd be a perfect leader. I only want to be sure you won't mind associating with a so-called 'society band.' It's a very commercial operation, and you'll have to smile a lot. We don't have to pretend it's anything great musically. It isn't bad though."

"It's a big step up from Vita-Crunch," he pointed out.

Ann smiled. They quietly thought for a while.

"Al," she said.

"Yes?"

"Were you in the service?"

"Yes. During the war."

"I thought so. What happened to your little finger?"

"I'd rather not talk about that."

"I understand."

A few moments later she spoke again.

"Ouch," she said. "What *are* you doing? Ooh, that tickles!"

"It's meant to."

"Mmm," she said.

SIXTY-THREE

In Transit, 1951

Al rented a car and they headed south. They were in a rapturously festive mood, happy to be alive and together. They marvelled at the scenic wonders of the Jersey flats – the swamps, the flames from the refineries, the hoardings advertising Broadway shows.

"The history of mankind!" Al observed, as they sped along the elevated highway above the primitive landscape, the industry and the promise of musical comedy.

"Utterly brilliant!" Ann said, for it was a phrase they often used.

A State Police patrol car chased them and eventually caught them and flashed its red light, stopping them at the verge of the New Jersey Turnpike.

"Where's the fire?" the trooper asked, who had evidently been supplied for the occasion by Central Casting.

"In my heart," Al replied; and, immediately perceiving that he would have to keep things simple, he added: "We're going to a wedding, officer. We're going to get married."

The trooper shook his head, grinning, as he put away his book of tickets.

"For that you shouldn't hurry," he said. "Take my word for it. Keep the speed down, fella, or you could end up going to a funeral."

Ann gave the trooper one of her most radiant smiles, and he waved them on.

"Get going," he said, "before any of us have second thoughts."

As he drove on, Al said:

"I've had second thoughts, and third thoughts, and they're all as good as the first thoughts. I love you."

"I love you, too," she said. "Aren't we fortunate?"

Crossing the Delaware, Ann said:

"I'm suddenly getting nervous. I bet Washington wasn't this nervous."

Al laughed nervously.

"He probably had a hotel reservation," he said. "But don't worry."

"I feel as though I'm abducting you."

"You are."

"How did you escape from getting married all these years?"

"I don't abduct easy. Nobody asked me."

"Louse!" she said fondly. She frowned earnestly. "You were the first one to talk about getting married."

"All right. Then I'm abducting you as well. But you were the one who thought of a justice of the peace in Elkton, Maryland."

"It's on the way. And it seemed funny at the time."

"It isn't funny now," he said. "This is the least funny day of my life. Up to now."

"You do mean that, don't you?"

"Yes. You aren't getting cold feet, are you? It isn't too late to back out. But if you want to you'd better hurry."

"No, I'm sure I don't. Do you?"

The conversation continued in this questioning and self-questioning manner. The miles of concrete smoothly hummed by. When they reached Elkton, they were both calm and resolute.

Though the J.P. recited the text parrot-fashion, while the witness, his wife, looked as if she were wondering about something she had left cooking on the kitchen stove, the words, apparently taken from some sort of *Reader's Digest* abridgement of the Episcopalian prayer book, exerted their ancient magic.

" '. . . so long as you both shall live,' the man said," Al remarked, as they walked slowly, arm in arm, back to the car.

"I'm game," Ann said.

"Me too," he replied, lightly kissing her cheek. "Provided you promise to let me die first. I know that's selfish of me."

"Do you know this part of the country?" she asked, as they drove on. "There's a lot of your history I don't know."

"It'll be something for me to tell you during all the long nights we're going to have together. I once spent some time in Virginia – Bull Run, Virginia. That hardly counts; it was a long time ago. As for Washington, I've only been through it. I spent a weekend there on the way to Carolina. That was long ago too. So the answer is no."

"Then you don't mind if I make a suggestion?"

"This is a partnership. Go ahead."

"Let's go down by way of the Eastern Shore of Maryland and across the Chesapeake Bay. That way we can spend tonight in Easton. I know a nice little hotel there, the Tidewater Inn."

"I don't want to stay anywhere you've stayed before," Al said.

"Staying with you will be completely different," Ann said. "We can't undo the past. I wouldn't want to try. It was the past that got us here. It would be silly to pretend we were born two weeks ago. But our life together is new. Together we'll make everything seem new. Besides, let's be a little bit practical."

"Must we? Already?"

"Yes, we must," she said firmly. "We're going to live in my house, aren't we? Or aren't we? We aren't going to abandon it, are we? I *like* it. I'm sure you will. It's ours now."

"I hadn't thought about that," he said.

"It'll be all right. I know it will."

"I'll *make* it all right," he said. "Show me the way to this Tidewater Inn."

SIXTY-FOUR

Washington, 1952

They both made it all right, better than just all right. They lived in a small neo-Georgian red-brick house in a small garden at the end of Ivy Circle, a small *cul-de-sac* off Connecticut Avenue, in Georgetown. Everything was small and perfect. Al called it neo-Georgetown : all the old houses had been renovated and refurbished. Like most of their close neighbors, the Dexters enjoyed the plain elegance of Early American furniture and the comfort of Late American mechanical convenience.

Al and Ann sat at the breakfast table in the kitchen, drinking their morning coffee and looking through the french windows at their single exquisite weeping cherry in the full bloom of their second Spring.

"You're not looking at television, are you?" Ann said. "Do you mind if I switch it off?"

"After the commercial," Al said.

"Is it one of ours?"

"Why else would I want to watch a commercial?"

"Vita-Crunch is the Lovers' Lunch!" sang a smooth, hip, closely coordinated quartet, like Mel Tormé in quadruplicate, with a cool, swinging accompaniment by French horn, flute and harpsichord. And by Al, snapping his fingers and waving his arm as though he were still conducting the group, as he had conducted it in the studio.

"Great!" he exclaimed at the end of the mini-performance. He pushed the *off* button.

"Though you say so yourself," Ann added with a wry smile.

"Though I say so myself," he acknowledged, smiling apologetically. "You must admit the new unit's good. If only you could imagine how much effort and how many takes we needed to produce that minute of film!"

"I can imagine. It took you a whole day and you were exhausted at the end of it."

"The jingle is a surprisingly demanding form," Al said. "People who've never tried it don't realize how difficult it is. On an LP you can take your time. With this, though, every second counts; every semi-demi-quaver...."

" 'Miniaturization to the nth degree,' " she said, quoting him. "But honestly, darling, the time has come for some maximization. You owe it to yourself. You don't need to do any more commercials. How about your real music?"

"Jingles are real music. They have to say a lot, very persuasively, in a little time. Writing them is the strictest imaginable discipline. But I appreciate what you're saying. And I'm planning to write something that can be somewhat more extensively developed."

"When, darling?"

"Soon. In the meantime, the band's shaping up well, you must agree. I'm seriously considering eliminating the strings and strengthening the brass section. But we don't want to alarm anyone."

"Heaven forbid!"

"And don't be sarcastic, sweetheart. It's the embassy party circuit that I need the strings for, and half our bookings come from your diplomat friends."

"I wasn't really criticizing what you've done with the band. It probably wouldn't have survived if you hadn't streamlined it. I was only thinking of you, of your music."

"I haven't forgotten it."

"Moses somehow manages to keep making the records he wants to make."

"It was partly to pay Moses all the money I owed him that I went into the jingles business."

"But you've paid him, so that's all right."

"Every time I hear the Vita-Crunch theme it's like hearing the clatter coins into Louis' piggy-bank."

"The flutter of hundred-dollar bills," Ann said. "Not that I begrudge him a single penny of it."

"I'll call Moses one of these days," Al said. "Maybe he and I can get together and work something out musically."

"I wish you would."

"I love you," he said.

"I love you too."

SIXTY-FIVE

Baltimore, 1956

Al Dexter & His Orchestra (formerly the Bob Faraday Orchestra) played most of their gigs in the Washington area. However, since Al had established several smaller subsidiary groups, the organization was now able to take on a greater variety of engagements and to venture farther afield. The official and semi-official social functions of the Government, the diplomatic corps and their numerous hangers-on and would-be hangers-on continued to constitute the basis for the company's growing prosperity; but Al also catered to country clubs, fraternal organizations, wedding parties, bar mitzvah celebrants, college students, trade associations and even to the herds of slightly used débutantes pushed forward on offer to society.

On this occasion, Al had brought the full orchestra, a Greyhound busload, to provide the music for a débutantes' cotillion in the ballroom of a downtown hotel. It was a high-budget affair, with all the pomp and circumstance the traffic would bear – all the courtliness of a royal occasion without the royalty. Al had not seen such a vulgar display of flowers since Chicago.

The program chairman, a severely corseted dowager with the facial complexion of an albino crocodile and anglophilic *a*'s so broad that they threatened to dislocate her dentures, simpered at Al in a formidable effort to charm him. The effort failed. Immediately after he had paid his formal respects to her, he committed the orchestra to the capable hands of his deputy, changed into his street clothes and left the hotel.

He found a bar nearby, on Eager Street, and drank a restorative Jack Daniel's on the rocks.

"Where's the best place in Baltimore to hear some jazz?" he asked the bartender.

"I don't go for it myself," the bartender said, "but hold on a minute." He crooked a forefinger at a black busboy, who came over with the frown of a man who did not wish to take on any extracurricular duties.

"Hey, Jefferson," the bartender said, "you're always singing that jazz music. Where's the best spot in town for jazz, the gentleman wants to know?"

"That depends," the busboy said, giving a cursory glance.

"Real jazz," Al said.

"Well, if you want some *real* jazz, you're in luck. Lady Day's in town."

Al got the address and thanked the boy and gave him a dollar and hurried out.

"O.K., Jefferson," the bartender said behind Al's back. "I'll take a piece of that." He took the bill and returned fifty cents.

A taxi took Al up Pennsylvania Avenue, in North-West Baltimore, where all the pedestrians were black. The taxi stopped in front of a nightclub.

"Are you sure this is the place you want?" the white driver asked.

"This is it," Al confirmed.

"It's a nigger joint."

"Billie Holiday's singing here," Al said, getting out and handing money in through the window of the taxi. "She only comes to Baltimore once a year."

"I wouldn't go in there if you paid me," the driver said.

"I wasn't offering."

"Nigger-lover!" the driver commented and trod hard on the gas.

The club was so dimly lighted that when Al first entered it he could see nothing but the bandstand, a narrow platform inside the hollow rectangle of the bar. There she stood, herself, alone, in person, Billie Holiday, a black-haired brown woman in a tight white dress, in a white spotlight, singing "Them There Eyes".

"What can I do for you?" asked a black man in a black tuxedo near the door.

"A table, please," Al said, "or a place at the bar – anything."

"How many are you?"

"Only me."

"Come this way."

As Al's eyes adjusted, he could see that the place was crowded, but there was a small table by the wall close to the singer.

"There's a cover charge and a minimum," the head waiter said, as Al sat down.

"Sure. Fine. Thanks."

Now that he was near her, he could see that Billie Holiday looked older than the recent pictures he had seen. She was only forty-one years old. She looked at least fifty. Her short, black curls were shiny, with a white flower over her left ear, but her shoulders were plump and flabby, the flesh under her arms bulged over the top of her dress, and her face was bloated and furrowed with anguish.

Booze, Al thought. Heroin. He recognized the painful look in her eyes from his own mirror of not so long ago, and his heart ached for her.

She was singing "Fine and Mellow", a blues she had written about a man who did not love her. The music and words were low-down and wretchedly sad, and yet she made misery inexplicably exhilarating.

She finished the song and bowed her head to the applause. Al clapped hard.

A waitress brought him a highball.

Drinking, he looked around at the other tables beside him and in front of him. He was the only white person in the room.

"Thank you, thank you," Billie Holiday said. He wondered how clearly she knew what she was doing. Her voice sounded tired. "And now I'd like to sing 'Strange Fruit'. The words are by Lewis Allen."

After the flat, unemotional announcement and the brief and simple musical introduction, the slow, terrible words about a Southern lynching hit Al like a series of slow, heavy blows. Worse, in that company, the brutal details of the lyric ("the bulging eyes and the twisted mouth") seemed to be directed at him, like the particulars of a criminal indictment. He felt that he was surrounded by angry hostility.

Moses, he thought, where are you? How could Al explain to these people around him that he was a friend? There was no way he could assure them of his good faith, his liberal credentials.

The song ended.

The room was silent.

Billie Holiday looked at Al.

She slowly stepped down from the stand. She slowly walked toward him. She seemed to float toward him in slow motion, while everybody else sat still, silently staring at him.

"Hi there!" Billie said, and gave Al a big fat kiss on the lips. They had never met before.

The whole room relaxed.

Al stood and asked her to sit down. She sat beside him.

"What will you have to drink?" he asked.

"Nothing, thanks," she said. "I'm not drinking."

That evening, Al telephoned Moses.

"We've got to write some songs together," Al said. Moses said he'd like to do that.

"Duke Ellington and Billy Strayhorn often collaborated by telephone," Al said. "Why shouldn't we?"

"Why shouldn't we?" Moses said. "I'll be Duke and you can be Sweat Pea."

SIXTY-SIX

London, 1960

O n his first morning in the city after the flight from New York, Moses had a late breakfast in a café in Shepherd Market, near the May Fair Hotel, where they were staying. It seemed strange to be in a place where so many people spoke with English accents. This was London long ago.

The October air was damp and chilly, so he didn't walk as far as he had thought he might. He decided to return to the hotel and take it easy until it was time for Louis' press reception.

In the lobby, another English voice came surprisingly from a bespectacled, bearded young white man dressed in a khaki Nehru jacket and a Nigerian beaded hat.

"Excuse me, sir," he said, standing in Moses' way, "if you're with the Louis Armstrong All Stars, could you spare me a few minutes?"

"Sure," Moses said. "What do you want?"

"If we could sit in a quiet corner for a moment, I have a few questions I'd like to ask you."

"Why don't you wait a little? Then you can ask old Satch himself. If you're press, that is."

"Oh, I am, I am," the young man assured him. "I represent *The Free Jazz Quarterly*. Our first issue's coming out next month. I'd rather speak to you alone. He'll be mobbed up there by the dailies. I have to get my own exclusive angle."

"O.K.," Moses said with a sigh. They sat down in armchairs with a small round table between them.

"Would you like a cup of tea or anything?" the young man asked. "I'm on expenses."

"No, thanks. I just had my first cup of English coffee. My stomach's all confused "

"You wouldn't mind if I have some, would you?"

"No. Go ahead. Have a ball."

The young man rang for a waiter and ordered hmself some tea. He opened his large notebook and opened a ballpoint pen.

"By the way," the young man said, "my name's Abdullah Ibn Safim. I've got a press card. I can show it to you, if you like."

"That's O.K.," Moses said. "I like to live dangerously."

"What's your name?"

"Just plain old Moses Decatur."

"Please would you spell it? I want to make sure I get everything right."

Moses spelled his name and Abdullah Ibn Safim carefully recorded it. Evidently he was a conscientious interviewer. He had some questions written down. Now he posed them.

"Mr. Decatur, would you say that Ornette Coleman's white plastic alto saxophone is a magic wand that has liberated jazz?"

"No, Mr. Safim, I wouldn't."

"Oh. Well, do you feel that by breaking away from the established traditions of European and American musical culture and by embracing those of the Third World we may look forward to a new Free Jazz better able to express our awakening consciousness of the economic, political and social problems of our time?"

"No."

"Oh, dear," Mr. Safim said. "I was rather hoping you would. Our whole editorial philosophy is founded on that concept."

"I'm sorry."

"Never mind, Mr. Decatur. I'm sure it's not your fault. Let me ask you this: you do recognize, don't you, that the antique structure of melody, harmony and rhythm has been smashed, that solo instrumentation has been absorbed in improvized collectivism, and that the contemporary emphasis is on pure energy and feeling and tone color?"

"No, I don't."

"Oh, Mr. Decatur, that really is too bad. It was our understanding that Mr. Armstrong is taking his band on a forty-five-concert tour of the new nations of Africa."

"That is correct, pops."

"But Mr. Decatur, surely you aren't telling me that Mr. Armstrong is planning to take the shattered fragments of the antique structure of melody, harmony and rhythm to the peoples of the emergent nations?"

"No, I'm not telling you that. Satch has been around for a long time – sixty years – and so have I. Africa's been there for quite a while too. We've found that most people like a beat they can pat their foot to and a tune they can sing under the shower."

Abdullah Ibn Safim put his notebook and pen on the table. He looked shocked.

"Mr. Decatur! The State Department of the United States is sending Mr. Armstrong abroad as an ambassador of goodwill to offer *that*!"

"The State Department and the Pepsi Cola Company. Don't forget Pepsi! Louis says the last time he toured Africa, four years ago, he ran into some very thirsty weather down there."

"What are you in the band?" the young man asked exasperatedly, apparently disturbed by what he regarded as Moses' frivolous attitude to a serious subject.

"On this happy occasion, you might say I'm going along for the ride with my old buddy. I'm the band boy. I'm taking care of the travel arrangements, keeping an eye on the instruments and the rest of the baggage."

The young man's eyes brightened with angry tears of frustration.

"Why didn't you tell me that in the first place?" he asked.

"Why didn't you ask me? I advised you to go talk with Louis. You still can. If we go up now, we'll be able to catch most of the press shindig."

In the Monte Carlo Suite, television and press cameramen and reporters were crowding around Louis Armstrong and his fourth wife, Lucille. It was the twentieth anniversary of the night they had got married, in St. Louis, Missouri. They looked very happy. He was posing, pretending to play his trumpet. She, an orange-rinsed matronly lady in a quiet gray suit, was showing a man her gold bracelet, from which dangled charms symbolizing some of the countries Louis and she had visited on tour with the band. There was a lump of green jade from Hong Kong and there were gold models of the Eiffel Tower and Big Ben.

"Moses!" Louis called out when Moses entered the throng. "Thought we'd lost you! There's someone somewhere pouring brandy and Benedictine if you want one."

"Would you be willing to play in South Africa?" a reporter asked Louis.

"I'll blow my horn anywhere my manager books me," Louis said. "Going to Leopoldville's just the same as going to Hoboken, New Jersey. It's just another one-night stand. It'd be the same with South Africa. But I got no business with politics."

Once more, Abdullah Ibn Safim winced, as if Louis had blasphemed.

"We've got men to take care of that," Louis persisted. "I just blow. I don't care where I do it – in my back yard or in Africa. Them cats down in Ghana, all the chiefs and all the ordinary people, everybody, they really dig our music and, daddy, I dig swinging for them. We played an outdoor concert for a big crowd of them, and we played 'Royal Garden Blues', and I played some of them high notes – you know? – and some of them pretty notes, and they really dig all that. There was one old fella, about a hundred and ten years old, and he was really wailing. He danced all over. When we left that country all the cats came to the airport and sang 'Satchmo, good-bye.' There were nine trumpets, all playing for me, so beautiful, and I played with them, and they sang 'All for you, Louis, all for you.' So of course what we want to do now is go on back down there and lay it on them again."

"Have you been playing more commercially in recent years?" another reporter asked.

"What is commercial?" Louis answered. "What's jazz? All music's jazz, if you want to play jazz. My biggest number in Germany is 'The Vie en Rose'. A note's a note in any language, daddy. Miles Davis – I buy his album because he sounds good. But it was Joe Oliver who taught me how to *live* music. And that reminds me : where's that Humphrey Lyttelton? Where's Wally Fawkes? What's the good of coming through London if I don't get to see my boys?"

Another reporter was interviewing Dr. Alexander Schiff, of New York, Louis' personal physician.

"I've sent ninety-three pounds of medical supplies ahead to Accra," Dr. Schiff said. "Louis isn't a hypochondriac, but he does like pills, especially a good strong physic at the end of every day."

"Louis has always been a big laxative man," Moses said. "Ever since he was a kid back in New Orleans."

"Louis' lips have tough spots, like corns," Dr. Schiff said. "But they're in good shape."

"Every night, after he's taken his pills, Louis sterilizes his trumpet mouthpiece in witch hazel and puts it away wrapped in a handkerchief, safe from germs," Moses said. "Captain Jones taught us a lot of hygiene at the Waifs' Home."

"Do you practise?" a reporter asked Louis.

"I touch that horn every day," he replied. "You got to keep your chops eulogized."

"What do you think of progressive jazz, Mr. Armstrong?"

"Oh, God," Moses protested. "Here we go again!"

Abdullah Ibn Safim held his pen in readiness.

"That reminds me of a groom in a New Orleans livery stable who attracted a lot of suckers long ago," Louis said. "He put up a sign offering for a dime each to show them a horse with its tail where its head ought to be. He'd just turned that old horse back to front. You can get away with that just one time."

"Hallelujah!" Moses exclaimed.

Louis grinned and eased his way through the crowd, leading his wife by the hand.

"Come on, Mo," he said. "That's enough of that. Let's go and grab some chow."

On the way through the lobby, Moses said:

"I wonder where I can buy a postcard. I promised Louis I'd send him one from every country."

"That's a lot of postcards!" Louis Armstrong commented. "Where is he, Mo?"

"I hoped you'd ask," Moses said with a smile. "He's in his second year at Juilliard."

"Best music school in the business," Louis said.

"Someone in the family has to learn how to read and write music properly."

"You've always seemed to manage all right. That's nice for the boy though, the Juilliard School. Must set you back a pretty penny."

"It doesn't cost me a cent," Moses said. "You know who's paying his way? Vita-Crunch, that's who."

"There's a cop," Louis said, as the three emerged from the hotel. "Mo, ask the man where they keep the steaks in this town – the big ones."

Abdullah Ibn Safim gave up eavesdropping in despair. Why couldn't jazz musicians talk the way they were supposed to talk?

SIXTY-SEVEN

Washington, 1969

"Mo?" Al said, calling from the telephone beside the piano in his music room. "Are you busy?"

"Oh, hello, Al. I'm not busy. But if you've called to ask for ideas you sure have called the wrong number. I haven't had an idea for a month. I've just been sitting by the pool and staring. Is it hot down there?"

"In Washington in August? But you don't mind heat, do you?"

"I'm bored. Do you think maybe we're getting old?"

"Nonsense. How would you like to take a trip?"

"I can be packed in ten minutes. Where to?"

"Which country in Africa did you like best, when you went with Louis that time?"

"Ghana. He figured that's where we came from. It was like a family reunion. Tens of thousands of relations, all stomping!"

"Ghana then. Would you like to go to Ghana?"

"Did I hear you invite me to Ghana just now?"

"You did."

"Sun hasn't got to you? You're not on the sauce? Isn't this the time of year most people down in Washington are heavy into juleps? Isn't it kind of early in the day?"

"This is for real, Mo. You know Ann and I see a lot of the State Department people. It's part of the job, and some of them are friends. We were having dinner with a couple of them the other night, and we were talking about the usual things, such as the bad taste Vietnam's put in a lot of mouths and so on, and someone mentioned how much jazz has done to brighten our image abroad, and then, of course, some of the obvious names came up – Duke and Dave Brubeck and Louis et cetera. Anyway, these friends of ours thought it would be a good idea for State to get someone to shoot a movie of American jazz in the Third World and distribute it for television world-wide, instead of sending a band on a world tour. Using film, they could get a lot more mileage, more exposure, faster and cheaper. All they'd have to do is send a band to one country. They said it should be an African country – kill two birds

297

with one stone, help cool the inner-city ghettos while they're at it and – "

"And you got the job, and you're looking for a house black but you'd settle for pale brown?" Moses said.

"You have such a clear way of putting things, Mo. It's something like that. The next day, State called about Louis Armstrong. He was so successful on every overseas trip he ever made. But, as you know, Joe Glaser's death put a lot of extra strain on Louis, and Louis' health hasn't been good."

"Joe was more like a father than a manager."

"I know. Then they asked me. They said they'd like to send a small group, like the All Stars. There were only six or seven of them, weren't there?"

"Trumpet, trombone, clarinet, piano, bass and drums."

"I've written a special 'Third World Jazz Symphony.' "

Moses laughed.

"A symphony for a sextet? The Government isn't that short of cash, is it?"

"I have a secret weapon, Mo. Electronics. Some exciting ideas. I need you, Mo. You've made the African scene. You've been to Ghana. How about an encore? It'll be a quickie – there and back. The Government *isn't* short of cash, Mo. We'll be well paid. And we'll be seen all around the world. What do you say?"

"Tell me more about the electronic bit."

"But say yes."

"You know I'll say yes. Of course yes. O.K., yes. Now tell me : what's your diabolical scheme?"

"Get down here, Mo. I'll explain everything on the way to Africa."

"Well, it'll beat sitting and staring at the pool," Moses said.

SIXTY-EIGHT

Accra, Ghana, 1969

"When R. A. Moog developed his synthesizer, back in the late fifties, he really started something," Al said, his eyes agleam.

"I wish he hadn't," Moses said.

"Wait till I show you."

They were standing on the stage of the big new civic auditorium, one of the biggest indoor arenas in all of Africa, on the evening of the premiere of Al's "Third World Jazz Symphony". There were still a couple of hours until show time. They had agreed that the concert should be held under cover because the film crew said they could not afford to risk the interference of rainfall on an open stadium. Moses had his trumpet with him but he had not yet taken it out of its case. Al was supervising the installation of his electronic musical equipment, whose bulky control consoles, speakers and other components took up a considerable part of the great stage. Moses was in attendance as an observer, or kibbitzer, offering unsolicited criticism and advice.

"Music is human," Moses said. "This synthesizer in inhuman. How can it make music?"

"Don't be such a reactionary," Al said. "Think young. The jazz musician of today is like an astronaut at the controls of a spaceship. I'm showing you the way into new dimensions of space and time. The music we're going to make is the music of the spheres."

"Would Buddy Bolden have liked it?" Moses asked.

"Buddy Bolden cracked up. Perhaps he cracked up because he imagined jazz beyond the limited capacity of his horn. At last we have the means to create jazz that goes all the way. The synthesizer's capacity is infinite. As Joachim Berendt, the German jazz authority, said, when writing about Terry Riley, what we have here is 'music for a person's aura rather than for his ears.'"

"I hear you talking, Al. But what do you mean?"

"You've heard Sun Ra's Arkestra, haven't you?"

"Garbage."

"That's narrow-minded. How would jazz have progressed to its present state if everyone had resisted change the way you do?"

"It wouldn't have. It would still be right where it belongs – down by the old main stream." Moses sang the last phrase in the style of an old barbershop quartet, but Al was not to be diverted.

"Sun Ra used a clavinet, a rocksicord, an electra piano, a spacemaster – "

"Even just the words give me the heeby-jeebies."

" – and, of course, the Mini Moog, a compact, cut-down model of Moog's original synthesizer. I think the Mini Moog is too restrictive. That's why we're using Braun's new Great Synthesizer for tonight's performance. Take a good look at this, Mo ! This isn't only today; this is the future. In the future nobody'll be beating on things and plucking things and blowing through things. Jazz will be made by jazz programmers and jazz engineers. Look !"

Al pointed at the vast gray box in the center of the imposing array of machines.

"It looks like Houston Control," Moses observed disgustedly.

"Many a true word said in jest ! The same computer people were consulted," Al said. "The best."

The Great Synthesizer had an extremely complex instrument panel, all nickel-plated steel and illuminated glass and rows of toggle switches and knurled knobs.

"You're happy with that ?" Moses asked.

"Why wouldn't I be ?" Al demanded. "It's only the most powerful, versatile, innovative, sophisticated, technologically advanced custom-built music machine of all time, that's all. It runs the whole gamut of the spectrum of sounds – twenty-nine tone colors, everything from the electric harpsichord effects, through all the strings and wood-winds, to the vibraphone, gongs, chimes, bells, blocks, cymbals, tambourines and drums, and finally the fattest brass you can possibly imagine, like World War Three coming at you, for the big, *big* band effects. Not only that, this ultimate synthesizer can produce all the non-instrumental sounds, like those weirdo outer-space whoops and bleeps – all that the human ear can register, and more. There's a whole bunch of sounds you can only feel the vibes of, deep in the gut."

Al patted the gray steel of the cabinet, as a horseman of an earlier era might have patted the neck of his trusty steed.

"This synthesizer has a solid-state echo unit for repeating arpeggios and for vocal doubling, to infinity. There's a built-in fuzz-wah volume pedal with an automatic noise-gate. You want to bring in the sine-wave tone of the oscillator? Easy. There's an insulated glide switch."

"You wouldn't want to be without one of those," Moses said.

"They mocked Einstein," Al chidingly reminded him. "There are *four* tuneable octave dividers, with sympathetic cut-off, and synchro-mesh glissando and reverb control, plus overdrive you can rev 'way up if you want. There's enough power in this baby to fly this auditorium all the way to the Goddamn *Moon*! And the amplifiers are guaranteed against thermal fatigue. Well, Mo. Aren't you a little bit impressed?"

"Why did you want to bring the rest of us? That's my only question," Moses said.

"For contrast," Al said. "The trumpet, trombone, clarinet, piano, bass and drums will represent the past. You know I've always loved jazz, Mo, at all the stages of its evolution. Just because I have this Great Synthesizer doesn't mean I have no regard for our beginnings. I'll always have the greatest respect for old-fashioned man-made music."

"You've always dug the latest gimmick, haven't you, Al?"

"It's a case of progressing or perishing," Al said.

"O.K., Al. I said I wanted to come, and here I am. I won't let you down. But I must admit this is far beyond my worst nightmares. I never thought you'd join the electric-jazz crazies."

"Would you help me set up the music-stands and distribute the scores, Mo? Time's running short."

"O.K., Al."

"I'm surprised you call them 'electric-jazz crazies.' You wouldn't call Miles Davis crazy, would you?"

Moses stopped what he was doing, adjusting one of the stands, and stood upright and faced Al.

"I suppose Miles Davis has been one of the most influential jazz musicians ever since he began," Moses said. "I suppose he's the most successful jazz musician we have now, individually, in commercial terms – certainly the most successful trumpet player."

"Without doubt."

"His success doesn't bug me, Al, I swear. Maybe this makes me square in your opinion, but let me tell you something: I hereby pronounce Miles Davis's famous sensitivity a pain in the ass. And that goes for Cecil Taylor, too, and double for John Coltrane. So sue me. But give me old Satchelmouth any day."

"I've always admired your loyalty," Al said.

"So I'll finish handing out the part of Al Dexter's 'Third World Jazz Symphony'," Moses said. "And I hope you won't be too disappointed if the people don't dig it."

They were interrupted by the arrival of the man who represented the State Department. He had accompanied them all the way from Washington. He was a pale-faced ectomorph in a charcoal-gray, drip-dry, miracle-fiber tropical suit. He was a dedicated, professional worrier.

"Everything under control, Mr. Dexter?" he said. "One hour and forty minutes to go. We didn't have to give away any tickets. The concert's a complete sell-out. The President and his wife will attend, and the whole of the Cabinet and all *their* wives. The diplomatic corps will be fully represented. The media will all be here. They've been flying in all day. The film guys are on their way over from the hotel. Are you almost set up, huh, Mr. Dexter?"

"We're almost ready, Mr. Winthrop," Al said.

"Like cool," Moses said, putting on his black jazzman act, because he knew it would make the man sweat blood.

"If there's anything I can do . . ." Mr. Winthrop said dutifully.

"Nothing at all."

"The Voice of America's putting you on tape. They want to do an interview later."

"Fine," Al said.

"Well, good luck then," Mr. Winthrop said.

"Luck doesn't come into it," Moses said. "Jazz is a science. Or hadn't you noticed?"

Mr. Winthrop smiled uneasily.

"Ghana's security people have been very cooperative," he said. "They've gone over the building with a fine-tooth comb. They also used Alsatians and mine-detectors."

"Make sure the audience all check their weapons at the door," Moses said. "You know how emotional these Africans are."

Mr. Winthrop went away, courageously biting his lower lip. Al and Moses, having completed the setting-up, went backstage to their dressing rooms to change into evening dress.

By the time the concert was due to begin, movie cameras were established in the wings, at one side of the footlights, half-way up the central aisle and at the front of the first balcony. Every seat in the great auditorium was occupied. A couple of hundred more people were allowed to stand in the back, before the fire chief called a halt and hundreds more had to be turned away from the doors. The atmosphere of expectancy became more highly charged minute by minute, during the preliminary formalities and while speeches of mutual congratulation were made by spokesmen for the State Department and the Government of Ghana.

Al sat at the controls of the Great Synthesizer in the middle of the stage. The other musicians sat in an orthodox configuration to one side of him.

The first movement of the symphony was to feature the synthesizer alone. Al threw the master switch, the control panel lighted up pale green, and he started playing.

There was a low, rising hum, like the approach of a hostile swarm, a cloud, an all-engulfing plague, of jet-propelled hornets. This huge, oppressive buzz was suddenly pierced by a long, thin, keening screech, as of superheated steam being pumped through a tin whistle. The effect was not merely disturbing; the sound's high pitch approached very close to the threshold of pain. This threshold was actually surmounted by a vast brazen crash, Force 99 on the Zildjian Scale, like the explosive demolition of a glass skyscraper, but much noisier. That was the overture, which had been composed with the intention of catching the listeners' attention.

Their attention was then subjected to the burden of a longish passage of almost unbearable monotony : to the accompaniment of a slow, rhythmically repeating thud, like the enormously amplified heart-beat of a dying robot, there was a duet of incompatible electrical appliances, the dirge of a tubercular vacuum cleaner and the muted clamor of an alarm clock trapped in a thick woollen sock.

This was even worse than Moses had feared it might be. Not even the most polite of audiences will tolerate boredom placidly for long. And this was not a case of simple boredom; it was acute, first-degree boredom, with the complications of the disappointment and irritation caused by the unexpected lack of promised jazz. Moses could sense the mood of discontent. He shared it. If nothing were done about it, it would certainly intensify. Resentment might soon find an outlet in active expression. There was a danger of a united slow sarcastic clapping of hands. There could be catcalls.

303

He uneasily contemplated the extremely large size of the audience and the largeness of the people in it. A riot was not beyond the realm of possibility. He looked apprehensively in all directions. Then, having made up his mind, he hurried silently out into the wings.

Al was undertaking a difficult and dreary pianissimo passage that sounded like nothing more than the faint chirruping of a distant radar beacon, and the audience was audibly grumpy, when the electric power was cut, plunging the auditorium into darkness and the Great Synthesizer into silence.

It was so dark that Al could not see even the machine's control panel, which was only inches away. He was wondering what he should do, when he heard the hoarse, urgent rallying cry of Moses Decatur:

"O.K., you cats! Let's give them 'Saints'! One! Two!"

And Moses' splendid trumpet, a loud, fierce, thrilling clarion call in the dark, led the way, and the others eagerly joined in, playing "When The Saints Go Marching In".

The old jazz hymn had never before been played, and had never before been acclaimed, with such passionate jubilation.

Al felt his way over to the piano before the end of the first chorus. When he gave the rhythm sections the benefit of his strong left hand and introduced some wildly happy new ideas with his right, he heard Moses' exultant yell of approval. Al responded with an invisible grin and by pounding away at the piano with unprecedented fervor.

After phenomenally energetic and ingenious solos on every instrument in turn and the triumphant final ensemble, the auditorium seemed to rock and palpitate with an uproarious tumult of applause. According to one local newspaper commentary the next day, the applause must have astonished the good people of Ghana all the way down the coast as far as Takoradi.

When the cheering had diminished sufficiently for him to make himself heard by his fellow musicians, Al said:

"All right then! 'Tin Roof Blues'!"

During the third chorus, which was devoted principally to the clarinet, Al noticed that the sextet was temporarily without a trumpet.

That was when the lights came back on.

The audience cheered.

The green lights of the Great Synthesizer were glowing once more. Al got up from the piano. The audience gasped. He walked over to the synthesizer and switched it off.

The movie cameras were all whirring, as the President, himself, rose to his feet, and his Cabinet and the rest of the audience also rose, to give Al an ovation in acknowledgement of his generous act of self-abnegation.

The sextet went on to play a comprehensive program. They played some more of the jazz classics. They played outstanding jazz of the middle years. And they played some new things. In a solo piano interlude, Al played Thelonious Monk's "Functional" and Duke Ellington's "Laying on Mellow", from his *"La Plus Belle Africaine"* suite.

The evening was a tremendous success.

At the official Government reception after the concert, the President heartily shook Al and the other musicians by the hand and lavished praise on them. This heart-warming scene of international amity was recorded by a hand-held camera of the State Department film unit.

Mr. Winthrop said that frankly he was overjoyed.

"And I know they're going to be overjoyed back in Washington," he told Al. "The evening could have ended in chaos and tragedy. First, I thought your equipment had blown the fuses. But the stage manager said somebody apparently got into the wings and pulled the plug, as he put it. He said you sent out one of your men to put it right. That was quick thinking. I don't know how to thank you. I can't imagine how those Communist terrorist *provocateurs* succeeded in infiltrating the building, after all our precautions. They'll stop at nothing in their attempts to discredit us. The way you played on throughout the crisis unquestionably averted panic and disorder – and who knows what casualties. The whole Government of this country was imperilled, and you saved it. You will not find me unappreciative, Mr. Dexter."

Al found Moses by the bar.

"Mr. Winthrop said the power failure was caused by Communist sabotage," Al said.

"That was real sneaky, wasn't it? Still, everything turned out for the best."

"Yes, Mo, it sure did. I guess the best way to thank you is by swearing I'll never, never touch another synthesizer or have anything more to do with electronic jazz as long as I live."

"That makes the whole trip worthwhile, daddy-o!" Moses said.

"You've completely cured me, Mo, I guarantee."

"That's cool. As my friend Adam C. Powell always said, 'Keep the faith, baby!' "

SIXTY-NINE

A nn had been complaining of a slight pain in her left arm, so
Al drove the car. They arrived at the south-west gate of the
White House at five minutes past ten, five minutes late for the party
in his honor.

"I forgive you," said President Nixon, in evening dress, shaking
Al's hand and holding his forearm. The politician's double grip
signified extra-special friendship. Simultaneously, the President
smiled warmly at Ann. "Geniuses have to be allowed plenty of
leeway. Isn't that right, Mrs. Dexter? That's what I keep telling
Pat."

"Do I hear my name being taken in vain?" Mrs. Nixon said,
approaching with a big toothy smile.

"I'm afraid it's my fault we're a little late, Mr. President," Ann
said, clinging to their lateness as a comfortably non-controversial
topic. "I usually drive, but my husband had to drive tonight."

"Do I detect feminism raising its lovely head?" the President
quipped devilishly. "You know, somebody ought to do something
about this Washington traffic. There ought to be a law."

They all laughed.

"But seriously," he said with an earnest frown, "is it still sleeting
pretty bad out there?"

So they discussed the January weather at some length. It was
that sort of evening – a quiet, cosy get-together with Dick and
Pat at home.

"Many's the time Pat and I have danced to your music,"
President Nixon told Al.

"Thank you, sir," Al said.

"Real smoochy music," the President said, reaching for his
wife's hand and giving it an ostentatious squeeze. "Sometimes we
leave the record-player and let it turn itself off."

"The kids go for your quartet," Mrs. Nixon said.

"Yes, that's right. The hot numbers," the President said.

Al's smile was rather strained, as it usually was when strangers,
however well they meant, complimented him on his work. Ann

307

wondered how he thought he could keep it private. Since his return from Africa, there had not been much let-up. He had been persuaded quite easily to do a television special. But the LP of the Carnegie Hall concert had resulted in more offers than he needed. And now this. She was beginning to wonder whether her judgement had been altogether sound earlier in the week when Eamonn Andrews, the Irish TV personality, had telephoned from London and she had agreed to help inveigle Al to fly over to visit Ronnie Scott's jazz club there. When they showed up in the Soho club one night in March, the master of ceremonies would startle Al by confronting him with a broad grin, a red-bound volume and the celebrated declaration : "This is your life. . . ." For a bandleader, Al was still sometimes strangely shy. Of course, the Nixon White House was enough to embarrass *anyone*.

"Here's Mr. Balliett," President Nixon said. "Mr. Balliett come here a minute, so I can introduce you to our guest of honor and Mrs. Dexter. Al, Whitney Balliett, of *The New Yorker* magazine, wrote a very nice piece on the little birthday wing-ding I threw here last April for Duke Ellington. The Presidential Medal of Freedom I presented to Duke was the first one of my Administration. Maybe if you and Ann are real nice to Whitney he'll give you a write-up too. That'd be quite an honor – the Medal of Freedom and *The New Yorker* both in one week."

Whitney Balliett managed a smile.

"The President has given you the same size band as he gave Duke – ten pieces," he said. "I see there are some good repeats. Gerry Mulligan and Paul Desmond both made it again, and Milt Hinton's on bass, the same as last year."

"One of my favorite bass players," Al said.

The President made his brief speech near the microphones in the glare of floodlights. He read the citation. He gave Al the medal, "for swinging services to America's special relationship with the freedom-lovers of Africa and all the World." Al thanked him. The President shook his hand again, for a long time, for the cameras.

The rest of the evening was a fine musical party.

Many of Al's friends were there. Moses wasn't, but he had sent his son.

Louis Decatur congratulated Al soon after the presentation. At the age of twenty-eight, Louis looked more like a football pro than an associate professor, which was what he was. Juilliard had talked him into returning to the school as a member of the faculty.

"Dad was very sorry he wasn't able to make it," Louis said. "He hasn't been feeling too well. He sent his love, and so did Ma."

"This medal should really belong to him," Al said. "Did your father tell you the story of what happened in Ghana?"

"Yes. We had quite a laugh over it. He gave me another message for you. He said you mustn't think you're such hot stuff, getting the medal instead of him. He said the President had to give it to you. A black cat copped the first one, so tonight it had to be Whitey's turn."

SEVENTY

New York, 1976

On one of his increasingly rare visits to the city, Moses late
one night stopped by Gregory's, a small musical bar at the
corner of First Avenue and Sixty-Third Street. He knew it was a
place he could rely on for good jazz. He was no longer able to tolerate any sort of jazz he considered bad.

On this occasion, the Brooks Kerr Trio was playing music
by Duke Ellington. Brooks Kerr, a blind, white stride pianist in
his early twenties, had total recall of the entire Ellington *œuvre*.
He could play anything that Ellington ever wrote, and he could
play it right, note for note as Ellington wrote it. Indeed, during
the present long engagement, Brooks demonstrated an inflexible
preference for not playing anything by any other composer. Close
to the upright piano there were two other active practitioners of
Ellingtoniana – Russell Procope, alto sax and clarinet, who played
with Duke during some of the best years, in the middle of his
career, and Sonny Greer, the drummer, who was a charter member of Duke's original Washingtonians, in Washington in the
1920's.

Brooks recognized Moses' voice by the first few words of salu-
tation.

"Sit down by the piano, man," Brooks said. In accordance
with the hallowed traditions of jazz, he used his piano as a bar.

"How about 'Drop Me Off In Harlem'?" Moses suggested.
Brooks tilted his head to one side for a moment, as though listening
to a celestial choir.

"You mean the one that goes like this?" he asked, romping
into action. Yes, it was the one that went like that. He was joined
in this pleasant venture by Russell Procope, who played his alto
sax sitting with his back rigidly straight and his face as inscrutably dead-pan as Johnny Hodges' had always been. Sonny Greer
gave his support by briskly stirring a snare drum with wire brushes.

"Yeah!" Sonny confirmed.

Of the trio, Sonny was the musician whom Moses had known
longest and best. During the next time-out, they bought each
other a few glasses of Canadian Club on the rocks.

"How old are you, Sonny?" Moses asked.

"That's a difficult question," Sonny said. "At this time of the evening I'm eighty-five, but I'm about ninety-five after midnight."

Sonny in his eighties was still lean and trim and energetic, like Moses at the age of seventy-six. Unlike Moses, whose hair was now the silver-gray of steel wool, Sonny still had black hair. He looked amazingly young. When he climbed agilely behind his traps and the trio bounced into a jump rendition of "You're Just An Old Antidisestablishmentarianismist", Moses found the spectacle of the athletically swinging octogenarian extremely encouraging and, in the most admirable possible way, downright laughable. Why get old? seemed to be the gist of the message. Moses wondered why some of his more elderly Long Island neighbors, who were always discussing the symptoms of their geriatric decay, didn't take up jazz drumming.

By the end of the session, Moses agreed to meet Sonny and Tasty Parker the next day for lunch with Raymond Carroll, the United Nations correspondent of *Newsweek*. Tasty Parker was a trumpet player. Moses and he had often jammed together. Tasty had got his nickname, he had explained, because "when they ask me to blow four choruses I give them two – just a taste." He was always a trumpet player of such high principles that sometimes, as now, he was unemployed. At such times, he was willing to serve as Sonny's chauffeur.

When Tasty collected Sonny from his apartment on Central Park West, the drummer was wearing a red, white and blue necktie as glorious as a flag, in commemoration of the bicentennial of the United States.

"Looking sharp," Tasty commented admiringly.

"Going to the U.N., you *got* to look sharp," Sonny said.

Raymond Carroll and Moses met them, as arranged, at the entrance to the U.N. Secretariat, in the Headquarters compound, on the shore of the East River. Carroll showed his identity card, and introduced his guests, to the blue-uniformed black security guard inside the doorway.

"Mr. Greer, Mr. Decatur and Mr. Parker," Carroll said.

"Mr. *Sonny* Greer?" the guard asked.

"Right on," Sonny said, shaking the guard's hand.

Carroll led the way up an escalator, along wide corridors and across great expanses of carpet, to the Delegates' Lounge. A long wall of glass overlooked the sunlit river. At one end of the lounge there was a long bar. They sat on white leather sofas beside a glass table. Carroll fetched drinks on a silver tray. Sonny sipped his Canadian Club and surveyed the large room. He saw delegates of various colors, some of them dressed in African, Arab and Indian national costumes, conversing in small, mixed groups.

"Cats from all over," Sonny observed. "How about that?" He chuckled. "I like this place."

A black American in a tweed suit approached Sonny with a tentative smile.

"Excuse me," the stranger said. "Aren't you Sonny Greer?"

"That's right," Sonny said, smiling as he stood up and shook hands.

"I caught your act at Gregory's."

"That's me," Sonny said.

"Welcome to the U.N."

A few minutes later, the conversation was interrupted again, by two fans from Madagascar; and a few moments after that by a Canadian.

"I've been lining up to hear you play all over the world for the past thirty years," he said. "And here we are, meeting at last. It's a great honor."

"It's an honour for me," Sonny said.

An African came over. This one was for Moses.

"Mr. Decatur," the man said, "you probably don't remember me – Mike Ngomba. We met at the President's reception in Accra back in nineteen-sixty-nine, after that wonderful concert. I've been buying your records ever since then – yours and Al Dexter's."

Moses felt that he had scored a few points. He thanked his well-wisher.

"I had no idea so many people would know us here," Sonny said.

"The building's full of jazz-lovers," Carroll assured them.

In the Delegates' Dining Room, Carroll ordered a round of the special cocktail of the day, white rum, dry vermouth and Curaçao, called "El Presidente".

"That's smooth," Sonny said. "You could drink that all day."

They had some more.

Sonny recalled the time, more than forty years before, when

he had met the Prince of Wales at a party that Lord Beaverbrook had given in England. Duke Ellington and his orchestra were among the four hundred guests.

"The prince brought me a bottle of brandy and a bottle of champagne and sat on the floor beside me on the stand," Sonny said. "He stayed there all night. Everybody wanted to meet him but he stayed with me. We got kind of tight together. I didn't have time for 'Your Royal Highness' and all that junk, so I just called him 'Wale'. Whenever I saw him after that I always called him 'Wale'. I think he was proud to have that nickname. He was very enthusiastic about jazz. He was a very nice guy. Everybody liked him. He thought he was quite a drummer. He drummed a Charleston beat. I could teach a kindergarten child to drum like he did. He was a real enthusiast though and that was what counted. I let him play my drums, and he was nice to me. What I say is, 'Bread cast upon the sea comes back buttered toast.' "

Carroll took them on a tour of the other buildings. Sonny admired the Security Council chamber.

"Peace!" Moses said.

"That's what it's all for," Sonny said.

In a corridor, a black woman in a bright yellow suit recognized Sonny and greeted him. Carroll introduced him and Tasty and Moses to Madame Annie Brooks, the ambassador from Liberia, who had been the President of the General Assembly in 1969.

"Let me show you gentlemen where the General Assembly meets," she said.

"This is a beautiful room," Sonny said, looking around the great empty hall.

He climbed the podium and stood at the President's lectern.

"Well, will you look at this?" Sonny said. "Here I am. Isn't it wonderful that someone raised on the sidewalks of New York should be honored this way, standing where the President of the General Assembly of the United Nations stands?"

He pointed at the hundreds of seats in the gallery.

"I can see all my friends here," he said. "Duke, Harry Carney, Johnny Hodges, Barney Bigard, Tricky Sam Nanton – all of them."

He turned to Madame Brooks of Liberia.

"This is it, baby," he said. "This is where all the nations meet all the other nations. You got to make it, baby!"

Moses looked with him. To him, too, the chamber seemed to be thronged with the ghosts of jazz musicians.

"Don't go back this afternoon," Sonny said to Moses, when they were back in Tasty's station wagon. "Call Mae and stay one more night. We have some music to play for you at the club."

Sonny taught the bartender at Gregory's to make "El Presidente" cocktails. The bartender called the drink "Sonny's Dream".

"We may be old," Sonny said. "But we aren't *too* old."

"We've had a good run, you and I," Moses said, with a sentimental smile, as he raised his glass once more. "As Satch used to say, God rest him, 'If it all stopped tomorrow – hallelujah! Everybody's had a good time.' "

SEVENTY-ONE

After Ann died, Al moved into the Madison Hotel, in the same block as the *Washington Post* building. It was a quiet, comfortable hotel.

Selling the house was easy. The real-estate agent told Al he was lucky to be offering it for sale early in the Spring, the best time of the year to put it on the market. It was cherry-blossom time. The weeping cherry tree in the garden was in full bloom.

"A good neo-Georgian house in Georgetown is never a problem, of course," she assured him. "But don't let anyone try to tell you the season doesn't make a difference. Washington is always at its best at this time. It's a funny thing : those pink blossoms on your tree are probably worth about five thousand dollars. It's a psychological thing."

Ann had achieved death as easily as possible. Their doctor, an old friend, had permitted her to stay at home to do it. Al used one of the guest-rooms for the last couple of months. Ann remained in their double bed. During the days she was propped up with extra pillows. The nurses tactfully were as unobtrusive as they could be.

"I'm so tired," she said.

"I know you are," he said, kissing her. "But you'll be all right, after a good, long rest."

"I've been thinking. You shouldn't stay here after I've gone. It'd be so depressing, living in this house on your own. You'd be so bored. And you can't even boil an egg. You know what you should do ? You should go to live in New Orleans."

"Don't be silly," he said. "You aren't going anywhere."

They looked close into each other's eyes and she patiently smiled.

At the time, he had not been able to imagine doing anything without her, anywhere, ever.

He had an early dinner in the hotel restaurant. At the desk, someone gave him a folder containing his tickets – by air from Washington to Memphis; by steamboat from Memphis to New Orleans.

He sat in an armchair in the bar and drank two brandies. He went up to his room and took an Oblivon. He lay for a long time in a deep, hot bath.

He lay in bed in the dark, unable to sleep.

Being an urban man, he did not attempt to overcome his insomnia by counting sheep. Instead, through his mind passed the names of some of the jazz musicians whose music he knew. The slow procession was quite a long one :

. . . Buddy Bolden, Freddy Keppard, Joe King Oliver, Jelly Roll Morton, Bunk Johnson, Manuel Perez, Lorenzo Tio, Alphonse Picou, Honoré Dutrey, Oscar Papa Celestin, Kid Ory, Moses Decatur, Louis Armstrong, Henry Red Allen, Jimmy Noone, Barney Bigard, Sidney Bechet, Baby Dodds, Billie Banks, Sharkey Bonano, Red McKenzie, Adrian Rollini, Zutty Singleton, Earl Fatha Hines, Fletcher Henderson, Luis Russell, Eubie Blake, James P. Johnson, Fats Waller, Bunk Johnson, Johnny St. Cyr, George Lewis, Tommy Ladnier, Mezz Mezzrow, Ida Cox, Ma Rainey, Bessie Smith, Muggsy Spanier, Nick LaRocca, Red Nichols, Miff Mole, Leon Rapollo, Frankie Trumbauer, Bix Beiderbecke, Pee Wee Russell, Jimmy McPartland, Jim Lanigan, Frank Teschemacher, Bud Freeman, George Wettling, Dave Tough, Moses Decatur, Benny Goodman, Joe Sullivan, Gene Krupa, Eddie Condon, Jack Teagarden, Don Redman, Benny Carter, Bennie Moten, Walter Page, Count Basie, Hot Lips Page, Ben Webster, Bunny Berigan, Jimmie Lunceford, Chu Berry, Coleman Hawkins, Roy Eldrige, Teddy Wilson, Willie The Lion Smith, Lionel Hampton, Charlie Christian, Billie Holiday, Joe Smith, Alberta Hunter, George Pops Foster, Art Hodes, Sidney De Paris, Vic Dickenson, Johnny Dodds, Lil Armstrong, Lawrence Brown, Mike McKendrick, Yank Porter, George Oldham, Itzy Riskin, Eddie Lang, Joe Venuti, Chauncey Morehouse, Jimmy Dorsey, Rex Stewart, Buster Bailey, Keg Johnson, Russell Procope, Horace Henderson, Walter Johnson, Eddie Heywood, Crawford Wethington, O'Neill Spencer, Bob Ysaquirre, Big Sid Catlett, John Trueheart, Frankie Newton, Trummy Young, Juan Tizol, Lester Young, Illinois Jacquet, Chick Webb, Ella Fitzgerald, Andy Kirk, Buck Clayton, Jo Jones, Freddie Green, Dickie Wells, Stuff Smith, Art Tatum, Yank Lawson, Bobby Hackett, John Kirby, Charlie Shavers, Billy Kyle, Cootie Williams, Johnny Guarnieri, Johnny Hodges, Harry Carney, Tricky Sam Nanton,

Bubber Miley, Sonny Greer, Moses Decatur, Otto Hardwicke, Jimmy Blanton, Billy Strayhorn, Ray Nance, Paul Gonsalves, Duke Ellington, Jimmy Hamilton, Sam Woodyard, Freddy Guy, Wellman Braud, Jimmy Yancey, Cow Cow Davenport, Bob Zurke, Pinetop Smith, Mel Powell, Meade Lux Lewis, Joe Turner, Zoot Sims, Eddie Durham, Charlie Ventura, Max Kaminsky, Albert Ammons, Pete Johnson, Georgie Auld, Lucky Millinder, Ruby Braff, Leo Watson, Rod Cless, Wild Bill Davison, Jess Stacey, Joe Bushkin, Johnny Sparrow, Irving Fazola, Pete Brown, Eddie Miller, George Brunis, Teddy Bunn, Billy Butterfield, Israel Crosby, Cutty Cutshall, Jimmy Giuffre, Buddy De Franco, Edmond Hall, Tommy Dorsey, Ray Bauduc, Bob Haggart, Barney Kessel, Eddie Cleanhead Vinson, J. C. Higginbotham, Milt Hinton, Wingy Manone, Joe Marsala, Marty Marsala, Matty Matlock, Moses Decatur, Jimmy Rushing, Buddy Rich, Slim Gaillard, Slam Stewart, Carmen McRae, Mary Lou Williams, Sarah Vaughan, John Lewis, Peanuts Hucko, Blossom Dearie, Arthur Whetsol, Vido Musso, Hymie Schertzer, Herb Ellis, Lee Konitz, Ray Brown, Louis Bellson, Cat Anderson, Rudi Blesh, Wilbur De Paris, Betty Roché, Pete Fountain, Roy Liberto, Paul Desmond, Joe Morello, Dave Brubeck, Chet Baker, Gerry Mulligan, Dizzy Gillespie, Thelonious Monk, Bud Powell, Sonny Rollins, Stan Getz, Charles Mingus, Miles Davis, Charlie Parker, Art Blakey, Bobby Brookmeyer, John Coltrane, Archie Shepp, Oscar Peterson, Erroll Garner, Milt Jackson, Max Roach, Sonny Stitt, Lennie Tristano, Cannonball Adderley, Eddie Lockjaw Davis, Wild Bill Davis, Chico Hamilton, Herbie Hancock, Charlie Rouse, Shelly Manne, J. J. Johnson, Toots Mondello, Curley Russell, Willie Humphrey, Moses Decatur, Josiah Frazier, Allan Jaffe, Percy Humphrey, Narvin Kimball, Louis Armstrong, James Miller, Duke Ellington, Frank Demond, Moses Decatur. . . .'

Al slept.

CODA

Jazz endures.

Conceived in slavery and born in poverty, jazz survived and grew up in spite of many hazards, handicaps and humiliations.

Jazz overcame the disapproval of its own parents, harassment by the authorities, commercial exploitation, racial and social bigotry and discrimination – and the ineptitude of a large number of bum musicians.

Jazz was molested and preyed upon by madames, pimps, whores and gangsters; show-business promoters, managers and agents; union officials, radio and record-company executives, Hollywood and Broadway producers, proprietors of nightclubs and dance-halls, landladies and short-order cooks, dope peddlers and critics and countless other parasites and rip-off artists.

But jazz endures.

Jazz is a means of personal expression, a means of breaking down barriers between peoples, a means of universal communication. Jazz is fun.

In a beloved, shabby, little, old room in the French Quarter of New Orleans in the Spring of 1979, The Preservation Hall Jazz Band was giving its usual evening concert.

Al Dexter was at the piano.

The other veteran musicians were playing trumpet, trombone, clarinet, banjo, tuba and drums.

Like the others, Al was dressed casually in brown with a flashy tie. A straw skimmer was balanced at a debonair angle on his white hair. His spectacles had thick lenses; he could not see without them. He had a new white moustache.

"What now?" the trumpet man asked.

"Why don't we play this one?" Al said, offering a few chords. So that was what they played – "Do You Know What It Means To Miss New Orleans?"

"There's no doubt about it," a serious young tourist said in the ear of his wife, who was standing close beside him in the throng. "They're good all right, in their way. But these old guys are so unadventurous. They must have been here for ever. Why don't they ever go any place and find out what's new?"

318   *

BIBLIOGRAPHY

The French Quarter, by Herbert Asbury, Mockingbird Books, 1976.

Storyville, by Al Rose, Louisiana State University Press, 1976.

Le Voodoo à la Nouvelle Orleans, by Jerry Gandolfo, Laborde, 1975.

Satchmo: My Life in New Orleans, by Louis Armstrong, Peter Davies, 1955.

From Satchmo to Miles, by Leonard Feather, Stein & Day, 1972.

Louis, by Max Jones & John Chilton, Mayflower Books, 1975.

Really The Blues, by Mezz Mezzrow & Bernard Wolfe, Random House, 1946.

Hear Me Talkin' to Ya, by Nat Shapiro & Nat Hentoff, Dover, 1966.

The Bootleggers, by Kenneth Allsop, Hutchinson, 1961.

Blues People, by LeRoi Jones, Morrow, 1963.

Stomping The Blues, by Albert Murray, McGraw-Hill, 1976.

The Jazz Book, by Joachim Berendt, Lawrence Hill & Company, 1975.

The Book of Jazz, by Leonard Feather, Dell, 1976.

The Making of Jazz, by James Lincoln Collier, Hart Davis, MacGibbon, 1978.

Ecstasy at The Onion, by Whitney Balliett, Bobbs-Merrill, 1971.

My Life in Jazz, by Max Kaminsky & V. E. Hughes, Harper & Row, 1963.

Jazz Masters of the Twenties, by Richard Hadlock, Macmillan, 1965.

Jazz Masters of the Thirties, by Rex Stewart, Macmillan, 1972.

Jazz Masters of the Forties, by Ira Gitler, Macmillan, 1966.

Jazz Masters of the Fifties, by Joe Goldberg, Macmillan, 1965.

Music Is My Mistress, by Duke Ellington, W. H. Allen, 1974.

The World of Duke Ellington, by Stanley Dance, Scribner's, 1970.

Lady Sings The Blues, by Billie Holiday & William Dufty, Lancer, 1965.

Bessie, by Chris Albertson, Stein & Day, 1972.

John Coltrane, by Bill Cole, Schirmer Books, 1976.

Beneath the Underdog, by Charles Mingus, Knopf, 1971.

Jazz Is, by Nat Hentoff, W. H. Allen, 1978.

Jazz at Ronnie Scott's, by Kitty Grime, Robert Hale, 1979.

Second Chorus, by Humphrey Lyttelton, MacGibbon & Kee, 1958.